Lise Leroux was born in Montreal, Canada, and has subsequently lived in the United States, Holland, England and France. She is a full-time writer and illustrator and a long-time jumper out of perfectly good aeroplanes. She competes in international formation skydiving events, and divides her time between London, Paris and her computer. *One Hand Clapping* is her first book.

One Hand Clapping

LISE LEROUX

Illustrations by Lise Leroux

PENGUIN BOOKS

PENGUIN BOOKS

Published by the Penguin Group
Penguin Books Ltd, 27 Wrights Lane, London w8 5tz, England
Penguin Putnam Inc., 375 Hudson Street, New York, New York 10014, USA
Penguin Books Australia Ltd, Ringwood, Victoria, Australia
Penguin Books Canada Ltd, 10 Alcorn Avenue, Toronto, Ontario, Canada m4v 3b2
Penguin Books (NZ) Ltd, Private Bag 102902, NSMC, Auckland, New Zealand

Penguin Books Ltd, Registered Offices: Harmondsworth, Middlesex, England

First published by Viking 1998
Published in Penguin Books 1999
1 3 5 7 9 10 8 6 4 2

Grateful acknowledgement is made to Editions Gallimard
for permission to use the quotation from André Gide's *Journals*

Set in Monotype Fournier
Printed in England by Clays Ltd, St Ives plc

To Zebediah
himself,
upon whose tiny and insubstantial shoulders this book rests

Acknowledgements

To all those who said I couldn't,
spurring me on to prove I could,
To all those who said I could,
and were proud of me when I did.

My mother, Kami, Chris, Rachael and Murray. Thank you.

Carol Henson and Shelley Singer. Your support and editing assistance were invaluable.

Temple Grandin, whose book about autism, *Thinking in Pictures*, and whose description of the 'hug box' created in my mind such an unforgettable picture.

Contents

Part One

*Fish die belly-upward and rise to the
surface; it is their way of falling.*

ANDRÉ GIDE

One Hand Clapping

MARINA

*Clouds, mists and mountains are
unimportant beside the wear on a
threshold or the print of a hand.*

THOMAS HARDY

Growing a human ear on a mouse's back seemed to Marina presumption of the most monumental proportions. She sat up in bed and watched the mouse lumbering awkwardly across the television screen. The unwieldy construction on its back seemed an almost insupportable burden. A cool vanilla woman's voice-over spoke about the revolutionary medical advances being developed by the Hurtigger Institute.

'. . . so you see, this was a red-letter year for us. For this little chap here, too.'

'How could they do that?' Marina whispered, aghast. Her voice made the man next to her stir. His snores whiffled the sheet covering part of his face. It was a handsome face, she supposed. Long straight nose with flaring nostrils. Not too many errant hairs escaping from the nostrils. Full, petulant lips. Dark hair. Darker stubble. One of her own long strands of butter-coloured hair lounged across one eyebrow and fluttered across his face when he breathed. She longed to reach over and steal it back but she didn't dare. He'd wake and despite the positive effect of his individual features the total was unsettling.

Marina watched him in the dim strands of morning light. If he stirred again, she'd have to leap out of bed. He seemed quiet now. She closed her eyes and ran her fingers through her fine hair, combing out the tangles. 'Relax,' she said to herself, 'it's what you wanted.' Suddenly, she froze. One callused fingertip was running itself down her arm, raising the hairs on it as sharply as slivered glass.

'We could have another go,' the man said.

Marina tensed as the hand continued down her arm. 'You have

two seconds,' she said, in tones as ominous and certain as a greased guillotine. 'Two seconds to take your hand off me or I'll surgically remove it.' The unwelcome touch removed itself so quickly that a hand-shaped imprint seemed to shimmer in the air between them. The man's confusion washed over her.

Touch has become a prostitution, she thought. *I am only touched when commerce is to be conducted.* She shivered, feeling the cold winds of the man's fingertips still running down her body.

This was the fourth faceless man she'd picked up at a Transport station and brought home in two weeks. She couldn't remember the last time someone had touched her who hadn't wanted sex. A friend, tapping her on the shoulder to get her attention. A child, holding her hand because of the strength and comfort to be found there. What friend? What child? She had neither. When she was younger, the lack of affection hadn't bothered her so much. But now that she hadn't been able to find a job in months and had no family, this lack was taking over her life. She must find a way to do without these men. She was beginning to despise herself as well as them. Besides, if she considered statistics, she was bound to start running into problems. Social diseases had finally been eradicated, but violence certainly hadn't. She waved in the direction of the TV to increase the volume. Perhaps if she ignored him the man would get up and go.

'Look at this . . .' a voice on the TV said from the other side of the room.

Marina looked.

A white-coated man held a box which he tilted towards the camera. The mouse inside slid awkwardly towards the viewers. Its claws skittered across the slick bottom of the box as it tried to regain a toehold. It couldn't establish any sort of balance. With the cumbersome weight of the ear on its back, the mouse repeatedly fell over on to its side. Its legs fluttered weakly in an effort to right itself. The man had to help it up each time with one gloved finger. Whenever the mouse faltered to its feet, the man would tip the box again.

'Look at it go,' the programme's interviewer said, with awe.

The white-coated man laughed. 'Looks like a sailboat, doesn't he?'

The man in bed next to Marina laughed, the sound serrating her consciousness. She turned to look at him coldly, and he looked up at her with sleepy half-lidded eyes.

'I bet when that mouse puts a shell to its ear, it can hear the earth move.'

'There's the door,' she said, pulling the covers up to her chin. 'Don't slam it on your way out.' The man's reawakened confusion washed between them as he slid out of bed. Marina lay rigid underneath the duvet, while the silent affronted sounds of his dressing beat against her like wings. She heard him walk over to the door and pause. She willed him silently to go out *out* OUT.

'Don't you even want to know my name?' he asked.

'Not really.' *Please go.*

'It's Addy. Short for Addison. Can I call —?'

'No.' *I'm sorry. Really I am.*

He went, slamming the door with hurt emphasis. Marina sagged with relief into the duvet.

After getting up and showering with the hottest water she could stand, she nodded to the telephone screen to switch it on. It purred as she repeated the Institute's numbers given on the programme. As she uttered the last digit, the screen went green and she was connected. Quickly, she told the telephone to turn off the visuals. The Institute's receptionist came on the line. After haltingly telling her what she wanted, Marina was told to come in and fill out an application form to determine if she were a suitable donor. The Hurtigger Institute would pay her 300 City Credits plus tax for every body part she grew.

'Is it possible to have a hand instead of an ear?' Marina asked. Sitting down at the table, she picked up a pen and started doodling. Squiggles. Ears. Hands.

A doctor, who had obviously been listening to the receptionist speak to Marina, broke into the line at that point. 'There is a constant shortage of good-quality reliable hands,' he told her, with barely controlled excitement. 'Lots of industrial accidents, these days.'

'How . . .' Marina paused, the pen slippery in her hand ' . . . how do you take the implant off once it's ready?'

'Snip it off, quick as a flash,' he replied. 'You come in when the hand is matured, we put you to sleep, and then we slice it off.'

Marina stared out the window, silent.

'Are you worried about the scarring?' the doctor continued, his words tumbling past her silence. 'Usually women grow a hand underneath a breast or two. Good uplift.' He laughed but stopped abruptly at Marina's cold silence. He raced on, 'That way we can disguise the scarring from its removal. We cut just along the fold beneath the breast. Are you worried about what your husband or partner will say about the scars?'

'No,' she said. 'I have nobody who will mind.'

After she had nodded at the telephone to hang up, Marina sat in the darkened room with both arms wrapped around herself. Disparate parts of the faceless men from the past few weeks jiggled through her tired brain. *Could it work?*

An hour later, Marina found herself ensconced in an old rattling lime green taxi-moto, hurtling towards the Medical District. She had flagged it down, almost changed her mind, but climbed in after it beeped impatiently.

'The Medical District, please.' She addressed the back of the metallic head-like dome.

The dome swivelled towards her. 'Certainly, ma'am. And isn't it a lovely sunny day?' A tinny American-accented voice erupted from a rusted speaker on top of the dome.

Marina snorted. 'It's raining. Have your sprockets been checked recently?'

The dome didn't answer.

After five minutes of whooshing stop-and-go traffic, the taxi-moto pulled up in front of a pink stone building.

'Twelve City Credits,' the dome announced, with sunny certainty. Marina peered out of the window. Taking a deep breath, she waved her hand at the meter, letting the taxi-moto know it should deduct what she owed from her City Credit account. She hoped she hadn't gone above her unemployment limit this month. She got out and stared at the building.

'Have a nice day,' the taxi-moto chirped after her.

'Yeah, right,' she muttered, as she walked towards a revolving glass door with foot-high gold letters above it. 'Hurtigger Institute,' the letters trumpeted. As Marina pushed through the door, she was blinded by blue spotlights that flashed into her face and eyes. They felt hot and intrusive.

'Sorry,' a voice called. 'I can't get the lights working.'

Marina looked towards where the words had come from. Sitting at a large oval silver desk, with swooping wing designs tapped into its metal front, was a young woman operating the controls on a small laptop switchboard. *She can't be more than eighteen. How has she managed to find a job so young?*

Marina walked in the direction of the desk. She felt messy feelings of resentment leak towards the receptionist, who was smiling at her with glossy red lips arrayed over glistening teeth. Sweeping a sheaf of tea-coloured hair from her shoulder, she waved several turquoise-tipped fingernails at Marina. 'Can I help you?' Inexpertly she fiddled with the blue lights and finally just switched them off. 'I mean, *may* I help you?'

'I'm here to see Dr Hurtigger.'

The woman picked at her nail polish, flicking bits of blue across the silver desk. 'Do you have an appointment?'

Why am I here? I should go. 'No. Do I need one? I called before. I'm here about the implants.'

'Oh!' The blue bits stopped flicking. 'You're the . . . Just a sec. Don't go away. Let me call . . . please have a seat.'

Before Marina could sit down, the receptionist waved a pile of papers at her. 'Can . . . will you fill these out, please?'

After two hours of forms, forms and more forms, Marina was accepted with alacrity into the programme.

She was astonished at the range of questions on the forms. Requests for information she hadn't thought a doctor would need to know. But then again, what did she know about doctors anyway? He probably needed to know about all of it in case anything went wrong. Carefully, she checked the boxes following the various questions.

Questions about sex. *None of his business.*

Questions about her family. *Easy. None.*

Her genetic background. *How am I supposed to know about that?*

But mostly there were questions regarding her emotional state. Did she experience happiness? Contentment? Passion? Disappointment? Sadness? Depression? Hate? The questions made her feel odd. She drew a heavy black cross in the boxes next to all the negative ones. She hadn't felt the others in a long time.

As Marina was finishing, she felt her flesh creep. It was as if someone was watching her. Looking up in suspicion, she glanced at the receptionist. No, it was only her imagination. The girl was fiddling with the lights again.

The operation would be performed immediately by Dr Hurtigger himself.

'No sense waiting, now, is there?' His smile was wide, but Marina noticed that it didn't extend to his eyes. They had a calculating glint, which made her shiver. They looked familiar, too. Nothing else did. Just the eyes.

Doesn't matter about him, you're getting what you want. 'Could you explain what you're actually doing? I know you're growing something on me, but I don't understand how . . .'

Dr Hurtigger sat forward in his chair. Excitement made his nostrils flare. He reminded Marina of a horse. A balding horse with tiny, piggish eyes.

'Growing is the operable term. Think of it like a garden.'

Marina pressed herself against the back of the chair. She didn't like him invading her personal space. 'A garden?'

'Have you ever heard of grafting tree buds?'

'I think so.'

He pushed his glasses up his nose. 'It's like that. We surgically implant or graft body parts from one person, called the donee, on to another person, the donor.'

'So I would be the . . .?'

'Donor. Then, after the body part is matured, it's removed and replanted back on the donee. They're usually better than the original ones. Colour, size, shape and quality are far superior.'

'But how . . .?'

'The two parts grow together into a single grafted unit. Make sense so far?'

Marina nodded. *All I want to know is if it hurts.*

The doctor leaned back in his chair and picked up a pencil. After sketching for a silent minute or two on a piece of paper he had ripped from a pad, he passed it to Marina. He'd drawn a woman with a hand curling over her breast. She was naked, and looked pale and lonely in the middle of the page. Her hair frothed around her face, partially obscuring her eyes. It looked as if a man were standing behind her caressing her with gentle fingers. Surprisingly, the hand didn't look horrid or intrusive at all. It looked comforting.

She looked up at him. 'Does the grafted thingy have a name?'

'The scion.'

'What?'

'S-C-I-O-N. It's pronounced sigh-on. Nice name, don't you think?' When Marina didn't answer, he continued, 'We try to keep everything organic so as not to frighten people. Like planting. Growth.'

'What do you call the other parts?'

'Well . . . the areas of the donee where the scions will be cut from are called "budsticks" or "budwood". You, as the donor, will be called the "rootstock". And the part where the scion and rootstock heal together is called the "union". Is that clear, Marina?'

'Yes.'

'My procedure saves years of waiting time. Only three weeks into fully grown scions.' His face glowed and Marina was caught up in his enthusiasm.

'How does it mature so fast?'

'Scions are cut from already mature people. They know physiologically they are mature, and they remember where they're from, in spite of being grafted on to another person. The scion certainly doesn't become absorbed into your own system. It isn't part of your body.' Dr Hurtigger laughed. 'It's just borrowing you for a while.'

'Three weeks to be exact.'

'Precisely.'

'When will you do it?'

'Now?' The doctor's small eyes bored into her.

'Mareeeena. Marina?' Dr Hurtigger's voice cajoled. With her eyes closed, Marina thought his voice sounded sticky. Like gum stuck on your shoe.

'Marina?'

'Uhhhhh.' *Wrigley's spearmint gum.*

'Are you awake, Marina?'

'No. Yes. I don't know.' *I feel sick.*

Marina opened one eye. 'It hurts.'

Looking like a small boy with an overabundance of urine, Dr Hurtigger hopped from one foot to the other. 'Not for long. Would you like to see the hand bud?'

'No. I've changed my mind. I've . . .'

'Look.' Dr Hurtigger reached down to Marina, and swept the covers from her chest, leaving her bare to the waist except for one small bandage. Without noticing Marina's angry face, he ripped off the bandage.

Despite herself, she looked down. The hand bud lay underneath her left breast. It looked like a baby's fist implanted just underneath the skin. The fist, the size of a walnut, pushed up against her skin as if it were straining to get out. Marina could see movement from the spider-like fingers. She felt an odd skittering sensation in addition to the aching pain from the incision and closed her eyes, repelled. Although Dr Hurtigger had warned her what to expect, the reality was shocking.

'It's alive,' she moaned.

'Of course it is!' He was horrified. 'We wouldn't implant a dud bud. A dead hand. It's trying to push its way out. Like a Bird of Paradise, it will be looking to rise from the ashes of your ribcage to burst into the light . . . to soar . . .'

Marina didn't appreciate his flights of fancy. She groaned.

'The young have no imagination,' he said.

'Not so young, Dr Hurtigger. I'm thirty-one.'

He laughed, his eyes twinkling. 'Pah. You're a child! I'm twice that.'

Take it from me. I am old. I feel old.

'The first week is crucial,' he had said. 'It's touch-and-go if the hand will take. You can't go out until at *least* the second week.' At Marina's inquiring look, he went on, 'You can't run the risk of bumping into something or catching a chill.'

'Why?'

Dr Hurtigger took off his glasses and rubbed the red marks they left on his nose. 'If the hand bud gets bumped, it could start growing inwards. A fist could grow around your heart or . . .' he paused for dramatic emphasis ' . . . possibly a bony finger could poke you in the lungs. You wouldn't want that, would you? If it doesn't take or becomes ill, it will die while it's on you. If that happens, we'd have to cut it off immediately.'

'And if you don't cut it off in time?' Marina dragged her fingers through her hair nervously.

Dr Hurtigger put his glasses back on and stood up abruptly. 'If one of you dies, the other could die.'

Marina looked horrified.

'Stop worrying. I haven't lost a patient yet.' He had patted her on the shoulder and led her to the door.

The hand grew at a remarkable rate. It slowly pushed through her pale, faintly freckled skin, which peeled back in strips as if it were sunburnt. It didn't hurt, exactly. Just a dull sort of pressure. Dr Hurtigger had given her some special pain cream that supposedly pushed the skin cells and nerve endings aside. The hand bud seemed to try to keep its fingers close together when coming through, so as to make as small an aperture as possible.

Despite its care, her skin split like an out-of-control episiotomy. Some of the splits went beyond the area where she'd spread pain cream, which convinced her at once of its efficacy. She spread on more. Marina worried that the opening would become a huge asterisk-shaped scar. *What am I worrying for? Scarring is the least of my problems.*

The skin of the hand was waxy at first, its fingernails indistinct. After the first week, the nails hardened and the skin became pink and firm. The hand was restless and unsure of itself, as clumsy as a child, even though it was destined for a woman pianist of sixty. Marina tried to ignore it as she went about her business inside her small apartment. She slapped the flailing hand away when it tried to wrap itself around her breast for comfort. It was so needy, it was driving her mad.

'Get off!' *The ultimate intrusion. A hand that I can't repel.*

The hand lay quiet, sweating slightly with fright and confusion.

'What have I done?' Marina cried, with scorn for herself, bitter and green as rancid olives. It isn't working. This hand can't hold or comfort me! I can't stand its touch. What was I thinking of?'

On the eighth day, Marina had a check-up at the Institute. She wasn't sure what to wear. It wasn't a problem at home, as she could just wear a robe in order not to constrict the hand. But to go on the bus without people noticing it? She thought for a moment and went to the kitchen. Rummaging inside one of the drawers, she pulled out a pair of rusted scissors, two unmatching red wool socks, and an unread palmistry book someone had given her several years before, and found what she was after. A dusty roll of Vordrop's extra-strength cling-film.

Grimacing with distaste, she flattened the hand up on to her breast and wound long silvery sheets of cling-film around herself. She looked at the result in the mirror and felt guilty. Maybe the hand wouldn't grow correctly. Besides, she didn't want it to think she was ashamed of it. She unwrapped the cling-film and pulled on a loose sweater and jeans. She reached under the sweater and tucked the hand under her left armpit. It tried to resist, and she had to clamp her arm tightly down on it.

'Down, girl!'

She wasn't about to risk the looks she'd get from people if they saw a hand waving at them from inside her sweater.

'Gotcha with the armpit manoeuvre.' Marina smiled to herself.

Going over to the CompuLook machine, she blew the dust off the keyboard. She couldn't be bothered to use the machine most days. Besides, it wasn't one of the new upgraded versions with non-touch sensors. This one you actually had to key in the physical features that you wanted for the day.

She couldn't have her neighbours looking. What if they spotted the hand? Especially that nosy woman across the street. The one who did horoscopes or auras or something like that. Her eyes peered out constantly at Marina. She could feel the woman's eyes on her whenever she stepped out of her front door. Probably something to do with all the men she brought home.

She shrugged. Her morals were nobody's business but her own.

Picking quickly, she chose a short black bobbed haircut and thin lips. The opposite of her own looks. What else? Blue eyes. Pointed face. Tinted glasses.

That would do. Different enough to disguise her, but nondescript enough not to cause comment.

She felt relief when the hand was cut off after the third week. As Dr Hurtigger had said, it was in and out, quick as a snip. The only reminder was the soreness under her breast, and the stiff bandage that teased the tender skin. When she took it off, the incision looked like a faint pink smile surrounded by a starburst of silvery lines.

After dressing, Marina went to the front desk to check out.

'You're not having another implant?' Sandra, the blue-tipped receptionist asked, her pen poised over the form.

Marina wavered. *Sandra must think I'm some sick freak*, she thought. *Perhaps I am. A silly frigid woman who can't bear to be touched, even by an isolated hand.* It hadn't worked. It hadn't felt like the Transport men touching her at all. There wasn't any affection in the touch. Just blatant, excessive need. Then again, with the men there hadn't been affection either. Just blatant, excessive want. She couldn't go back to that. Maybe the implant hand had felt strange because it was by itself. Just one felt like an aberration. Perhaps two would have felt more real. More balanced. More like a real person.

Sandra coughed and Marina felt shamed by the derision she thought she could sense. Those men weren't real people either. She couldn't go back to what she'd been doing. All those anonymous hands and penises and . . .

'Sign me up for a multiple implant,' Marina blurted, the words forcing themselves from somewhere within her. *Kill or cure, that's the ticket. Immersion therapy.*

Sandra looked surprised, the derision replaced by something that Marina couldn't quite identify, but felt more comfortable with. She hoped it was respect. It was odd, though. The woman was staring at her as if she knew her. *I've never seen her before in my life. Quit staring. It's rude.*

As she didn't trust herself to come back, she asked if it were possible to get the multiple implant done that same day. Sandra seemed pleased, as well as Dr Hurtigger, who appeared to be breathing hard when he arrived in the outer office. She noticed a tiny smear of lipstick on the corner of his mouth. Was it the same colour as Sandra's? *Dallying during business hours, eh?*

'Marina!' he cried, delight making his words sound more gum-like than usual. 'Our star donor site.' He tried to take her arm but drew his hand back when she flinched. He shrugged. 'Follow me.'

In the beginning, the multiple implant had almost sent her around the bend. For the first week, she lay on the faded sofa in her living room, the ten hand buds pushing their way out. One hand grew under each of her breasts, one below each shoulder blade, and four curled around her waist like a belt of knuckles. Two perched on her shoulders, parrot companions to her swashbuckling pirate.

They rarely stopped their incessant fluttering. Grimly, she thought that if she was a depraved silly frigid woman instead of just a silly frigid woman she could have had the hands placed more strategically.

During the second week, the feeling of mass intrusion lessened. It was fascinating to watch the hands. It occurred to her that she hadn't once thought of the faceless men since ID, Implant Day.

At the thought of the men, she flinched. The hands inside her dressing gown began to scrabble wildly, the movement against the loam-coloured silk as unsettled as her mind.

Marina soothed the restless shifting by cupping the worst offenders around her waist between her own cool, capable hands. She leaned forward and rocked as she held the hands, sheets of pale hair sweeping forward and enclosing them.

She let go and reached inside the folds of her dressing gown to the trembling hand on her left shoulder. The others seemed to relax, but this one wouldn't settle. She flattened her palm against the dry, curled fingers, pressing the hand with steady firmness into her shoulder.

'Be still, my hand,' she whispered.

It still seemed uneasy. Perhaps it needed comforting. She uncurled the hand and traced her fingers across the cup-shaped palm, over the lines that radiated across it.

'What do we have here?' she asked.

When Marina hadn't been able to go out during the first hand's incubation week, she'd flipped through the book she'd pulled out of the kitchen drawer in her search for cling-film. She wished she knew who had dropped it outside her flat. Had her mother sent it in some pathetic form of reparation? It was around the time of her birthday when she'd found it. Her sister Wynne? No. Wynne never bought books for birthdays. She had too many of her own. Electrician's manuals, mostly. Just thinking about Mama and Wynne caused Marina pain. Neither of them would have sent her the book. They hadn't wanted her around, after all. She'd been sent away. *Stop thinking about them. The book. Look at the book.*

'Palmistry for Life', the cover proclaimed. The letters of the title wove across the cover, as golden and mysterious as Egyptian hieroglyphics. Marina turned to the first page. 'Major lines of the palm illustrated' ran across the top. Fascinated, Marina pored over the illustration. If the life line crossed the palm completely, the owner would have a long life. If it was short or broken, they'd die young. Having a sun line under the ring finger denoted success. The heart line showed whether they'd have a happy emotional life.

Curiosity compelled her to look at her own hand. Her heart line was, as she had suspected, short and stunted. She closed her eyes and leaned her head back. She wasn't cut out for relationships. Never had been. She'd thought she was once.

No. She wouldn't think of that particular man either. He'd left her, saying that she had no warmth. He had felt frozen by her lack of response.

She blew warm breath gently onto the hand that was still trembling on her shoulder. It seemed much less self-sufficient than the others. She looked again at its palm. Maybe she could read to the hand. Maybe her voice would soothe it. She'd read to it from the book. Palmistry certainly hadn't interested her when she'd only had two palms. But such a plethora of them to work with now! A veritable feast of palms. And all with seemingly disparate identities. She had thought they would be just inanimate things, as low on personality as a sock or a toenail clipping. But was it her imagination, or were they developing distinct personalities as they grew? She supposed that as the hand buds contained the genetic information of the 'donees', the people who'd had the accidents, they were developing the donees' personalities.

People with personalities need names. She couldn't just keep referring to them as hand-on-left-shoulder, third-hand-on-right-hip. She didn't know the donees' names, so she'd make some up. She would name them after the Italian heroes and heroines with whom Mama had peopled her childhood bedtime stories. Before Berri had left them without a mother, she'd read to the two girls every night.

'Wynne and Marina! Come sit beside me. That's right. Cuddle closely. Now once upon a time in a wondrous city called Florence, there was a prince called Giuseppe and a princess . . .'

Berri had yearned to be an Italian *principessa* married to a handsome nobleman. Even a gondolier would have done. But Herbert, a London Transport Scraper from Croydon, obviously did not fulfil her fantasies.

'You have the eyes of an adored *principessa*,' she whispered fragrantly to Marina. 'Don't tell Wynne. We don't want her to be jealous.'

Marina heard her mother whispering to her sister. ' . . . don't tell Marina. We wouldn't want her to be jealous.' Marina closed her eyes and inhaled. The smell of her mother comforted her. The warm scent of cinnamon . . . slight tang of lemon . . . a touch of creosote . . . with overtones of rubbery plastic from her omni-present overalls.

Berri had run off with Imolo, the man from the Italian deli on Wardour Street. 'Imolo is the man of my heart,' she murmured to Marina, moments before she left. 'It is fate.' She pressed her lips onto Marina's heated forehead. 'You can't change fate.' Marina's sniffed at the sharp scent of her mother's yearning which rose imperious among the other scents.

Marina failed to see what Imolo had that Papa didn't. Didn't Papa's soft mushroom-coloured hair sweep just as romantically as Imolo's? Just because Imolo had flashing black eyes and smelled like fresh basil, did that make him more of a man?

Was it Imolo at all? Perhaps Mama just hadn't believed her own strictures to Marina and wanted to escape her life as a Transport Scraper.

Berri had left one afternoon with Imolo and had never come back, effectively destroying her entire family with one blow. *I was the one who was sent away. It must have been my fault.*

Thinking of her mother made Marina's nervous rocking become more violent. The hands stirred. She stopped abruptly, wondering if hands could become seasick.

Names . . . let's see . . . 'You there, on my right shoulder. You're a sensible-looking woman's hand. Square palm. Long fingers. Not a flighty hand. I'll call you Donata. That's a sensible Italian woman's name. You, nervous worrybird on my left, I'll come back to you. Under my left breast, a delicate hand, aren't you? A woman's hand again. Delicate silvery fingernail tips. I'll call you Terza, for "third". The others, well, I'll wait until your personalities suggest something. Now, you on my left shoulder . . .' Her voice dropped to a whisper. 'I don't want the others to be jealous, but you're my favourite.'

Shy pride exuded from the hand. It leaned against Marina's neck.

'I'll call you Cecilio, or "Little Blind One", since you can't see.' She repeated his name to herself with pleasure. *Cecilio. Chee-CHILL-yo.*

Leaning back in the comforting folds of the sofa, she waved to the TV. It came on: a re-run about embarrassing video clips. A man getting slapped on the face by a fish. Marina giggled. At the same time, she felt strange vibrations coming from her left shoulder. She grabbed Cecilio, thinking it was sick. *Is it falling off? Is it having a fit?*

The hand patted her shoulder, pointed towards the TV screen and twiddled its fingers back and forth. Marina didn't understand what was happening, but eventually it dawned on her that the hand was laughing. It pointed to the TV screen at the funny bits, while the canned audience howled with laughter at the antics of the man with the fish. Cecilio clutched its fingers together and kept collapsing on to Marina's shoulder, as if it was unable to stand up.

'No more TV for you,' she said, with relief, finally understanding what Cecilio was trying to tell her. 'Next the doctor will accuse me of filling your head with junk TV.' She groaned. *Head?*

Cecilio touched her neck with one delicate finger. Marina tensed, but the hand did nothing further. Curling itself up into the hollow of her shoulder like a small bony cat, it felt to Marina as if it were purring. She leaned her head against it and smiled. Her smile muscles felt corroded and unstable. *A hand implant that can hear and understand. What will the medical profession think up next?*

Marina began to wake up every day with a sense of anticipation. Instead of the slight miasma of despair that fluffed her mental pillows every morning, she felt a strange, tight feeling deep in the pit of her stomach. At first, she thought it was indigestion, but to her amazement she discovered it was contentment.

All because of a hand?

'Are you part of me, Cecilio?' she asked it, feeling silly. 'Am I willing you to move? To have a personality?'

Was it her subconscious wish for affection that made Cecilio know exactly when she needed a friendly pat, a cheery wave, an impatient flick . . . a loving stroke? She didn't know exactly when the constant presence of the hands stopped feeling like a ghastly intrusion. Perhaps when Cecilio had shown her that it . . . he was a hearing, understanding entity? She'd always thought of hands as 'things'. Inanimate objects wanting something. It was strange that she felt more partial to Cecilio than the others.

The other hands felt like warm acquaintances, but Cecilio felt like something more. Why was he trying to communicate with her and not the others? Was it because he was on her shoulder? But then Terza was on her other shoulder, and she hadn't laughed at any TV shows. Marina rubbed her forehead in confusion. The other hands held her, but more as unknowing babies would seek comfort from their mother. Cecilio seemed to have a range of expression beyond theirs.

In a panic, she telephoned Dr Hurtigger. 'Tell me,' she cried, 'do the implanted hands have their own will? Their own personality? That of the person they're intended for? Or are they based on me?' She trailed off, unsure how to explain.

Dr Hurtigger's assured tones filled her ear. 'Of course they don't have a personality!' He laughed. 'Don't tell me you've been having intimate conversations with your implanted body parts?'

'Not really . . .'

'Now, Marina,' he chided her gently, 'I think you'd better take a break from any more implants. Perhaps the multiple implant was too much. After the ten are off, I'll find something extra special for you.' He paused. 'It's a good thing they're all due for removal starting next week.'

Marina felt a pang. 'Yes,' she said. 'I know.'

Although she knew Cecilio couldn't respond, she began to talk to him at length. It felt as though he understood. Marina's confusion mounted. She went over the same questions again and again. She didn't know why all the other hands felt like short-term visitors and this one felt like the hand of a man she could care about. Cecilio held her like a man would. Not like a Transport station man at all. He held her like a man who loved and wanted nothing from her.

'Nothing that a parasitic extra body part would want,' she said aloud. 'I must retain my perspective. I am *not* in the middle of some bizarre surrealistic romance novel.'

She sat in the darkening room. Cecilio tapped her on the cheek and pointed to the lamp. Marina's eyebrows raised. *Can you see, too?*

She nodded to the lamp to switch it on and rolled her eyes. *I guess my naming you Little Blind One was inappropriate.*

Marina thought to herself what a supple wrist he had. Graceful yet strong. He was gaining strength daily. Sometimes she felt the weaker of the two.

'I like it dark. I can pretend you're a real man sitting next to me, talking to me, touching me on the neck like you do.' She twined her fingers through his. 'Although if I confess to having feelings for a hand then I'll have to admit I'm crazy.'

Stung, Cecilio drew himself back and crouched on her shoulder as if turning his back on her. He looked unsure whether to sulk or not, but then straightened up. He appeared to have made a decision. He pointed to the other hands, quiescent at the various staging posts on her body.

Making a dismissive gesture, he seemed to be saying, 'They're inanimate hands. I'm Cecilio, and I'd want to be with you whether I were a hand or a man.' Exultant, he flexed his fingers, as if surprised at what he felt. He began to make odd hand motions. Marina recognized that he was using sign language as she'd seen it on TV, but couldn't understand what he was saying. She'd never learned to read it. His donee must have learned it somewhere. He spelt out the same words over and over, but when she indicated her confusion, he clenched his fist with frustration.

For the last few days before the CDs, or Cut-off Dates, Marina tried to spend quality time with the hands. She sat in the bath for hours and watched them fan little ripples in the water. Humming to herself, she felt like a longboat with five rowers on each side. '*Row, row, row your boat, gently down the stream . . . merrily merrily merrily merrily, life is but a dream . . .*'

Using the book for reference, she read their palms.

'Terza,' she said, to the hand on her right shoulder, 'you're going to a fine young woman. See this sun line? It means you'll be highly successful in a public career. Dancing, I bet. You've got dancer's fingers. Let's look at your love line. Ahhh! You've had trouble with men. You're going to be a woman who's a bit of a flirt. Two husbands and an affair. Be careful, Terza. One of them might hurt you.'

Only one hand could be harvested at a time. Three per day for the first three days, and then the man's hand last, by himself on the fourth day. Terza was removed first. Marina sent a note with the hand. Warning the young woman on whom Terza was to be implanted about the affair. She didn't want her to get hurt. She hoped the doctor would give her the note.

'Donata, you're such a down-to-earth person. Very grounded. You'll have problems with your weight. Don't let people tell you what to do. And stay away from the criminal element.'

Marina sighed. 'Now, hands . . . try to avoid taxi-moto accidents – they cause a lot of accidents. If you have to take one, be careful. Take an American one. The British taxi-motos are like British motorcycles. They look better than the American ones but they break down or go out of control more often.'

The belt hands were next. On their last evening together, they clutched her waist sadly. She read the fate lines on each palm. She looked at her palm for her own fate line. Indistinct. Unimpressive.

The others were gone now. Just Cecilio was left. It looked as if there would be a gap of a few days before he'd be taken off, though. Apparently his donee was in the hospital having problems with infection.

Good. She didn't want the donee to get his hand. She liked it where it was. The thought of her soon-to-be-empty shoulder filled her with velvety green gloom.

Time for Cecilio. Dr Hurtigger wanted Marina to come in the next day. The donee was ready. His infection was under control. Marina must read Cecilio's palm for him. It was his last evening. *Cecilio's Last Stand.*

When she traced the lines with her fingers and looked at what the book said, she gasped. Cecilio had a short life line. Didn't this mean the man would die soon after his hand was implanted? What a waste! Why couldn't she keep him? If he'd only die anyway . . . She thought long and hard.

I could give the City Credits back. Dr Hurtigger couldn't force the donation. They could grow another hand for the donee. She paced back and forth in a frenzy of indecision. Cecilio clasped her shoulder, as if in the grip of some strong emotion. She leaned her head towards him and brushed her cheek softly across his knuckles. He twined his fingers around a clutch of her hair.

On the scheduled CD, the incessant door banging and telephone ringing started an hour after her appointment time came and went. Marina unplugged her telephone. Locked the door.

Let them ring. She felt dizzy and full of unaccustomed emotion.

Four days later, Marina panicked. Cecilio was ill. His healthy pink skin had become a dark, furious purple.

He couldn't die! She couldn't let that happen. She'd have to take him back to the hospital, after all. Perhaps she'd waited too long already in her selfishness. Four days when she could have saved him. The fate line was right. He was dying. Surely Dr Hurtigger would help them.

She ran all the way to the Medical District, spurning the taxi-motos that beeped at her. She ran past Sandra, who was flicking purple, and burst into Dr Hurtigger's office, ripping open her jacket. She was only momentarily embarrassed to notice that she'd forgotten to put anything on underneath. Cecilio huddled, crouching weakly on her shoulder, an insubstantial mauve-coloured spider. You could almost see through his fingers, which seemed thin and weak as crumpled tissue.

'You've got to do something.'

'You've been avoiding us, haven't you?' Dr Hurtigger smiled thinly. 'I was about to come and fetch you myself. You can *not* keep the hand. The man requires it. We have a contract.'

'But he's going to die anyway.' She felt clammy with sweat.

The doctor's eyebrows disappeared into the hair carefully combed down to cover his baldness. 'To what do we owe this amazing foreknowledge?'

'I've read his palm.'

Sandra snickered from the doorway.

'I've changed my mind. Here are the City Credits back.' Marina thrust the envelope towards him that she'd stuffed in her jacket pocket before leaving her flat. 'I want to keep the hand.'

He took the envelope and absently flipped it back and forth. 'If the hand can sign a living will, giving up its right to donation, we will consider it.' He pushed a piece of paper towards her.

Marina sagged with relief. 'I thought you'd try to take him from me. He'll sign it right now. Can we borrow a pen?' *It was almost as if he'd expected this.*

'Certainly,' he said, soothingly, handing her one. He looked past her towards Sandra, who nodded slightly and came forward with a hypodermic needle. 'Lie down, and we'll give you an antibiotic shot for the hand. Maybe that will help. Its colour's terrible. Good thing you came in when you did. You both could have died. Just a little pinch now . . .'

Marina handed the pen to Cecilio as Dr Hurtigger gave her the shot. She felt dizzy instantly. When her eyes started to close, she fought the drugs that she guessed were certainly not antibiotics.

'Sign their form, Cecilio. Don't let them take you!'

Through her haze, she saw Cecilio trying desperately to operate the large black pen. Dr Hurtigger reached over and took hold of it. Cecilio lost the tug of war, his tissue-paper fingers crumpling against the onslaught of Dr Hurtigger's strength.

'Gotcha!' Dr Hurtigger's voice became faint, as did Sandra's answering giggle.

Marina slept.

When she woke Cecilio was gone, They told her it had been too late. They hadn't been able to save the hand. Marina touched her newest incision, the shape of a tiny smile, and felt empty. They told her to come back in a week to have the stitches out. 'We'll be ready for you then,' they said to her. Dr Hurtigger and Sandra both smiled at each other.

Marina walked home, feet stumbling against each other and tried to feel happy that she had her own space back. She wouldn't have to share her body with anything else. But when she ran her fingers across Cecilio's incision, she felt like howling in pain. Crossing both arms against her chest, she hunched down by the side of the road and rocked. There was nobody to complain. There were no hands to avoid making seasick.

An odd tingling coming from the incision interrupted her misery. It felt like a pulsing electric current. Was something wrong? Surely the tingling couldn't be this strong without him being alive? She laughed at her appalling lack of grasp on reality.

Now you've got a hand trying to contact you by ESP! Next it'll be telekinesis. Could Dr Hurtigger have been lying? She straightened up, ignoring the wary looks from people who had been watching her. With her head held high, she stepped smartly back on to the walkway and hurried home. She'd have to think about this.

When she arrived at her apartment and took off her jacket, she heard something crackle. She reached into her pocket and pulled out . . . the City Credits envelope she'd given back to Dr Hurtigger. She stared at it then held it to her cheek for an instant, motionless. She dropped it to the floor and threw her jacket on again. She had to know.

They wouldn't have given me back the envelope if he hadn't survived.

It took her seven hours to go to all the hospitals near to the Hurtigger Institute. She went from ward to ward, looking for men with fresh incisions around their wrists. Marina pretended to the nurses that she was a visitor for each man who looked likely. 'I'm his sister,' she said. 'I'm his wife.' When she went up to each man's bed, she smiled at him and told him she was a nurse's aide checking his pulse. When she picked up each hand, looking for the short life line, she hoped she wasn't hurting its owner. Every life line was frustratingly long. When she saw that, she'd place the man's hand down next to him with as much gentleness as possible, although she wanted to hurl it down.

After searching the last hospital with no success, she sagged with fatigue and despair. Perhaps it was too late. Had he already died? Had Dr Hurtigger been right? She walked towards the exit, gloom surrounding her like a viscous black cloud.

'Out of the way!' an orderly cried, as he shoved past Marina, pushing a wheeled stretcher. A man lay upon it, loosely wrapped in a sheet, his face a white blur.

'Emergency! We need a resuscitation team. STAT!'

Three people in white appeared from what seemed like nowhere and they all rushed past.

Marina watched them duck into one of the emergency-ward cubicles. The curtain wasn't quite closed and she watched them putting things that looked like miniature tennis racquets on each side of the man's chest.

'Clear!' they shouted, and a terrible thunking noise erupted from the racquets. 'And again!'

Marina watched the man's body arch upwards and his arms flop weakly to his sides. Strong brown arms, one with a fresh scar around the wrist. The hand attached to that wrist was an odd mauve colour.

She stayed.

Marina waited, barely able to breathe, for what seemed like hours. When the orderly finally came out of the cubicle, she grabbed his sleeve and begged him to tell her what had happened to the man.

'Are you a relative?' His beeper went off and he continued down the hall. Not waiting for her answer, he went on, 'He had a hand implant from one of those sicko people who sign up to be donor sites.'

Marina flinched.

'It was put on too late and the hand resisted implantation. It kept trying to pull itself off or sumthin' weird like that. Maybe it wanted to go home to its mummy.' He grinned at her over his shoulder as he sprinted off down the corridor.

'No!' Marina paled. She went back to the emergency cubicle and pulled open the curtain. It was empty of medical workers but filled with the hollow beeping of his ventilator. A clear tube led from it and curved down the man's throat. A piece of white tape held it steady against his mouth.

'You can't be him,' Marina whispered to the man, as she carefully stepped over the electric cable leading to the ventilator. The man's eyes were closed, and he was as pale as the sheets he lay upon. She forced herself to look from his hands to his face. Black hair curled onto a broad forehead. Full lips, dry and cracked. Smile lines. No straggling nose hair, from what she could see through the tubes and catheters cluttering his face. She sat down abruptly on the orange plastic chair next to the stretcher. His was not a face to inspire fear.

'Cecilio?' she whispered.

Nothing.

'Cecilio?'

The man's eyelids flickered.

'*Cecilio?* Is that you in there?' She felt silly and looked around to see if anyone was listening.

Marina picked up the hand lying at his side. *Poor man. He looks so weak.*

He also looked slightly Italian. Very Italian. She steeled herself to look at his palm. Vicious disappointment slammed her. Long, straight, impossibly healthy life line. She dropped the hand and put her head down on the bed and moaned.

She felt something. A hand twining itself gently into her hair and tugging. A familiar touch. Or was it? She was so afraid to look up. The misery would be too much to bear.

She drew a ragged breath.

She felt a weak tapping on her cheek and then a hand cupping her shoulder. As Cecilio had done.

She sat up abruptly. The man looked at her from behind all his myriad tubes and sticky tape. His eyes blazed. He made a sound. She leaned closer. He made the same sound. Uh-Ee-Uh. *Marina?*

In a panic, she looked at his hand again. The long life line mocked her. She looked at her own hand to check that she was looking at the right line. And looked again at the line running next to the life line.

Her fate line had changed. It was crossing the love line. Before, they'd been distinctly separate. She recalled what the book had tried to say. Some rubbish about lines changing if you changed your current circumstances. 'Your life is not mapped out in stone,' the book said. 'You can alter your own future.' *Mine changed. Could Cecilio's?*

His life line could have been short before because of her. In keeping the hand from the man, she would have been his killer.

She held the mauve hand tightly with disbelief as the ventilator monitor beeped on. The man made a sound in his throat. An imperative gurgle, trying to bypass the tube curving down his throat. She looked up. He pointed to his face with his good hand.

He pointed to his other hand, trapped between Marina's, and patted himself on the chest.

'*I* am Cecilio,' he seemed to be saying. 'Not just my hand. It is part of the whole man. He is me.' He patted his chest again. 'I am him.' All the tubes and catheters couldn't hide the exultant look on his face.

He held out his good arm, shaking with the strain. She waited only for a second before she leaned down and let herself be enclosed by it.

Mama, she thought. You were wrong. You *can* change fate.

The beeping of the breathing machine echoed the rushing of blood in her ears and Cecilio's beating heart as she lay against him. But then it was only his heart she heard. Nothing else. The beeping had stopped. The lights went off, and the air-conditioner hummed to a halt.

You can change it . . . CAN'T YOU?

Cecilio, you can't die twice.

Pressure Tactics

WYNNE

*Her own mother lived the latter years
of her life in the horrible suspicion
that electricity was dripping invisibly
all over the house.*

JAMES THURBER

'There's been another incident on the Piccadilly Line,' Wynne called to Colton, as she followed him up the tracks. Playfully she shone her torch down at where she estimated his feet would be. 'So watch what you're stepping in, Col!' Colton's steps faltered slightly as she laughed. She could always get him with that one, even after ten years of marriage. Being a Scraper himself should have made him immune to it, but he had never become comfortable with some of the grimmer aspects of the job.

'Knock it on the head, you.' Colton called from the darkness in front of her. Wynne laughed again and bent down, spotting an errant hair on the grimy steel track. Her new white plastic overalls crinkled as her knees bent.

London Organized Transport Inc. – or London Occasional Transport, as most people referred to it – had instituted new overalls for its city-wide crews of Scrapers. They were supposedly much more hygienic, but damned if they didn't make her feel like turkey wrapped in cling-film. The uniforms also included fluorescent yellow plastic turbans to prevent their own hair from joining the bags of detritus they scraped off the tracks every night. As she'd tucked hers in tonight before starting work, Colton had come up behind her, clucking admiringly. 'Very sexy. I don't know why they didn't make us wear these years ago.'

Wynne ignored him. Her thick dark hair refused to stay trapped inside the turban and insisted on springing out.

Colton leaned up against her and snaked his hands around her huge distended stomach. 'Our boy will have to get used to wearing them as well, won't he?' He patted her stomach. 'Our bowling ball, that is.'

'Our girl,' Wynne said, primly pursing her lips. 'Don't forget I put in a gene request for our child to be a girl. They were so glad to get a request from me after so many years that they gave me the choice.'

Colton's eyes, the colour of fresh-squeezed orange juice, dimmed to a dull tangerine. 'I'm still not convinced having a child is a good idea –'

'I am. Come on, Colton, one little baby,' Wynne interrupted. 'Surely you won't mind just one eensy weensy baby?'

He looked worried.

Wynne knew he'd get used to the idea eventually. His reasons for not wanting children were so silly. Just because he'd been adopted or had had an awful childhood, or something like that. He'd get used to the idea. She could tell from the way he kept touching her stomach, despite his words to the contrary, that he was as excited as she was. She finished packing her hair into the turban and carefully wrapped duct tape around the wires sprouting from the back of her jump-suit.

'Anyway, we're having a child and it's too late to cancel the gene request, so stop moaning. You'll be a great father.'

'Yes, but the gene manipulation is only ninety-eight per cent effective. There's a risk of having a deformed baby. You never know. The boy could be . . .' Colton fiddled with Wynne's wires as he looked down.

'What boy?' Wynne chucked him on the chin. 'I couldn't run the risk of having a little boy like his father running around loose. Cause havoc among all the young girls. It'll be a girl, and she won't be deformed, take my word for it. Maybe mentally deranged, like her father.'

Colton had tickled her through the plastic and they'd both been late for work.

Wynne couldn't remember a night when she hadn't walked the tracks. Night after night for the past twenty years, eight months and twenty-eight days. At first, when she was ten, it had been behind her mother and father as they showed her how to handle the long claw-like scrapers.

You had to straddle the de-electrified rail, both feet a good distance away from the metal just in case it still held an errant charge. The tunnel wall must be on your left and the platform to your right. You placed the business end of the scraper on the rail and nodded towards a green optic light along the stem. The light operated the claws, which opened like arthritic fingers to clutch the rail. You then pushed the scraper ahead of you along the rail with an elegant swoop. When the claw had gathered enough detritus, you nodded at the light to open the fingers just enough to release the rail. Next, you twisted the stem gracefully to keep the foreign matter in the cup-shaped palm of the claw and swooped it up into the air behind your right side. You had to manage to drop the claw's contents behind you into the large garbage sack clipped to the back of your uniform without clunking yourself on the head. Then you kept the swoop going and brought the claw round to your left side against the tunnel wall. As the scraper's impetus pulled it downwards, you scraped as much of the wall as possible.

All in one great ungainly circle, over and over again, without missing a beat. So many times she'd been unable to lift the heavy claw high enough and she'd smacked herself painfully on the head. LOT always made trainees wear protective helmets for the first few months, just in case. Sourly, she could tell from her father's shaking shoulders that he found her efforts exceedingly funny. She would sulk for several minutes, and flip her grounding wires at him with glum irritation.

The wires had driven her nuts at first, until she'd become used to them. Just as annoying as wearing her first bra had been. They itched like crazy, but you got used to them. Bras. And wires.

She was certainly good at scraping now, though. Twenty years of being one of LOT's tribe of thousands that came to life after the electricity was shut off for the evening.

When trains rushed through the tunnels, the burst of wind swept round the sour-faced commuters standing on the platforms, playfully sweeping away errant hairs and flecks of dead skin, which would drift on to the tracks and tunnel walls as the trains escaped the platform. It was important that the rails remained pristine to facilitate the movement of the trains. That was the Scrapers' job. Keep the rails scraped. The walls, having less to do with the actual operation of the trains, failed to receive the same attention. Over time, the flecks on the walls built up to a patina of seemingly living, breathing new skin.

Unless they were scraped, of course. LOT didn't like human walls.

The first time Wynne had brushed her hand against the grease-encrusted white tiles of the tunnel walls without her protective gloves on she had been shocked at how human they felt. As she grazed her fingertips along them, the surface felt like the soft, fuzzy skin of a peach.

Hair and skin. It seemed sometimes as if they were her whole life. Besides Colton and the baby, she thought hastily. Hair and skin. Sometimes she was tempted to leave one tiny strand of hair over a rail just to see what happened. *Would the train screech to a halt, throwing all its occupants into the air? Would it derail horribly, carnage ensuing?*

No. All that would probably happen is that the train would delay between stations as usual, and there'd be an incomprehensible announcement to the public: 'We are . . . ufhgs . . . gseuwl . . . sorry to announce that the wrong kind of hair is on the tracks . . . sgpuw . . . we apologize for the delay.'

Just like that winter LOT had bleated about the wrong snow on the tracks causing the two-week system breakdown. And the wrong leaves one autumn. LOT had a phenomenal range of excuses, from mundane to so absolutely fantastic you couldn't believe it was possible they'd made it up.

The wrong hair on the tracks, indeed. Wynne sniffed. Scrape. So many years of the same. Scraaaapppppe. She'd wanted to be something different once. When her mother had told her she had to serve out the contract, she cried bitterly. 'No!' She was appalled. 'You can't mean it. Twenty years?'

'Don't fight it,' her mother replied, resignation coating her words like a thick blanket. 'No sense in fighting when you can't win. Accept your lot in life. Stop wanting more. It will only disappoint you in the end.'

Once a Scraper, always a Scraper. LOT had decreed that since declining numbers of people were applying to be Scrapers, the job would pass from parent to child, and then on again from child's child, to child's child's child.

'Who else would want the damn job?' Wynne muttered under her breath.

'What was that, Wynne?' Scandalized, her mother swatted the back of her legs.

'Nothing.'

'Do you want your mouth washed out with soap? Don't be ungrateful. Jobs don't grow on trees.'

The contract had been signed. Every mother signed over her child on the day of its birth. The only way to avoid signing was for the mother herself to be in another job before she gave birth. Not much chance of that: after twenty years of hefting a scraper claw, it was unlikely you could get a job doing anything else. Who'd hire a Scraper? In London's employment caste scheme, Scrapers were untouchables.

Wynne had made her token resistance to signing over her own child by refusing to become pregnant until her own contract was finished. Even though Colton kept insisting he didn't want children, she knew he did. She had refused to give in and request a child before now. It's just . . . all of a sudden, having a child seemed so important. *I want the illusion of choice.*

At least she'd been able to choose Colton. She'd decided when she was a little girl that she'd marry him when she grew up. When had he arrived in their scraping section? She couldn't recall much of her early childhood. She thought she could remember being taken care of by an unpleasant baby-sitter or something.

In some way or another, Colton had always drifted on the periphery of her life. He used to have the same wish to escape life's assumptions. To escape life as a Scraper. Wynne had seen it in his eyes. His air of rebellion had excited her. She'd noticed him at a Scraper Meeting she'd attended with Aunt Estra. Her parents had been fighting again, so her aunt had volunteered to take her.

'Aunt Estra.' Wynne had tapped her arm. 'Look at that boy over there. The restless one with the orange eyes.'

Aunt Estra was distracted. 'What? Oh, yes.' She laughed, the sound gurgling over the voices of the others. 'He looks as if he wants to run somewhere very hard and very fast. Like a palomino.'

Wynne didn't think he looked like a horse at all, but she didn't want to hurt her aunt's feelings. She was old, after all. Almost forty, she thought. Ancient.

'Sure thing. Like a horse. Uh-huh.'

She rolled her eyes and sneaked another peep at the boy. His hair looked as if it refused to lie down without a fight. When his eyes eventually rested upon her, during their restless search around the platform, she had smiled at him until her face hurt.

'Wynne?' Colton's voice sounded impatient. 'Strike a trot, will you? We have to finish this stretch before my hair goes grey.'

Wynne couldn't figure out where Colton's rebellion had gone. He'd tried to get out once, but had returned almost before he'd gone. His eyes were grim and his hair chastened. It lay obediently along the top of his head where it was supposed to. Wynne felt cold sand trickle into the pit of her stomach. She ached to mess his hair up again and make it erupt from the top of his head as it used to. Something had happened while he was gone but she didn't know what. All she knew is that after that, Colton had allowed LOT's hairy mantle to embrace him without resisting.

She still possessed remnants of her rebellion. Somewhere.

'I wanted to be an electrician,' Wynne whispered to Colton's retreating man-shaped blackness. 'I did. I could have been.'

Her mother's betrayal bothered her still. Berri had told her and Marina that you had to make do with what you were given. But it had been a lie. Her mother hadn't stayed where she belonged. She'd broken away. *Was it my fault she left?* It must have been Marina's. After all, she'd been sent away. *You only got sent away if you did something unforgivable, didn't you?*

She walked on, her hand brushing the damp steel of one of the escape doors.

'Ouch,' she cried, as sparks flicked her arm and chased up to her shoulders.

She'd forgotten to check her omnipresent grounding wires. She and her family had become so used to her being different over the years that they all tended to forget about her wires. *Especially me.*

Ever since she could remember, she'd had the unlucky propensity to be filled with some kind of errant electric charge. Whenever she touched anything, she experienced a painful, teeth-juddering shock. Her mother took her to the family GP, Dr Lupus, but he was stumped. He scratched his head in bewilderment and suggested that it might be caused by incipient puberty. He added hopefully that it might go away when she had her first period. Random poltergeist electricity, perhaps.

Her periods came and went regularly from her thirteenth birthday, but the electricity stayed. Eventually she and her family got used to it. It wasn't any stranger than their next-door neighbour's bratty child, who screamed and stuck a finger up each nostril when you said hello to him. She tried to avoid touching people without warning them.

It had frightened Colton, the first time he touched her.

'Jesus!' he cried. 'Something's bitten me!'

He had become used to it eventually, and even suggested the bundle of grounding wires Wynne now wore clipped to herself wherever she went. They made a tremendous difference in her life. Since she couldn't touch anybody without administering a painful electric jolt, she'd experienced a considerable lack of affection as a child. Wynne could look back on it now with a degree of equanimity, but she shuddered to think of how alone and unloved she'd felt. Like some kind of electric pariah. Sometimes she thought it had done permanent damage to her, deep inside. Every once in a while she felt strange glimmers of unease.

Colton had changed that. Wynne felt a glow when she thought of him. Usually before he reached over and touched her in the night, he checked that the tell-tale wires were snuggled round her neck and touching the ground. Naked but for the wires, adorned like a human Christmas tree, she'd lean against him. The parts of her that touched him would sizzle pleasantly from pleasure rather than random voltage.

As she ran her fingers through his hair and down his strong back, rippled by oddly shaped scars, every part of her felt electric with feeling. He'd come back from his escape attempt with those scars and he never wanted to talk about them. Looking at him with sympathy, she decided he'd tell her some day, when he was ready.

Maybe he'd tell her about the box, too.

The wires dragged behind her when she walked, the small rubber marbles at the ends bouncing merrily like tumbling lottery balls against the damp floors.

Pregnancy made her absent-minded, though, and Wynne kept forgetting to check that the wires were in constant contact with the ground. She reached behind her now and, as she had thought, they'd become caught up in the refuse sack.

Viciously, she straightened it and flung the wires over her shoulder. One grey rubber marble flicked her cheek, leaving a faint pink mark on the paleness. *Scrape. Scraaaapppppe.*

Wynne continued down the tunnel until she stepped on something soft. It felt unusual. Making a face, she bent to see if it was a dead rat. There were millions of them around. More of them than people in London, supposedly. She reached one gloved hand down towards it. Small, pale and oblong. It wasn't a rat. It was a . . . Wynne snapped upwards, her unborn child performing internal gymnastics. *It's a human finger.*

That incident on the Piccadilly Line that she'd teased Colton about. She hoped she wouldn't find any more grisly bits. Aunt Estra had once found a smiling head. A jumper leaped in front of a Central Line train during rush hour. The police managed to find most of the sections, but the head stuck to the front of the train, without the driver being any the wiser. It eventually dropped off, for Aunt Estra to come upon during her nightly Central Line trawling. Poor Aunt Estra hadn't been the same after that.

'What's that in the track ahead?' she'd mutter to herself constantly. 'A head?' People steered clear of her.

The poisonous realization that she'd be a Scraper the rest of her life stretched before Wynne, a cold tunnel filled with freezing liquid and human body parts sucking around her ankles.

'I can't do this to you,' she cried to her unborn child.

Wynne jogged up the track awkwardly to where Colton was closing another filled bag. Her huge stomach swayed alarmingly, so she held it as she ran. In a rush of nervous words, she told him of the finger, of her dissatisfaction and what she wanted to do. When she finished and looked up at his white face, the normally relaxed features were pinched with upset.

'Why?' he cried towards her, the pain evident in his voice. 'By saying you don't want our child to be a Scraper, you're saying that what we do isn't valuable. What's wrong with a job for life? Security . . .'

'Security is strangling me,' she said quietly. 'I want our child to have a choice.' If he said no she would scream. Everyone always said no.

'It isn't possible,' Colton replied.

Wynne's head ached as the words sank into the pile of negatives she had collected assiduously throughout her life.

'No,' her mother had said, 'you can't go swimming. You'll electrocute everyone in the pool. No. You cannot be an electrician. I signed a Work Contract for you while you were still unborn. Don't you understand what I've given up for you? No. You will be a Scraper, as I am, as my parents were, and as your children will be.'

No. No. No. Wynne looked up at his face. 'Colton, please. I . . .' She braced her body for flight. If he said no again, she wouldn't be able to keep from pushing him away from her. Silence. She started to feel angry. A buzzing sensation crawled up her neck. A furious warmth.

'All right,' he said, his voice low and unstable. 'If you want to leave your job, go to LOT and try convincing them to accept you into the electrician's training programme, I'll support you. I know you've wanted to leave Scraping for years.' He sagged. 'I hoped you'd forget about it when you forged my signature and requested that baby. I wasn't angry. I thought a baby would make you feel happier. More settled. Obviously not.'

Wynne let out her breath. She hadn't realized that he knew you had to have both signatures on the gene request form.

'I'm sorry.'

Colton picked at one edge of his scraper with a fingernail. 'When will you go?'

Wynne smiled carefully. 'I can't wait. I'll go tomorrow morning.'

Colton's face darkened. 'Aren't they closed for the weekend?'

'No. They're open until ten.' At Colton's surprise, she shrugged. 'I'm a fount of useless information.'

'I suppose you have to go tomorrow. Isn't your Birth Clinic appointment on Sunday morning?'

He knew more than she'd thought. She shot him a wary look. He seemed to have accepted the situation with resigned grace. His eyes were sad, though. As if he thought he wasn't enough to keep her happy.

Wynne sighed. 'I know. It's not much time. I'll have to stay awake after we finish work, and take the Transport into the West End to Central Headquarters.' She leaned against him in the darkness. 'Wish me luck.' She'd make sure he knew how much he made her happy. After she had done what she had to do.

Colton reached down and brushed a dark smut off her white plastic. 'I wish you both luck.' He turned and started walking away, towards the Northern Line gates flickering in the distance.

'I love you, Colton,' Wynne said softly in his direction. As she looked at him, she felt warm glimmers of electricity bouncing around under her turban, rustling among her hair like a mouse in clover. Strong emotion got the currents going. They got in the way sometimes, but they made her feel special.

It was a long night. Pregnancy made her clumsy and easily tired. She wished she could have afforded to take the last week off work.

When the shift ended at seven a.m., she tried to doze for an hour before setting off. She'd use Colton to make sure she didn't oversleep: his nose was a superb alarm clock. Every morning, when they went to bed together, he'd fall asleep exactly one hour after he had lain down and his nose would whistle like a banshee. It sounded like her mother's antique electric kettle. *Wheeeeeeeeeee!*

Normally it drove her nuts, but this time it would be quite helpful.

When Colton's nose whistled, she got up. She hadn't slept at all. She blew a kiss in his direction and got dressed carefully in the gloom. Without windows, it was always so dark underground.

What did one wear for an interview? She hadn't a clue. Best not wear her ubiquitous white plastic, though. She didn't have anything for an interview. She'd never *had* an interview. That faded yellow dress with the drowsy red poppies? Too much? She couldn't be sure. *Why not?* Flowers would give her courage.

After putting on the dress, she ran a comb through her unruly hair. She peered into the CompuLook screen and cocked her head. Did she want a different look? A rounder face? Different-coloured eyes? She decided against it as she didn't want to risk any software bugs. The machine broke down more often than it worked. Sometimes you couldn't tell if you were walking around with one blue and one green eye. She wished she could afford the upgrade.

Despite the immense bulge of her daughter spreading out the poppies on her dress, she thought she'd do. She clipped her wires carefully to the collar and smoothed them down one side. She paused. What would they think? Everyone down here was used to her attachments, but LOT certainly wouldn't be. She tucked the wires down inside her dress. They dribbled out from the bottom of her skirt in an odd way but that would have to do. If LOT said anything she'd tell them she had a magnetic personality.

Going to the door of their small neat apartment, she looked back at Colton. He lay covered up in all the blankets, whistling away. She almost softened. Giving in was easy. Maybe she shouldn't bother. The child kicked her hard, as if to remind her. 'Thanks,' she said, 'I needed that.'

She pulled on her jacket and went to the door, pausing to cough painfully. She didn't want to think about what her lungs were like.

Probably coated with human skin just like the walls of the tunnels. Layers and layers of London's finest were gathered inside her. People crawling down her throat and into her lungs. She coughed again, hoping to dislodge them before they could get down any further. *I need a number 10 bus from Tufnell Park to King's Cross.*

She talked companionably to herself as she rode the escalators up to ground level. After she got off the number 10, she'd nip on to a Piccadilly Line Transport bound for the West End. Simple twenty-minute journey. *No problem.*

Her steps slowed as she approached the bus stop on Junction Road. A mass of people crowded round every red double-decker that warily approached. People spilled on to the street and surrounded the buses, preventing them from leaving. People shouted obscenities at each other. Screamed. Fought for a place on a bus, pushing each other off back on to the street.

Wynne stopped, horrified. It couldn't be. Not today. She groaned.

Another Transport strike crippling the City yet again. She hadn't known, being underground and involved in her own affairs. Every summer, for the past, well, ever since she could remember, Transport drivers had gone on strike. Better pay, shorter hours, the wrong cheese in the canteen sandwiches. It was always something. She hadn't known this summer's first strike was today. She never did know when there was a strike until she went scraping and found the tracks pristine and untouched. No hair. No skin. Because she slept during the daytime, she rarely came into contact with the effects of the strikes. Although there was far less work during one, it was also a lot more boring.

Her mother had told her, before she left, that back in her day *all* people-conveyance companies, including the buses and trains, went on strike one hot summer. London's murder rate escalated exponentially. So did incident counts.

'People jumped, or were pushed from anger and frustration,' her mother had whispered to Wynne as she tucked her in. 'You couldn't tell after a while.'

Wynne couldn't countenance the thought of all three companies going on strike. One was bad enough. When one went on strike, it threw the others into turmoil.

Look how badly the bus system is coping with this Transport strike.

There were too many people in London for the number of buses. She tried to be charitable. She used to feel sorry for Transport drivers being taken advantage of by LOT. She knew how its management could be. Then she felt sorry for LOT, as they always appeared so contrite and lost so much money – so many billions of City Credits per strike day. She did try to be charitable.

But charitability was not getting her a bus. She needed one *now*. She had to get to Headquarters by ten. Wynne tried to push forward in the scrum, but was beaten back by hundreds of people shoving past her with rough urgency. Each passing bus disgorged one or two sweating lucky people, and four hundred tried to force their way past the frightened conductors.

'Only five standing!' they shrieked. 'Ten up top and five standing below!'

Everyone ignored them. Nobody paid the City Credit bus fee. Taking four hours to get to work was driving them mad. *Talk about road rage. People are filled with strike rage.* As she was. Impotence and fury saturated her, as the ten a.m. deadline got nearer. She managed to heave her unwieldy self on to the eighth bus that inched forward in the snarl of traffic, not without receiving many sharp-elbowed attacks. She held on to the rail as the bus crept down the street. The wind sucked at her skirt and whipped the poppies into a frenzy. Wynne held fast to the rail, relieved she was on despite the uncertain hold her toes had on the running board. If the bus went over a bump, she'd fall off. If she did, she'd be trampled by hundreds trying to take her place.

People pressed into her from all sides. Indistinct body parts nudged her. She couldn't be sure which parts they were. At one point, something that felt like a blunt umbrella mashed into her side. It seemed to have a life of its own. It moved. She edged away. It followed, and glued itself against her amorously. She couldn't move any further. Carefully, she took one hand off the metal rail and reached behind for her grounding wires. She lifted them up until they no longer touched the floor of the bus. The umbrella pressed warmly against her and its human owner screamed. 'Jesus!' he cried. 'Something's bloody bitten me.'

Wynne looked around with wide innocent eyes. Good thing he'd moved off. He shouldn't upset her. Anger did funny things to her electricity. She'd never let it go too far before as it scared her – but it wasn't good to upset her as she wasn't too clear on how to control it. High emotion started growth inside her. Something electric travelling up her spinal cord. Growing. Pushing. Becoming warm and alive. Almost like the birth of something . . . but not like a birth. Bemused, she patted where she estimated her daughter's head was. She hoped she wasn't patting the child's rear end.

When she got off at King's Cross, trembling from strain, it was nine thirty. She still had to catch another bus into the West End. She pushed through the crowds, feeling sweaty and tired. Trudging to the next bus stop down Euston Road, she passed the barricaded gates to Euston Transport Station. A man, whose large damp face gave the impression of a plate of soggy scrambled eggs, barred the way in. His LOT uniform looked too small for him. Sweat stains spread from under his waving arms. He was standing on a stool and yelling at the furious crowds, his hands cupped like a megaphone over his mouth.

'It's them!' he cried, in a voice thin as skimmed milk. 'Management! They keep refusing our demands!'

Next to the man was a newspaper kiosk. The headline of the first edition of the *Evening Standard* read: 'Transport chiefs offer deal. Unions say no.' A small girl kicked the man's stool, almost toppling him off. He hung on desperately to the gates behind him as he whined, 'There's another arbitration meeting at Headquarters this morning. Please. It's not my fault.' He was practically in tears with all the people shouting at him.

Five buses passed Wynne, stuffed full of people.

'No room, sorry!' The drivers tried not to attract any of the waiting crowds as they did a running stop to let a few off. 'No more people!'

Wynne started to pray. 'Pleasepleaseplease may the next one have some room.'

The next one had no room. Nor had the next. Or the next. Ten minutes to ten. She crushed a fold of the once brilliant poppy-strewn fabric in her fist, and tears of frustration carved her face. Bile made her insides roil.

Wynne stood in the middle of the crowd, looked up into the smog-choked sky and let out an almighty cry of frustration. Defeat gestured rudely at her. She'd have to go back a failure. She couldn't do anything. Warmth boiled up her spinal cord. This time she didn't try to damp it down. It seeped ever higher, filling the spaces between her vertebrae. Sparks shot from her like fireworks.

'The Transport strike has sentenced my child to twenty years of scraping hair off tracks. Thank you, Unions! Thank you, LOT!' Her voice spiralled above the crowd. People backed away from her. *Mama, why did you leave us? Why* . . .

'Look aboot there, Dysis!' a broad flat Canadian voice said right behind her. 'One of those street performers. Give her some City Credits or something. Wow!'

Wynne stopped her tirade in mid-spark, gasping for breath, and looked over to where the voice had come from. The electricity felt curiously reluctant to retreat this time. A large pink person. A tourist, obviously – he looked too happy. As he smiled at her, she noticed how white and healthy his teeth were. How thick and shiny his hair. She found it difficult to respond as a representative of her country should.

'What do you bloody want?' she snarled at his pinkness.

'Oh, sorry,' the pink man stuttered. He put up his arm protectively and then took a step back.

Wynne felt bad. This was probably his first trip abroad and here he was getting verbally flayed by an electrically charged pregnant frustrated whale in a flower-spattered dress.

'It's the Transport strike,' she managed to say between clenched teeth. 'They're holding the public to ransom yet again. I could kill them.'

Tsking in concerned tones, the man stepped forward and patted her comfortingly on the shoulder, trying to avoid the sparks that fizzed intermittently around her. Wynne explained to him about the strike. She didn't want to tell him why it upset her so, but his wide friendly face looked so interested that she found herself telling him about the baby. And the job.

'I think you should go for it, don't you, Dysis?' The man – Ricker, as he insisted she call him – looked for his wife. She was somewhere behind him in the crowd, apparently.

'Go to the headquarters. Tell them that it's their fault you couldn't get there on time. Make a fuss. A big stink. Go on!' His voice became more and more excited, and he punched the air with a large pink fist. 'Use pressure tactics.'

'Pardon?'

'Back in Montreal public utilities aren't allowed to go on strike.'

Wynne was disbelieving. 'No?'

'They're not allowed to disrupt the public, so they use pressure tactics.' He nodded with certainty.

'Which are?'

'When the police went on strike five years ago, they stopped shaving their beards.' At Wynne's incredulous face, he laughed. 'I know it sounds weird, but it worked. Their bosses and everyone knew that they were upset, but they did their job. Nobody suffered. Then the ambulance men, well . . . they stopped washing their ambulances.'

Wynne shot him a doubtful glance.

'And the postal strikes. The postmen wore their caps backwards.' Ricker beamed at Wynne.

'But wasn't it ineffectual? Didn't people think how silly they were?'

Ricker shook his head. 'Oops, sorry.' As he had been talking, he hadn't paid attention and he'd stepped on one of her wires. 'Dysis always tells me I'm a clumsy clot. Feet like a drunk elephant.'

He looked back into the crowd. 'And a late one, too. I better go find Dysis. We're supposed to have met our group and be

48

doing the Tower of London by now. We'll have to walk at this rate.'

As they said their goodbyes, Wynne hugged him impulsively, careful first to check that she was grounded. 'Thanks,' she said.

'What for? I didn't do anything.' He looked bemused.

'You did. Take my word for it.'

As Wynne walked away from him, she looked back once and was surprised to see him still looking at her. He wasn't smiling and seemed less pink somehow. She decided he must be worried about missing the Tower of London.

Instead of heading home, Wynne walked the rest of the way to LOT Headquarters. It was the building next to the grim Victorian hospital, which always looked haunted. She looked up at its shuttered windows: they were medieval and unwelcoming. She shivered and hurried past an adjoining pink-stoned building. Some clinic or other. Colton always told her she had too much imagination.

The main Headquarters door was bolted, bearing a sign stating that they were closed for the weekend. 'Arbitration Meeting in Progress' cringed across it. Wynne sniffed and went round to the alley next to the building. She knew that one of the Transport tunnels went underneath this building and reappeared next to LOT's service entrance.

There it is. She unlocked the tunnel gate with her pass-key and closed it behind her. She walked downwards, ignoring rats skittering past on their way to some unknown destination.

The tunnel intersected with the main electric control room for the headquarters building. Wynne used her key to open its locked door. Scrapers needed access to all Transport tunnels and control rooms, so nothing was out of bounds. She walked up to the main electric panel and stared at it with dismay. A multitude of wires coiled snake-like on a huge flashing panel behind thick glass. Ranged around the panel were security cameras, showing the rooms in the building above.

Wynne inserted her pass-key into the electric panel lock. Maybe if she could get at them, she could plan what to do next. Her inbuilt current must be good for something. Maybe it had given her some sort of inherent electrical ability. Perhaps she could cut the lights to the Arbitration Meeting. She wanted to do *some*thing to express her dissatisfaction. She turned the key.

It didn't work. It must be only for doors and gates, not for electrical panels. She rocked on her heels, not knowing what to do next.

The glass and wires glimmered with taunting cruelty. Wynne leaned forward and pounded on the panel with her fists. *Nothing. Not a crack.*

Frustration and rage overwhelmed her. The eager warmth in her spinal cord flared. It felt grateful to be let loose. It had been reluctant to retreat before. She looked at herself in the glass, which had a strange bevelled effect. Her reflection was hazy and distorted. Her head and feet were tiny and her stomach was the size of a Volkswagen. Her child. Twenty years of giving in erupted. Wynne looked at the security cameras, and found one showing the meeting room. She reached over and snapped the volume switch upwards.

'No!' a tinny voice squeaked. 'No. No. No. We won't settle.'

Nonononono. Wynne braced herself with one hand placed against the camera and the other against the glass of the electrical panel. Anger and frustration roiled within her. The electric thing inside her passed the point of no return. It gripped her skull with metallic fingers and her hair felt hot. She wiped a pearl of sweat trickling down the side of her neck. When her hand met her neck, something crackled. A small drop-shaped flame oozed out from between her fingers and spat towards the glass in front of her. Slowly, Wynne brought up her other hand. Both hands now encircled her neck. She smelled singed hair and hoped it wasn't hers. The smell of burning skin. She was surprised not to feel pain. The heat felt good. The flames became less drop-like and developed brighter red knife-like edges.

Moving closer to the camera and the electric panel, she felt as if she were burning up. Something was escaping and wanted further release from her. The flames became a conflagration encircling her head like a crown. Wynne took her hands away from her neck and pressed one on the camera and the other on the panel. She didn't know what would happen but she felt that some great effort was needed. She had to push. She did. Smoke curled from her hands. Grimacing, she focused all her attention into making the final hard thrust.

Tiny figures flickered in the eye of the camera. The meeting appeared to be in stalemate. Both sides sat obdurately with arms folded, eyes narrowed to small angry slits. The two elected leaders of the opposing sides waited, wordless.

'Well?' the arbitrator said. 'Have we a deal?'

Both leaders spoke at once; the besuited President of LOT, and the union leader in his 'Power to the People' T-shirt.

'No!'

Wynne felt the release. The glass panel in front of her shattered and electricity slithered on to the wires and licked them with slavering hunger. *That's better.*

She felt a twinge from the child.

Everything happened at once. As the word 'no' left both leaders' lips simultaneously, a bolt of bluish electric current shot up from the air vents in the floor, crackled up each chair leg and into their nether regions.

'Jesus!' they both cried. 'Something's bitten me!'

They looked around, suspicion mottling their features. To their annoyance, the crowd of people in the room, spectators and journalists included, were desperately trying to control trembling lips. One smallish woman at the back failed to hold back a short hysterical giggle. 'Thank you, God, that was just what I asked for. A bolt from the blue!'

A taller man, standing next to her, laughed. 'Religion's got nothing to do with it. They needed a kick up the —'

'We will adjourn until later,' the President spat, and tried to get up. Horrified, she looked down as bands of current criss-crossed her lap, effectively roping her to the chair. She screamed, her mouth opening impossibly wide. The other leader chortled until he noticed that the same thing was happening to him.

The small woman yelled from the back, 'Why not get on with the meeting? Looks like you're not going anywhere!'

For the rest of the meeting, which ended surprisingly quickly, whenever 'No' was said by either side, the issuer received an electric shock of increasingly monumental proportions. The shock seemed alive somehow. Very soon, both leaders were saying, 'Yes,' to anything the other side proposed, to avoid the painful pinching bursts. The Arbitrator smiled and smiled.

'Yes.'

'Sure.'

'Yep.'

'Fine. Whatever you say.'

'Me too. Super.'

'Fine.'

'Yes,' the two leaders said finally in unison.

'Settled. Call off the Transport Strike!'

Yes.

Wynne took her hands away from what was left of the camera and the glass panel. Tiny crystalline shards winked at her. She reached in and untwisted one of the wires. The blue one looked loose and she didn't want to start a fire or anything.

Feeling fragile, she went back up the tunnel and round to the front door. She walked brazenly past the receptionist, who backed away from her in fright. After she knocked tentatively at the door, one of the journalists opened it. Wynne stepped in, her dress in all its poppied glory charred into unrecognizable smears of red and black. Tufts of burnt hair sprang up from her smoking head every which way. The people in the room turned to look at her.

'Oh, so sorry,' she said, stepping back slightly. 'I thought you'd have finished.'

'And *who*, may we ask, are *you*?' the criss-crossed President uttered, fatigue and electrical current redolent in her voice.

'Just Wynne,' she replied, shyness causing her to speak to the ground. 'Wynne,' she said in firmer tones. 'I've come from below.'

The small woman crossed herself, as Wynne continued, 'I'm here to apply for a job as an electrician.'

Part Two

*What we call our future is the shadow
which our past throws in front of us.*

MARCEL PROUST

Cartons of Chaos

COLTON

*For he counteracts the powers of
darkness by his electrical skin and
glaring eyes.*

CHRISTOPHER SMART

Putting a mouse into each ear wasn't drowning out the noises from the room next door at all. Settling back into the pillow, Colton cupped a grubby hand around each small warm body and nudged them closer to the sides of his head. The scrabbling of Bonnie's feet tickled his ear and he giggled, trying not to catapult both mice up into the air. 'Be still, sweetheart,' he whispered as he stroked her tiny chocolate-coloured head with one finger. 'You too, Clyde.'

He whispered because lately his voice had started to crack with alarming regularity. One minute he sounded like any normal kid and the next he sounded like a growly-voiced adult. The thought of the puberty-induced changes to come horrified him. Dysis had sat him down a few weeks ago and explained the Facts of Life. She must be making it up. That stuff couldn't be true. *Yuck*.

'Hush,' he murmured, as Clyde made an inquiring 'urp'. Colton didn't want to scare his family with his wildly careering vocal pitch. He reached both hands up to his head and simultaneously scritched under each family member's chin. Colton made sure that he gave them both exactly the same amount of time and attention. He didn't want to show any favouritism, although secretly he thought Bonnie had softer fur and smelt sweeter. Clyde smelt as if he'd stayed in a few rough mouse-holes in his day. Colton breathed in. Bonnie smelt of fresh grass. Plus, she had a smoother tail and shinier eyes. Colton felt ashamed of himself that he seemed to be basing his preference on looks alone, so he tried to understand where the other mouse was coming from.

Clyde must have been the black mouse of the family. Although he was a conservative tan colour with splodges of darker tea-stain brown, he had that rough-and-tumble look of a mouse who hadn't had life easy. Besides possessing a minute cow-lick, which shot his already erratic fur into obstinately diverse directions, he rarely groomed himself. In addition, he must have trapped his tail in a door or something because there was a kink at the end of it, which looked like a crooked finger.

The two mice made the small chittering that Colton knew meant they were concerned with what was going on next door, but they were trusting him to take care of whatever it was.

Bonnie went to sleep first. Colton could tell from the rhythmic snuffling in his left ear. Clyde reorganized himself into numerous configurations with the ear, trying to get comfortable. His kinked tail kept poking Colton in the eye.

Colton tried to be patient. Clyde took a long time getting to sleep. His stress level was higher than Bonnie's. Definitely not a relaxed mouse. A Make-My-Day, Clint Eastwood sort of mouse. Colton tried to imagine Clyde with a tiny Mexican serape and a matchstick-sized gunbelt draped over him, but failed miserably. He sensed the small black-eyed gaze upon him, even with his own eyes shut.

Eventually, Clyde's snuffles matched Bonnie's and he slept. Colton listened to the bubbling mouse snores echoing stereophonically on both sides of his head.

He was surprised at their relative equanimity. How could they sleep through the noise? Didn't it bother them? It was louder and more erratic than usual. Were Ricker and Dysis trying something new? The garbled sounds crept past his furry earmuffs and scraped a macabre melody on the inside of his brain. Loud . . . loud . . . louder . . . sssssooooft moan . . . loud louder loudest . . . ssssoft moan. Monday music.

Sighing, he wished that new arrivals weren't kept in the room next door. He never got any sleep. But then, Colton reflected, someone had probably been annoyed by him when *he'd* been the new one. Mentally, he apologized to whoever it was who had been interrupted when he'd arrived.

*

Mondays were Experiment Days for the new ones. Newbies. Dysis always had loads of energy for experimenting after resting during the weekends. She prided herself on her youthfulness and vigour.

'Impressive for my age, aren't I?' Dysis' pink face, surrounded by waves of thick silver hair, glowed with wholesomeness and well-being. Her eyes were the clear blue of the innocent, although Colton thought that if they were any closer to each other they'd merge into one great big Cyclops eye.

Horrible old trout, Colton thought sourly. She had to be at least thirty or forty years old. That was the oldest he could imagine.

Colton hated Mondays. He also hated the way Dysis hummed as she ate her breakfast. He could hear them when they left the Newbie room to go upstairs. It must be the kitchen up there. Although he'd never seen any of the other rooms, that was where the food smells usually trickled from. Besides the laboratory, the kitchen was where Ricker and Dysis spent most of their time.

Ricker was always coaxing her to finish her egg and chips.

'Finish up every bit of that nice egg, that's a dear,' Ricker clucked. 'An empty stomach is begging for problems. Just one more bite . . . we've got to keep you from getting too skinny.'

Dysis would giggle girlishly. 'Stop fussing, you old worrybird.'

'Well, don't come running to me if you lose one of the kiddies through inattention because you've been hungry.'

Colton also hated the way they spoke to each other like two-year-olds. Although he knew they did the bed stuff – he'd heard them often enough – they squabbled like brother and sister.

Colton hoped Dysis would keep her strength up. Egg and chips better be packed full of nutrients. He didn't want her going hypoglycaemic half-way through her Monday-morning activities.

'Your turn, sweet thing,' she had warbled to him when he was a Newbie.

He wasn't sure if she was his real mother or whether he was someone else's boy. Colton couldn't remember anything before Ricker and Dysis. He tried, but anything before them was as wispy and insubstantial as the cobwebs that wafted from his ceiling. Back when he was a little kid, Colton had been convinced he was someone else's. He was old and cynical now. He was nobody's kid. Old, cynical and weary.

He guessed he must be somewhere between ten and sixteen years old. He had to be. Didn't your voice crack somewhere between then? He wished he could narrow down the range, but he hadn't much room for comparison against anyone else. Whenever he looked into the small mirror in his room, he just looked like himself. No special age jumped out and smacked him in the face. Colton sighed. Ricker was older than him, that was for sure. Ancient.

It was funny. Ricker was bigger physically than Dysis, but Colton was more scared of her. Ricker never looked any of the Newbies in the eye. He looked past you, to a spot a few inches behind your head. Dysis . . . Well, she *always* looked at you, and your spine shivered like trickling ice cubes when it was your turn.

Colton wished he knew his age. It was an important thing to know. You weren't a person unless you knew how many years you'd been hanging around. Endlessly, he gazed at his palms whenever light splattered through the grimy window-panes of his small room. *Could you tell your age from your palms? Like the rings of an oak tree?*

From the fine lines criss-crossing his palm, Colton figured he must be about a hundred and four. Specially on Mondays.

'Roll over, sweetie-pie. This will just feel like a teeny weeny little pinch,' Dysis had always said. The egg and chips obviously gave her a sense of humour on Mondays, because the teeny weeny pinch of the anaesthetic injection felt as if an elephant with steel-toed boots had kicked him.

Colton wished he'd never complained, because Dysis narrowed her eyes at his yelp and never gave him any more anaesthetic. He hoped the elephant would come back and stomp on her. It would make the electricity easier to bear.

After the first shocking Monday faded slowly in his memory, Colton never again gave her the satisfaction of hearing him cry.

'Scream a little,' Dysis coaxed, becoming more and more exasperated.

Or the satisfaction of hearing him scream.

'Just a little whimper for Auntie Dysis . . .' Her rosy-pink complexion became an angry red.

Or even talk.

Colton stopped speaking at all. Whenever they talked to him after that first Monday, he glared up at them with what he hoped were hate-filled ray-gun daggers. *Blam! Zam! Kapow!* He pictured them clutching their throats and falling down in a hail of killer beams, pain creasing their features in hideous torment. Unfortunately, Colton's imaginary ray-guns didn't do anything in the short term. He hoped the cumulative effect would get them in the end. Ricker and Dysis would turn all purple and gasp for breath and stuff and then fall down dead.

One could always hope.

After Dysis' failure to get a response out of him in the beginning, she had become concerned. Colton heard her nagging Ricker about him while he lay face down in bed, recovering in his room. Her voice rose and fell in the kitchen, sinking heavily and dripping down through the ceiling into Colton's room.

'Ricker,' she'd start, 'I think we've got a dud one here . . .'

Colton lost the next bit of dialogue. Dysis thumped over to the other side of the room. Her ponderous elephantine tread faded.

Ricker's voice boomed just above him, 'You're right. We need a couple a new ones. These latest have been . . .' *Mutter. Mutter. Mutter.*

'I want good ones. Talking ones. Girls this time. You know. You've got to start the project . . .' Dysis thumped and faded. Louder. Thump thump thump. 'No more dysfunctional aut . . .'

Making them think he was autistic had been a stroke of genius. A *coup de foudre*, he thought proudly. A 'bolt of lightning'. He hoped some day he'd have a chance to use some of the foreign words he read in his books. Impress a girl with his worldliness. After all, living in one room your whole life, he wouldn't be able to impress her with his rippling biceps or knowledge of geography. Sighing, he eyed his skinny arms with resigned dejection.

Maybe he *was* autistic. Perhaps autism was as cumulative an effect as death ray-guns hopefully were. Did it mean you were autistic if you spent years screaming until you were hoarse inside and keeping your outsides silent and cold as frozen ground? So be it. At least they left him alone mostly now.

It had been lonely in the little room, year after year, until he'd found Bonnie and Clyde in the small wardrobe to the left of his bed. They'd been curled up one morning in one of the dusty mismatched shoes piled up at the back. He'd been about to drag out all the kids' shoes and try to juggle with them when he'd spotted two sets of tiny black eyes staring contemplatively at him.

'Hello,' Colton said, delight raising the hairs on his arms. *Friends.*

He could swear they smiled at him.

Before Bonnie and Clyde, it had been just him and the dust balls under the bed. Sometimes he raced the dust balls and placed bets on which one would tumble to the other side of the room first. He blew and blew and provided breathless whispered commentary at the same time. 'Aaaaaand he's off! Dust Bunny number one . . . No, it's . . . the dark horse from the back catching up . . . and passing . . . but wait . . . Number one has snuck round the straight and pulled ahead . . . aaaaaaand the winner is Dust Devil number two!'

After blowing and commentating at the same time, he just about passed out from hyperventilating. It was fun. He felt light-headed after a race, but exhausted. It was nice under the bed, too. Dark and confining, but nice.

When he wasn't being seen to by Dysis, chatting to the two mice or puffing dust balls into the final home stretch, he read. There were billions and gezillions of old books lining the walls of his tiny room. They must have belonged to the previous occupants. They couldn't be Dysis and Ricker's books. He'd never seen Dysis read a word and Ricker only read boring old medical journals. They were both pretty stupid. Maybe Dysis couldn't read? They must figure *he* was stupid because he didn't speak. Stupid or verbally challenged. Or both. They had taken to alternating their visits, leaning very close and shouting into his face.

'Speak, honeybun!' Spittle flew from Dysis towards Colton's face. It was agony not flinching.

'Kids these days. Sheesh! You do all you can for them, and look what happens.' She clucked sadly.

Colton stared at her, unblinking. Ray-guns blazing. *Ping. Ping. Kapow. Steeeeerike!*

It was handy being autistic. They forgot to watch what they said around you because they figured you were stupid and couldn't understand.

'. . . all right, Dysis, but how? They'll recognize you at the hospitals. Too many went missing before.' Ricker sounded concerned. 'We can't keep on depending on the prison and that helpful nurse to keep supplying us. We have to establish our own source of supply so we don't run out. If I don't get my project started, we'll be too old to appreciate it when it comes to fruition!'

Thump thump thump. Dysis stumped across the kitchen. Pause. 'What about pregnant women?'

'Pardon?'

'Nurse Johnson sneaked me over some of that labour-inducing stuff from next door.'

Ricker chuckled. 'And how do you intend to convince them to take it?'

Impatient, Dysis ignored the sarcasm. 'No problem. I'll follow them when they're catching a Transport or something. When they're not looking, I'll creep close, pretend to sneeze and spray them with the stuff. It's supposed to work fast.'

'Won't the other people be a problem?'

'Shouldn't be. People usually walk by if there's trouble. If you're that worried, you can show her your fake Ph.D. papers, pretend to be a doctor and whisk her away.'

'Nobody would believe us. I don't look a GP.' Ricker sounded doubtful, but then smiled. 'I'm strictly a research and development man, as you well know.'

'We can do anything we want to do. Don't be so negative. Think positively! We can watch reruns of those old TV medical shows. You know . . . *ER. Casualty, General Hospital.*'

'Those antiquated old shows? Don't be so stupid. Doctors don't actually *treat* patients if they give birth on the street. All those lawsuits put a stop to that.'

Stung, Dysis' voice became high-pitched and venomous. 'I don't see you suggesting anything better.'

'I didn't mean to doubt you. Sorry, sweetheart, Give Rickypoo a kissy-face.'

Besides forgetting to censor what they said, they figured he wasn't with it enough to try and escape. They forgot to lock his door sometimes. They must have sensed his complete capitulation.

If that was the case, it was time to go.

'Bonnie? Clyde? C'mon.' Tucking the squirming handfuls into his pockets, Colton smiled to himself. It was great to have a family at long last. He had been scared of mice at first. He had read about all the diseases they could carry, such as Weil's disease, which rats gave you if they peed on you. As if! He couldn't imagine even Clyde would be mannerless enough to do that. Plus, mice weren't rats. Totally different. Mice had feelings. Colton patted both pockets respectfully. *You wouldn't pee on me, would you, honeybees?*

He could guess Bonnie's indignation if she knew what he was asking.

He had looked deep into her mysterious eyes the first time she'd trusted him enough to let him pick her up. He willed her to give him a sign if she had the plague or anything. Nothing. And he could swear that she smiled up at him, her little brown face crinkling. The flirt! A sweet, innocent mousy kind of smile.

Colton hoped they'd stay with him for ever. Luckily, Ricker and Dysis hadn't noticed them. They came less and less often these days to take him into the room next door. Usually Dysis just passed him food through a mail slot Ricker had built into the wall. Sourly Colton wondered if they were afraid he'd give them great big horrible germ-ridden cooties if they came into contact with him too much. He thought probably they came to get him now more out of sentiment than from any real hope of usefulness after all this time.

It was time to go. He knew he'd lingered long enough, waiting for the perfect opportunity.

Tiptoeing to the door, he shushed the chittering coming from his pockets. All was quiet. Ricker and Dysis had stopped their bickering and gone to bed. He could hear Ricker's rhythmic snoring from somewhere above.

If it's this loud through the ceiling, how can Dysis sleep through it?

Tonight he'd warmed up his muscles specially for what was to come. He hopped off the bed and marched around the room smartly, making sure he brought his knees up high on every step. After thirty circuits around the room, he supposed his legs were ready to roll. He'd tried to keep them exercised in constant readiness for the Big Run. He flexed them as much as possible. And the feet. Left ankle up. Round and round. Point the toes. Back. And down. Right ankle up . . . march round the room. Back and forth. Six steps across. Six steps back. As he marched, he stretched out his hands as wide and flat as possible until they looked like human starfish. At each step, he curled one finger into his palm. Step one. One finger down. Step two. Two fingers down . . .

He'd stretched his arms as much as possible, too. By reaching up both arms over his bed and pushing his fingers through the little metal food flaps and air holes in the walls of his room, he could pull himself up a few inches off the mattress. Up. *Down.* Up *down.* Up *down* up *down. Me and Jane Fonda.*

He had wanted to be strong to escape, and now here he was doing it. Escaping. His stomach curdled with anticipation and he carefully opened his door. Looking into the hall, he saw that all the other doors were closed. Slipping off his shoes, he tiptoed towards the two doors at the end of the hall. One led above ground, the other to a Transport tunnel. Dysis had told him about it. She'd threatened him with the tunnel.

'You'd better scream or we'll lock you underground to be eaten by nasty tunnel mice!'

He wasn't afraid. Some of his best friends were nasty tunnel mice.

The cool night air reached out from beyond the cracks of the above-ground door and tickled his nostrils. That was the door leading to freedom.

Colton placed his hand on the doorknob and turned it, ever so slowly. Afraid for his life that the door would groan, waking Them up. Or maybe it would be Them standing outside grinning maniacally at him.

'April Fool!' they'd say.

Go. Do it. Run. Throwing open the door, Colton plunged out into the darkness. And fell.

Not from any obstruction or discombobulation of his feet. Not from any leeching of strength from his jail-sapped muscles or synapses.

The utter lack of restraint hit him in the solar plexus, as hard as anything Dysis could have given him. Harder. He couldn't breathe. The air and space and birds trees car noises blaring horns silent screaming inside threatened to come boiling out from within.

Falling to his knees, he cradled his head in his arms and moaned. The Monday music became louder and more discordant, each individual note swelled inside him and became huge balloon-like segmented worms, which throbbed and shrieked. Closing his eyes tightly, he hoped that by wishing as hard as possible the worms would go away, and when he opened his eyes again he'd be away from here.

Away away away. Every fibre in his body wished.

After two full minutes of wishing, he cracked open one eye. Reality smacked him in the face. Nothing was different. He was crouching on a cement path leading away from Dysis and Ricker's small brick house. His nose was running and the contents of his pockets were chittering worriedly. Don't be an idiot, he snarled to himself. Only little kids think wishing changes things.

Crawling back inside took ages. When he closed the door, it snicked shut with a hollow, final sound. Going back into his room, he pulled Bonnie and Clyde out of his pockets and placed them on his pillow. A sharp jagged-edged blow of despair bent him over at the waist and forced him down on the floor. He crawled underneath the bed, disrupting the newest dust balls collecting in anticipation for more games. The darkness embraced him with warm comforting arms and the mice's chittering soothed him from above. The worms retreated, scathing, contemptuous scorn apparent in every undulation.

When Dysis passed him his breakfast through the food slot the next morning, Colton felt sick with disgust at himself. *Wimp. Idiot. Coward.*

He stared at the paper plate filled with artistically arranged tempting titbits, wrapped in cling-film. If he hadn't needed the food for Bonnie and Clyde, he would have flung it back at her. With lacklustre glumness, he unwrapped the plate and looked at it without enthusiasm. Two white tortillas, dusty with flour, swirled thickly with peanut butter and dotted with plump raisins. Celery sticks with pineapple cream cheese piled high and cinnamon sprinkled on top. A Canadian's version of *haute cuisine*. He knew that Ricker and Dysis were Canadian. He'd heard them talk often enough about how much they missed Montreal. They constantly bitched about everything in London being shorter. Smaller. Inconsequential. Smaller refrigerators. Tiny pints of milk. Little people. The only thing they seemed enthusiastic about was the upping of the electricity voltage from 110 to 220.

The thought of Canada horrified Colton. Canada must be a land of huge pink healthy people with big teeth and greying hair who stuck you with electric cattle prods. He didn't think he'd like to go there on holiday.

Thinking of holidays forced him to think of what he'd avoided all night and all this morning. How could he ever escape if he couldn't face the horrifying chaos that freedom presented? The lack of walls around him had made him feel as if all of himself was leaking out into unlimited space. There was nothing to contain him. To hold or protect him. He wished Bonnie was big enough to put her arms around him. He bet that she'd hold him, rocking him back and forth. She'd pat him on the back and murmur, 'It'll be all right, honeybee,' in the ear she'd crouched in earlier.

Oh, Bonnie.

After breakfast, Bonnie and Clyde indicated by way of huge jaw-cracking mouse yawns that they were much more interested in having yet another nap than going exploring. Colton wished he could sleep his life away as easily. He cupped his hands around the two mice so they wouldn't get cold and cuddled them up to his ears. His room could get draughty sometimes. When the mice settled, Colton reached for a book from a box next to his bed.

He wasn't a fast reader, but he had lots of free time. He'd read most of the best ones over the years. Now that Bonnie and Clyde were part of his life, he decided that he should take a gander at the animal books he'd passed over. He'd thought they were kids' books and had just given the ones with pictures a cursory glance. He used them to practise his right hook from across the room. His accuracy had improved in the past few years. Nowadays, he could generally pitch nine out of ten books right into the box, even when he threw with his left hand. He pretended the box was either Dysis' or Ricker's face, depending on his mood.

He took some of the books out of the box, trying not to jiggle the bed, and spread them around him in a huge fan. Opening one after the other, he couldn't believe he hadn't paid attention to them before. There were wonderful glossy 3-D interactive books about nickering zebra-striped unicorns. Lop-eared pink and white spotted rabbits with twitching noses. Gleaming liquorice-tinted Labrador dogs with raspberry spit-shined noses and tails wagging with so much momentum their bodies shook from side to side. The book started shaking so hard, Colton had to turn the page quickly. On the next page, a greying palomino turned to look at him with huge soft eyes and flaring nostrils. Colton yearned to run with him, tangling his fingers in the horse's mane, feeling the rippling muscles in its neck as they ran together.

There was another book which he'd only noticed as it left his good throwing arm. Its fluttering pages didn't have many pictures, so he'd never been tempted to look further. It was about cows. Farming. Animal husbandry. Colton didn't know what husbandry meant, but he figured it was something to do with cows getting married. Doing their business, like Ricker and Dysis must be doing when they weren't both snoring. Doing the Facts of Life. Kissypoo with Rickyface. *Yuck*.

Flipping through the pages, Colton yawned. *Boring. Booorrrrrrring*.

Animal husbandry. Cows and their feeding habits. How to keep them happy. Dewormed. Disease-free. It wasn't like he could return the book in a huff, though. Demand a replacement. A racier plot.

He read the cow book. With reluctance at first and then with growing fascination.

When cows were herded into killing pens to be slaughtered, they somehow sensed their fate. They moaned. A low, keening cow moan originating way down in their secondary stomachs. Not in their normal stomachs, but down where the grass came to be ruminated. He wasn't quite sure. Rumenmated? Rumournated? Colton's brows drew together and he flipped to the next page.

After they began to moan, the cows thrashed about. Hoofs flew. Teeth gnashed. Valuable animal flesh became damaged.

The farmers had looked for a solution and found the answer. *Chaos boxes*.

If cows were led down a tunnel that closed in on them, they'd settle. The roof imperceptibly drew down, the sides closed in and soon they plodded in single file. They calmed. Eventually each animal came to the end of the tunnel, which was blocked off. A trap door slid down behind each one until each was sectioned off with not an inch of space below, above or on any of their sides.

Each cow eventually stood totally enclosed in a tiny dark box. The walls pressed against them without a smidgen of light. The cows, far from being traumatized by mass waves of claustrophobia – why, they loved it! Colton caught his breath and looked at the cow's face in the book's one picture. Its eyes were calm and its nostrils unruffled by stress. Colton could swear it winked at him.

The cows felt safe while enclosed. Give a cow space to breathe and room to roam and it went nuts. Stick a cow in a dark box and it felt comforted. As if hugged by its mother. If cows *could* hug, that is. Colton let out a snort. Clyde, who had been dozing on his shoulder, jerked in fright.

After Colton had reassured Clyde, he lay back on his pillow and thought about the cow in the picture. Were cows incredibly stupid or just bred into a MacDonald's-Styrofoam-box mentality?

'I am food, therefore I should be in a box.'

If it worked for cows, would it work for humans? Would it work for him?

Maybe he could make a chaos box. If he put it over himself before walking out of that door, maybe he could stop the terrible panic that had buffeted him when he tried to escape. Just thinking about it made every drop of saliva in his mouth turn to ash.

It might work. He didn't have the same panic attacks when Dysis took him to the Transport tunnel. They'd started that a few weeks before.

'After all . . . he's autistic.'

'Are you sure he won't run off?' Ricker sounded concerned.

Dysis laughed. 'If he could have, he would have done it long ago, honeybee. Not after all these years. We've got him trained just like cattle. And he'll be perfect bait.'

'Bait for what?'

'A Scraper child would be perfect.'

'Like the ones you see wandering about the tracks at night after the electricity is shut off? Won't they scream? Children are told not to go off with strangers. Even Scrapers know that.'

Silence. They both clumped down the stairs and Colton's door opened. Dysis smiled with every one of her postage-stamp-sized teeth at Colton. He barely had time to hide Clyde under the covers. 'Time for walkies,' Dysis breathed sweetly. She looked expansive, as if they were giving him a gift of inestimable value.

It took four scouting trips before they struck gold. Two little girls out with their busily scraping mother. When Dysis spotted them, she waved at Colton to stay close behind her until she was ready.

'Don't let them see you yet,' she breathed. 'Wait.'

Colton watched the two girls with fascination. He'd never seen any other children. Just heard them in the room next door to his. The two girls were laughing together. One threw a roll of tape at the other. Colton felt a strange pang somewhere inside. The girl throwing the tape was beautiful. She had long blonde hair and a sweet pale face, but the other girl was even prettier. Her face looked like peppermint candy that he yearned to lick. All red and white and flushed with excitement. Her head of dark curls looked like it never stayed still. The blonde girl was giggling now, her mouth wide and happy.

Their mother was preoccupied, so the two girls continued to walk along the track. The distance between them and their mother lengthened. Shadows played between them and sectioned off large areas of the tunnel and tracks. The tunnel curved to the left.

Dysis and Ricker held their breath. Colton felt their excitement and smelt the adrenaline rolling off them in acrid waves.

When the girls reached the bend in the tunnel and were briefly out of sight of their mother, Dysis gripped Colton's thin shoulder with steely fingers. She shoved him towards them. 'Go!'

Colton walked towards the two girls. Dysis had made sure he knew explicitly what he was supposed to do. Last Monday. His shoulder-blades still ached. He didn't dare refuse. Hearing the blonde girl laugh, bitterness swept through him. Why should he refuse? What had those two girls ever done for him? Which one should he try for? Both? It's not like he owed them anything. He reached into his pocket and felt Bonnie. Which one? He felt Clyde in the other pocket. Which one? He closed his hand around Bonnie and gently pulled her from his pocket.

Stepping towards the blonde girl, who spotted him first, he waved. Smiling broadly at her, he held out Bonnie in his other hand.

He felt terrible afterwards. They'd made an awful fuss. Ricker had grabbed both girls before their mother had even noticed they were gone. Dysis was ecstatically polishing up her beakers now and choosing the best electrical currents to try out. Colton could hear her rattling about upstairs.

They'd forgotten to lock his door again. Colton went to it and peeped into the next room. There were two cartons like the one he'd been put in when he'd first arrived. Big heavy cardboard boxes that used to hold cauliflower. They were pulsing with live cargo at the moment.

Colton was struck suddenly with another *coup de foudre*. He could make a chaos box out of one of those containers. He'd wait till the girls were taken out and then he'd try to get one of the boxes before Ricker threw them away. Colton wondered why they kept Newbies in boxes when they arrived. Maybe Dysis was trying to calm them down like the cows. It wasn't working at the moment. An apricot-coloured frill from the dark-haired girl's dress was caught in the edge of the box. She must have struggled when she was put in. *Doesn't she realize?*

There was no use in struggling. He watched the sides of the boxes heave with their futile efforts to get out. He wondered what experiments were planned for them. Dysis was humming upstairs. That was always a bad sign.

Colton saw the multi-plugged electric cable creeping on the floor past the two boxes. It reminded him of a slavering, poison-fanged snake.

He wished the dark-haired one had escaped. She was so pretty.

Hearing Dysis clump down the stairs, Colton retreated back into his room and waited.

It was ages until Dysis got the girls installed in their room. Colton lay in bed with both mice pressed up against his ears. The sounds were worse when you could picture in your head who was making them.

Ricker and Dysis took for ever to go to bed that night. They were thrilled about the new acquisitions. Colton could hear Dysis gibbering excitedly as they went up the stairs. They kept talking about the two girls being the beginning of the end or something like that.

When their snoring began, he tiptoed out into the hall.

Dysis had dumped the two cartons outside the other room. Colton dragged one into his room and set to work.

Ten minutes later, he walked up to the two front doors. He put one clammy hand on to the doorknob leading out above-ground. He started to turn the knob. Bonnie chittered. Colton stopped. Took his hand off the above-ground door. She was right. He went over to the other door. The one leading down into the Transport tunnel. It would be easier. He'd stay underground.

Turning the knob, he opened the door and stepped through. He had to turn sideways to go through while wearing the box. He stopped and straightened it as the lopsided holes he'd cut for his neck and arms kept shifting. Colton began to jog, the box shifting back and forth. Bonnie and Clyde complained bitterly in his pockets.

As Colton descended into the tunnel, panic swirled inside him. His breathing accelerated and finally he had to stop. He knelt down on the ground, and pulled his head back inside the box like a turtle. He pulled his arms inside and put his hands over his face. Corrosive air rushed in and enveloped him. He squeezed his eyes and waited for the air to crush him. He clenched his fists and waited. Clyde let out a squeak and interrupted Colton's spiralling panic. Lifting both mice from his pockets, he held them against his face. Bonnie's cold nose brushed his cheek with affection.

'Thank you,' Colton breathed. And understood what he was thanking them for. His panic had subsided. He could breathe again. It wasn't really outside, after all. The tunnel protected him.

His panic retreated. It was replaced by something else. Something sharp and glassy. Blue-coloured. *Guilt.*

Colton looked back towards the door to the house. It was him or them.

'I'm sorry,' he said, towards the closed door, then turned his back on it.

Chaos couldn't follow him down into the dark of the tunnel. Maybe he could find the Scrapers and see if they'd break their family rule and give him a job. He'd work for nothing if he had to. He couldn't go back and he couldn't go above ground. However, he'd make it with his box and the tunnel.

Colton walked deeper into the tunnel. The face of the peppermint girl haunted him. Her laughing mouth. He pushed the pictures away.

His steps were heavy and his feet felt like they were someone else's altogether. They should be pointing the other way. He should be saving the two girls. Not leaving them to Ricker and Dysis. He jammed his hands in his pockets in misery.

Clyde's kinked tail curled around his left hand and Bonnie pushed her head sympathetically into his right hand. Colton felt warmed.

The two mice had helped him.

All right! He'd find a way to go back and help the two girls. Maybe they would be his friends.

Hardly recognizing the sparkles of joy that fizzed around him, his steps lightened, and a gigantic unaccustomed smile creaked across his face. Freedom felt like budding flowers bursting open in his head.

He would make it up to her. To them both.

He'd never tell the peppermint girl that he'd traded the two of them for his own freedom. Still smiling, he made an exploratory leap into the air just to see if he could. His box leaped with him.

Not liking the sensation of being airborne, Bonnie and Clyde complained bitterly.

Stigmata

ESTRA

Pale hands, pink tipped, like lotus-buds that float
On those cool waters where we used to dwell,
I would have rather felt you round my throat
Crushing out life; than waving me farewell!

LAWRENCE HOPE

Snowflakes of blood littered the bluish-white landscape of her body. Carefully, she opened her eyes and flexed one hand to see if she still could. Tiny mosaic-like shards of russet and crimson floated into the air, settling slowly in intricate dusty patterns upon her. Estra was afraid to move further. What was it they said after a terrible accident? You must assess the damage. You had to see whether you still had all your arms and legs. What did they also say?

'*Always wear clean underwear, just in case . . .*'

No, that was her mother's voice intruding. Estra smiled slightly and closed her eyes. If she concentrated, she could just see her mother's shiny nose and permanently misted rose-tinted glasses. Everyone said Estra was the clone of her mother. The same slight build and swathes of roan-coloured hair, the same wide-set grey eyes and aura of apology. As a child, she worried that people thought she *was* a clone of her mother. Luckily school taught her that cloning had been discontinued due to sheep duplicating problems in the nineties. The medical profession now concentrated on body-part cloning, not entire people. Or sheep. She'd felt reassured.

'Safety pins,' her mother's Italian-accented voice intruded again, tight with horror. 'Unsightly gaps! Rips! Uneven colour due to mixing brights with whites!'

What would happen if – horrors – a safety-pin sprang out viciously, greying knicker elastic smiled up at horrified ambulance men, or unidentified discharge peeked out with guilty abandon? Pristine. You must be unsullied. No discharge or safety-pins allowed. To avoid certain annihilation by embarrassment, you had to avoid wearing underwear at all. Keep the damn things wrapped in plastic, tucked away from any nasty prying fingers of light or human intervention. Walk around naked, clutching your bag of clean underwear with air whistling up your private parts. Or you could always cork yourself up. Stop yourself exuding. Perspiring. Oozing.

She could feel the cuts oozing now. Throbbing. Her hands felt dipped in boiling oil. The pain had never been this bad before. She tried to uncurl her left hand, which had been pressed lover-like into her chest. Stiff as a pack of new playing cards, the fingers unfurled, nail edges grimed with blood. Her untouched palm passively stared up at her. The slight keen of pain she was making changed. As she stared at her palm, the keening became a snort. Delighted laughter came unremembered from deep within her and burbled out, effervescent and caramel. She lay back in the gloom and waved her hands back and forth swirling the iridescent ruby snowflakes around her.

'You shouldn't marry him,' Berri had urged, her eyes filled with uncertainty. 'He's not . . . I don't know. There's something about him that scares me.' She took another bite of the apple she was holding.

Estra stuck out her tongue and crossed her eyes at her sister. 'Like this? Does he scare you like this?'

Berri huffed and threw the half-eaten apple at Estra. 'I thought people became smarter when they were adults but you're worse than ever. You deserve everything you get. I hope he turns into Bluebeard, chops your head off and sticks you in the back of a taxi-moto.'

Estra giggled, picked up the apple as if it were a dangerous axe and made threatening gestures towards Berri. Seeing Wynne, Berri's youngest daughter, peeping round the bedroom door, which was slightly ajar, Estra growled dangerously and hacked away with the apple. A shriek was heard and the patter of small running feet and scattered marbles disappeared down the hall.

Berri smiled ruefully at Estra. 'Good thing you didn't do that with Marina on the other side of the door. She would have had that awful blotchy stress rash for months. You know how funny she's become.' Berri picked up the white plastic overalls she had been mending with sticky tape before Estra had interrupted her.

'Go on, get. Sicko!'

Estra waltzed around the room with an imaginary partner. 'I'm not sick. I'm in love.'

'In lust, more like. You've been scraping too many dark tunnels. It's warped your brain.'

Estra swept out the door. 'At least I *have* a brain!' As she slammed the door shut, she heard the roll of sticky tape hit the other side with a thud.

Estra had seen Daniel at the monthly Scraper meetings. You went with your family and your family's family to see what new and exciting developments had burst forth in the field of rail scraping. As if there were anything new about the removal of human hair and skin off the tracks.

Give me a break, she thought. I've been doing this job for the last I don't know how many years, and when have they ever come up with anything new to make our jobs easier?

Cynically, she thought that LOT conducted the meetings to force motivation up and absenteeism down. Still, it was a chance to see everyone dressed in normal clothes for once without the omnipresent plastic.

'Come on, Wynne, strike a trot! We'll never get a good seat under the anti-SADS lights unless you get a move on!' Estra shooed Wynne towards the front edge of the platform where the lights were. Getting a boost from the hot glare of the anti-depression lights would set her up for weeks. People used to use them in the winter, when darkness descended with the moods. LOT took them over for permanent staff usage after one of the strikes. The Scrapers didn't get more money, but at least they got light.

Playfully, Estra swatted her small niece's plastic-clad back. It was nice of Berri to let Estra take Wynne around with her. Estra liked pretending to be Wynne's mother. It gave her a good feeling of what it must be like. Berri was eager to get Wynne out of the apartment tonight. Berri and Herbert were arguing. Something to do with Marina, Wynne's older sister, who was holed up in her bedroom as usual. Poor kid. She'd had things rough. Wynne, too, but she seemed to have come out of it better. At least she never spoke about it. It was almost as if she'd just blocked the whole thing from her memory.

Thank God the boy and I got them back. Before they could sustain any lasting damage? She hoped so.

She'd caught the boy, Colton, sneaking out of the tunnel one night wearing a box over his head. Why? She didn't know or care. She'd been walking along the tracks, unable to sleep. She hadn't seen him before. Was he someone's cousin? He appeared to be having trouble at the exit door. He'd step out and then step back in again.

'What's up?' she'd said, coming up behind him.

The boy jumped and turned to look at her. His face was panicked, and sweat ran in rivulets from his hair.

'You're Wynne and Marina's aunt, aren't you?' he said.

Bemused by the box, she nodded.

'Can you help me?' he asked. 'I know where they are.'

She'd gone with him more out of sympathy than belief that he knew where her kidnapped nieces were. The police couldn't find them and it had been three weeks since Berri had come back screaming that she'd lost them.

Colton told her about Ricker and Dysis as they flagged down a taxi-moto. About his years in captivity and how he'd seen Wynne and Marina when they were brought in. She noticed that he contradicted himself sometimes, but she attributed that to his youth and inexperience. She put her arms around him and rocked him. 'I'm so sorry,' she said. 'Why didn't you tell me before?'

He had tried to get them himself. Apparently he had no belief that the authorities could help. After all, they'd never come to his assistance. Estra was too grateful to him to be angry. She figured he must be traumatized by his own experience.

When they arrived at the brick house Colton indicated, she marched up the front walk and banged on the door. Colton hung back.

'What's wrong?' she said, and felt stupid. *Of course.*

'It's . . .'

She hugged him. 'I'm here. I won't let them take you again.'

Funnily enough, the man who answered the door was pleased to see them. 'Why, look who it is!' He turned back to the hall behind him and called, 'Dysis, honey, look who's back for a visit!'

Estra noticed that Colton flinched at the mention of Dysis.

'We're here to take Marina and Wynne home.' She paused and drew back her shoulders. 'I'm their aunt.' She brandished the scraper claw that Colton had begged her to take for protection.

The man tilted his head and looked at them. 'What could I have in exchange?'

Estra felt cold. She'd brought no City Credits. She had no jewellery. 'I'll take their place,' she said bravely. 'You can hold me as hostage in place of my nieces. If you're trying to hold them for ransom, I'll stay until you can get payment from their parents. I warn you, though, they don't have much money.'

Colton tried to speak but she shushed him. He seemed intimidated by this man, but Ricker wasn't nearly as frightening as she had expected.

'No,' he said finally, with a genial smile. 'But I've thought of something else. Come in.' At their hesitation, he continued. 'I won't bite.'

They stayed where they were.

'Don't worry, Colton,' Ricker said, 'I'm not interested in having you back. You wore out years ago. Thanks for the trade, though. Two fresh young girls for one useless worn-out husk of a boy.'

Trade? What trade?

They edged their way in and he led them down a hallway. Estra could feel Colton trembling behind her. The sides of his box knocked against the wall.

Ricker waved them into a room. 'Colton, you look like a turtle in that box. Were you wearing it for protection?' He chortled.

Colton made an unintelligible sound.

Ricker motioned for them to sit down.

'What kind of deal?' Colton asked, with belligerence.

'Well . . .' Ricker drawled. 'Your arrival is rather timely. I'm running out of space, and I don't need them any more until . . .'

Oh, God, what has he done to them?

'Besides, teenagers make a lot of noise and eat way too much. Don't you agree?' Ricker beamed at them.

After Colton's brave start, Estra thought he wasn't contributing much to the negotiations. But he was only a young boy. What did he know about negotiating in risky situations? She laughed hysterically. What did she?

'You can have them back in exchange for . . .' He swallowed noisily. 'Two things.'

Estra and Colton leaned forward in their chairs.

'I've been doing some medical experimentation on them,' he continued.

Estra made a sound at the back of her throat. Colton sucked in his breath.

'Quiet, please,' Ricker said. 'I don't have to give them back, you know.'

'Sorry.'

He continued, with oily smoothness, 'Due to slight inattention on my part, I've overexposed Wynne to electric current. You'll have to ensure she never becomes angry or upset. There has been some . . . uh . . . residual damage. Side effects. I wouldn't recommend that she become pregnant either. That could cause problems. Now, Marina. She had the full whack. I've implanted a self-destructive device inside her and I can't reverse it. She will explode if she stays with her family. Genetically similar contact will trigger it off within one or two years.' He seemed amused by how horrified they looked. 'Sorry. I was trying a few new things, and they didn't work out. I got carried away. You'll have to send Marina away and watch Wynne closely.'

Estra couldn't think what to say. Colton seemed incapable of speaking.

'Well?'

'I'll do it,' she said. *Dr Lupus will be able to find out what it is and stop it. And I can report this man to the police.*

Ricker stood up. 'I'll get them for you. Of course, you can't contact the authorities. If you do, I'll set Marina and Wynne off by remote control.'

He went over at Colton, who shrank back inside his box. 'You haven't told her, have you?'

'No.'

After they had led the two shocked girls out and down the street, Estra tried to make him tell her what Ricker meant. He insisted that he didn't know. He had seemed so frightened that Estra let it drop.

They'd been back now for several months and the girls were much improved. They had some time before they'd have to think where to send Marina.

Estra looked fondly at Wynne. At least she could help by taking the child away from her warring parents for a while. Take her to this Scraper meeting. She felt a special kinship with Wynne. Maybe because she resembled Estra when she was young. She wanted to give her all the encouragement she could, as Wynne had just started the Scraper training. Ten years old. She couldn't believe it. Seemed like just yesterday Wynne and Marina had been born.

As the little girl smiled up at her, Estra felt a pang. At thirty-nine, it was too late for her. She only had three more months to meet someone, fall in love and make a gene request to the Pregnancy Board. An impossibly tall order.

Estra saw Marina and Berri come on to the platform. She tried waving, but there weren't any more seats so Berri indicated they'd stand at the back. Marina's pale head stayed close to Berri's dark one. The girl was afraid to go two steps away from her mother in case she was taken again. She had been so lively and assured before. Her eyes had glowed.

Had Marina blocked out the memories, too? They both denied any memory of what happened. They were different, though. Quieter. Marina's eyes didn't glow any more. She looked like an old soul, her eyes dark and cool. Not like Wynne, who was always there open-faced, arms and palms outstretched.

'Hug me!' she'd demanded imperiously as a baby. As a child. As a newly fledged ten-year-old Scraper. She never seemed to get enough affection. Probably to do with that weird electric current she now had.

Estra leaned down and hugged her, careful to check the child's wires touched the ground. *Crinkle crinkle.* White plastic made so much noise when you hugged somebody wearing it.

Sliding across the long benches, Estra took a look round. This month they were meeting at Mornington Crescent Transport Station. As it had been closed again for repairs, it was the perfect meeting site. Since privatization, at least 50 per cent of the stations were usually shut for repairs. Some permanently.

Closed to save costs, she thought cynically.

Mornington Crescent hadn't changed much. Still that smell of rotting damp and oozing walls. It was as if the tunnel had a permanently runny nose. Estra shivered. Even the anti-SADS lights didn't dispel the dark greasy atmosphere. Good thing LOT had given in on the lights issue. You couldn't have hordes of depressed people working next to electrified tracks and rushing trains.

No indeed. The instant Estra felt depressed, she made for the lights. Turning your face up to one of them and shutting your eyes, you felt as if you were on a sunny beach in Ibiza. Not on a dank platform somewhere underneath North London.

'Aunt Estra!' Wynne shook her arm impatiently. 'There's someone new!'

So there was. 'Mmmmahha,' she answered noncommittally.

It wasn't often you saw any new faces. Since Scraper jobs were passed within families, it wasn't as if new job applicants popped out all over the place. She shared Wynne's excitement and almost stood up herself in order to see better. Remembering that she was an adult and should be a good example for Wynne prevented her, though. Besides, some cranky old Scraper behind her was muttering his complaints. She'd better just hunker down and try to see what she could between the heads of the people in front of her.

The man stood apart from the LOT management team, on the other side of the platform across the track. Management never mixed with Scrapers. They said it was to establish authority, but she could sense the slight *moue* of distaste in the back of their throats when they looked at Scrapers. Even when you were standing face to face with someone on the management team, it felt as if they were looking down at you.

The man wore black denim. Odd enough, in a room full of black-suited management and Scrapers in their Sunday best – but extremely odd as denim had been barred from the Transport tunnels for ages. It was declared far too insanitary. Denim attracted skin flecks instead of repelling them. Estra remembered what it was like to wear denim. When you slapped your leg, a cloud of skin flecks and dust would puff up from the fabric. Plastic was less prone to carry disease.

He was wearing black denim. Worn black denim with a sheen of charcoal flannel. The jeans were tight on the man's legs. Tight enough to matter, but not tight enough to scare you off. The jacket edges were soft and curled, as if his jacket had been crushed and rolled many times to make a pillow. Soft folds and mysterious pockets. Estra wondered what was in the pockets of his jeans. And blushed furiously when she felt Wynne's eyes upon her.

Estra pretended to look straight ahead at the LOT team gathering up their papers and preparing to speak, but instead kept looking at the man waiting patiently. His face was a pale smudge in the darkness. Dark soft hair and eyes. At least, his hair looked soft, she amended. She couldn't tell if it was brown or black from here. The gloom in the tunnels shrouded everything in a darker hue. Dark shadows played across his face.

'Look at his eyes, Aunt Estra.'

Estra looked. Surprisingly enough, you could see some colour from where they sat. The eyes weren't dark at all. They were the colour of the antique turquoise glass perfume bottle on her bedroom bureau. The one she ran her thumb across, over and over the unreal colour. It looked as if it could be rubbed off. Achingly blue. The colour of the real sky before they'd pumped those dull grey artificial clouds up to protect what was left of the ozone layer. To her, blue eyes had always been the colour of trust. And his were staring right at her.

How could she resist a man with eyes like that? After the LOT team introduced him as a Scraping Supervisor from the Paris Métro System, Estra applauded dutifully. LOT was trying to bring new blood to the clapped-out Scrapers in London, she figured. Perhaps they thought London's scrapers were unequal to the task that lay always before them. Either there were more people taking the Transport or hair and skin were getting looser.

Sourly, Estra wished that everyone would become bald and skinless, so that she wouldn't have to keep scraping their by-products off the tracks.

The man would be stuck-up anyway. French. It figured. Bloody French. He probably thought he was better than them.

'Aunt Estra! Stop pinching me!' Wynne pulled her arm away from Estra, who was surprised at the pressure she'd been exerting. They both listened to the speakers, Estra ducking behind the heads in front of her so that the man wouldn't see her. Wynne rocked from side to side, trying to get a good look. The speakers went on about scraping technique. They were always on about improving skills and productivity. About avoiding head-smacking injuries.

As she listened, Estra picked unconsciously at her dry cuticles. Running a finger along her opposite thumb, she caught a tiny serrated piece that needed removal. Carefully, she edged her fingernail under the rough edge and worried it off, flicking the piece of skin on to the ground. Without thinking, she continued to search for bits that needed removal. Picking soothed her agitation.

Thirty minutes later when the speaker coughed and took a sip of water, she gazed down at her feet and felt mild embarrassment: around them lay a faint halo of skin flecks. And the damage to her hands. As she stretched them out, the ends of her fingers glowed rosily red where she'd picked at them. It hurt. She wished she didn't have such an unattractive and painful nervous habit.

'My meat-grinder hand syndrome!' she had laughed with Berri. 'Looks like I stick my hands into a slicer dicer.' When things were going well, her hands would heal and she'd show them off to Berri. Fluttering like pale pink-tipped birds, the hands would be up for public consumption. During a bad week, the birds would be kept in cages of her pockets, clenched tightly to avoid being seen.

It was embarrassing. People gave you disgusted looks when they noticed. 'Your hands are *bleeding*,' they'd cry, their faces twisted in disgust. 'What in heaven's name have you *done* to yourself?'

Estra knew they were wondering how she could do it to herself. It was better than some other bad habits she could name. Like smoking. Or farting.

During the entire meeting Estra felt the man's eyes on her. *What's your problem?* Was she dribbling? Did she have something disgusting on the end of her nose? She felt uncomfortable under the constant blue regard. It felt like he was touching her. She did up the top button of her shirt, avoided his gaze and looked everywhere else possible. Having someone's fingerprints all over you before you'd even met them was thoroughly disconcerting.

At last the meeting ended and Estra hurried towards the exit, dragging Wynne behind her.

'Excuse me?' A touch on her arm and a voice stopped her. She looked round, knowing instantly who it was. She felt Wynne's unspoken excitement beside her. The man cleared his throat and tried again. '*J'ai envie de* . . . uh . . . I have wanted to kiss those lips since I saw them across the track.'

Estra coughed, incredulity catching in her throat. 'You saw them all the way across the track?' Frenchmen were so predictable. 'Are they that big?' *What a pick-up line.*

Wynne giggled. Estra pinched her.

He had seemed taller across the track, but up close he was exactly Estra's height. He reached over to her, the frayed edge of his denim jacket falling back. His hand looked strong and brown. Swooping whorls on the fingertips. Deeply etched lines criss-crossing his palms. She tried not to flinch. He touched her bottom lip with one finger. The finger was warm. Her lip burned where it touched her. The man let his hand drop to his side.

'Don't pretend you don't feel it,' he said.

She smiled at him with innocent complicity. She knew.

After years of being alone by choice, she knew after three weeks that she wanted to marry Daniel. The duck convinced her.

He'd been telling her about the Paris Métro. The roasted-nut smell crackling down your throat. The mélange of odours. Perfume, sweat, engine grease, and excrement. You tasted the smells on your lips as you walked along the platforms. The way the tunnels curved round so you never saw your destination.

He'd started scraping at the age of ten, as she had. He'd been a dark denim-clad boy who had refused to change his clothes or wear plastic overalls. Being French, the people in charge had waved their hands around and yelled a lot. Eventually they had just let him get on with things. They decided to let him discover the impractical nature of denim for himself.

'I found a duck.'

Estra laughed. 'Cooked?'

'No.' He put his hand up and ran his finger down her arm. The tiny russet hairs on it stood up.

'It marched down the track towards me one night. I found it when I was scraping line four. Porte de Clignancourt. Up in the north side of Paris by the Périphérique. I could hear cars rushing over me . . .'

'You couldn't possibly. You can't hear cars from down below when you're scraping. Your eyes are turning brown they're so full of . . .'

Daniel laughed and interrupted her. 'All right. I added that bit for effect. I couldn't hear them. But I could sense them around me. The weight of them was unbearable. My heart felt heavy –'

Estra pulled her arm away. She couldn't concentrate when he

touched her. She loved the way he spoke. Perfect English with only a hint of a French accent. And the words he used. It beat the 'wanna have a shag?' approach from men here. Grimly, she thought that she hadn't had much opportunity to see what they were like lately. She hadn't wanted to.

'—up he walked, bold as brass.'

'The duck?'

He nodded. 'Yes. He —'

'He was a he? How could you tell?'

Daniel leaned over and placed his lips gently against Estra's. For a second he just let them warm against hers, a delicate intrusion. He put one hand around the back of her neck and pulled her head roughly towards him. The tip of his tongue brushed her lower lip. Not an intrusion at all. He sucked gently at her lip and she felt tiny shocks of pleasure crackle inside her.

After kissing her thoroughly, Daniel pushed her away. '*Ma dulcinée*, I know the difference between male and female. The French always know.'

Estra was shaken by the kiss. 'Even among ducks?'

'Of course.' He looked down at his hands. 'I'd always wanted a pet. The only animals I'd ever seen were tunnel rats, and I wanted a dog. Or a cat. A rabbit.'

'A duck seemed a reasonable alternative?'

'Why not? I hunched down and put my scraper behind me. I didn't want to scare him. I reached into my pocket and found some chocolate Florentines the people I lived with . . . uh . . . my grandfather had given me earlier. I offered them to the duck. He trusted me enough to come up and eat them.'

'A hungry duck.'

'Starving. His feet were black from tunnel grease and cigarette ash. I don't know how or where he'd come in. He looked exhausted. Perhaps from the Marché aux Puces – the flea-market up the end of the line. Probably from a butcher's stall. Queuing up to have the duck executioner lop his head off and hang him upside down by his feet.'

'Sold to a discerning buyer.'

'I couldn't let it happen.'

Estra was relieved that the duck had escaped such a horrid fate. Not that she didn't enjoy a dab of *foie gras* on toast. Or was that from geese?

'What did you do with it?'

'I had a piece of string that I'd found on the track a while earlier. I made a leash for it.' He saw Estra's concerned face.

'I didn't tie it tightly around his neck, I assure you! I led him along the tunnel to where my . . . grandfather and I lived. Underneath Les Halles Métro station. I was so excited.'

'I bet you were. A boy and his pet duck out for a walk.'

'Don't laugh,' Daniel said, scrunching his eyebrows together into stern lines.

'I had big plans for my duck. He would accompany me on my rounds every day. I would train him to pick up garbage. To have him earn his keep.'

Estra laughed. 'What did your grandfather say about it?'

'He was great at first. Expressed admiration at what a fine fat duck I'd found. Even offered to watch him while I finished my Clignancourt round.' Daniel looked grim.

'And?'

'He told me I shouldn't ignore my responsibilities just because I'd brought home a friend for dinner.'

'Oh, no.'

'Oh, yes. When I came back, the duck was gone. The piece of string hung there, tied to the chair where I'd left it. The loop was empty. Grandfather said the duck had escaped.'

'Did you believe him?' Estra felt sympathy-pains in the pit of her stomach.

'I did until I saw the fresh pots of *confit de canard* that appeared in the pantry the next day.' Daniel's eyes hardened. 'Grandfather had a sneaky look in his eyes and duck-liver crumbs on the edges of his moustache.'

Estra choked. She put a hand on his shoulder, a hand that had been remarkably pick-free for the past few weeks. 'Bastard.'

'Yeah. I got him back for it, though.'

He wouldn't tell her what he meant by that, and she didn't press him. Families could be horrible sometimes.

After they'd married, Estra's hands stayed relatively damage-free for a while. The pink tide receded and skin healed. Fingers became smooth and calm. Estra felt unfamiliar strains of contentment. She made sure never to cook duck for dinner.

'You were wrong, Berri,' Estra taunted her sister. 'I'm perfectly happy.'

'Is he good to you?' Berri frowned.

'Last night he told me what wonderful skin I had.' Estra smiled to herself.

'Wonderful *skin*?' Berri snorted, the burst of air sounding incredulous. 'A Scraper? Telling you that?'

'Well, it was strange, I admit. But nice.'

'Isn't it what men say when they don't want to say how beautiful you are?'

Stung, Estra glared at Berri. 'Just because I'm overweight doesn't mean he doesn't find me attractive.'

Berri sighed. 'I didn't mean that. For the millionth time, you are *not* fat. A pencil is obese next to you. How many times do I have to tell you?'

'I just need to lose a couple of pounds.' Estra pulled up her shirt and pinched a fold of the skin that stretched tightly over her ribcage. *Blubber-guts*. 'See?'

Berri looked at her with exasperation. 'You're nuts. Are you happy at least?'

'Of course.' *Most of the time*. Except when he got in *those* moods. Even anti-SADS lights didn't protect Daniel from the plushy darkness that could descend in an instant. At first, Estra tried to tease him out of them.

She stopped doing that the time he turned to her with hatred-filled eyes. She had never been afraid of him before. She was then. She took a step back involuntarily, and the look of fear on her face must have woken him out of whatever shadow he'd gone away hand-in-hand with. His eyes changed back to the antique bottle colour she knew and felt familiar with. The colour of trust.

Of course I trust him.

He began doing illogical things.

'Pepper!' he yelled at her. 'Give me all the pepper we have in the kitchen.'

Estra thought he was kidding. 'What are you going to do? Salt and pepper yourself into a better humour?'

'Shut up,' he said. 'Or I'll shut you up permanently.'

What?

Shakily, she handed him three bottles. One of ground white pepper, one of extra-strong finely ground black, and one of whole green peppercorns with which she'd made a sauce the night before. He emptied the bottles into his mouth, with Estra looking on in horror. He stuck out his tongue at her and she couldn't help giggling. It looked like *steak au poivre*. Daniel sniffed the pepper up into his sinuses. He fell backwards, hitting his head on the floor with a harsh thump. He smiled up at her, an odd, sick sort of look. 'That's better,' he said.

Estra didn't tell Berri. It was probably just a one-off. It wouldn't happen again. Sucking pepper for forgetfulness? Whatever happened to sniffing glue? Was this more environmentally friendly? The glimmers of anger she sensed rising within Daniel would ebb if she just made him feel safer. More loved.

She sensed him watching her. Not with the warm brush of approval she'd become used to, but with cold evaluation. One night as Estra was getting undressed for bed, she felt his eyes on the back of her legs. It was a measured glance. A measur*ing* glance. As she took off her shirt, Daniel's glance chilled her. She turned, her nipples becoming frozen grapes in the shadow of his regard. Her bra straps tightened, the flesh puffing out in indignation at the criticism implied in the look. She felt the curves of her body, which he had once touched with loving ardour, become embarrassed fleshy protrusions.

She turned and quickly unsnapped her bra. She sensed his eyes tracing the harsh red marks streaking across her pale back. Burning. Not the red marks. His eyes.

'Too fat,' she knew he was saying. 'Look at that bulging flesh.' He was looking for reasons to feel glad that he'd decided he no longer loved her. That must be it. He wanted to use her in his search for escape.

Estra did her best to avoid setting him off and stopped undressing in front of him. She didn't replace the pepper. Daniel searched for other things to try. She wasn't sure, but she could have sworn she had had a full bottle of bleach before. *Surely not?*

Things went missing. The bottle of peppermint schnapps, in her family for generations, was a predictable hit.

'Dance with me,' Daniel slurred an hour after he'd finished it, his breath sweetly familiar and sour with the schnapps. 'I want to dance with my wife.'

Estra felt his approval waft over her. Perhaps her love for him would fill the spaces that had been slowly emptying. Fright was a good emptier. Wrapping her arms around him, she averted her face from his breath, and danced with him until he fell. He tried to kiss her, the peppermint mixing with her own breath until Estra couldn't tell where his breath ended and hers began.

The lighter fuel he drank next made him vomit. When she tried to help him up, he struck her for the first time.

She hit the back of her head against the metal door frame. She cried more from shock than from pain. Daniel cried with her, vomit and tears mixing on his face. He tried to hug her, but the smell of lighter fuel made her gag.

'You shouldn't have stood in front of my fist,' he choked out. 'It was your fault.'

Whoever's fault it was, it seemed to happen a lot.

The red tide returned. Daniel slapped her once when he saw her doing it. 'Stop the goddam picking!' he yelled.

In order not to let people see that the redness and damage were migrating down her fingers, she started on her feet. She lay in bed, listening to Daniel's tortured breathing, carefully drawing a knee up to her chest. She ran her hands lightly over each toe, across the arch and around each narrow heel – until she found a spot needing attention.

Scraaaaape. Scrape. Scrape. She worked a nail under the edge of the jagged bit and ripped it off, carefully saving each twisted curl of skin next to her in bed. She let one of the curls drop on to the floor one night. Daniel had stepped on it in the morning. He snatched up the hardened pigtail of skin.

'What the hell is that?'

It hadn't been a good day. Berri had asked why she was limping.

Eventually, she ripped through the first layer of skin on both feet. It hurt like hell, but it distracted her from the confused pain she felt when she looked at Daniel. How could he have changed so much? What had she done to set him off? Had her perception of him been off in the first place? She couldn't see through his eyes to the man he'd been before.

Estra's limping became more pronounced. By day, she wore three pairs of thick socks under her Scraper boots to make walking more bearable. By night, she methodically ripped.

She knew her sister assumed Daniel was abusing her. It wasn't as though he hit her very often. Just when the moods struck. Estra couldn't tell her sister that she picked her feet. Berri would worry. It was hard enough making jokes about hand picking. She couldn't show her the furrowed bloody gouges on her feet.

Estra peeled so many layers of skin that some became infected. She sluiced her feet with contact-lens disinfectant solution containing hydrogen peroxide. The wounds boiled. Throwing her head back, she screamed soundlessly. When the bubbling stopped, she smoothed Vaseline over the worst gouges and wrapped her hands and feet with cling-film. Hopefully, it would keep the raw skin on her feet protected and keep her hands from picking.

Daniel taunted her. 'You're like a piece of fatty beef wrapped in cling-film.'

They didn't dance any more. Or, rather, Daniel danced with his fists. His angry mouth. His stranger's blue eyes. It was her fault. All of it. All of what? She wished she knew. She crept around, not knowing what it was she wasn't supposed to do.

Pick pick pick.

Working in the Camden Town tunnel one night, she forced

herself to think of the alternatives. She couldn't possibly admit to herself, Berri and everyone, that she'd made a mistake. Besides, she could feel her child slipping away from her. The child she'd requested from the Gene Board. She and Daniel had filled out the form the day after their wedding, and had waited the requisite month before sending it in. Daniel had posted it on the way to work.

She couldn't divorce him. The gene request would be cancelled. Only if the husband died would they let the request go through. That was the only way. Estra thought it was quite amazing that Daniel hadn't died yet after ingesting half the apartment's chemicals. Listening to herself, she was appalled at what she was thinking. This man she loved.

Used to love. She wasn't sure she did any more, but she was damned if she'd lose everything. Self-esteem, husband and child in one fell swoop.

Dying was better than divorce. So many people died around Transport stations.

The next day Estra went up to the Tufnell Park platform when the trains started running. She stood close to the platform edge while people gathered for the early-morning commute to work. A man stood next to her who was probably going home after doing a night-shift. His hair was thin and he kept reaching up to straighten it when the air rushed through the tunnel. When the Charing Cross train boomed its way into the station, Estra watched the man step off the platform. The train driver's face was a horrified white blur behind the glass. Estra stood there, the screaming behind her muting into a dull blur of white noise.

The Scrapers had a lot of work to do that night. Body-part detail. They found everything but the head, which had stayed on the front of the train, scaring an old lady at the next station into fits. Estra went to the station in question and retrieved it. She used her pass-key to close down the track electricity temporarily. She descended on to the rails, and reached up to where the head perched on the train's nose, thinning hair disordered in the breeze. Using her scraper claw, she tugged it off and put it in a refuse sack.

The funny thing was, when she had been standing next to the man on the platform, before he jumped, Estra had been thinking of doing it herself.

'Jump,' she said to herself. 'Jump! Solve your problems. Step off. Now. Jump. Juuuuump.' Eyes closed, she had concentrated with every fragment of her self-control and willed herself to jump. When she had just about decided that perhaps it could wait until another day, the man had jumped.

Before he did, he turned to look her full in the face for an instant with a look of terrified collusion.

'Estra?' His mouth had framed her name as he jumped.

She had meant to take a nap when she got home. Her head felt as if a truck had run it over. A ten-gallon headache. Pushing open the front door, she gasped.

Her blue-glass perfume bottle lay in pieces on the kitchen floor. Daniel had obviously tried to drink the contents. He must have been furious when he discovered that she'd filled it with tinted water when the perfume ran out. The refrigerator was on its side, its contents spilling out everywhere. The smoked turkey she had prepared earlier that day was missing from its platter. Daniel was clutching it to his breast. Holding on to each of the turkey's legs delicately, he whirled around to music that only he could hear.

He was waltzing with a cooked turkey. Estra forgot to be careful. She laughed.

Daniel stopped in mid-swirl and glared at her over the turkey's plump shoulder. 'Excuse me? You haven't filled out my dance card. Get out of my way.'

He clutched the turkey to him with romantic fervour and swung it in a flamboyant twirl meant to impress. He whirled around the room, coming closer to her. She went towards him to see if she could grab the turkey when it swooshed by her on one of its turns. Daniel swung towards her and she reached out. The turkey smashed her on the side of the head. She fell among the shards of antique blue glass.

Estra lay on the floor with the turkey, her left cheek pressing against the linoleum. She could see triangles of blue glass sparkling and something white underneath the kitchen cabinet. She listened to Daniel humming to himself across the room. She dragged herself closer to the cabinet and retrieved the crumpled piece of paper. Opening it up, her finger brushed a smear of blood on it as she smoothed out the wrinkles. It was the gene request form she and Daniel filled out with such optimism the day after their wedding. The one he had posted. *Had said he'd posted.*

Estra crumpled the paper with one hand and picked up a shard of glass with the other. A long, knife-shaped piece of glass. What right had this man to come into her life like he did and make it a misery? She fingered her weapon, constructed from trust. The trust she'd wanted to pass on to her daughter.

The smell of cooked turkey sickened her. Estra's finger hurt. She laid down the glass knife and put her finger into her mouth. She didn't know whether it hurt from her own picking or from being cut.

She did know that Daniel had to go. If the man on the Tufnell Park Transport platform could be convinced to jump, perhaps she could convince Daniel to go away. Somewhere he'd really hate. The worst place possible. Where could she wish him to?

'I'm glad your grandfather ate your duck,' she muttered, her voice thin and insubstantial.

Estra picked up her knife and looked through the blue glass. She ran it up and down between her fingers, wincing when she came to a raw patch. She concentrated as hard as possible. She still couldn't think of where to wish him to, but hopefully the intention would send him to a place he'd despise. As long as he was away from her, she'd be happy. *Go.*

Estra was surprised to find she'd slept. It must have been for quite a while, because she felt stiff and bruised. There was no sound from Daniel. Her hands felt as if they were dipped in boiling oil. The pain had never been this bad before. She tried to uncurl her left hand, which was pressed lover-like into her chest. Stiff as a pack of new playing cards, the fingers unfurled, nail edges grimed with blood. Her untouched palm gleamed up at her.

An eye stared up at her from the centre of it. A bloodshot eye. Furious. Scared. Blue. The colour of sky. Of trust. The keen of pain she had been making changed. As she stared at her palm, the keening became a snort. Delighted laughter came unremembered from deep within her and burbled out, effervescent and caramel. She lay back in the gloom and waved her hands back and forth swirling the iridescent ruby snowflakes around her.

'Gotcha!'

She'd really done it this time. By wishing her husband to a place he'd despise, it hadn't occurred to her that place was herself.

I've managed to wish him inside me?

It was Daniel's eye staring out at her in horrified recognition. Estra spat on the eye and it blinked furiously.

'Shall I poke you with a sharp stick?' she asked the eye. 'But then,' she giggled, 'You'd get annoyed and take nasty nips out of my pancreas or something, wouldn't you?'

The hand picking stopped. She didn't want to dig her way in to him. Her feet healed for the first time in months. The red tide on her fingers receded. Tiny rough edges of skin were no longer worried off under nail edges and flicked away. Aureoles of skin flecks stopped surrounding her chair after she'd been sitting there.

Estra stopped laughing when the picking started again. This time it wasn't her picking. It was Daniel. He was picking his way out to get to her.

Fear of Flotation

ADDY

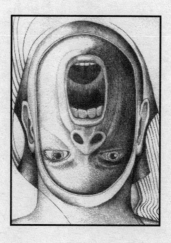

Heat not a furnace for your foe so hot,
that it do singe yourself.

WILLIAM SHAKESPEARE

Why did women always resist when you pushed their heads down towards something that was just expressing its admiration for them? All he was doing was accelerating the process and they got all stroppy and started struggling. Addy rolled his eyes. You wouldn't get much satisfaction after that. Their lips would go all floppy and unenthusiastic.

Silently, he rested within the dark wetness of the flotation tank. Terza was his wife. You shouldn't have to force a wife to do something she should be doing without his asking. She always offered that token argument about wanting to be given the illusion of choice, but he knew better. Women functioned more efficiently when they weren't given any options.

Addy clenched his fists. Terza apparently operated under the illusion that she had choices when it came to men, too.

He tried to relax and unclench. He'd lose the benefits of the flotation tank if he got worked up about it. Things were in motion. Addy waved his hands in the water, feeling the soft ripples against his legs. He snorted, the bubbles exiting his mouth and nose and rising to the surface. He felt like a porpoise. 'With rippling muscles.' He smiled to himself. 'And all my hair.' He was proud he hadn't lost any of his abundant turf of black curls. Most of his friends had.

He had been in a bad mood when he began his float session. When he shut the domed lid on top of his tank, he caught the soft fleshy part of his thumb on a sharp edge where the rubber had worn away. He winced and stuck it in his mouth. If he died of massive blood loss, it would be far too easy for Terza.

Terza. His wife. He pressed hard where he estimated his heart was. He ached at her deception. She thought she had him fooled with this birthday present. A series of relaxation sessions at Tarvoy's Float Centre sent anonymously. Oh, well. He'd let her think he was fooled. For now.

Closing his eyes, he considered the first weapon in his arsenal of revenge. Proud of the analogy, he reached down between his legs to the small soft handful that floated amiably between them. His first punishment for her was set in motion.

It hadn't worked as well as he envisaged. Being kicked out of the woman's flat hadn't been part of the plan. Prostitutes weren't supposed to do that. Well, no. She wasn't a prostitute. He was just angry at being turfed out like an unwelcome cockroach.

Thinking of the woman made him harden. The cool saline water surrounding him felt like her touch. His soft handful became a turgid armload. As if! he thought to himself wryly. More like a sodden handful. Moving his hands up and down, he groaned, bubbles fizzing from his mouth and nose. The gurgling of the saline pump next to the tank kept time to the rhythmic swooshing of his hands.

The woman had stood by the Camden Town ticket counters, rocking back and forth on small boot-clad heels. It was her hair Addy noticed first. Soft lemony clutches of the stuff. He was about to buy an adult return to King's Cross when the woman's hair made him stop dead. He had to restrain himself from walking up to her, burying his nose in it and taking deep sniffing gulps. Smells were his *raison d'être*. His reason for living.

Her hair would have the aroma of chilled lemonade with mint leaves crushed slightly to release their scent. Mint and lemon pulp swirling in a glass with crushed ice. The smell rose to his nostrils. He wished it did. His teeth ached with want. He loved long hair. Terza had cut hers without asking him. Nastily, he guessed her other men liked a short chop. He allowed her to think he didn't mind. He gave in on issues that didn't matter in the scheme of things. He just gritted his teeth and didn't touch her head when she performed her duties. Short hair made Terza look like a boy with breasts. Damned if he wanted to be in bed with a bebreasted boy! *Heck, no. I'm no pervert.*

Relationships are all give and take, he reflected.

Addy fiddled with his wallet, licking his dry lips. He watched the woman from the corner of his eye. She fascinated him although he couldn't work out why. He hadn't intended on finding one this early, figuring that most prostitutes would be centred around King's Cross.

If she *was* a prostitute. He wasn't sure. Her posture was that of one. Slouching body. Roving eyes. Hips forward. Glossy pink lips. But the lips hadn't the practised mobility that prostitutes usually pouted with. Nor had her eyes the clouded resentfulness that those of women in the biz possessed. Her eyes were uncertain but clear. Addy noticed that she kept her arms tight to her body. The dress she wore was made of the rubber stuff that had been in fashion years ago. She must not be a successful prostitute if she was wearing that. Didn't she know how insanitary it was?

It wasn't as if he *had* to go to prostitutes. It would teach Terza a lesson. Besides, he liked the notion of keeping his hand in. Keeping his eye on the female pulse. Plus, he wasn't blind. He could appreciate a good-looking woman. That's how he'd met his wife. He'd noticed her in Sainsbury's and threatened her with a loaf of ciabatta until she had laughingly agreed to go out with him.

Would this woman at the Transport station go out with him? Worth a shot.

'Hello,' Addy said to her. 'Are you lost?'

The woman looked up at him, her eyes wary. 'Do I look lost?'

Addy laughed uncomfortably. 'Are you waiting for someone?'

'Yes,' she replied.

'Sorry,' Addy said, feeling dull warmth creep up his neck. He started to back off. 'I've got the wrong end of the stick. Sorry . . .'

'I was waiting for you,' she said.

He could play at Terza's game.

*

When Addy woke up the next morning, he couldn't remember where he was for a second. It wasn't his and Terza's Spartan flat in Finsbury Park. He could tell without opening his eyes. It felt warmer. Womb-like. Different from theirs. Terza liked white space. She loved dancing around their apartment, arms outstretched, without having to worry she'd sweep things off tables. He used to like watching her dance.

He felt warm and enclosed now. There was a body next to him in bed. An unfamiliar body. Not Terza's cool angular bones and sculpted muscles. This body was warm and smelled of cinnamon. The warmth was seductive. Addy could hear the television buzzing in the distance.

'Remember, three hundred City Credits. Call this number or come in. The Hurtigger Institute on Arrabo Street.' An officious man's voice.

'Thank you, Dr Hurtigger. It's been . . . uh . . . an education having you on our show.' An attractive-sounding woman's voice.

Addy opened one eye and peered at the screen. Not a hint of a woman. Some goddam freaky mouse with extra body parts. Nothing there that interested him. He was far more interested in what lay next to him.

The woman's hair didn't smell lemony. It smelled like woodsmoke. He breathed in happily and asked himself if he was up for another go. He felt a turgid fullness reawakening. Yep. She'd be happy for another round. She wasn't a prostitute. She . . . Marina, she said was her name last night, had been waiting for her friend. She had been attracted to him from the start. Addy sucked in his stomach. Even though it was fashionable for men these days to be a touch porky, he hated the gelid feeling of a pot-belly. Whenever he turned on his side, his stomach slid down like bread dough. At least he still had his looks. He was a robust and impressive thirty-seven. Terza told him she'd talked to him in Sainsbury's because he looked so safe. So nice. *Nice*.

What a word. He almost laughed. He reached over only to have Marina swat his hand away.

'Quick, hand me a pencil. I want to write that phone number down,' she said.

'You can't be serious. Why do you want an extra body part? I can give you all the body parts you need. Look, I've got one here for you . . .' Addy grabbed Marina's pale hand and placed it where he thought it could do the most good.

The painful squeeze she gave it wasn't what he had in mind exactly.

'Ow! You didn't have to do that. It was just expressing its admiration for you.' Addy gave her the sexy half-lidded look that always got Terza going.

'Don't you have to be somewhere or something? Work? A wife?' she asked.

The look must not be working. He had to give it one more try. He didn't want to get up yet.

'We could have another go . . .' He reached over and squeezed her pink-tipped breast.

Her voice was clipped and frozen. 'You have two seconds.'

Addy chuckled. They always played hard to get. 'For what? Not long enough for what I have in mind.'

'Two seconds to take your hand off me or I'll surgically remove it,' Marina continued.

Addy decided that it would be advantageous to take her advice. Who wanted to take the chance that she wasn't playing hard to get?

'You can't mean that.' An incipient whine curled around his words to his surprise. 'Last night you didn't mind . . . and you asked me to hold you all night.'

'That was then. This is now.'

'You're kicking me out?'

'Finally you understand.'

'But you had two –'

'Never mind! The door's over there. Don't slam it on your way out.'

It wasn't right for her to kick him out as if he was some errant turd. He was the one that should be doing the kicking out.

Unfortunately, he was in her bed. In her flat. He was running out of options. Better try being pathetic.

'Whatever I did, I'm sorry.'

'It's nothing you did. It's just . . . what are you doing?'

Addy hadn't been able to resist. Her woodsmoke smell was getting to him again. Besides, he was always turned on by resistance. 'You've got such silky hair. The colour of butter . . . the colour I'd imagine real butter to be.'

Marina snorted. 'The colour of butter? That's a new one. How would you know? Dairy products disappeared years ago.'

'I've read about it. Before those pre-millennium cows got their marching orders from Brussels, people used to spread butter on their toast, not petroleum by-products.'

'Yeah, right.'

'Supposedly, butter was yellow, not the lard-white of the petro-margarine. The colour of sun. Of honey . . . of . . . of skin warmed by . . .'

A small hand came towards him. He held his breath.

Which expelled sharply when he hit the ground. His fashionably acquired extra pounds should have protected his bones from the hard floor, but no such luck. When you were shoved out of bed, you didn't have time to arrange padding in appropriate places.

'Bitch,' he muttered.

'I told you not to touch me again.'

Resigned. 'I get the message. I'll go.'

'Thanks.'

He didn't know what he'd seen in her. 'I don't get it. What did I do?'

Addy got up and scrabbled around for his boxer shorts, flung off last night with such happy abandon. As he bent over to look under the bed, he stubbed his toe on the edge of something sharp.

'Bloody hell.' He winced.

No sound from the bed.

'Where are my shorts?'

A voice crept out from under the duvet. 'In the other room with –'

'The rest of my clothes. Cheers. Thanks for your consideration.'

Addy stomped into the other room, making sure he made as much noise as possible on the hardwood floors. After pulling on his black all-in-one, he undid the top button of the trouser section. *Oof.* That was better. He pulled on his leather flight jacket, did up the zip and picked up his keys.

'I'm going now,' he called.

A small voice came from the bedroom. ''Bye.'

He walked to the door, opened it, and paused. Wistful, he thought of the smell of her hair. 'Aren't you going to stop me?'

'No.'

He hadn't thought so. 'Don't you even want to know my name?'

Her silence must mean she didn't. Slamming the door, Addy went out, running down the stairs two at a time. His stomach rumbled uncomfortably. He hadn't had time to go home and eat dinner last night. He wondered if Terza had noticed. She better had. He wanted her to ask him where he'd been. He wanted to tell her. Irritated, he got in his car and slammed the door. Revving the engine, Addy hoped he'd wake up all the neighbours.

What had gone wrong? He couldn't figure out where his technique with women could have disintegrated. It hadn't been that long since he was the scourge of the night-clubs, delighting the Chosen with his beaming regard. His friends were always so admiring. 'How do you do it, Addison? You pull all the best birds!' He knew they were jealous about Terza. She was gorgeous. That's why he had married her. Because his friends wanted her. She was damned attractive, though. That was the problem.

It was all her fault. *Bloody women.*

He hadn't expected to fall in love with her after they'd married. It was so inconvenient. He had never given a stuff before what women got up to when they weren't with him.

But Terza was different. So many other men wanted her, which was why he had to exert his control so often. Terza had to realize that she didn't have the upper hand in this relationship. It was driving him nuts, though. What she must be doing.

Thinking about all the men, he put his foot down so that he'd get home before she left for the dance class she taught. He checked his watch.

Too late. When he walked in, Addy saw her note telling him she'd gone to class. She always signed it with a smiley face. He hoped she was worried about him and wondering where he was. Did she care?

Throwing his jacket on to the angular white leather sofa in the lounge, he went looking. He'd find evidence this time. After checking her date book, the answering machine, her drawers, looking under the bed and scrutinizing the sheets, he went to the laundry room. He picked up the dirty-clothes basket, poured everything on to the floor and sifted through it carefully. His own socks and undershirts he put aside, pinching his nostrils shut with one hand: in warm weather, things smelled ripe. A scrap of pink lace. Her underwear. There must be evidence in there. Foreign discharge. A single hair of a different colour. Semen had a particular smell, especially when it was somebody else's. He'd know evidence if he saw it. Addy knew Terza was cheating on him with men from her class. And he knew what she was planning to do to him. She pretended that she wanted him to come to class with her sometimes. A clever subterfuge.

'Come to class with me, honey.' Terza scooped a handful of glittery gel and ran it through her boyish curls. 'I'd love you to come.'

I bet you would. 'You know I don't dance that pansy hip-swinging stuff.'

Terza sighed. 'Salsa isn't for pansies. Look at all those macho Latin American men out there swinging their hips. None of them look effeminate.'

Which one are you doing it with? 'Salsa is for poufs.'

Terza came up to him, put both cool hands on either side of his face and kissed him. 'If you won't come, then I'm off. I'm trying to get the new combinations practised so I can take off a bit early next week. We could go out to dinner.'

That must be where she's planning to do it.

At least Addy knew what she was up to. He'd decided three

days before that a private investigator was the only way to know for sure. He couldn't stand the thought that Terza could be having it off with one of those horrid salsa-dancing creeps. Or, even worse, with one of his friends. He watched the way they looked at her. Slavering acquisitive looks. He didn't speak to them any more.

A private investigator would help him. Waving to the *Yellow Pages*, he asked them to recommend one in his area. With a hum, the *YP* asked in a bored mechanical tone for his search criteria and then printed out a list. There was only one on the list within his price range but he supposed this private dick looked okay. The guy was cheap and just down the road at Kentish Town. Not wanting anyone to identify his car, Addy thought he'd better take the Transport. Kentish Town was only two stops away on the Northern Line.

After trotting down to the Transport station, Addy sighed at the inconvenience. Another of the omnipresent strikes creating havoc on the roads.

Grinning to himself at the turmoil going on, he shoved his way on to a bus attempting to plough its way down Junction Road. Extra body mass had its advantages.

Addy hung on to one of the straps suspended from the ceiling of the bus and looked around him with pleasure. One surprising benefit of the strikes was its effect on personal space. Usually people needed at least ten feet of personal space around them. Sometimes when he was bored, he'd edge up to people in Food Bank queues and watch their shoulders twitch. They felt it when he crossed their personal-space boundary, even by an inch. It was fun to do it to women.

People never touched any more. Unless you were having sex, or embracing family members, you forgot what bodily contact was like.

Except on Transport strike days. He grinned hugely and waited, hardly daring to exhale. The excitement was electric.

When the bus turned a corner, Addy allowed himself to sway along with everyone standing in the middle aisle of the bus. They were all hemmed in tightly. It was impossible to move. It was like lying full length with your body pressed against several people at once. You felt everything, from soup to nuts. What was in their pockets. What religion they were. You looked deep into their eyes and knew if they had just woken up, reluctant sediment still littering their eyes. What they smelt like. Addy wiggled his toes with delight and sniffed.

The scent of stress was the pervading one. People were upset . . . had run for the bus . . . had fought to get on . . . had silvery snail tracks of tears drying on flushed cheeks. Shirts were untucked. Flesh gaped. Breasts and buttocks flattened him from all sides. There had better not be any men rubbing anything against him. He was no homo. Bodies pressed familiarly into each other, their faces and eyes trying to look uninvolved. Uncaring. As if this invasion wasn't happening. The air in the bus was redolent with distaste and unease.

A faint scent of perfume wafted up to Addy's nose from somewhere to his right. He looked around and down. The scent exuded from a smallish woman crushed up under his right armpit. He hoped he didn't smell bad. He tried to sniff himself, and didn't notice anything offensive. Edging sideways so that he pressed into her back, he let her other smells caress his nostrils. Along with the faint flowery perfume and the smell of soap, he smelt something else.

Carbolic? Creosote. The stuff they used to paint on fences to prevent horses chewing them. Now it was used for track scraping. Scrapers painted it on rails to repel rats from eating the hair and skin they scraped up. Addy shivered at the thought. She must be a Scraper. *Ugh.* Rats were one thing. But everyone knew Scrapers weren't really people. They couldn't be. Who'd apply for a job like that?

Still, this Scraper was awfully round and cute. She was hugely pregnant, like a mammoth beach ball. Pregnant women were sexy. It always brought to mind what they had done to get that way. The woman was wearing a filmy dress with floppy whorish flowers all over it. It looked like Terza's night-gown. The other thing about pregnancy was that it gave women the most incredibly big breasts.

Addy peered down the front of her dress. Yes, he sighed with delight, he was right. The whitest, most edible, marshmallow-coloured breasts he'd ever seen. He ached to slip one hand down her beckoning cleavage. There, between the flowers. His fingers would become wet with the warm perspiration that the woman's fight to get on the bus had generated. Her nipples would be large and flamboyant, like fuzzy cherries. He licked his lips. He could almost taste them, rolling around in his mouth.

The bus swayed, and Addy moved against her. He felt his penis engorge. It had been perking up as he thought about her breasts, but now that he was leaning against her, it was even better. She'd probably think it was his umbrella. Was she wearing any underwear? He nudged between the warm cleft of her buttocks. The thin fabric started to seem an unwelcome obstruction. Addy wondered if he could get away with slipping up the fabric of her dress surreptitiously. It had always been his fantasy to touch up a woman on a bus. Maybe she'd welcome it. He flexed his fingers in preparation.

The woman moved, noticing something intruding that wasn't as random as it should be. It was too consistently there. Unfortunately, every time she tried to push away, the bus was so packed that she was pushed right back on to Addy. He groaned slightly at the start of her resistance. So entrancing. Her buttocks rhythmically flattened against him as she tried to move. He fought to retain control. His hand slowly rucked up the skirt of her dress, the flowers crumpling ever so slowly into his sweaty palm. The captivating scent of perfume, sweet perspiration and creosote filled his nostrils. He leaned his head back waiting for the bus to go over a bump. When it did, he'd pull her skirt right up and press himself into her moist flesh. Nobody would see and nobody would know. Just Addy and the woman.

Suddenly, an electric shock of the most monumental teeth-juddering proportions shot through his body, curling his toes and other extended body parts. He screamed, his voice high and terrified.

'Jesus! Something's bloody bitten me!'

Addy didn't press against anybody else after that. What was left of the throbbing erection he'd been nursing had retreated shyly into the depths of his jauntily striped boxer shorts. Haughtily, he avoided the disgusted looks of the people standing next to him and stayed well clear of the woman. Something was definitely strange about Scrapers.

Nursing his toasted testicles at least kept Addy's mind off his main problem. What to do about Terza. When he got off the bus, he read the address the *Yellow Pages* had printed out for him. '83 Tollington Park Way,' it said. When Addy squinted and looked up at the nearest building numbers, he saw 160. He sighed heavily. The numbers wouldn't correspond across the street. They never did in London. Whoever had planned the streets originally must have been smoking something pretty damaging. He looked across the street.

Just as he thought: '25.' When he went to the next corner, he let out an exasperated grunt. The street name had changed. *Bloody hell*. He crossed back and went the other way. This time the numbers went up. Was it him, or were they not making sense?

At number 240, Addy noticed a small blue sign painted with white letters. 'Madame Berengaria', it extolled. 'Fortune Teller – Palmist – Horoscopes. No appointment necessary.'

'Rubbish,' he muttered. The goddam detective agency was nowhere to be seen. How was he going to find out about Terza? He couldn't read her thoughts.

An idea struck Addy and he scratched his crotch thoughtfully. Perhaps a fortune teller could read Terza's mind? They could discover if she was bonking one of his friends. Find out what she was thinking. If she was thinking about George or Essel, he'd kill her.

Terza always read horoscopes. She swore by them. Just yesterday she'd come up to him while he was taking a bath, meditating on which friend she was sleeping with.

'Addy, listen. This is yours today.' She licked a finger and turned the page of the magazine she was holding.

'"Lucky Taurus, you'll discover at long last what's been bothering you. You'll be shocked when you find out but it'll be worth it."' She giggled and looked at him from underneath her lashes. 'Now me. "Gorgeous Gemini, you'll be the centre of all eyes. The eye of a storm. Centre of a maelstrom." What's a maelstrom?'

Addy grunted and sank into the water. Centre of all eyes, huh? He knew it. It must be George. He was long-sighted and wore glasses that made him look as if he had huge alien bug's eyes.

'Dunno,' he had replied. 'You know I don't believe in that rubbish.'

Addy's fingers fluttered inside his pockets as he followed the horoscope palm woman who had let him in. They walked down a dark hallway, the smell of cats tickling his nostrils as fluff brushed his fingertips. There was nothing much in his pockets. He just liked fiddling in them sometimes. A nervous habit, really. What else was in there? A crumpled bit of paper.

Ouch! Something sharp. A thick crescent of fingernail he had ripped off in a frenzy of nerves on the way to the front door. He dropped the fragment outside the woman's door but when he saw it grinning obscenely up at him, he scooped it up and put it back in his pocket. He didn't want to leave anything the woman could use for voodoo or anything like that. Addy giggled nervously. No pins stuck into him, thank you very much.

He clenched the sliver between nerveless fingers, as the woman gestured for him to sit down.

Addy looked around as he did so, thinking how dark and cosy the room was. The windows were covered up with thick curtains, and the glow from the one light was dim. He went to sit where the woman indicated. The cat he sat on complained bitterly and shot off into the gloom.

'Sorry, Madame Ber–'

The woman smiled. 'Berengaria. Don't worry about the cat. He thinks he owns the place.'

Addy nodded when she asked him if he'd like his palms read.

While she went to do whatever initial ablutions palmists do, he looked around again. Photographs were arranged with careful symmetry on a high shelf. Displayed in ornate gilded frames, they looked the only things in the room kept dust-free. Boring old family photos, most likely. Addy couldn't see from where he was sitting. Photos of kiddies. Yuck. Give him a couple of breasts any day.

He couldn't see whether this Madame Berengaria, whatever she called herself, had any breasts when she came back. She was completely covered up from the top of her coiled silver hair to the green snakeskin slippers she wore. Her feet shuffled as she walked. Slap slap slap.

Old slapper.

The robe she wore was of a purple-coloured wool, a colour he thought was called hyacinth. It was thickly woven with a silky blue slub flickering here and there. Whenever he blinked, the colour changed. Blue. Green. Blue again.

'What do you want to know?' She smiled at him as she took his hand in hers. She had a charming smile for an older woman. He felt himself smiling back.

'I've got a problem . . .'

Addy told her what he wanted and was astonished at how angry she became.

'I am not the police! You can't use me to check up on your wife!' She seemed appalled and shook her head vigorously, her silver hair coming out of its previously neat coil.

'Please? I need to know.' Addy shot her his most winsome expression. 'I can't be a loving husband to her when I think she's up to something with my friends.' He allowed his eyelids to flutter in despair.

Madame Berengaria looked at him for a long moment. Her flustered expression cleared. She still looked angry, but a calculating look had come into her eyes. Addy hoped she wasn't going to charge him more.

She didn't raise the price. Instead she told him what he had to do. He felt sick. He knew it. Somehow, he had hoped that Madame

Berengaria would tell him it was all his imagination. Addy felt so betrayed, tears sprang to his eyes.

He knew it, but to hear it in words made it so final.

'You have no choice,' she continued, her face serene behind its careful smile. 'You must.' She raised one pallid hand towards her throat, and made a sharp sawing motion with one finger.

'You can't mean that.' Addy leaned forward. He saw, with sick fascination, the long curled fingernails, grimed underneath with something dark and viscous. He placed his own hands on the table between them, as if to repel her.

'You read all that from just my palms?' He clenched the palms in question.

Madame Berengaria narrowed her eyes and continued. 'Like I said, she killed you in a previous life.' Suddenly she reached over and touched his neck. Her hand felt surprisingly young. Smooth. Scented with almonds.

'Here. She wrapped a length of wire around your throat. Can't you feel the psychic remnants? The choking?'

Addy shot backwards in his chair, away from the fingers that fluttered towards him like diseased pigeons. As he backed away, his hands went up to his throat involuntarily. He felt himself choking. A rancid wash of bile crept down his throat as he tried to swallow.

'She'll do it again.'

Madame Berengaria's words followed him, as he yanked his jacket from the chair, trampolining off the cat which had settled on it.

'Your wife and all of her lovers. Quite a few of them. You'll have to kill her first before she gets you.' She chuckled and sounded as if she relished the dire nature of the situation.

'No,' he whispered. 'Not my wife.'

He got up and ran for the door.

She called after him, 'No charge for that one. I enjoyed it.'

Terza had killed him in a previous life. Addy walked all the way back roiling with furious perturbation. At least he had proof now about the men. Unless that palm stuff was all rubbish. Wasn't it? But Madame Berengaria had known about all the men without him even telling her. Surely that gave her legitimacy.

Addy let himself into the house and stopped himself from checking Terza's laundry as usual. He didn't need to know now. He felt sick. He had proof. Did he? Perhaps he needed to consult another fortune teller. Palmist. Whatever. To cross-reference.

Picking up the prostitute had been to make him feel better and do to Terza what she was doing to him. The woman hadn't been a prostitute in the end, and he didn't feel much better since she'd kicked him out, but still. The intention had been there. It was the first time he'd slept with another woman since he and Terza were married. He hoped she'd feel terrible when she found out.

No more searching for clues. His head told him what his heart already knew. What that palm reader told him was true. If more evidence was needed, well, he'd heard her on the telephone yesterday laughing about him to her friends. His head hurt. Rummaging in his pocket, he pulled out the Tarvoy's Flotation coupons. There were still a couple left. What he needed was a good soak. That would give him the energy to decide what to do next.

Addy pushed open Tarvoy's door, walked up to the desk and slapped his coupon on the red vinyl counter.

'I'm here for a bloody good soak.' He winked at the receptionist, whose name tag stated that she was pleased to be of assistance and that customers could call her Rita. You never knew. Now that he was paying Terza back for what she was doing, he could sleep with whomever he chose. Even Madame Berengaria, if he wanted. Not that he would. Addy shuddered.

'Regular or Fear?' Rita smiled at him, her green contact lenses glinting. Addy sucked in his stomach happily. *Yep, the magic still works*.

Leaning on the counter casually, so that Rita could get a whiff of his pheromones, he winked at her. 'I had the Regular last time,

Rita.' He checked his coupon. 'That's all my wi– uh, friend bought me. Coupons for the Regular float tanks.'

Rita appeared overwhelmed by his pheromones.

'Fear flotation costs more, but . . .' she dimpled ' . . . maybe I could slip you in.'

You certainly can, he grinned to himself. 'I'd love to be slipped in, sweetheart. If you've got an opening, of course?' He winked again.

Rita twinkled at him and handed him a towel. 'This way. I'll let you have the deluxe Fear soak. It's been empty for a couple of days waiting for my boss's brother to come and do up the room a bit.'

'There's nothing wrong with it, is there?' He hoped it had some kind of reclining couch or sheet they could roll around on. He was too old to frolic on the bare floor.

'No, no, it just needs sprucing up. The tank's our most popular one and it's showing its age.'

As Rita led him down the briny-smelling tunnel, Addy watched her hips moving in front of him like oiled ball bearings. Encased in tight white shorts, the creases of her buttocks smiled at him and begged to be touched. When she stopped at a door and turned, Rita caught him looking at her. This time, she winked at him.

'You first.' She beckoned.

Addy peeled off his clothes with glum deliberation and climbed into the tank. So much for fantasy. Things never worked out like you expected. And she had looked like the type he wouldn't even have to force to get her head down. Lovely mobile lips.

She had given him a special deal with this float thing, at least. He tugged on the rusted dome above him. Was it stuck? He pulled harder and finally the lid closed with a clatter, just missing his hand. He glared at it and sank backwards.

Floating in saline solution was surprisingly addictive. The first time he'd been here, being afraid of water, he had been wary. But the man with the Dumbo ears serving him told him it was good to face your fears.

'It's the point of our whole company . . .' he started.

He had been about to elaborate, but Addy had cut him off. He didn't have time to listen to any milk-faced creep going on about holistic crap.

It was wonderfully relaxing. It almost took his mind off the trauma he was going through. Should he leave Terza or kill her before she got to him?

After settling into the water, Addy pressed the green button on the right side of the tank. That, Rita had said coolly, would release the nerve drops into the water. The ones that elicited random fears or worries you had and drew them out into the water. Whether it was arachnophobia, claustrophobia, or whatever-phobia, the embodiment of your fear would develop into some kind of nerve gas facsimile. Huge waterlogged spiders would gyrate around you in the enclosed tank, or the tank would shrink, getting smaller and smaller, closing in . . .

Whatever you were afraid of, you faced it alone. And in facing it, you dealt with it and were freed. At least, that's what Rita had promised.

'It's a marvellously relaxing experience,' she said to him, her eyes unreadable. 'You feel rejuvenated, fear- and stress-free afterwards. Like when you have a toothache. Don't you wiggle the tooth? You relish the pain. When the pain is over, it makes the feeling all the sweeter. Besides, fear is never as bad when you face it.' She smiled at him.

'I'm not afraid of anything,' Addy boasted, keeping his stomach carefully in. Big was in. Flab wasn't. Perhaps he could still convince her to have a quick one. Maybe up against the flotation tank.

'We'll see . . .' she said.

'They're not real, those things in the water with you, are they?' he asked. Addy wasn't afraid, but there was no sense in being stupidly foolish.

'No trouble at all, as long as there aren't any electrical problems.' A cloud crossed Rita's filtered gaze and she looked out of the window. 'That could activate the fear objects.' She saw his face and laughed.

'You're not afraid, are you? Such a big, strong man . . .' She reached over and chucked him playfully under the chin.

Addy looked around him at the dank walls and rusted equipment, and wasn't surprised that it needed fixing up. The tank looked like some kind of ancient rusted blimp. Was it safe? He guessed they'd keep their standards up so they didn't get sued. Probably why the room was free. Rita had said it was booked up solidly most of the time.

'Don't catch anything valuable on that sharp edge where the rubber's worn away,' she said. 'Nothing you wouldn't miss if you lost it.' Addy laughed and winked at her. Rita had smiled thinly.

Addy waited as the nerve gas trickled in. What would show up? You couldn't choose. You got whatever fear was most on your mind at the moment. Addy didn't think he was afraid of much, but you never knew. Spiders didn't bother him. Small spaces, no . . .

As he waited, Addy's mind drifted back to the telephone call he had overheard. Terza was speaking on the mobile phone in the bedroom when he'd come in.

'No. No. I don't think so.' Terza laughed.

I knew it.

'He loves it when I do that.'

She's talking about sex. I'll kill her.

'Yeah. Treat 'em mean to keep 'em keen . . . yeah.' She laughed. 'You too?'

The bitch.

'He likes the others to want me. I'm more valuable that way.' She laughed. 'Men!'

Addy peered through the crack in the door edge. Terza faced away from him, smoothing a hand down her flat stomach.

Her laughing at him had been the last straw.

Addy shut his eyes and sank into the water. Terza's smooth brown stomach undulated before his closed eyes. He thought of her dancing. The way her body twisted as she twirled. Even though he hated other men touching her, he loved seeing her dance with them. She held her arms above her, as light as air. The men grasped her hand and spun her around. She gyrated, the only point of contact being that one magical hand. That hand that had given him so much pleasure. She twirled, spangled skirts flaring. Again. One. Two. Her head went back and her mouth opened. She was laughing. Again she twirled. He'd like to cut that hand off.

He could have her meet him there at the flotation tanks and suggest she have a Fear soak. He wouldn't tell her about the missing rubber edging. When she went to climb in, he'd slam the cover down and trap her cheating hand. That would teach her to touch those other men.

Jealousy scrabbled its burning fingernails inside Addy's guts. Terza really wound him up. Always these men after her. She could be sleeping with more than one . . . my God, with every one of his friends! The ones he'd cut off to restrict their contact to her. The thought of them with her disgusted him. Addy could picture them. In and out. One after the other. Hundreds of them.

In the water next to him, pale fleshy objects began to bob like bath toys. First one. Then two. Then the tank filled with them. They pressed against him from all sides. Addy couldn't believe it. He splashed around to get the things away from him. He was no shirt-lifter! He turned his head and reached towards the tank lid's latch. A huge one stared him in the eye, its foreskin flared like a cobra. He opened his mouth to scream and felt the back of his head being inexorably pushed forward by the others.

Tiberius Maximus

ZEBEDIAH

Cruel, but composed and bland,
Dumb, inscrutable and grand,
So Tiberius might have sat,
had Tiberius been a cat.

MATTHEW ARNOLD

When the electricity blew and plunged the laboratory into darkness, the mouse screamed. Not in pain this time, but from gibbering, cautious relief. He wasn't stupid enough to think that he was off the hook, though. It had to be yet another painful surprise the Man in White had for him.

Backing up until he hit the chilly wires of his cage, he sagged to the floor and rested his nose on one paw. He must gather his thoughts and remember who and what he was, in case he ever escaped.

'I am Tiberius Maximus,' he mumbled.

No. That wasn't it. *Zebediah*. Zeb to his friends.

One minute, he had been scurrying back and forth, enjoying seeing tourists gasp as they spotted him on the tracks, nosing through fluffs of hair and skin flecks, and shifting bits of garbage to make the Scrapers' work harder. Just for fun. Not from any sense of vindictiveness. The next minute, a dark square box-thing was slapped over his head. As he looked up in terror, wondering if the end of the world was nigh, a metal sheet sliced underneath his paws to block his escape. When he looked back down at them, frantically sliding, he was scooped up like an errant cockroach.

Shifting from side to side in the box-thing, he tried not to panic. After all, he was a family mouse of reasonable intelligence and acceptable lineage. Only ignorant mice freaked out when they were caught the first time. Granted, this seemed worse than just dodging a trap or some phonily scented poison. Calm. He must remain calm. Keep his marbles about him and all his nuts in one basket. He giggled, his voice high with nerves. *Calm*.

After what seemed like ages, the box-thing opened. Artificial blue light poured in, making him blink. A hand with plump gloved fingers and whorls of hair sprouting from the edge of white sleeves reached in, approaching him with a white cone-like object. Zeb shrank as far as possible into the corner of the box. Coming down . . . oh, the smells! Of heat and disease. Something else. Some medicinal smell. Formaldehyde or someth–

Black . . . white . . . orange flame-like pain in his back. Limbs torn asunder. He was flayed . . . split open . . . something was put in. Steely shards of grey-blue steel. *It hurts, Zimne!*

After the pain eased, the finger began. Prod prod prod. 'Get up,' it seemed to say. 'Give us a couple a circuits round the track.' The cage, rather.

He was in a cage sitting on the floor of some kind of laboratory. The ground was damped-down earth, which smelt peaty and moist. The wires of the cage were thin and silvery, but strong. He'd tested them with his teeth, not with any real sense of hope but he couldn't just sit there. His gums were bleeding and there was a nasty taste of tar in his mouth from the wires. He licked his dry lips upon which he could taste the tang of creosote. Wasn't that what humans painted on fences to make horses not nibble on them?

Am I a horse? He thought furiously.

The finger came back.

No! How can I get up?

Prod prod prod.

I don't care how bad it tastes, I'll bite it, I will. I hope he dies in terrible convulsions. He. The man. That great spawn of the devil.

Later, Zeb was put back in his cage. Drained, he lay on the uncomfortable wire cage bottom and watched the Man. He sat on a stool and wrote things in a notebook for a while. As he wrote, he kept twitching his foot. Zeb wished he would stop. It was bloody irritating. The Man got up finally, checked his watch, and waved at a TV screen in the far corner of the laboratory, turning it on.

Oh, God, there were two Men in White. And Two Zebs. They were on TV. Now he knew he was going crazy. Hadn't Zeb teased Zimne about how important he was when he'd first met her?

'You'll see! I'm a mouse that's going places.' Proud as a politician, he puffed up his chest and blew air out of the sides of his mouth to set his whiskers wiggling. 'I'll be on TV some day.'

Zimne had snorted. But she'd snuggled a bit closer to him.

Yeah. TV. He was on TV now. Sourly, Zeb thought that he'd pass next time. He decided to watch what the TV star Zeb and Man-in-White were up to.

A cool vanilla woman's voice was speaking. '. . . revolutionary medical advances. So you see, this was a red-letter year for us. For this little chap here too.'

I look awful. And there's a . . . there's a thing on me. An ear. Zeb fainted, the tiny thump unnoticeable in the room. When he opened his eyes again, he blearily watched the screen.

The interviewer sounded repelled. 'Didn't legal action against animal testing back in the nineties preclude this kind of thing, Dr Hurtigger?'

Man-in-White answered, 'We decided that it was worth the risk. Look at him. Can't you just imagine the benefit to mankind?' Dr Hurtigger looked terribly pleased with himself. 'It brings forward my experiments with multi-donors.'

'Multi-donors?'

'People who can generate more than one scion – uh, donated body part.'

The woman looked interested. 'What kinds of experiments?'

'They're still in progress.' He laughed. 'It depends on the public's reaction to this mouse. And, of course, whether I can get further funding. Such a valuable project, don't you think?'

'I can see that it opens up all kinds of possibilities, but I'm sure our viewers are concerned with how the mouse feels about this.'

That's right, think of me! Zeb sat up.

'I can assure you, he doesn't feel a thing.'

Says who?

'You've asked him?'

'We couldn't exactly get him to sign a waiver. But look at

him. Does he look distressed at all?' Both the woman interviewer and Dr Hurtigger on the screen turned towards the mouse. The camera zoomed in.

Now people will see how miserable I am. Zeb grew excited.

The camera panned in on an unconcerned TV star Zeb. A whisker twitched here and there and there was a glassy look in the small black eyes.

If you didn't know better, you'd think I didn't give a damn! Appalled, Zeb shut his eyes. *He must have recorded this while I was drugged.*

He heard himself squeaking and the sound of his claws skittering over a hard surface. Next came munching noises and several minutes of happy mouse music. Zeb opened his eyes and watched with sick fascination. The camera played with the mouse on the screen. Zoomed in. Raced out.

Stop that, you're making me dizzy.

The camera returned to the woman interviewer's face. She appeared to be forcing a look of businesslike matter-of-factness to cover the repugnance she felt. She brushed back a strand of hair and held out the microphone to Dr Hurtigger.

'Dr Hurtigger, ethical considerations aside, do you really believe this is the wave of the future?'

He chuckled. 'Of course. When you think of all the people out there who have accidents or illnesses requiring the amputation of body parts, I can assure you the preponderance of people would be willing to grow a little ear for their fellow human beings.'

I'm going to be sick. Zeb tried to cover his ears with his paws, but he couldn't drown out the voices.

'Sick people everywhere will regain hope. We can grow them new ears, new hands – anything they need. All we lack are willing donors. We must find a way to convince more people to volunteer. Either that or create our own source. I wasn't supposed to talk about this yet, but I think it's important.'

The woman laughed. 'I don't suppose you can grow a human leg on a mouse.'

Dr Hurtigger ignored the sarcasm. 'I'm hoping that people

seeing this programme will come into the Hurtigger Medical Clinic and sign up to be donors. We are in such desperate need.'

'Why would anyone want to do anything like that?' The woman looked back at the mouse on the screen. 'I for one can't imagine signing up to have a huge ear the size of a Volkswagen implanted on my back.'

'Come now, size is relative – although you've probably heard that before from most of us men.' He paused to allow the canned audience laughter to be heard. 'You'd have a regular-sized body part implanted on you. We couldn't implant a mouse ear on a mouse. That wouldn't have been challenging enough. Do you remember when they grew a human ear on a mouse back in the nineties? They were on the right track, but they didn't take it far enough. Plus, the ears weren't totally authentic. They were fiddling around with fake cartilage moulds and ridiculously backward stuff like that. No, no . . . my experiments are much more advanced. We're talking the real thing here. Viable ears which can be used to help the suffering of millions –'

'Millions of what?' the woman interrupted. 'Earless humans wandering around in dire need of assistance?'

'– and we have to test them on something.' Dr Hurtigger pretended she hadn't spoken. 'You know how people get about human testing.'

'Still . . .'

Zeb decided he liked the woman. She didn't look convinced.

Dr Hurtigger continued, a fatuous smile creasing his features, 'Think of the satisfaction of knowing you're helping someone to live a whole and productive life.'

'And?' The woman prompted.

'We'll pay. Three hundred City Credits per body part they grow.' Dr Hurtigger hesitated. 'Negotiable for group discounts.'

'That should make a difference. With unemployment up where it is these days, it might convince a few. Why, look at our phones lighting up!' The camera panned over to a group of women in black manning a switchboard. Orange pinpricks of light flickered on it, and the women nodded at the board to answer calls. As they came in faster and faster, the women's nodding became more and more frenetic, and they looked increasingly like toy dogs bobbing in cars.

Dr Hurtigger took off his glasses and rubbed the red marks on his nose. 'Besides, it's not like it's for ever. All we need is their body as a host for about three weeks. We implant the bud, which includes genetic information of the person it's to go to. Three weeks, that's all we need. When the body part's matured, we snip it off, quick as a flash. It leaves a tiny little scar. Hardly noticeable.'

The woman snorted. 'I think I'd notice.'

Dr Hurtigger laughed, his eyes cold.

Businesslike, the woman continued, 'What were you saying about group discounts? You could have more than one?'

'Sure. A person can grow as many body parts as they have space for.'

'For three weeks, you've got parasitic extra ears or whatever all over your body?' The woman looked sick now.

Oh, gross.

Dr Hurtigger sounded defensive. 'It could be advantageous. Think of the hearing you'd have with an extra ear. Or the shopping an extra hand could help you with.' He grinned out at the audience.

Zeb bared his teeth and growled under his breath.

'Remember, folks, three hundred City Credits. Call this number or come in. The Hurtigger Institute, Hurtigger, that's me, on Arrabo Street.'

'Thank you, Dr Hurtigger. It's been . . . an education having you on our show.' The woman turned to look at the camera, smiling with every tooth possible. Credits rolled. The happy mouse music and squeaking sounds were brought up and faded as the TV star Zeb filled the screen.

One of the omnipresent advertising commercials for the daily lottery came on after the show ended. 'It's YOU!' a voice boomed. Dr Hurtigger waved at the screen to turn it off.

It's you. Me. I. I am Tiberius Maximus and . . .

The finger came towards him again.

I could bite it. Zeb's muzzy head cleared. He'd tried before when he woke up from the anaesthesia. When the finger prodded him for the first time, Zeb had turned and sunk his teeth into it as hard as he could manage without passing out. The Man jerked back his hand sharply with Zeb's teeth still embedded in it. Zeb hung on, drawing back his lips to avoid the horrid medicinal taste of the Man's gloves. The hand snapped back and forth and Zeb had fallen heavily back into the cage, landing on his side.

Grimly, Zeb's past experience told him that he'd better hunker down and keep himself to himself. He had to try to get used to walking with the abomination on his back. It was like learning to walk again. He must look so stuuuupid. How embarrassing.

Good thing Zimne can't see me. She'd leave me for sure, if she hasn't already. Slowly, he got up. One step at a time. Take it easy. He had to avoid pitching over on to his side. How humiliating it was to lie there the first time, helpless, making small mewling sounds of distress until the Man had come back.

After three steps, Zeb grew tired. Depression and hopelessness crashed down upon him. *What was the use?*

His head hurt, angry tears made him blink rapidly and the sense of displacement and uncertainty started to descend.

Who am I? Tiberius Maximus. I can't be what I was before. Not possible. Was I? Was. Wasn't. I must be him because I can't be Zebediah any more. I want to kill the one who has done this to me. I who am now an emperor. God of mice and men. I can rule with this thing on my back. I am a Roman emperor. I am more than the others now. I, who had never wanted more, now have more than I ever could have imagined.

Zeb cried, the tears trickling down into the fur which he hadn't the energy to try to clean. His skin was so cracked and stiff. He hadn't the energy to care. He tried to shake away the displacement and hold on to the dwindling sense of normality he sensed ebbing away. He could hear the crazy side of him talking to the normal side. He'd heard about that kind of thing. Now, besides being a mouse with a human ear on his back, he had a Multiple Personality Disorder as well. Was that fair? What would his family think?

They'd come to save him right after he'd first been . . . uh . . .

enhanced. Three of them. Zimne, his brother Synda and oldest boy Teebe. They slipped in from outside and ranged themselves outside Zeb's cage. God knows how they found him. He was still out of it from the surgery and could only look at them helplessly, the ear wafting from side to side in the breeze coming in through a high window. When his family saw him, their eyes became rolled green marbles and the shock paralysed them for an instant. Teebe screamed and ran out of the room. Synda looked horrified and ran next. Zimne looked after Teebe and Synda. Back at Zeb. Pity, disgust and love warred within her eyes. Footsteps. The Man must be approaching. Zimne looked sorrowfully at Zeb, turned and ran.

The rejection by his family hurt terribly. He didn't blame them. He'd have done the same.

The Man came in after his family had gone. The Finger arrived. Prod prod.

If he prods me to get up and walk again, I'll kill him. I will. I'm so tired. My joints hurt. He missed Zimne's warm touch. Every time Zeb closed his eyes, he saw their faces staring at him. They hadn't come back. He wanted to die. He would. Maybe he could will himself to die. That would annoy the Man. He'd have no experiment to play with then.

Two hours after the TV show ended, the thumping started. Zeb wished it would stop. He was busy trying to die and the noise disturbed his concentration. It hadn't worked yet, although he had a raging case of stress-related indigestion mixed with hunger. He hadn't been able to eat any of the unappetizing seed stuff Dr Hurtigger had placed in his cage.

Thump thump thump.

Zeb sighed. He couldn't even die in peace.

The sounds were coming from beneath him. Not from a room below, but buried right underneath him. Zeb didn't know what was under the laboratory. Earth could hide anything.

Dr Hurtigger could have carted it in so I wouldn't pee all over his precious carpet or something.

Maybe there was a basement underneath the laboratory. Was

there something down there? Some other poor captured mutant. Zeb closed his eyes. This time he invited the displacement.

I'm a star. I'll be shown on TV screens around the nation. Nobody will see me or be affected by it, though. A mouse with a human ear on his back. Who will notice? Who would care?

I am Tiberius Maximus, after all. I am the judgement seat of the almighty. God gave me this ear for a reason and has given me the power to judge the Man's deeds. I shall crucify you all in the name of the Father, the Son, and the Holy Spirit.

For your deeds against the mousehood, I, Tiberius Maximus, Emperor of the Roman Empire, do hereby proclaim this cell block to be CRUCIFIED in the eyes of the public to bear witness of their atrocities against the Roman Empire.

I am Tiberius Maximus, Roman Emperor at the time of Christ. I have reincarnated into this body. You know him as Zebediah. All of you shall be nailed to the cross. You are neither mice nor men. I will and shall cast judgement and take your stewardship away. For I will show no mercy to those who ask, or give hint to. May whomever you believe in, son of God or whomever, have mercy on your sinful lives.

Thump thump thump.

Zeb could hear so much more than he used to. It was not a boon. Sounds poured into his body through the ear and roiled around his insides like snakes in a frying pan. There was nowhere for them to go. His body couldn't digest them.

Dr Hurtigger was back. Zeb heard rubber gloves snapped on to freshly washed hands. Snap snap snap. Bitterly, he knew that Dr Hurtigger was putting them on to protect himself from mouse germs. What a laugh. Not the other way round. The cage door opened. Zeb squeezed his eyelids shut and played dead. Maybe he'd go away. No, the Finger was back. He could smell it through the rubber. It smelled of hair oil . . . and ham. He must have had ham and cheese for lunch, with lemon mayo. Zeb's stomach gurgled.

Prod prod prod.

No, I won't get up all right all right I will if you pick me up and dangle me in the air like that I will.

Zeb was placed down in the cage again. He tried to remain standing, although every fibre of his body demanded that he give in and collapse. Every time he took a step, the ear's perambulations sent shock waves throughout his body. It wasn't as if he had been in the best shape of his life before this. Zimne had hinted that he was getting a bit porky just the other week. All those rich pickings on the Northern Line.

He could hear thumping again. *Doesn't the Man hear it?*

A horrified thought struck him. The Man was probably responsible for it. Zeb sneaked a sideways look up at him, carefully, not to be seen looking. He didn't want to annoy the good doctor any further.

Look at what he did to me the first time. Jesus Christ on a stick. He might implant me on the forehead of a moose for all I know.

He wanted to remember the doctor's face. As if he could ever forget. Huge mossy furrows of eyebrows under a bulging domed forehead. Soft strands of hair optimistically swooped from one side of his head to the other, unsuccessfully covering what appeared to be an extreme lack of hair. The sum total of all the hair on his head wouldn't make up the minimum requirement for the most rudimentary nest, Zeb reflected. The eyebrows were adorned delicately here and there with snowy chunks of dandruff. Massive chasm-like eye sockets, hiding behind round panes of shiny stuff.

'Glasses,' he knew they were called. He found enough broken examples of them on the Transport tracks. He had even tried putting on a broken pair once. The shiny stuff had been all broken off. He crawled through one of the rims and stood up on his hind legs, calling to Zimne.

'Look! I've got my own hula hoop!' Zimne looked disgusted and made disparaging comments about his mental age compared to those of their children. He squeaked at her when he realized he was stuck in the damned things. That's when Zimne had gone on about him becoming porky. Cheeky bitch.

The face and finger retreated. The gloves unsnapped. Zeb sagged with relief.

What no jogging around the track? No blowing in my ear, peering into it with lights? Exploring my guts? Checking what I had for lunch the other day? I can't stand this.

I am Tiberius Maximus . . .

Thump thump thump.

He couldn't even concentrate on going nuts, much less dying. The thumping was coming in patterns. *I don't want to know.*

Zeb sighed. What would Zimne think of this craven avoidance? And the babies? What would they think of him if he just gave up? Maybe if he could hear the thumping more clearly he could decide what to do. He counted to three and then leaned. As he did so, he felt the ear start to fall with its massive weight, pulling his own insubstantial frame after it. What a hideously helpless feeling.

The ear slammed down on the ground, raising clouds of dust at the bottom of the cage. Zeb's legs dangled helplessly as he coughed. He knew he wouldn't be able to get up again by himself but he knew, as sure as Scrapers scraped, that the finger would be back soon. It would prod him back into righteousness. Uprightedness. Upright. Whatever.

With the ear flat on the ground, all the sounds funnelled painfully right into his guts.

THUD THUD 'HELP.'

Wait a minute. He cuddled against the floor and listened with all the effort he could muster.

'HELP. ME. SOMEBODY.'

Help somebody else? Why should he help whoever the heck it was? He had enough of his own problems. And, besides, it was another one of Them. It wasn't an animal. It was a person buried in there. Was Dr Hurtigger trying to make a human *foie gras* out of somebody?

Zeb lay thinking quietly for a few minutes. Normally he would have run away. Mice did. It was their nature. A pang reminded him of his family's visit. He didn't suppose he had the option of running away. He was stuck here by dint of a huge human ear. And a cage, of course. That didn't mean he had to try to help whoever it was, though. What universal rule said that mice must help humans? After all, humans only made mouse lives miserable. They ran around shrieking when they saw mice and set traps. No. He'd ignore the thumping.

Since he couldn't get up until the Finger came back, he stretched his head along the dirt at the bottom of the cage. At this low vantage point, he caught sight of something he hadn't seen before. Electric wires ran into the cage, ending in tiny bulldog clips. Zeb tried to see where they came from. He peered into the gloom. There still wasn't any electricity, which was what the doctor was probably doing. Sorting out the electricity repairmen.

The wires gathered together outside the cage. They were wrapped into one big cable with black electrical tape. Zeb had seen some and tasted it before. The cable snaked up and ended in an electric plug attached to a socket in the wall.

What is he up to? What experiments can he be planning? It wasn't some sort of electric cattle prod, was it? It took a few minutes before Zeb could breathe normally again. He squinted up at the socket and noticed that it had two cables coming from it. Not just one. The other ran along the cage next to Zeb's cable, but then just disappeared into the ground through a little opening in the earth right above the thumping.

By rocking back and forth, Zeb managed to edge closer to the side of the cage. If he could just manage to look down that opening to see if it was actually a person under there or not.

The rocking made him feel sick. His empty stomach complained, and as the ear swayed back and forth from Zeb's effort, it pulled with an awful ripping sensation from somewhere inside him. He hated to think what it was connected to.

Maybe I could rock the thing off. It would probably kill me in the process, but I suppose that would be better than trying to will myself to death. Or I could –

Zeb was struck by a better idea.

If he could reach those electric wires, he could chew them.

Either it would fry him, helping him to escape from this misery, or he could burn the laboratory up and escape. Maybe help the person below him to escape. Or maybe not. If he could see more, he'd be able to make up his mind.

He rocked the rest of the way to the side of the cage, next to the opening in the floor. He could almost see into it. He tried edging just another few centimetres. *Just ... almost ... ah, there ...*

He raised his head to get a better view and looked down into the opening.

When he'd screamed at the electricity blowing out before and plunging the room into darkness, it had been nothing compared to the shriek he let out when he saw what was below. Gibbering with fright, he rocked backwards in an effort to get away.

It's a she down there. A woman. He could see her eye looking up at him. A scared eye, red-rimmed from crying. Electric scorch marks striated zebra-like across the part of her face he could see. Dr Hurtigger's work, Zeb thought grimly to himself.

There was something else that must be the Man's work. The woman had something implanted on her, like Zeb did. Something far worse than an ear.

She wins. She's Tiberius Maximus. She would have to be with something like that on her.

His ear didn't feel so bad now.

Trading Teeth

CECILIO

*In every deed of mischief he had a
heart to resolve, a head to contrive,
and a hand to execute.*

EDWARD GIBBON

'Cecilio? Come back . . . Cecilio?'

The voice crept out of the plushy darkness of the prison cell and chased Dario down the corridor, nipping at his heels. He stopped, his shoulders hunching in distress.

'Don't call me that,' he spat over his shoulder into the gloom. Only Mama was allowed to call him Cecilio. It was a stupid babyish name. Little Blind One. *She* was the blind one, after all – not deaf, as her own mother had been. Mama appeared abruptly in front of him as if summoned. Her face wavered in the steam from whatever she'd just been cooking. Her milky sightless eyes gazed lovingly towards where she estimated he would be standing.

'Cecilio?' she called and held out her small arthritic hands to him, slightly too far to the left. Cecilio wanted to rush over and tell her he was here – to the right. He'd love to be back safe in her kitchen, his own hands held like captured birds within her crippled ones. He would spell out the words in a language that she had tried over and over to teach him. 'I love you, Mama. *Ti amo.*' He couldn't say something like that to her, even in sign language. He'd never said it to anyone. Once he'd tried to say it into a mirror to see if he could, but he just looked stupid.

'Cecilio? Where are you? I can't find you,' she called, confidence in him redolent in her voice.

Mama had started calling him Little Blind One after he told her that he wanted to be blind just like her when he growed up. She'd laughed softly and brushed the dark curls from out of his still babyish eyes.

'No,' she said, 'you don't, *caro mio*.'

'I do, Mama!' he begged. 'Please show me how.' Smiling winsomely, he cuddled against her. 'Pleasepleaseplease?'

He wanted to be like her. To smell like her. She smelled of comfort and immediacy. He wanted to feel like her. Her skin was firm when you pressed into it. Not mushy like some mothers. She felt like she'd be able to back you up if that bully down the street, Patrizio, threatened to beat you up.

Cecilio never understood why she wouldn't help him become blind like her, no matter how much he begged. He didn't believe her when she gave him that tosh about it being the result of illness. She didn't smell or feel sick. Sick would be mushy. He pressed a surreptitious fingertip against her arm every day. Surely, if she was sick, the fingertip would indent and the flesh would stay pushed in. But no, his finger made a red mark and her skin sprang back.

She was probably lying to him to protect him. Like she always protected Papa.

He'd have to blind himself, if she wouldn't help him.

He scrabbled around in his untidy drawers to find something to blindfold himself with. A T-shirt? It would fall off. Socks? Too small. Underwear? Ugly old Y-fronts. He hated them. He never could manoeuvre the various folded-over flaps and stuff when he had to go.

'*Per amore di Dio*,' Papa said, 'you can't pull your pants down like a woman!'

Unfortunately, it was usually too late by the time he got the flaps organized in a manly fashion. Peeing on yourself was manly?

So, okay, the Y-fronts would redeem themselves at long last.

Cecilio blocked off the window in his bedroom with his red blanket, and put the underwear over his head. They fitted like a snug skullcap, the elastic waistband settling down over the tops of his ears. Perfect. Twisting them round, he made sure the detested flaps were out of harm's way at the back of his head, and the leg holes to the sides. He didn't want to risk any light coming through.

Closing his eyes, he commenced his blindness. Stretching out his arms, he bumbled around the room, barking his shins painfully against the bed frame. He tried not to open his eyes even when he stumbled into the still open wardrobe, tripped over his shoes and games equipment and hit his nose hard on a clothing rail. He let out a mighty oath.

Good thing Mama isn't here. She'd smack him for saying that.

He heard a stifled giggle.

Mama was there.

Dannazione! Cecilio ripped off his blindfold and spun round. Mama was standing in the doorway. Although she couldn't possibly see him, she was laughing, giving up any attempt at stifling it.

'Your sounds of distress . . .' She started laughing again. 'The muttering . . . the swearing as you kept smashing into things. *Mio caro* Cecilio, being blind is not a privilege!'

She'd just about laughed herself sick.

Cecilio no longer wished to be blind. He saw how his father had taken advantage of Mama's inability to see. Thinking of it angered him. Seeing how it angered him annoyed him further. He thought he'd dealt with the whole family issue by leaving Italy when Mama died and moving to England. Here he was, a young man with youth, looks and intelligence. Twenty-eight was relatively young, his mother had thought he was handsome and he was intelligent on a good day. Except in language learning, of course. He could still be flung back into the dumps by thinking of Papa.

The father who was attempting to drag him back into his life.

His father's voice called again, plaintive now instead of peremptory.

'Please come back, Cec– uh, Dario. I'm sorry.'

As much as his mind urged him to flee from the voice, Cecilio found his body turning on automatic pilot and returning to the source of the call. Arriving again at the cell door, he felt disgusted with himself. Why couldn't he write him off? His father couldn't even call him by the correct name.

Even after years of begging both parents not to call him Cecilio, his father never remembered. Cecilio figured Papa did remember, but chose to ignore his requests in some paternal power trip. He had finally allowed his mother to call him that babyish name with bad grace, only because it didn't come out of her lips like an insult. His father uttered it now to manipulate him. To establish warm family feeling and remind him of his mother.

Cecilio reached up and curled both hands around the cold steel bars to steady himself. Flakes of rust fluttered to his feet. Warm family feeling, indeed!

'Why should I bother with you?'

The voice in the darkness coughed.

'Nice try. I'm going . . .'

The voice came closer and solidified into a small figure with a huge moustache, dressed in prison grey. 'I'm your father, that's why.' He coughed again, bending over slightly.

Cecilio felt exasperated guilt. 'You sound terrible. Have you got a cold?'

His father laughed and wrapped both skinny arms around his chest. He waggled his eyebrows up and down. 'They don't believe in cosseting you in prison. No tucking you into bed with lemon tea and hot compresses, that's for certain.'

'Like Mama used to.'

'Son . . .'

Cecilio was suddenly furious. The small man in front of him, hugging himself, used to be so much bigger. He had spent so many years despising this man. Loving him with reluctant fervour. Being afraid of him. And here Papa was in prison, making him feel guilty. How did he manage it? Cecilio narrowed his eyes and looked down at his father. Giuseppe Insenga. At the leathery face, the crinkly laugh lines around the mouth and eyes, the bushy eyebrows like wads of black cotton and the still silver-free black hair sweeping back abundantly from a lined forehead. It wasn't fair. He had more grey hair than Papa did. It was probably from the stress of having Giuseppe as a father.

'Son —?'

'What do you want?' Cecilio said rudely.

'You can't talk to your father like that!' Scandalized, Giuseppe reached out to slap him in the face. All he managed to do was bruise his knuckles on the rough bars. Putting one of his scraped knuckles in his mouth, he looked at Cecilio with hurt reproach.

Cecilio didn't understand why he'd even come in to visit his father. He wasn't required to. The letter he'd received from Kingston prison last week had just asked for an answer and an authorization signature. The Canadians were transferring his father from Canada to England. At Giuseppe's request. To be near his son. Proximity to family was supposed to make his rehabilitation faster. Amazingly enough, the resident head shrink at Kingston prison had agreed. Wormwood Scrubs prison in London had accepted the transfer. How was that possible? Cecilio didn't realize you could request a jail transfer. Was it like being in a fancy hotel?

Squinting into his father's cell, he didn't *think* it looked like a luxury hotel. London didn't have them for high-profile criminals. Not any more.

The cell looked dingy, from what he could glimpse. It was hard to see into it because of the darkness. The room controls panel on the left-hand wall looked old-fashioned. Papa must have cleaned up in anticipation for his visit because the bed button had been pressed, withdrawing the sleeping board into a wall slot. The paper blankets had been dissolved with antiseptic spray and the remnants sucked down through the myriad holes in the concrete floor. The only things that remained in the three-sided concrete block were a shiny steel bucket with little wheels on the bottom, a few rolls of toilet paper and a row of photographs stuck on the wall.

Cecilio couldn't see who the photographs were of, but he could guess. Which ones were they? He hoped his mother was at least one of them.

'How did you convince them to transfer you?'

An odd smile played around Giuseppe's lips. 'I'll be right back. I have to . . . don't go away.'

He had probably started playing up. Becoming obnoxious and they'd wanted to ship him out somewhere. Anywhere. Maybe he'd flirted with the female prison guards. You never knew with Giuseppe.

Cecilio shook his head in disgust and waved at Giuseppe to take his time.

'You won't leave, will you?' Giuseppe paused. 'I'll be with you in a sec.' He retreated into the darkness at the back of his cell.

Cecilio sighed and leaned against the wall facing the cell. He resented being pulled back into his father's confusing orbit. His normal routine was out of whack now. He was trying so hard to be someone his mother would be proud of. To adapt to his new adopted country. To learn English. It was the least he could do for her.

Everything had been fine until last Tuesday.

Cecilio had been trying to turn under the frayed edges of his good black jacket. The letter was pushed by an unseen hand through the rusted letterbox on his front door. It fluttered to the floor, beckoning him with impatience and oozing with importance. Cecilio tossed his jacket on to the lumpy single bed, went over and picked it up. Turning it over and over in his hands, he was tempted to throw it away unopened. The gold crest of Kingston prison's logo gleamed at him balefully from the corner of the envelope. It couldn't be good news. Sighing, he knew he'd better open it. You had to take responsibility for these things. It must have something to do with his father.

The letter took ages to interpret, even with the help of his dictionary. After six months, the intricacies of English grammar, syntax and pronunciation were still refusing to become clearer. Even after hours and hours of homework, every time he opened his mouth and attempted some form of communication in English, verbal garbage erupted. Sure, verbs and pronouns and stuff came out, but never in the right order. From the uncomprehending look on people's faces and the quizzical height of their eyebrows, his mouth and tongue had obviously not twisted themselves around the correct pronunciation.

It drove him mad. He wanted to speak English more than anything. He adored his new adopted country. The pale whimsical people. The charming circumlocution with which they expressed themselves.

'Excuse me for bothering you. I wonder if you wouldn't mind possibly giving me a hand. I seem to have had a bit of an accident.'

The bit of an accident could be that the man's leg had been cut off in a terrible disaster, and blood could be spurting out of the stump in huge gouts. But the gentleman would still tap you on the shoulder politely. 'Excuse me . . .'

And the Transport system! It was fascinating to sit on one of the frayed fabric seats and look around him. He felt he should be paying somebody just for the privilege of being allowed to absorb the atmosphere. Besides handing over City Credits for the ticket, of course. The range of people, languages, accents and cultures stunned him. He had to be careful, because people here weren't used to being stared at. It wasn't like Italy. He had to make sure he looked down and just peeped out from under lowered eyelashes. The long lush eyelashes he'd always despaired of proved an effective screen for the fascinated study of his Transport companions.

It could be anyone. A man sporting a felt hat shaped like a loaf of bread, plastic Sainsbury's bag tucked neatly around it for rain protection, long curly sideburns like fat sausages framing his face. A woman robed in black from head to toe, kohl lining her huge dark eyes, glimmers of gold tantalizing from between the black folds of her outfit. French people . . . German . . . Chinese . . . Americans . . . Canadians.

Despite having been told several times, he still couldn't differentiate the Canadian accent from the American. North Americans from British. New Zealanders from Australian. It was hopeless. He tried listening to the vowel sounds, as instructed by his English books, but as he was still having trouble understanding *what* word was being spoken, he couldn't differentiate between vowels.

He wouldn't be able to get a job if he didn't speak English. He'd have to redouble his efforts. Or, at least, that's what he had thought before he saw the ad for Talk-Lang Inc. 'English without Pain', the ad promised. 'Especially for people with no language

145

ability whatsoever. For people as thick as two or three short planks.' At least, that's what Cecilio had thought the ad said.

Talk-Lang wasn't a teaching method.

No indeed. Much easier and more painless than that. It was a computerized language implant chip.

He would never have spent his dwindling supply of City Credits on something so frivolous, but his difficulty in interpreting the prison letter had thrown him.

When he'd pressed the additional-information button on the Talk-Lang advertisement, a woman with a seductive tone promised him that he'd be able to interpret letters, deal with any verbal English communication, and correct his abysmal pronunciation. He had thought that was what she said. He had to press the button about fifty times just to get that information.

At least, now that he had the language chip, he'd be able to interpret letters from the prison authorities and negotiate with them on his father's behalf. How could you bribe an English prison guard if you couldn't even speak their language? Cecilio was furious that he was having to think of such things. Oh, well. Besides helping him with bribery, hopefully the chip would help him pass his English competency exam so he could get a job in computer graphics.

The exam he should be studying for instead of lounging about in prisons. *Porca miseria!* Cecilio thought.

His language chip activated with a tiny beep. 'Bloody hell,' his brain and mouth whispered simultaneously. *At least the darned thing is working.*

Glumly, Cecilio thought the chip probably wouldn't help in the long run. He didn't have any language facility. He was too old. Your head became hard as rock after the age of ten. It was much easier for children to learn a language. How else could he have learned the intricacies of his mother's and grandmother's sign language? Not that he'd learned much. He didn't know how his grammar was. But Mama had always smiled fondly when he signed to her, *Ti amo, Mama.* He wished he'd said that to her out loud while she was alive. You always thought you had so much time.

Maybe the language chip would help him pass the verbal part of the exam. He had to get that job. His tiny store of City Credits was getting that sucked-in starved look.

The chip hadn't hurt going in. He was a wimp about pain and had been afraid he'd cry out. He hadn't been able to look when the Talk-Lang technician swabbed his upper arm with alcohol. Cecilio flexed both hands repeatedly, the nails cutting into his palms.

'Hurry up.' His teeth were clenched so hard, he thought they'd crack.

The technician swabbed again and clapped Cecilio on the back. 'All done.' He handed Cecilio a tiny keypad with coloured buttons.

'What's th–?'

'Keep this in your pocket. You'll need to press the green button periodically to clear any inaccuracies clogging up the diodes. If you don't, you might find some clangers erupting from your own mouth.'

Cecilio had placed the keypad in his pocket and kept his hand nearby. Just in case.

'I wanted to be near you.' Giuseppe broke rudely into Cecilio's thought perambulations. He'd still not reappeared, but he must have realized his tenuous hold on his son would fade if he didn't speak. 'Don't just stand over there like a lump, ignoring me. Talk to me, boy. Talk!'

Cecilio snorted. 'You never wanted to talk much before.'

'I can't keep apologizing for that, Cec– Dario. What's the use? You're never going to forgive me, are you?' Hurt silence wafted from the darkness of the cell.

Cecilio found himself feeling waves of guilt, which infuriated him. 'You did it again, didn't you?' he called, his voice cracking. 'One wife just wasn't enough.' Straightening up, he paced back and forth in front of the grimy bars.

Irritated silence leaked through them and splattered on the floor at his feet. Cecilio stepped closer and squinted into the gloom.

'Come out here! I know you're in there. There isn't anywhere for you to go.' He scowled down at his feet as if, by looking away, he could draw his father inexorably to him.

Giuseppe's voice trickled towards him, as dignified as it could be when its owner had been caught crouching over an ablutions bucket. 'I am not at home to visitors at the moment.'

Cecilio felt pained as the sound of his father urinating into the metal bucket reached him. Tinkle tinkle tinkle. Pause. Tinkle. Even the urine sounded reproachful. Cecilio closed his eyes and leaned his forehead against the bars.

'When the prison wrote to me, I didn't want to come.'

'Why did you? You don't have to do me any favours.'

'I came to see you for Mama's sake.'

His father's face appeared suddenly in front of him. Cecilio took an involuntary step backwards. With the combined darkness of his clothes and his cell, Giuseppe's face looked as if it was floating bodyless in a weirdly Hamlet type of effect.

'Your mama . . .' Giuseppe started, his voice an airless balloon.

Cecilio's face crumpled. 'That is, if you remember her . . . she –'

'Of course I remember your mother,' Giuseppe interrupted. 'You look just like her, after all. She was so *bella*.' He tried to smile, but his face didn't seem to be working properly. 'I loved her, you know.'

Cecilio looked incredulous. 'You can say that, after what you did?'

Giuseppe seemed tired of abasing himself. 'Come on, Cec– uh, Dario. She got me back in the end. She's the one who reported me. And she didn't take me back. Despite her illness.'

Cecilio couldn't imagine his tiny, inconsequential mother finally taking a stand against Giuseppe. He rubbed his tired eyes. 'She always took you back before.'

'Not that time. She took exception to the number eight.'

'So she should!' Cecilio huffed.

'She got me back.'

'Tooth for a tooth.'

Giuseppe sighed and ran his fingers through his hair, making it stand up in frothy disarray. 'Perhaps . . .'

A squeak came from the back of the cell, distracting them. Cecilio squinted past his father. 'What the hell was that?'

'Dunno. Rats. Mice. Who knows?' Disconsolate, his father leaned his head against the bars.

Horrified, Cecilio drew in his breath to yell for the guards, when he glanced back at his father's face and saw That Look. That teasing look. The one that had dissolved him into giggles when he was a boy. Cecilio let out his breath again and laughed ruefully.

'*Idiota!* You've got the makings for a snack, then.'

Giuseppe laughed. 'I'm not desperate enough to eat rat burgers yet. Actually, I could do with a snack. Your mother made the best *cannoli.*'

The sound of keys jingling interrupted both Giuseppe and Cecilio's mental images of *cannoli* dancing around the bars.

'Speak English, you friggin' Eyeties,' the guard snarled. 'Visiting time is over.'

After Cecilio left the prison, he tried to forget his father. He'd visit him once a month. Bring him some *cannoli*, if he could find an Italian deli that supplied them. Salve his conscience. He was busy studying for his exam, after all.

Fiddling with his keypad, he reset the inaccuracy button to clear any that had gathered since he had last pushed it. Cecilio walked out on to the street, avoiding the taxi-motos beeping inquiringly at him. He'd better walk and save his remaining City Credits for the *cannoli*. Just thinking of the crispy pastries filled with soft sweet cheese and chocolate made his mouth water.

He would try to keep his mixed feelings for his father clamped down for Mama's sake.

Why couldn't she ever leave Giuseppe in all the years she knew he was off with other women? *Didn't* she know about them? Cecilio resented her passivity. That's what it had to be. Maybe she was afraid to leave since she was blind. She'd gained the strength to report him in the end. Good for her. Cecilio couldn't stand passive women or those who couldn't take responsibility for their actions. His mother had. Yet how could she report her own husband? Cecilio's respect for her fought with his shock that she could do such a thing.

It wasn't as if he knew much about the female sex. The only women he'd ever had guts enough to ask out had laughed in his face. Naples was a small city, after all. Everyone knew about his father's activities, both Camorra and wife-related. When his father had fled Naples to Canada in an effort to escape jail, it had been in all the papers.

Giuseppe hadn't accepted the consequences of his actions. He still didn't act chastened enough.

Suddenly a horrible thought pushed its way into Cecilio's head. What if the weakness in both parents carried down through him? Were criminal tendencies and passivity genetically passed on? *Per amore di Dio!*

The computer chip switched on and made a funny high-pitched sound before switching off abruptly without giving him the translation. Cecilio figured it was a momentary glitch.

He'd never be able to be with a woman. His parents had seen to that. How could a woman ever love him unconditionally when she learned what his parents had done?

Napoli. He missed his home.

The chip switched on successfully this time and beeped. 'Naples,' it insisted.

Cecilio wished he could have upgraded to the newer Talk-Lang machine. He wished he could have upgraded his family too. Would different versions have made any difference?

After yet another embarrassing malfunction at the corner shop while he was buying a pint of milk, Cecilio shook the keypad. It wasn't working very well. Supposedly all you had to do was think the Italian phrase, the chip would spit out the correct English one into his brain, and he would speak it automatically. It certainly hadn't worked when he ordered his dinner at the café the other night. He'd ended up with eighteen pieces of toast with Marmite instead of the anchovy pizza he wanted. Yuck. Marmite. It tasted how he imagined a road accident would taste.

The keypad better work tomorrow. He was counting on it. This interview was terribly important. They wouldn't hire him to be a computer-graphics trainee if his English wasn't perfect. And this unemployment rate didn't leave much room for errors. He was going for the job without even passing the competency exam. With the chip, he should be able to swing it. He wouldn't have dreamed of promising he could speak perfect English without the chip. The darned thing had better work. Shaking the machine again, he heard a tiny clicking. He hoped it wasn't a loose wire.

The man at the interview had smiled at him. He held out his hand.

'Dario Insenga? Nice to meet you.'

Relief flooded Cecilio. He appeared friendly. Shaking the man's hand, Cecilio thought carefully to his chip. 'It is indeed a pleasure to meet you, sir.'

After Cecilio was bundled unceremoniously to the door by the guards, he worked out what it was that he had actually said. *Porca miseria.*

'Oh, hell,' his chip whispered.

'Shut up, you.' Cecilio shoved the keypad deep into his pocket, tempted to throw it in front of a cruising taxi-moto.

He couldn't *believe* what he'd said to the man during the most potentially important interview of his career.

'I really fancy the pants off you,' he had said firmly, as he shook the man's hand.

Cecilio could still see the odd shade of purple that wiped the man's face of the friendly introductory look he had been wearing. He snatched back his hand so fast that a hand-shaped imprint practically sizzled in the air.

Cecilio wanted to dig his fingernails into his shoulder and rip the chip from its mooring. He'd smash it to the ground and break it to pieces with his boot heel! He tried digging one fingernail into his skin and it hurt, so he stopped.

How would he ever get a job? He couldn't afford to upgrade

the damn translation machine. The newer version corrected inaccuracies automatically without saving them up to be cleared manually. Clearing them manually, as he had to do, there were always a few that wandered around waiting to strike at inappropriate moments. Cecilio cringed internally. Inappropriate moments. Yes, indeed.

The people who had sold the chip and keypad to him had said they were selling him the older version for a reduced price.

'Talk-Lang Version 2.2. Introductory English.'

Cecilio hefted the tiny chip in his hand. 'Does it work?'

'There are a few bugs in it, but what do you want for this price?'

Unless he wanted to spend another load of City Credits for the next upgraded version, 3.1, that was what he was stuck with. They assured him there wasn't a big difference between the two versions. A few bugs, and the lack of the automatic inaccuracy stripper. That was all. Not having a gezillion City Credits solved the problem for him.

'I'll take the buggy version.'

After all, it couldn't cause that many problems, could it? Cecilio would just think before he spoke. Upgrading wasn't an option.

Neither was upgrading his father. He'd given up wishing for one of the fathers you saw on TV all the time. A normal one. One who didn't tango around the house with his delighted mother during his childhood, dressed in flower-embroidered pyjamas. He'd probably learned to tango with all those other wives.

The flower stitches were a bit wonky on the pyjamas, as Mama had to estimate the stitch length since she couldn't see them. There were several dots of blood on the fabric where she'd pricked her finger. They never washed out. Neither of them ever told her.

'They're beautiful,' they both chorused when she proudly presented the matching pyjamas to them one Christmas. Giuseppe kissed his wife and her face was suffused with happiness.

'Stop! Your moustache is tickling me.' She'd laughed and turned away, pressing her hand against the glowing warmth in her face.

If Cecilio could upgrade his father, he'd still want one with a moustache. They gave great entertainment value. As a kid, whenever Giuseppe tried to take a nap in the afternoon, Cecilio would sneak up and commence his attack. When the snores started, Cecilio would push Papa's moustache up his nose with a pencil, tangling it with his father's long curling nose hairs. The sharp-ended black moustache hairs poked into the sensitive skin inside Giuseppe's nose. Cecilio watched him shoot up practically to the ceiling. Roaring, he'd flail around in sleepy fury. 'Where are you, Cecilio, you spawn of the Devil?'

Cecilio hid behind his helplessly giggling mother.

When he was twelve, Giuseppe told him about kissing. 'Not too wet,' he'd said. 'You don't want to drown them.'

Cecilio was grossed out. 'Yuck. Why would I want to kiss girls anyway?'

Giuseppe's face was suffused with adoration. 'Women are wonderful. You'll see.'

'I'm never going to want to kiss one.' What a repulsive thought. Cecilio had shuddered.

Cecilio smiled now, remembering his childish disgust. Would he have upgraded his mother if he could? Changed her for one of the perfect TV mothers? What defined a perfect woman, after all?

He'd seen a woman once in a Transport station. She was gorgeous, he remembered wistfully. Her looks were the complete opposite of his mother's. The woman had cool buttery blonde hair and pale creamy skin, where his mother had inky black hair and skin the colour of milky coffee. The woman had leaned against the barriers, waiting for someone.

Cecilio was struck dumb with wanting. He'd never felt like that before and it embarrassed him. He felt as if all his insides had turned inside out with need. What could he say to her? He had to go up and speak to her. He marshalled every single one of the introductory English phrases he'd been practising in his head. He stepped forward.

And stopped. What could he say? None of his phrases were

right. Ten minutes later, he still hadn't worked out what to say. Oh, hell, he'd just go up to her and see what came out. It wouldn't matter. He could sense that with her. She had a kind face. Sad, too. He stepped forward.

Porca miseria! The man she must have been waiting for arrived. He touched her shoulder and, after exchanging a few words, they turned and left. Cecilio watched the woman walk away and felt a pang of distress.

He had felt bereft and incredibly stupid for feeling so. How could he feel as if he'd missed the most magnificent chance in his life, just for want of a few English phrases?

Sitting at home in the dark feeling sorry for himself, Cecilio heard a letter being pushed through his mail slot. He got up and trudged over. Another bill? Picking up the letter, he felt irritation build up in him. He wasn't to be allowed to forget about his father. Wormwood Scrubs had sent another letter.

Pulling out the enemy keypad from his pocket, Cecilio put it on the table and opened the envelope. Unfolding the sheet of paper, he began to read aloud the English haltingly. The chip better not let him down. At least he was in the privacy of his own home. Nobody would hear him make any monumental errors.

The letter was chatty, in an odd sort of way. As Cecilio read, his chip whispered the interpretation in his brain.

Dear Mr Insenga,

Pursuant to our previous communication, it has been decided to inform you of the additional reasons for your father's transfer. In an effort to be flexible and to facilitate creative prison reform, it has been agreed between the two prisons that your father's punishment will be commensurate to his crime. Rather than incarcerating him for life where he could happily resist rehabilitation, or let him out to repeat his crime, we have decided that he is a habitual criminal. He needs further inducement not to continue his activities. Polygamy is no joke and the eight women your father has married are to be pitied for their gullibility.

Due to your father's efforts to escape the consequences of his actions committed in Italy, by attempting to repatriate in Canada, we have decided to turn our attention to his rejected country's prison-reform methods.

In an effort to work within your father's cultural background, we have decided to match the punishment to the crime, as it would be done in Italy. His interesting job contacts in Naples believe in some fairly detailed punishments. These people believe, like in many other cultures, that you pay back in kind. A hand for a hand. Tooth for a tooth. We agonized over the appropriate punishment to choose, and cogitated at length over what a multiple bigamist would hate to lose most. We came up first with castration. A rather over-obvious punishment, to be sure, but we couldn't think of anything better.

However, we don't wish to impose our ideas on him without attempting to be fair. He deserves consideration in this matter. We gave him the option of choosing which body part he'd care to lose. We gave him the attached list to pick from. Unfortunately he has felt unable to make a decision. Your father is a very indecisive man.

Therefore, we decided to let you, his eldest son, choose for him. Your father agreed, with evident relief. That's why we agreed to the prison transfer from Canada to England. So that you can decide upon his punishment for him. We apologize for letting you assume from the previous letter that we were transferring him in order to have your father closer to you. We do earnestly believe, however, that your proximity would be beneficial after your father's punishment has been conducted.

Let us be absolutely clear. You do not have the option of abstaining. If you do, he will lose the body part that we originally decided upon. We will castrate him. So if you do not wish your father to lose the part of him that was instrumental in your creation, you must choose for him.

We look forward to hearing from you at your earliest convenience regarding this rather urgent and highly sensitive matter. Please check off the body part below which corresponds most closely to the one which you would like him to lose.

The letter was signed illegibly with a signature that appeared to start with the letter H. Or was it a B? Cecilio couldn't read the rest of it. The loopy squiggle defied interpretation.

The list of body parts on the Schedule A page, following, horrified him. How could they think it would be possible for him to do this? What was better to lose? A toe? A finger? A nose? *Madre di Dio!*

He'd have to speak to them in person immediately. He couldn't just write to them. His English wasn't good enough. Fiddling with his keypad, he prayed it would stand him in good stead.

'Don't fail me now, machine,' he said.

He patted the site where the chip was implanted on his shoulder twice, for good luck, and looked in the mirror at the incision. The tiny curved scar smiled mockingly at him.

Blow the expense. Cecilio took the first taxi-moto that beeped at him on the street. Sitting back in the plastic seat, his head whirled. Frantic pictures of his mother and father battled for attention in the foreground of his brain. His father beckoned to him, still wearing those flower-embroidered pyjamas.

'Son?' he was calling.

Cecilio shook his head. *Go away. I can't choose for you. I couldn't possibly take that responsibility.*

That's what he told Giuseppe while he was clutching his father's flaking cell bars.

'I can't,' he said again, louder this time. 'Please don't make me.'

After a while Giuseppe lay on his bed board and refused to speak to him.

Cecilio stood at the bars for another hour, trying to make him understand why he couldn't choose. 'Take responsibility for your own actions, Papa.'

Frustrated, Cecilio gave up when Giuseppe pretended to snore. Viciously, he wished he could use that moustache-pushing pencil to stick up his father's nose so far, it would tickle his brain. He stomped off and went to the front desk.

'I ask – no, I *demand* to see the man who wrote me the letter.'

The guard looked at him, eyebrows rising. 'And who might that be?'

Cecilio thrust the letter across the desk. 'This man here. This squiggle. I need to see him immediately!'

'Hold your horses.' The guard got up, insolence oozing from him in great sweaty wafts. 'I'll see if he's free to see the likes of you.'

After twenty minutes, the man appeared and took Cecilio to his office. He sat down, took off his glasses and rubbed the red marks on his nose with one hand, waving the other at the remaining chair.

'Have a seat.'

Cecilio sat and launched into an explanation.

The man stopped him with an impatient motion. 'Wait a sec. Let me just switch the APD on.' At Cecilio's quizzical look, he continued seamlessly, 'Automatic Punishment Dispenser. Whatever body part you choose will be registered without possibility for change once you speak into this microphone.'

'But –'

'Speak loudly. The machine needs to hear you clearly.'

Cecilio felt nervous sweat collecting under his arms. This wasn't how he'd pictured the discussion going at all. Clutching his keypad tightly in his hand, he pressed the inaccuracy button.

'We have no time to waste, young man. Your father is waiting for his punishment to be decided. It is very unkind to make him wait any longer.' The man put his glasses back on and looked expectantly across the desk.

Thinking carefully to ensure that his chip had enough time to erase any inaccuracies, Cecilio thought, I *do* wish to give my father a hand in all this, but I don't see how I could possibly choose which body part he is to lose.

The chip beeped and spat out the results into his brain.

Cecilio's mouth opened and the words came out. They exited so fast, he couldn't keep track of the English verbs. They all came out in a tumble, like people in an overcrowded Transport fighting their way out of the opening door.

The words flew out and were sucked up into the APD.

The man beamed and switched off the machine. He shook Cecilio's hand. 'Thank you, Mr Insenga! We certainly never could have hoped for such self-sacrifice for one's father. Commencement of the punishment has now been set in motion.'

Cecilio gasped in dismay as his wrists were manacled.

What had he said? *What had he said?*

Fox Paw

BERRI

Fate is not an eagle, it creeps like a rat.

ELIZABETH BOWEN

The man's hand was the colour of melting raspberry sherbet. The woman hiding outside the emergency-cubicle curtains squinted and tried to see the two people inside more clearly. The peculiar thing was that the hand was only that colour up to the wrist. A chalky white bandage separated it from its sinewy tanned arm. The hand and the arm didn't look comfortable together. As if they'd just met through friends and hadn't yet been introduced.

Had the man burned his hand? What did her daughter Marina, sitting with such coiled tension next to the bed, have to do with him? Berri sighed, as quietly as possible. Her eyesight wasn't what it used to be. It was difficult to see between the crack in the curtains without attracting attention.

She tried to move her feet into a more comfortable position and almost tripped on some wires. Looking down, she noticed that a black cable snaked out from underneath the emergency cubicle's curtain and crept out into the main corridor. Looking behind her, she noticed that the wire crawled up the wall and ended in a vast spider-like plug, one of a huge knotted collection, all mashed into an overwhelmed central wall socket.

They must be short of sockets here, if they have to plug that many machines into one. Giggling to herself nervously, she supposed she'd better watch out. She turned back towards the curtain opening to see if she could deduce what the black cord led to. She followed the wire with her eyes, and finally located the source. A battered machine with several ominous-looking dents beeped frenetically next to the man she'd caught red-handed. She tittered at her pathetic attempt to cheer herself up.

The machine's pump went up and down like a sideways gypsy's

accordion. She supposed it must be his breathing machine. She tried breathing in time with its puffy burping sounds to further disguise her presence. It was more difficult than she had expected. She had to try to anticipate any irregularity of burping speed. She couldn't let them hear her.

Gingerly, she shuffled her feet to avoid stepping on the wires. Accidentally pulling out a plug at a hospital would *not* be a popular move. Besides, it would draw attention that she desperately wanted to avoid.

She looked again at the man. Red, white and brown was an odd colour combination for an arm. Like a tricolour flag from some foreign country, she mused. Which colours were on Italy's flag? The man looked slightly . . . it must be him.

A faint noise trickled from the cubicle. Struggling to see, Berri moved closer to the curtain opening. What was happening?

Marina had slid off her chair and was kneeling next to the man, leaning her blonde head next to the immobile tri-coloured arm. By the heaving of her back, Berri knew she was crying.

Such an inflamed angry-looking hand. *It looks as if it's been sunburned.* What was wrong with it? Berri heard Marina mumble and she leaned forward, almost propelling herself through the curtains.

Speak *up*, Marina! Berri thought. How many times when you were a child did I tell you not to mumble?

How bloody frustrating.

Berri wasn't cut out for this stalking stuff. How could a middle-aged woman with wobbly thighs, a bad back and greying hair possibly hope to keep tracking her daughter all these years? She was tired of being a bargain-basement private eye. It was so difficult to peer through curtains with bifocals. If only she'd had that corneal transplant operation they offered on TV, her eyesight might have improved. But you never knew about the long-term results of those operations. Your eyeballs could fall out after a couple of years or something dreadful like that. The doctors might forget to connect them at the back. Berri shuddered.

Besides, while you were asleep, the doctors could whip out your eyeballs and pop a couple of polyurethane ones in. For nefarious purposes. She didn't want nefarious polyurethane eyeballs, despite the good press they were getting. The new eyes were supposed to be better than real ones. Her old ones would do her fine, thank you very much. Despite getting bloodshot and fuzzy lately. And having to wear bifocals. Having a sister with perfect eyesight wasn't fair. Although she supposed Estra had enough problems of her own.

More movement from the cubicle. Berri leaned forward, careful not to slip forwards this time. More mumbling. From the man this time. How could he talk with all those tubes in his mouth? His face was turning the same fruity colour as his hand! Was he choking to death? Dying? Berri held her breath.

Watching him, eyes narrowed, she decided he was a man of colour extremes. Inky black hair, light cappuccino-coloured arms, and that crimson and white of hands and face. A handsome face, Berri acceded in grudging admiration. His eyelashes were so long, she supposed he must constantly tangle them when he blinked.

Berri surreptitiously took off her bifocals and cleaned them on her good blue LycraSyl skirt. It was the one she normally wore only for her palmistry clients, but she hadn't had time to change. The fabric was nice and colourful and didn't need ironing or washing, thanks to LycraSyl's self-washing element. Gold threads squiggled through the skirt and the fabric looked a deep blue-green in certain lights. She thought it made her look mysterious.

Mysterious my foot, she thought roundly, exasperated by her periodic bouts of pathetic romanticism. *Cheap and nasty, more like*. LycraSyl was all she could afford these days. The paltry amount of City Credits she received per palmistry reading didn't buy you real silk, cotton or even burlap sacking. *Pah*. At least she didn't have to wear white plastic any more. During her years as a Scraper, she had yearned to wear bright colours. White was just so demoralizing.

The man's hand moved. A finger fluttered. Two.

When Berri saw the trembling scarlet hand heft itself as if moving a monumental weight, she almost cried out. It moved towards her daughter's pale hair. Berri clenched her fists. Her palms burned, itching with some kind of poison. She wanted to rake her fingernails across the man's face.

'Don't touch her,' she cried inside. 'Get off!'

The hand appeared drunk, slightly weaving as it moved towards its target. The fluttering fingers came down and delicately brushed the back of Marina's bowed head. As if unable to restrain themselves, the fingers tangled themselves in the buttery fronds of hair and closed fiercely as if they'd never let go. Every movement looked excruciatingly painful, yet the sense of cautious joy and stunned relief that emanated from the fingers was almost palpable.

No. Leaning down, Berri scrabbled with her fingers along the linoleum floor until she found the electric cord leading from the man's ventilator. She had to protect her daughter.

'You can't be with her,' Berri choked, aloud this time. 'No!' Pulling the cord as hard as possible away from the bed, she hoped she was pulling the right one from the ventilator. She didn't want to pull the huge multi-plug out behind her.

At Berri's words, Marina's shoulders froze. She spun round, her mouth open in shock.

At the exact second that Marina saw Berri, the corridor was plunged in darkness. Berri listened, afraid of what she might hear. After a moment of silence, she let out her breath in harsh gasps. The ventilator stopped. She sagged with guilty relief. She hadn't thought she had managed to pull out the correct cable. As a matter of fact, she hadn't felt any resistance at that end. But she must have been successful. The results were all around her.

'Cecilio?' she heard Marina cry, agonized worry spiralling.

Nothing.

Incredulity strangled Marina's voice.

'Mother? Is that you?'

How can she have recognized me after all these years? She was only a little girl when I – Berri sprang up and ran as fast as she could down the dark corridor. She couldn't let Marina catch her. Not that she heard any running feet. Why wasn't Marina chasing after her? It was too late for the man. Berri ran anyway, ploughing through people milling about in the dark corridors.

'The generator!' one doctor with wild eyes yelled, with a horrified wobble in his voice. 'Why hasn't the back-up generator kicked in?'

Berri prayed that nobody else had been on life-support machines in the Emergency Department. She wouldn't want to be responsible for any more than one death. A life for a life, she thought. That unknown man's death for my daughter's life. I couldn't let him steal it unwittingly.

As she ran, tears streamed down her cheeks and flowed past her temples into the masses of silver hair. Her hair-pins fell and bounced on to the floor, leaving a trail of surrealistic breadcrumbs behind her. The heavy silver coil flung itself half-way down her back, surprisingly heavy for hair that should be thinning with age.

A life for a life, she thought. Tooth for a tooth. I've saved you, Marina. *I hope you don't wish me in hell for it.*

Hell is certainly where she'd been for the last who-knew-how-many years, with the Devil spitting in her eye and flames tickling her insteps. That's what she deserved after what she'd done.

Losing her sense of direction, Berri pelted through corridor after corridor. In her panic, they all looked alike. Her hair whipped in frantic silver wings around her head. With that and the effort of running, her bifocals steamed up, making it difficult to see. Noticing a large fuzzy crowd of white-clad people in one hallway pointing at her, she wheeled around and turned down the only way open to her. Almost colliding with the closed door at the end of the small corridor, she pushed with frantic desperation against it. A small printed sign on the door bleated, 'PRIVATE – Hurtigger Institute.'

Berri ignored the warning and pushed open the door. She also ignored the surprised-looking young woman she passed, painting her fingernails at a silver desk. Relieved, Berri spotted a revolving glass door that led outside.

After almost running up the heels of a couple who were shuffling through the glass doors, she erupted into the street. People stared at her curiously as she jogged the rest of the quarter-mile home, muttering to herself and clutching her sides in pain. Berri knew she was out of shape. Her ribcage heaved.

What did they do to murderers these days? It didn't matter. She had no choice.

Staggering up the front steps of the little house she'd lived in since she'd left her underground flat, she could sense her next-door neighbour staring at her. Taking a quick glance over her shoulder, she saw Mrs Murphy's rheumy eyes peering at her from behind the high dividing fence. Waving at the old woman briefly, Berri scrambled in her pocket for her key. Thrusting it into the front-door lock, she noticed that her carefully painted sign, 'Madame Berengaria – Fortune Teller – Palmist – Horoscopes. No appointment necessary', was slightly askew. Ignoring it, she went in. Deciding what to do next was more important than being house-proud.

Trying to catch her breath and calm her laboured breathing, Berri tried to feel good about what she'd done. Tracking Marina for all these years and trying to prevent the worst happening was damned hard work. She had to admit it was getting harder. It had been easier when Marina was younger and didn't go out at all. Now she seemed to alternate between promiscuity and signing up for strange hospital experiments.

Berri had her work cut out for her, trying to make sure the nasty men Marina picked up at the Transport stations were never more than one-night stands, as distasteful as she found the thought. Good thing she'd been able to rent the house across from Marina's flat. That way she could keep a constant eye on her. Whenever the men tried to come back, which they always did, Berri would run out and get rid of them. She wasn't surprised the men came back. Marina was lovely, after all. She took after her mother's side.

'Sorry,' she'd cry, tucking her skirt around her hurriedly, 'you aren't that other one . . . Paul, is it? No? Sorry. She told me to tell anyone else besides Paul to get lost.' At their confused, hurt looks, she always felt guilty. 'Sorry, dear. My daughter is a naughty baggage, isn't she?' Rolling her eyes, she would make a fluttering motion away from Marina's building. 'Get along now. She didn't say very flattering things about you.' Berri felt terrible. Lying made her feel sick to her stomach. It was for her daughter's own good.

The only time she'd had trouble was when one of the men had actually been *called* Paul. What horrible misfortune. Hurriedly, she had to change the name. 'Sorry, it was *Peter* she told me to find. I have to head off all the rest. Get along now.' Seeing the man turn, his shoulders dejected, made her feel depressed and relieved at the same time. *Another one bites the dust.*

Being the constant protector of Marina's purity and well-being was exhausting. She never had time for anything. When was the last time she'd seen Estra? Wynne and Colton? How could she arrange any consistent exercise classes when her schedule was constantly being interrupted by Marina's forays out of her flat? Berri certainly needed exercise. Placing a hand on her stomach, she wished it were flatter. It was all pooched out, making the blue-green material pull at the centre seam. She looked down at the hand pressing her stomach, at its softness and the faint age spots that had begun to appear like sprinkled brown sugar.

I'm only fifty-eight, she thought. I'm not old. At least I don't *feel* old. *Except when I jog a quarter of a mile in sensible heels with wild-woman hair flailing everywhere.*

Turning up the palm of her right hand, Berri ran her fingers across the two tiny lines on the left side, underneath her little finger. The child lines. Marina and Wynne. Her two daughters. The lines were still there, thankfully. The left hand would always carry the two lines, since the left carried the lines and the future you were fated to have. The right hand contained the lines pertaining to what you did with the fate you were given. Kind of a running total.

She tried not to think of the red-handed man clutching her daughter with such familiarity. Surely he'd been about to die anyway? She wasn't normally a murderer. Her palm didn't mention anything about that. Plus, murderers usually had the oddly disjointed thumb. She turned on the lamp and thrust her hand under the hot light to check her thumb. Poring over the lines on her palm, she tried to see anything new that would indicate the latest turn of events. After all, lines could change, depending on what you did with your life. Fate wasn't written in stone. She'd learned that since she had become interested in palmistry.

Becoming a palmist ten years before had been almost as much of a surprise to Berri as it had been to her neighbours. She'd been flipping idly through an Open University catalogue and had spotted the entry for 'Home Study Palmistry Course'. She was getting sick of sitting around the house waiting for Marina to go outside and she was extremely financially embarrassed. She could study palmistry at home, and then she could have clients come to her. Excited for the first time in months, Berri had immediately signed up.

It had taken her five years to pass the course. It wasn't just the studying: she had to wait until she could afford each section. On the first day of each month, when her City Credit account total registered positive, she'd send off a cheque for the next course instalment. When she passed the final exam and received the long-awaited diploma, she felt a brief flash of unfamiliar pride.

She went outside to nail up the sign she'd painted in readiness when she had started the course. Old Mrs Murphy next door looked askance at the lettering, too small for her to read. Looking through the slats of the white picket fence, she watched Berri hammer up the sign and then carefully straighten it.

'You there,' the old woman quavered, in a small but carrying voice. 'What exactly are you selling?'

Berri laughed. Funny how the woman hadn't bothered to speak to her in five years and only did now because she was worried about the tone of the neighbourhood being lowered. 'I'm selling good fortune. Do you want some?'

Mrs Murphy's face became mottled and suspicious. 'My husband and I knew there was something odd about you and your floaty bits of clothing. You'd better not be selling drugs.' Primly, she arched her thinly-pencilled eyebrows together.

Smiling broadly at her, Berri walked over to the fence. 'Give me your hand.'

Even the white hair on the old woman's head was indignant. 'Give you my what?'

'I'll tell your fortune. It won't hurt.' Berri stood back, raised her hands in the air and spun around. 'See? No drugs, no needles, no weapons.'

Mrs Murphy's curiosity got the better of her and she thrust her hand through the slats. Gruffly she ordered Berri to tell her something good.

Berri peered at her through the fence. Her Open University course had taught that you must read the person's body language. The way they were dressed. The expression in their eyes. The texture of their hands. You tried to deduce what they wanted to hear.

She saw the older woman stiffen when the sound of a door slamming reached them. Mr Murphy? The woman's husband. Berri saw Mrs Murphy involuntarily pat her stiffly curled hair and the look of sadness in her eyes.

That's it! Berri felt exultant. She could help.

'You know, Mrs Murphy,' she started, holding the woman's hand gently, 'there's someone in your life who's terribly sad. He thinks you don't love him any more as you only have sharp words to say to him. You haven't . . . shown him much affection for a few years, have you?'

Berri felt the woman jerk and try to pull her hand away. She didn't let go.

'It isn't too late, you know.' The hand quivered, then lay still as a tame mouse in her own capable ones. Softly, she stroked the ancient palm. 'See, look here. You have a rounded Mount of Venus. It means you were meant to live for love.'

Mrs Murphy looked embarrassed. She pursed her thin lips and looked unbelieving, muttering, 'But he . . .'

Berri reached through the slats and shook Mrs Murphy's shoulder in mock impatience. 'He won't ask again. He thinks you don't want to any more. You'll have to go to him.'

'But how?' the old woman wailed. 'I've forgotten how!' Looking down at her drab blue house-coat and matted greying slippers with fluff coming off in clumps, she frowned. 'Besides, how could he still want to?' Sighing, she reached down with her free hand and pulled up her long woollen underwear, one leg of which had crept down below the edge of her drooping skirt.

'When we go to bed at night, he turns his back on me.' She sniffled, resignation creeping into her pink-rimmed eyes.

Berri smiled to herself. The woollen underwear, although forbidding at such a quick glance, was a surprisingly girlish pink. It even had a froth of dainty lace peeking out from under the edge.

'Wear something nice to bed tonight,' she said firmly. 'And a splash of perfume. When he turns his back on you, put your arms around him. If he doesn't respond, stay where you are. Let him feel the warmth of that Mount of Venus.'

She patted Mrs Murphy's shoulder. 'Go on. He does miss you, you know.' *At least I hope so.*

Mrs Murphy gave her a tremulous smile and turned towards her own house. With a cautiously flamboyant little kick, she flung her right foot up into the air. The small grey slipper flew off and landed, a forlorn sparrow in the grass. Off went the other. Barefoot and shoulders well back, she marched up to the front door. Turning back to Berri, Mrs Murphy had given her a dazzling smile, which made her surprisingly sweet-faced.

'Thank you, dear.'

Berri tried never to make stuff up despite occasional provocation from irritating clients. It was a palmist's duty to help. All palmists went by an unwritten rule like the Socrates oath. Or was it the Hypocrite's oath? Hypocrates? She couldn't remember. Her exam had been a while ago.

You weren't supposed to frighten anyone. If you saw, for instance, that their life line stopped abruptly, you couldn't just blurt out, 'You're going to kick the bucket any day now.' After all, belief was self-perpetuating. If people thought they were going to up and die, they might go and jump in front of a train. Voodoo operated on the same principles. And she was no voodoo queen.

Berri tried never to tell bad futures. Maybe just gently warn people away from dangerous areas. Steer them on to the correct route. She'd made such a mess of her own and her family's life that she tried to make up for it by helping everybody else. Berri thought she'd helped a few. Even Marina. Berri smiled fondly. She was helping her daughter stay on the only right path, despite the pain she knew Marina felt at the constant rejection she encountered.

Hadn't she helped Mrs Murphy? The day after Berri had read the old woman's palm she had spotted Mr and Mrs Murphy holding hands in the garden. Mrs Murphy walked around for weeks with a smile playing about her face. Even Mr Murphy was slightly less mournful. Berri noticed a spring in his step.

Berri sighed, pleasure warming her frayed nerves. She liked having a positive effect on people's lives.

A small worm of thought niggled at her satisfaction. That awful man who had come to see her not long ago. Addison, his name was. Addy for short. How could she forget? She shouldn't have given him such an awful future. She hadn't meant a word of it, but he'd made her so angry! All that guff about his wife cheating on him. She couldn't bear to think about it. It brought back horrible memories of her own husband. Poor Herbert. How she'd hurt him.

Besides, she saw Marina go home with Addy. How could he be so concerned that Terza was cheating on him if he picked up Marina at the Transport station the next day?

Lifting her head proudly, Berri felt smug. She always knew where her daughter was. She knew her habits by now. Twice a day, she followed Marina when she left her flat. Berri had a telescope permanently trained on Marina's front door. It had taken her ages and hundreds of palmistry clients to be able to afford a second-hand one. It worked brilliantly. Whenever Marina went outside, the telescope's beeper would go off and Berri rushed out to follow. Sometimes she barely had time to pin up her hair or dry her hands on a tea-towel.

Poor Herbert, she thought again, her smile fading. If he only knew to what depths she'd sunk. Holding people's filthy palms, telling their hopeful faces all about the lucre they'd acquire, the nasty brutish sods they'd marry, and the zillions of baby crumb-crushers they'd bring up. Sourly, Berri thought she was losing her ability to stay detached.

At least she'd sorted out that repellent man. Addy wouldn't bother Marina any more. She'd seen to that. Sending him those Flotation coupons and signing them with his wife's name had been inspired. Terza. The man had muttered her name often enough in his rambling diatribe. The Fear tanks would take care of him. He'll be busy for a while. A small smile lifted up one corner of her mouth. Once plump and pink, her lips now felt desiccated and colourless.

Oh, Herbert. Life with you was never this stressful. I was never this vindictive.

In the bathroom, she popped a vitamin B and two Stress Vites. She rubbed her temples to try to ease her throbbing headache. The red-handed man had looked Italian, what with that dark hair and all. The strong nose. The dark eyes that had been looking at her daughter with such depth of feeling.

Italian. Yes. It was such a shame, really.

As the years passed, between stalking Marina and dealing with her sparse numbers of palmistry clients, she had tried to keep herself busy. Eventually, after eating herself out of all of her 'fat' clothes and having to wear a sheet wrapped around her artistically when a client called, she decided she should develop other interests besides food.

She'd learn Italian. After all, her mother had been born in Italy and Berri always had a fantasy about living there. The wine. The tantalizing landscapes. The dark-haired, chocolate-eyed people. Berri shuddered, a small feeling of guilt cropping up. She and Estra had gone there just before Berri's marriage to Herbert. She'd seen Italy on those posters LOT used to put up in the Transport tunnels before they decided signs attracted too many skin flakes.

'Visit the exciting thrilling fantastic country of Italy!' the signs emoted. Maybe she'd go back. Maybe some day. Not yet. She had to stay and watch over Marina. The self-combustion Colton and

Estra had warned her about all those years ago when they brought her back could not be allowed to happen. By losing Marina and Wynne in the first place, Berri had already done too much to her. Wynne was doing well now. Colton watched over her. But Marina was different. It had been too late. The damage was done.

Keeping her guilt at bay and making it up to Marina by preventing her from self-combustion or contact with anyone genetically linked were the only things in Berri's life that kept her going. She had to give up the Italian learning, as well as any contact with the remaining members of her family. She didn't have time.

A Talk-Lang chip had been inserted into Berri's shoulder so she could learn Italian more quickly. She hadn't been getting on fast enough by her own efforts.

Uno, due, tre . . . It would take her years to get up to *undici*. And that was only number eleven. *Damn*.

Talk-Lang promised, 'Language with No Pain'. Unfortunately, she had to get the chip removed. It kept malfunctioning during palmistry sessions with the few Italian clients she'd managed to secure.

'You will meet a tall dark handsome man,' she'd attempt to think and say.

Sadly, 'You will have a gender restructure and become a tall, dark, handsome man,' or the like would erupt from her mouth. People snatched away their palms so fast. *Oops*.

Talk-Lang created more problems than it was worth. Berri sighed. *Uno, due, tre* . . . *undici, dodici, tredici*. She never could get the hang of it so she'd had to knock it on the head. It still gave her an unsatisfied pang, one that she stored carefully next to the other far more major pangs she kept in neat labelled files inside her conscience. She had a big file labelled 'Daughters'. And a rather smaller but no less painful file labelled 'Herbert'. Berri hefted the Italian-language pang into the large antique chest called 'Failure' and closed the top with a thud. She knew the pang wouldn't be lonely in the chest because it had plenty of company.

Herbert had given her the name Berengaria. It was an obscure

Italian word for Princess. She'd been just plain old Beryl before that and Herbert knew she loved Italy. The name Beryl was not romantic at all.

Herbert. Every part of her, from the top of her greying head down to the crooked toenail on her left foot, still missed him. Despite his bland appearance and pale, almost anaemic features, she had loved his quiet, reassuring certainty. The way he laughed at his own mistakes. 'I've made another fox paw, Berengaria. Oh dear.'

They'd laugh together. 'Fox paw' was his phrase for French *faux pas*. Little mistakes. As Herbert scraped the tracks with her day after day, up and down with the scraper claw, right to left, Berri felt the inevitability of her life with him. Up and down. She'd always be with him.

Until she had to pretend to leave. For Marina and Wynne. And the cause of all the problems. Berengaria. Berri. Beryl. *Me.*

After the fiction of Imolo, she couldn't bear anyone else calling her Berengaria and the name Beryl disgusted her. She asked people to call her 'Berri', the name Estra called her.

At least I've managed to save my daughters so far.

She would never forget that Colton and Estra had brought her daughters back for her. Grateful waves of emotion enveloped her whenever she thought of what they'd done. During the weeks that Wynne and Marina had been in Dr Lupus's care, Berri had talked about it over and over with them.

'You can't mean it,' she moaned, pain contorting her words. 'Surely there's something else we can do. To fix what those people have done.'

Colton shook his head, his tangerine-coloured eyes hooded. He reached out and held both of her hands in his. 'At least we got Wynne out in time before the worst damage was done.' Something dark glazed his eyes and cast a shadow over his face. 'She'll have electrical problems, but if we don't tell her she won't worry. We'll just have to watch her for signs. We can't let her get angry.'

'How can I keep watch over Marina if we have to send her

away?' Berri wailed. 'And Wynne. How can I watch her at the same time?'

Colton tightened his hold on her hands. 'Don't worry. I'll be there. She's been inside my soul since . . . well, ever since I've known her. I want to marry her.'

Berri looked up at Estra, who didn't seem surprised at the statement the boy just made. 'Colton, you're only a boy.'

'I'm man enough to know. But that can wait. Estra and I will keep Wynne safe. But you'll have to send Marina away to prevent the self-combustion.'

Animal testing always made her feel sick to her stomach. Daughter testing was far worse.

Sending Marina away and cutting her out of her life had been the hardest and most painful thing Berri had ever had to do. She couldn't tell Herbert until the deed was done or he would have done something rash. She couldn't let him go after the Canadians – not after hearing about what they'd done. He wasn't the Rambo type. They'd hurt him, too. She couldn't risk losing him.

She hoped Herbert would understand and forgive her when she told him. They'd laugh about Imolo, the imaginary Italian, around the kitchen table eventually. But, for now, she couldn't tell either Herbert or Marina why she was doing this. And she wouldn't ever be able to tell Marina about the constant threat she would live under. She wasn't strong enough.

She had to hurt him and Marina to save them.

Oh, the pain. It was as though a rusting knife lay embedded in her chest wall.

Berri couldn't let Marina think there was any hope of reconciliation. She had to hurt her badly so that Marina would never return on her own. Berri had to make the poor girl despise her mother.

'It can't be helped,' she told Marina. 'I'm leaving with Imolo, a man from the deli counter on Wardour Street. He's got lovely curling black hair. Italian, you know.' *That sounded believable enough, didn't it?*

Marina had sobbed brokenly. 'What will Daddy do?'

Berri's heart hurt her so badly she thought it would crack. 'Daddy's upset. He's gone off, dear. I don't know where.'

'Wheeeerrrrrre?'

'I don't know. He'll be back.' She took a breath. 'It's fate, dear. You can't change fate.'

Leaning her head down and laying her cheek against the top of her daughter's shaking head, she held her as tightly as she could, despite Marina's struggles to get away from her.

'This means you'll have to leave, dear. *Your two years of safety are gone*. You can't stay and be a Scraper if the mother leaves. *Or if contact with your family will make you explode*. Wynne is older and past the age of consent. She can stay and will live with your Auntie Estra.' Berri paused and swallowed painfully. 'You'll have to leave and you can't come with me. I'll be with my new . . . lover.' She almost choked. 'You're a strong, beautiful girl who will grow up to be a strong, beautiful woman. You don't need me.' *I'm so frightened for you*. 'Believe me.' Berri listened to her daughter's quiet sobbing. 'I wouldn't lie.' *You must be as far as possible from us to elude genetic contamination. At least I hope to God you can. I can't tell you about the self-combustion and how I lost you in the first place.*

'You'll be okay. I promise you.' *I'll have to stay nearby and never let you see me. Watch you and keep you safe.*

'Goodbye, sweetheart.' *Don't hate me.*

It wasn't just another lie to Marina. Herbert *had* gone off. Berri was sure he'd return. She had to tell him Imolo was just a silly fiction.

Herbert hadn't come back.

Estra told her. Herbert had jumped in front of a train, thinking she was leaving him. Before she could explain it all to him. There was an odd look on her sister's face. Because she helped with the clean-up? Berri didn't know if it was her shock at the break-up of her sister's family, the death of her brother-in-law or something else altogether.

In the end, Berri left too, in an eerie reconstruction of the scenario she had pretended to set in motion to send Marina away to safety.

Berri sat in her living room, one hand on the telescope trained on her daughter's front door. She kept thinking of the man in the cubicle. The sudden silence of his ventilator shrieked in her head.

Silence. *Beep*. Silence. *Beep*.

He had to be the one. He looked so much like Giuseppe. She closed her eyes. Giuseppe Imolo Insenga. What a mistake.

Herbert, I've done such a fox paw. Forgive me.

Wallflower

GIUSEPPE

For I'm not so old, and not so plain,
And I'm quite prepared to marry again.

WILLIAM SCHWENCK GILBERT

'Guardia!'

Giuseppe's voice bounced along the dark prison corridor, pinging off the cell bars and trailing off into silence.

'Sentinella!'

He was getting tired of yelling into space. Why wouldn't they come?

'I demand knowing where my son Cecilio is! Why no you let him come see me? Many weeks pass . . . He come see me if he could. Where . . .?'

Giuseppe pounded his bars with frustration. He'd continue yelling in his broken English and causing uproar until someone came. They had to come eventually. He knew the guards could hear him. There were microphones in all the cells to register voices above a certain decibel level. In case of a prison disturbance. Ha! He hoped he was disturbing someone's lunch.

As Giuseppe curled his hands around the thick steel bars, he winced at the arthritis that the prison damp was exacerbating. His fingers felt thick and disobedient, with hot twinges of pain circling around the knuckles, searching for a convenient place to settle. Drawing in his breath, he opened his mouth ready for a fresh bout of yelling.

Suddenly, a voice rasped at him in Italian from the cell to his right, 'Shut up, will you? I can't even eat my bloody lunch in peace.'

Giuseppe was stunned. A woman's voice. *And* she spoke Italian! Hel*lo*. He was delighted. He wished he could see her. There weren't any chinks in the walls: the concrete was as solid as you'd expect in a prison. All the cells had three walls of dark grey concrete and a fourth made up of floor-to-ceiling steel bars. No privacy whatsoever. All you could see through the bars were slices of concrete wall opposite. The cells were staggered so that none of the prisoners could see or communicate visually with each other. The prison powerheads must have assumed that if the prisoners couldn't see, they couldn't foment unrest. Well, they'd failed this time. The opportunity to foment unrest with the prisoner on his right was irresistible.

'I didn't realize this was a co-ed prison.'

'You don't realize much, if your bellowing about son-loss is anything to go by,' the woman responded.

Giuseppe was stung. 'I haven't lost him.'

'No?'

'He hasn't been to see me in weeks. Something's wrong. I know it.' His voice tightened with frustration. 'I don't know if he's being prevented or . . . maybe he couldn't choose.'

'Choose what?'

'Nothing.'

The woman sniffed and clattered what sounded like her metal cup on to a lunch tray. 'Suit yourself.'

Giuseppe retreated back into the darkness of his cell and perched miserably on his bucket. If he balanced carefully on some folded-up pads of toilet paper over the rim, sitting wasn't too bad. You just had to avoid the sharp edges shredding your buttocks into spaghetti. It made a change from sitting on the cold floor. It would be easier just to up-end the damned thing, but then all the contents would slime over the floor. The indignity of it all. He was too old to be sitting on floors or tiptoeing around his own waste products.

Snippy woman. He heard her shoving her tray into the wall meal slot. He tried to picture what she looked like, then got annoyed with himself. He had infinitely more to worry about than what his next-door neighbour looked like. *Where is Cecilio?*

An hour later Giuseppe was still worried, but he didn't bother to resume the yelling. He was starting to lose his voice, and he didn't want to alienate his cranky neighbour. Worry corroded one's ability to get along in prison society. He rubbed his temples, circling his fingers in slow perambulations in an effort to get rid of the roadwork pounding within. He had such a headache. He thought he'd had one ever since he left Italy two months ago. And all for what? Escaping to his cousin in Canada hadn't served any realistic purpose. The police just caught up with him there. The Italian *carabinieri* had a long reach – especially when assisted by hordes of angry Camorra fathers. Two weeks of freedom and wham! Slapped into Kingston prison.

It was so humiliating to be reported by one's wife.

'Wives,' he reminded himself, with glum resignation.

Giuseppe leaned back against the gritty wall and listened to the muttering of the old harpy next door. If she was old. It was hard to tell from the few words she flung at him. He tried to listen to what she was muttering to get some clue as to her age.

'. . . *la terza vittima*,' she was saying. 'The third victim.'

What was that all about?

Dannazione. He wished the sound acoustics in prison were better. He was bored. Nothing to do but fiddle with his moustache and pace back and forth. He'd never been skilled at entertaining himself. He'd never had to. There'd always been plenty of volunteers.

'Excuse me,' he attempted, low enough to stay submerged below the prison's ruckus sensors. 'Pardon me for bothering you, but I couldn't help overhearing . . .' It paid to be polite. The harpy might tell him to shut up again.

The woman stopped muttering.

'Hello? Miss?' He'd get a response from her if it killed him.

'What do you want now?' Her voice was glacial, icicles slithering from every clipped consonant.

'I was wondering . . .'

'What?'

Giuseppe almost lost his nerve. She didn't sound as if she would be very forthcoming with information. 'How is it that you speak Italian?' It was so rare that he ran into anyone who did. He missed Napoli with a fervour that distressed him in its intensity. He stared up at the ceiling of his tiny box-like room, swamp-coloured stains chasing each other across the stippled surface. Was the sun up beyond there somewhere? He closed his eyes, trying to imagine its warm fingers stroking his face and ruffling his moustache.

The woman's voice crashed into his reverie just as Giuseppe almost convinced himself he felt the sun's warmth.

'My mother.' She sounded sad.

She must have decided that talking to him was the only way to shut him up.

'Your mother is Italian?'

'Was. Half. She taught my sister and me to speak it when we were small. I haven't spoken it in years.'

'But you speak it so beautifully –'

Her voice hardened as she interrupted his automatically generated insincerity. 'I was only speaking it here because I hoped nobody would understand. The guards –'

'– or the prisoners,' Giuseppe finished for her.

'Exactly. So do you mind leaving me alone to talk to myself?'

Giuseppe huffed. 'I was just trying –'

'– to be sociable. And yes, you are trying. Trying my bloody patience! This is not a Sunday afternoon tea party. *Capisci*? Understand?'

Giuseppe didn't answer. Hmmphf. He wasn't accustomed to being spoken to in that fashion by a woman. It was an unpleasant feeling.

After waiting ten minutes, Giuseppe knocked politely on the wall.

'Excuse me. What was it you said your name was?'

An exasperated sigh heaved its way through the bars. 'I didn't say.'

'So what is it? It's driving me mad just sitting here not speaking when I know you speak Italian.'

'Cleo-bloody-patra.'

'Such ill temper is not strictly necessary in the circumstances.' Silence. 'Okay. I get the message.'

'About time.' The woman gave a humourless chuckle. 'Took you long enough.'

Stung, Giuseppe didn't answer. He released the bars and flapped his hands in her direction dismissively, which made him feel better. Noticing the rust flecks and unidentified substances that came off his hands, he wiped them on his baggy grey prison trousers.

The woman obviously felt she'd been overly acerbic. 'I'm sorry. I'm not used to being here.'

'And you think I am? I'm sorry. I don't intend to be irritating. But it's been aeons since I've spoken to anyone. I'm sick of talking to myself.'

'I can see why. You do go on . . . sorry. I'm starting on you again.'

'I won't take it personally. I'm used to hearing abuse from my son. It means he loves me.'

The woman laughed, raspy huskiness curling around into his cell. 'If I abuse you verbally, it doesn't mean I love you, *capisci*?'

Giuseppe chuckled. 'I'll let you abuse me without expecting you to love me.'

'You're a flirt-and-a-half.'

He smiled to himself. She didn't know the half of it. He wondered what her problem was. Besides being banged up in prison. The woman, when she wasn't being obnoxious, sounded worried. And lonely. He stroked his moustache slowly with grimy fingers.

'So, tell me, what are you in this fine establishment for? Anything impressive? Creative accounting? Nicking the plastic garbage bin in front of your house? Writing bad cheques?'

'Murder.'

Giuseppe choked and almost poked himself in the eye.

'Attempted murder.'

'Oh.'

The woman sighed. 'It didn't work.'

'Did you *want* to kill whoever it was?'

'Yes . . .' She hesitated. 'But since I've never killed anyone before, I didn't do a good enough job.'

'Did they deserve it?'

The woman's cold silence was her only answer.

Despite his shock at what she told him, Giuseppe was caught by the sadness in her words. 'I'm waiting too. For my son.'

'Cecilio?'

'How did you – oh, yes, I forgot you heard me –'

'Several times,' she said.

'Sorry. I just don't know what to think. Is he being prevented from seeing me? Is he staying away to punish me? I think he's angry with me.'

'I'm sure he's not.'

Giuseppe looked down at his feet and noticed several holes in his best brown socks. What had been his best brown socks. One extremely unattractive grey toenail was poking through one of the larger ones. Disgusted, he bent down and tried to twist the sock so that the holes were underneath. *That's better.* He stood up again and leaned against the bars. 'He's been angry with me his whole life.'

'Why?' The woman sounded interested. Maybe he was getting her to forget her own problems. Her murder-victim problems, he reminded himself.

'I could never please anyone.' He started to feel sorry for himself.

'Don't whinge. I hate it when people are pathetic and whiny.'

'Sorry.'

'Why are *you* in? I've told you.'

Giuseppe brought his mouth up close to the bars. 'Come here.'

'Why?' She sounded suspicious.

'Just come to the corner of your cell, woman! I don't want to share what I've done with the whole world.'

'Is it that bad?'

Glum, he picked at some dry skin around the cuticles of one finger. 'Some people might think so.'

'Well?'

'It was a couple of things . . .'

The woman's voice crackled with impatience. '*Well?*'

'I was a Camorra kingpin.'

'You?' The woman chortled.

'What's so improbable about that?'

'I can't figure you for a Camorra kingpin. You talk too much. Aren't Camorra kingpins reticent and growly-voiced? You're as reticent as an auctioneer.'

Giuseppe punched the bars with one fist and stomped towards the other end of his cell. He brought his hand up to his mouth and winced as his tongue brushed the newest raw spot. He should learn not to keep whamming those bars. He always lost the confrontation. Haughtily he replied in the direction of the bars, 'I can be quiet when I want to.'

'What did you do as this, uh, Camorra kingpin?'

'I was involved in the highest echelon of Capos.'

'The Whatos? Sounds like a children's group. You know. The bunnies. The widdle wabbits. The capering Capos.'

'Why do I bother talking to you? The Capos are Al Capone's middle-management structure. The ones that get everything done.'

'What did you do for them, Kingpin?'

'I had an important position.'

'It's a very important job you'll be doing for us, boy.' The man had leaned towards him over the desk, jowls flapping. His acrid cigar smoke curled into Giuseppe's eyes, making them smart. 'What was your name again?'

When his new boss reached one meaty hand over to tap his cigar ash on the floor next to him, the boy tensed. He hoped he wouldn't say the wrong thing.

'Giuseppe Ing– Insenga.' The man's eyes boring into him made him almost forget. God, what a waste of space he was, what a wimp, a pillock –

'Glad to have you on board, boy. Now get lost.' The man's face rearranged itself into an approximation of a smile.

Relieved to have the initial interview over with, Giuseppe trudged off down the hall, frog-marched between two men with big guns tucked discreetly in their armpit holsters. They led him into a spacious white room with gleaming metal counters and shut the door behind him. Weapons hung on every available wall. Axes.

Knives. Ice picks. But mostly knives.

And spoons.

Giuseppe was fascinated. 'Is this the weapons armoury?'

One of the men had laughed at him, making a low rumbling noise. 'No, kid. This is the kitchen. Like the *padre* said, get to work. He likes extra chocolate in his *cannoli*.'

The woman laughed, incredulous. 'You worked for the Camorra as a pastry chef?'

'What's wrong with that? It was an honest living.' Giuseppe flexed one arm, looking at the almost non-existent biceps. He hated the way the skin on his arms looked so shrivelled and wrinkly. Like an old woman's breasts. He waggled his arm back and forth, watching the loose pouch of skin underneath flap.

'Did you get arrested for burning the apple tarts?'

Giuseppe dropped his arm. 'Don't be stupid.'

'I can't wait to hear what else you did.' The woman was sounding positively friendly.

Giuseppe felt foolish. 'I was married a few times.'

The woman hooted. 'They locked you up for that? You went from woman to woman, one right after the other?'

'They weren't one right after the other.'

'Go on. I can't wait.'

Giuseppe mumbled something in a small voice.

'*What?* I can't hear you.'

'Same time.'

'You're going to have to speak up louder. These concrete walls don't carry sound terribly well.'

'I MARRIED THEM ALL AT THE SAME TIME.'

'Oh.' She paused. 'How many?'

'Eight.'

'Jeez Louise.'

'I did love them all. I still do.'

'Of course.' She snickered.

'I did! And two of them were to the same person, so it's only seven.'

'A much lower number. Yes. I can appreciate your recalculations.'

'You see why I'm here?'

'You were a polygamous pastry chef.'

'Sort of.'

The woman started laughing so hard that she choked and had to get some water. A few minutes later she tried calling him again, but Giuseppe pretended he didn't hear her. He went and hid at the back of his cell. Sat on his bucket and put his head between his hands. Nobody had ever made him feel embarrassed about it before. She was laughing *at* him not *with* him. It wasn't a good feeling.

Giuseppe ignored her periodic tapping on the wall. It was time to get some exercise. That floppy arm had really put him off. He lay on the cell floor and took up a bar-bell in each hand. *A roll of toilet paper can be a bar-bell, can't it? With a bit of imagination.*

He raised each leg in turn into the air, flexed his foot round and round and slowly let it down. When both legs rested on the floor, he raised his arms and clonked the two rolls of toilet paper over his head. That would get both muscle groups going. He hoped. The rolls of toilet paper weren't as heavy as they should be, but you had to make do with the materials at hand, didn't you?

'Hey, you.' The woman's voice hissed next to the bars. 'Kingpin?'

Giuseppe raised his left foot and held it, despite the tremor that shook his leg after a couple of seconds. He stared at one of the holes in his sock, which had twisted back round to the front. His toenail glimmered at him. He wiggled his toe.

'I'm sorry I laughed at you.' She sounded genuinely contrite.

He lowered his leg and stared up into the air. Both hands hefted their rolls of toilet paper. One started to unwind as he held it skywards, the sheets tickling him as they fluttered in his face.

'My name's Estra.' Her voice sounded apologetic.

Giuseppe looked up at the ceiling. Should he get up?

'If you don't come over here and talk to me, Kingpin, I'm going to escape and come and rip your face off.'

Giuseppe got up with alacrity. 'You say the sweetest things, my darling.'

'Shut your mouth. You shouldn't cross me. I'm a murderer, you know.'

'Not yet, you're not.'

'Details, details.'

Giuseppe found himself telling Estra about Cecilio. Everything. Including the choice he'd asked him to make.

'Why do you call him Cecilio? Such a babyish name to call a grown man.'

'His real name is Dario, but my wife called him Cecilio. I call him that to remind myself what I've done to her. Sort of a hair-shirt nickname.'

'Does your son mind being your flagellation device?'

'He doesn't know,' he said dismissively. Anticipating her next question, he beat her to it. 'My first wife. My last one.'

'Probably the best one to be.'

Giuseppe was confused. 'Which?'

'Both.'

Shaking his head, Giuseppe skipped over that last comment. Although Estra was surprisingly good company, sometimes she said things he didn't quite understand. Maybe it was because she was English. They were different from Italians. Not any worse, he thought hurriedly. Just different.

'Do you miss her? The last one?' Estra interrupted his thoughts.

'Yes. She wasn't my favourite. That one went off to England. But the last one, the first one, she was my son's mother. That has to mean something.'

'What happened?'

Giuseppe twisted his moustache hairs. How could he tell her? She'd lacerate him verbally.

As if reading his mind, she spoke quietly. 'I won't criticize, Kingpin. Really I won't. I've done enough unforgivable things myself.'

'I married her when we were both young. She lived next door to my family on Via Benito. She followed me around when we were children. I hated it. My friends laughed at me and we tried getting rid of her by throwing rotten tomatoes at her. She just ducked and kept following. We finally just forgot she was there. I stopped minding having a permanent shadow when she turned into a beautiful sulky teenager with beckoning grey eyes. I pursued *her* then. She made me pay for her long wait, but I respected her for it.'

'Played hard to get?'

'No. I can't explain it. She didn't take any guff from me. I liked that.'

'So?'

'It was stupid. I started spending a lot of time at work. Being a pastry chef for the Mob was a time-consuming business. Very picky about their *cannoli*, they were. If the *panettone* was one bit dry, they'd fling it up in the air and shoot it with their pistols, until little bits of candied fruit and powdered sugar rained down upon your sorry head.'

'And?'

Giuseppe felt embarrassed again. 'One of the Capo's daughters started visiting me in the kitchens a lot. Then we – she jumped me when I was looking in one of the lower cupboards for the candied cherries. One minute I was deep into calculating possible cooking times for the new kind of marzipan and fruit cake I'd invented. The next, I had my kitchen whites rucked down around my ankles and this gorgeous black-haired girl with caramel skin was perched up on the metal counter with her legs scissoring around me. What could I do? I forgot all about the marzipan.'

'Oh, my.'

'Marzipan and flour went everywhere. I think I had egg white in my hair.'

'You sure it was . . .?'

'She kept coming back. I tried saying no.'

Estra snorted her disbelief.

'I don't know how it happened, but I ended up agreeing to marry her.'

'Forgetting about your long-suffering wife at home?'

'You don't understand the people I worked for!' Giuseppe was desperate to make her understand. 'You don't dally with a Capo's daughter and not marry her. I just had to make sure that I didn't get caught going between my two apartments.'

'Being a pastry chef must have been profitable those days.'

'Only because I received bonuses whenever I baked weapons and drugs inside cakes to be used as gifts for the Capos' friends.'

'Ah.'

'The problem was that my first wife, Amalea, didn't like spending time on her own. She went out one night to a party by herself and tripped on the street. She landed with her hand in some horrible dog's mess. It got in her eyes.'

'No!'

'I can't even pronounce the illness she had, but she was in hospital for ages. When she came out she was blind.'

'Oh, Kingpin, I'm so sorry.'

'So was I.' Grimly, he continued, 'And, shit that I was, I continued to go out with other women. Not just go out with them . . .'

'But marry them.' Giuseppe heard her taking a sip of water and tapping the empty cup absently on the bars in contemplation. 'Substantially worse than just messing with their marzipan.'

'I kept meeting Capos' daughters. They liked hanging around the kitchens and coaxing me to give them slices of cake and bits of frosting. They were terribly persuasive. Always wanting to lick the bowls. You always meet people you work with, don't you? I felt so guilty about Amalea that I stayed away from her as much as possible. The other women distracted me.'

'I bet.' The cup tapped again in amusement.

'There was always the worry I'd get caught by one of their fathers. At home, Amalea became dependent and clingy. She thought I would leave her. When I woke up in the morning, she'd be lying there, staring at me sightlessly. Her face was so sweet and her eyes so blank. She thought I wouldn't want to hang around an old blind bat like her. I loved her, though. To prove to her that I did, I married her again. Sort of an affirmation of vows.'

'Jeez Louise. I'm surprised you're still alive!'

Giuseppe smiled in wry humour. 'I had an accident in the kitchen some time later. I cut my hand on a knife that I was baking inside a *panettone*. It just about sliced my thumb off so I had to go to the hospital to get some stitches.'

'Divine intervention?' Estra giggled. The sound of it was surprisingly girlish. He smiled through the wall in her direction.

'Divine *something* was about ready to take care of me. All my wives came to the hospital, except for one who'd gone back to England. Cecilio drove Amalea, since she couldn't drive any more.'

'Oh, no!'

'Oh, yes.' He sighed. 'It was like one of those nightmares you always dream about. All your exes, or in this case all your presents, turning up at one party. They all huffed off to get their fathers. I should know Italian fathers. I'm one myself. If I had a daughter, I'd probably be the same.'

'I think you'd be an okay father, despite your over-enthusiasm for the marital state. I can tell you adore your son.'

'I do.' He paused. 'Can you blame me for heading off to Canada?'

Estra laughed hugely. 'Not at all. How did you get caught?'

'Amalea knew my cousin lived in Kingston. She reported me.'

'Ouch.'

'Yeah.'

'Can I see the scar on your thumb?'

'Why? Don't you believe me?' Giuseppe was hurt.

Estra sounded exasperated. 'Of course I do, Kingpin. It's just that I know about damaged hands. I want to see.'

Giuseppe wiped his left hand on his trousers, and ruefully examined the black unidentified sludge under the nails. Prison wasn't conducive to good hygiene. He was embarrassed to show a woman hands like that.

He thrust his hand through the bars. He felt a cool finger trace the still livid scar along his thumb.

'At least you didn't lose it,' she said.

'True,' he said gruffly, as he yanked his hand back in. He could still feel her touch. It burned.

Don't start, he told himself grimly. *Cecilio. Amalea. Cecilio. Amalea.*

'Kingpin?' Estra called softly from her side of the wall.

'What?'

'I hope your son comes to see you soon.'

Giuseppe tightened both hands around the bars. 'I don't think he'll come. He would have come by now. He's better off without me.'

'How do you know?'

'He's doing so well. He's even trying to learn English. I think he's got a job interview. I hope he meets a nice Italian girl. Do you have any daughters?'

'No.' Estra spat.

'Is that a sensitive area?'

'Yes.' She sighed again and clinked her cup against the bars. 'It's not your fault. I just don't want to talk about it.'

'Sorry.'

'Tell me about Cecilio. Why did you ask him to make such a difficult choice?'

Giuseppe had known she'd get round to asking him that.

'I didn't want him to be like me. I wanted him to have to choose my punishment, even if the choice was difficult. My problem was, and may still be, weakness. I could never choose anything. Nobody ever made me. I wanted to force Cecilio to make a decision that I knew was difficult. To make conscious choices. Besides . . .' Estra's silence washed over him like soothing hands. '. . . if he can punish me, it might make him forgive me some day. He's angry with me for his mother's sake. I can't blame him.'

'You're not so bad, Kingpin.'

'You're sweet. If you were in here, I'd kiss you.'

'If I was in there, we'd be arrested.'

'If we weren't already.'

'Of course.'

The jangling of keys stopped their conversation. The guard was on his periodic trawl through the corridors. Giuseppe went back and perched on his bucket, thinking about Estra. It was the first time he'd ever told a woman the truth. It felt strange. He didn't even know what she looked like but she had the familiarity of a friend. Underneath her prickly exterior, there was something. He couldn't understand how she could try to kill someone. They must have done something unforgivable to her.

After the guards had sauntered through the corridor, checking that all the prisoners were safe and accounted for, Estra asked him again about Cecilio. 'Have you told him any of that stuff you told me?'

Giuseppe was indignant. 'Of course not. I'm his father. He'd think I was weak. I have to be a good example for him. Stoic. Reticent.'

'Yeah. Like you're such a good example for him now, Jail-bird.'

'I want him to choose. To be strong.'

'If I were him, I'd choose you.'

'You're sweet.'

'Go and play in the traffic.'

Giuseppe wished he could see her face. He couldn't even imagine what she looked like.

'How old are you, Estra?'

'What a question to ask a woman.'

He was horrified at his insensitivity. 'I'm sor –.'

Estra was laughing at him again. 'I'm kidding, Kingpin. You're so gullible! No wonder all those women convinced you to marry them.'

'It wasn't just them . . . I let myself be convinced. It was my –'

'I know. I can hear it in your voice. That's why I think you're okay.' She spoke quietly.

Giuseppe couldn't think of anything in response.

Estra coughed. 'Fifty-six.'

'Pardon?'

'I'm fifty-six.'

'Same as me.'

'A good age.'

'Yep.'

Companionable silence leaked through the bars. For some reason the dark wasn't so oppressive.

'I wish I could see you,' he said to the wall. 'At least put one of your hands through the bars. It's so strange just talking to air. I can't believe you even exist.'

'No.'

'Just no? No reason?'

'Exactly.'

'Oh.' Giuseppe felt hurt.

Silence. 'Sorry. I don't want to. My hands are in bad shape after the . . .'

'That's all right.' Giuseppe chuckled. 'I forgive you.'

'Phew.'

'This time.'

They both laughed.

'I forgive you too,' Estra said, in an odd tone.

'For what?'

'For being married to all those women.'

'I'm glad someone does.' Giuseppe said. 'Actually you're wrong.'

'About what?'

'I'm not married any more to any of them.'

'No?'

'Every single one of them divorced me except for one. I don't know where she is, though.'

'That must have been a blow.'

'Yes.'

'So you're single now?'

'I'm sure I am. My third wife must have divorced me too. She probably just couldn't find me to send me the papers. Why? Do you want to get married?'

'No chance. I've done my stint.'

'You were married before?'

'Sort of.'

'Being "sort of" married is like being "sort of" pregnant. Impossible.'

She ignored him. 'I don't think I'll ever be able to remarry. My husband was so psycho that I'm forever going to wonder what's waiting behind the nicest face and thickest façade of normality.'

Giuseppe was struck with an idea. 'Was it him you tried to kill?'

'Noooo.' She hesitated. 'I was trying to get his help with the murder.'

'You wanted a psycho to help you murder someone? Interesting choice.'

'You'd understand if I explained.'

'So explain, sweetheart.'

'Stop flirting.'

'Sorry. Habit.'

'OK.'

'I may be a flirt but at least I'm not a psychopath.'

'True.' There was a smile in her voice. 'You're a polygamous pastry chef.'

'It has a nice ring to it, don't you think?'

'At least your faults and weirdnesses are all hanging out front for everyone to make up their minds about you.'

'My son wouldn't agree,' he said sadly.

'I like not seeing you while I speak to you. Your face would distract me. I'd be searching for signs of psycho-ness.'

'Thanks, I think —'

'You don't have a normal façade.'

'Now, wait a minute. Nobody's ever complained before.'

'Just kidding.'

'Harpy.'

'Annoying creep.'

'If you were over here, I'd sweep you into my arms, push you against the bed, well, there's no nice bed in here, I'd have to push you against the concrete and ravish you.'

'Oh, to be ravished up against a urine bucket – my life's dream.'

'Be romantic, why can't you?'

'I'm fifty-six. I don't do those things any more.'

'You hadn't met me.'

'You're flirting again.'

'Am I? I didn't realize.' Giuseppe laughed happily.

She was silent for a moment. 'You have a very seductive voice.'

'Now who's flirting? Fast woman.'

'Don't get excited. That's all you get.'

'One can always hope.'

'Go to bed.'

'With you?'

'No, stupid. The guards have switched off the corridor light. Lights out.'

'Goodnight, Estra.'

'*Buonanotte*, Kingpin.'

In the middle of the night. Giuseppe was woken by Estra's panicked yelling.

'Estra?'

No answer.

'Estra. Answer me,' he called.

'*La terza vittime!*'

'What?' Giuseppe leaped off his bed board, tripped on his own foot, and staggered over to the bars with groggy uncoordination.

'I dreamed about them again.' Her voice was small and distant. 'The woman in the box. Her name is . . . it rhymes with hookah. What is it? Sambucca. Or Luca. Something like that.'

'Who?'

'And the mouse with the human ear. I won't even *attempt* his name.'

'You're not making sense.'

'I don't know who the woman in the box is. I have to get out. Something bad is going to happen to people I love. I keep having these dreams about them.'

'Estra?' There was no answer. He called again, urgently, 'Estra?'

'What?'

'I wish you'd come over here and give me your hand.'

'Why?' Her voice was agonized. 'Do you want to gawp at the damage?'

'I don't care about any damage. I just want to hold your hand. It sounds like nobody's held it in a long time.'

'Go away. Don't make me like you. You should be terrified. I'm a murderess.'

'Only an attempted one.' Giuseppe was desperate to get her back to her normal snippy self. 'How'd you try to kill him?'

'Him?'

'Or her. I don't want to be sexist.'

'I sliced him to ribbons.'

'How?'

Estra ignored his question. 'I tried. Both of them.' Her voice was a low monotone, stripped of emotion.

Both? Giuseppe was confused. 'You tried to kill two people?' She was ignoring him again. *Did she even hear him?*

'My hand hurts,' she said.

'Why?'

'You know, when I was a child, I used to paint Elmer's white glue all over my palms. It would dry totally clear within a few minutes. It felt as if I had protective gloves on. If I was careful, I could peel each of the gloves off in one piece. They looked like exact copies of my hand, lines and all. I used to leave them all over my room. Drove my mother nuts when she came in to straighten up. "Why can't you leave sticky fingerprints like any normal child?" she'd yell.'

'I never did that,' Guiseppe said in a lofty tone.

'You were busy leaving your sticky fingerprints all over the girls in the neighbourhood.' A faint echo of a laugh beckoned in her voice.

Relieved by it, he looked around his cell for inspiration. Nothing except his bucket and bar-bells. He went over to the middle of the room and picked up the toilet paper, which needed rewinding. Taking it back to the bars, he pulled off the last square and started tearing bits to keep his hands busy.

'I wish I had some glue to give you.'

'Thanks.' She paused. 'I have cling-film wrapped round my

hand now. It's the only thing that helps. It traps him in, among other things.'

'Pardon?' Giuseppe's fingers paused in their folding.

'Didn't I tell you? My husband's inside me.'

The toilet-paper origami crane Giuseppe had been attempting became totally crushed and fell from his hand. He didn't move for the next ten minutes. Estra told him what had happened, haltingly at first, and then with resigned diffidence. When she finished, her silence was tense and expectant. When he laughed, she was furious.

'Why are you laughing? What kind of a life can I ever have with him inside me? What man would ever want me now?' Tears filled her voice. 'He took care of that.'

Giuseppe was laughing in great whoops.

'What the hell are you laughing about?'

'How could a man like me complain about one husband more or less? I've got eight wives knocking about.'

'True.'

'You might think about it. If you really want to annoy him, make love to another man. Think about how he'd feel being prodded by a random penis that wasn't his.'

Estra's giggle was infectious. 'When I first saw him blinking at me from the middle of my palm, I wanted to thrust an ice pick into him. Poke him in the eye with a sharp stick.'

'You have a nice laugh.'

She ignored him. 'At first I was afraid of the pain.'

'At first?'

'But then he started picking his way out to get to me. The rage in his eye terrified me. I had to do something.' She was still laughing, but hysteria was creeping in.

'I wish I could help you.'

'I don't need anyone.'

'Don't you?' He listened carefully.

'No.' Her laughing became an almost indistinguishable sob.

Giuseppe felt pain deep in the pit of his stomach for her. 'Don't cry.'

'I thought I could prevent him picking his way out if I could hurt him.'

'How? Surely not by sticking an ice pick in your hand.' Giuseppe was horrified.

Her voice became harsh. 'Do you want to see?'

Suddenly she thrust a hand out of her cell towards him. Giuseppe looked at it with consternation. It was delicately wristed and finely boned, with long fingers clenched tightly in a fist. Around the hand was wrapped a snowball of iridescent film.

'Take off the cling-film!' she ordered.

Giuseppe was afraid to touch her. She was holding out her hand as if it didn't even belong to her. Tentatively, he reached his own through the bars and touched one of her curled fingers. It twitched slightly then stilled. He almost lost his nerve. He was trembling and almost forgot to breathe.

He could smell her hand's scent. Underneath the prison grime, it smelt like fruit. Not fresh fruit, but jewelled nuggets of the candied fruit he used to keep ready-mixed in his kitchen. Glowing tangy chunks of lemon folded in with thin slices of crystallized ginger, mixed with fat red cherries and scattered with raisins. Scooping up a handful of the knobbly mixed fruit and dropping it piece by piece into the cooking bowl, he had relished the sticky-sweet feel of them. The smell lingered on his hands for hours, no matter how many times he washed them.

The smell made him bolder. He touched the thin bones of her wrist. Her hand shuddered, but didn't draw back. *Will she let me?*

His hand moved up further. He stopped breathing. His little finger slid under the crinkled edge of cling-film. He pushed slightly, feeling resistance. Still she didn't pull away. He slid three fingers under the cling-film and down into the moist depths of her palm. He wanted to go all the way in. He did. The edge of the silvery film eased back and revealed the beginning of the pinkness. He panted.

He slid his fingers out of the slick dampness, feeling cold after the warmth of her palm. Delicately, he unwrapped the cling-film, until a silvery tail trailed on to the floor.

Eventually he unwrapped all the cling-film. It dropped to the ground, unnoticed. Giuseppe felt sick. Her fingers were livid and red, but that wasn't the worst. The worst was the furious eye glaring out at him. It blinked, the eyelashes clumped together. Not with tears, but with blood. Estra had taken a razor to her own hand. The eye had slash marks in it, but none that appeared to be fatal. Surrounding the eye, the skin was bubbling, as if a tiny mouse were skittering under the carpet of her palm.

Bile rose in his throat. The man was indeed trying to pick his way out. The bubbling must be Daniel's fingers picking. A tiny corner of something metallic flashed from one of the deep cuts in her hand.

'*Porca miseria*! He's got a razor in there!' Giuseppe dropped her hand in horror.

The hand withdrew itself from sight, and reappeared down near the floor. It snaked out and retrieved the discarded tail of cling-film. Giuseppe watched her drag it back into her cell.

Estra's voice reached him from the back of her cell where she must have been rewrapping her hand. 'I don't know how, but he sucked the razor away from me. One minute I was slicing away, trying to kill him, and the next the razor was gone and his eye was triumphant. Daniel will kill me if he can.'

Giuseppe couldn't think of a word to say.

After a moment, Estra continued, 'I tried to use his anger against the person who has destroyed my family. Daniel isn't important. Nor am I. But my family is. Wynne. Marina. Berri. I can't let the other man continue. I decided to use Daniel as my secret weapon.'

'How?'

'I thought if I got him angry enough he'd be able to get out. Tempt him out with a bit of symbolic cheese.'

'How would tempting him out help you with the other person?'

'I hoped that, by taunting him with more razor blades, I'd incense him so much that he'd leap out slashing without looking. If I followed Ricker, as soon as I felt Daniel ready to leap, I'd just hold my hand in front of his face. I was hoping Daniel would kill Ricker instead of me. Slash *his* face with the razors.'

'And?' Giuseppe was almost afraid to ask.

'It almost worked. I felt him lash out and I tried to get in front of Ricker in time.'

'It didn't work?'

'You see the results. I'm here. Daniel is still inside me and angrier than ever. Also, I think I've loosened something. He managed to swipe the razor. He cut the man's face. He has two razors now!'

'Better keep that cling-film on.'

'It's not holding him back like it used to. He's stronger now. I'm thinking of having my hand removed. Getting one of those donor-implant things.'

'Oh, no! I've heard they don't work very well.'

'It can't be any worse than this. I've lived with him inside me for fifteen years. I couldn't bear another fifteen.'

'But even if you cut your hand off, wouldn't he still be inside you?'

'I don't know. At least I wouldn't have to look at him. He can't get out anywhere else. Only my hand for some reason. Probably because there's a weakness there from all my picking.'

'Picking?'

'Nervous habit.'

'I've got nervous habits.' Perhaps he could cheer her up.

'Not like mine.'

'You don't think polygamy is a bad habit?'

She chortled. 'Not as bad as some.'

'I smoke cigars sometimes. Pick my nose when nobody's looking. Estra? Are you listening? I even fart in bed. Very loudly.'

'You're right. You are disgusting. I don't want to marry you, after all.'

'Were you considering it?' Giuseppe felt unfamiliar warmth creeping up his neck and into his cheeks. He picked up another square of toilet paper and started to fold.

'I've got to try to help my family.' Estra sounded tired. 'The third victim. I have to prevent unspeakable things from happening.'

'I'll help you.'

'How? You're in here.'

'I'll get Cecilio to help. He's a smart boy.'

'Smart, maybe, but absent.'

'Perhaps they'll let me telephone him. He'll come if he can. You'll see. He's a good boy. I've got to get to him before he chooses a body part for me to lose.'

The sound of jiggling keys made them both jump. Giuseppe picked up his toilet-paper arrangements. 'Quick, Estra. Give me your hand.'

'Why? You've seen it already.'

'Hold out your hand and stop arguing.'

'Forceful, aren't you?'

'I'm waiting.'

The cling-film-wrapped hand crept out from between the bars. Giuseppe reached out and rubbed his fingers tenderly on her wrist, the only area that wasn't damaged. Then he withdrew his hand and picked up what he'd been folding in his lap. Closing his hand around it carefully, he reached out through the bars and dropped it into her hand.

An intricately folded rose fluttered in her nest of cling-film, petals delicately curving up from the thin sheaves of toilet paper. At one end was a twisted paper stalk. From some of the twists, tiny pointed thorns peeped.

'Kingpin . . .'

'Take it and shut up. It's my promise to you. We'll get out of here and try to protect your family. You leave it to me.'

'Kingpin?'

'Yes?' The jangling keys were getting closer.

'When we get married, will you bake our wedding cake?'

'What do you take me for? Of course.'

The jangling keys, accompanied by the tread of several people's footsteps. They stopped in front of Giuseppe's cell.

Giuseppe had been looking down at his own hands, flexing the arthritic fingers slowly. His eyes were damp. When he realized that the sounds had halted in front of his own cell, he looked up.

Was it too late? Had Cecilio already chosen?

Losing Your Place

SANDRA

I inhabit a weak, frail, decayed tenement,
battered by the winds and broken in on
by the storms, and, from all I can learn,
the landlord does not intend to repair.

JOHN QUINCY ADAMS

Spearing a yellow-orange cloudberry on the end of one blue sparkle-tipped fingernail was easy. Swooping it out of its plastic punnet and thrusting it into her lips before either the mobile security camera or any of the other shoppers saw her was another story. Sandra got the berry three-quarters of the way up and had just parted her mouth, ready to lob the thing in and savour its juicy sweetness, when she heard them coming.

A little boy rounded the aisle corner at speed, with his mother trailing behind him like the owner at the end of a dog's leash. Sandra almost blinded herself with the cloudberry. It slid off her fingernail and landed on the floor with a small plop.

What a waste. Now she'd have to throw one over her shoulder for good luck.

'Mummy, look at that woman! Wannahavearazzwherry. Canne-yecanneye?'

As the child started shrieking, the harassed mother threw Sandra an evil look. It must be the work of an afternoon to calm the kid down.

'Shush, Robby. They're not raspberries. They're nasty old Swedish cloudberries, and at two City Credits each, you'd have to go out and mortgage your little body before Daddy and I could afford a punnet of those.'

'But she —'

'Oh, do shut up, Robby.'

Sandra giggled. With finicky precision, she plucked another thumb-sized cloudberry from the punnet, examined it carefully on all sides and popped it into her mouth. Throwing the woman an arch glance, Sandra pushed her trolley past them. 'The cloudberries aren't ripe. I wouldn't buy any, if I were you.' Shaking her head with disgust, she addressed the security camera that had swivelled towards them when the child started making so much noise. 'They're trying to sell us underripe cloudberries. I'm going to have to report that.'

Sandra felt two pairs of eyes besides the mechanical one clamped on her back as she hurried past them. Maybe they'd think she was a quality-control inspector. She'd better get out of there before they sent out the Grocery Guards or the Food Police. Speeding back to the main part of the hall, she felt rattled. She hadn't wanted to leave the fruit department yet. Usually, she stayed twenty-two minutes. Angry that the woman and her child had destroyed her fragile peace and meticulously arranged shopping routine, Sandra shoved the metal trolley in front of her with irritation.

Clackety clackety clackety. Why was it that she always got the one with the wonky wheels? Did the trolleys see her coming? Did they nudge each other with steely humour and lie in wait for her? 'You can have that one . . . she's a fuck-up,' the trolley had probably said to its neighbour. Like Dr Hurtigger always called her. Muck-up. Foul-up. Mess-up. *I'm fed up.*

Sandra gave the trolley a vicious shove and then raised both hands. *Look, Ma, no hands – see?*

There it went, zooming to the left. Life could go in that direction too. Sandra smiled with dry humour as she corrected the trolley's deviation. *I'm not just a receptionist. I'm a philosopher.*

Philosophers needed peace and quiet. That was why she was here. She'd had a bad morning. Whenever she felt her stress level rising, she came here at the first opportunity. Grafton's Grocery. Not just to stock up on supplies for Dr Hurtigger's office and shop for herself but to soak up the atmosphere.

Leaving the fruit section, Sandra decided to take the transport switcher rather than walk all the way to the main food hall. No sense wasting time when she could be transported there in a second. She walked up to the grey metal cage and waited patiently in the queue while the other people in front of her winked out, one by one. As she stepped on to the transmission platform, Sandra pressed her palm on the grimy entrance panel.

'Main food hall, please.' Nothing happened. Sandra pressed the panel again, more firmly this time. Just her luck. The transport switcher must have decided, along with everything else, to ensure that her day deteriorated as fast as possible. 'Main hall, please!' she said.

The panel's lights flickered once and then went out. She slapped it with a bag of tangerines. The lights came back on again and the platform jiggled. The menthol feeling of coolness that enveloped her told her that she'd winked out. *About time, too.*

The panel's electronic voice cleared its throat and spoke. 'Main hall. Floor B-18. Please proceed to the left, remaining always on your right to avoid oncoming traffic. When you arrive at the main entrance, take a trolley from the stack on your left.'

I already have one of the bloody things, thank you very much.

The main food hall opened in front of her as she walked in. Descending from the electric walkway, she looked out over the huge maze-like area with a tight feeling of anticipation. She could see tiny heads bobbing up and down as people selected their products. Trolleys glimmering with either silvery efficiency or stubborn recalcitrance. *At least I'm not the only one with wonky wheels.*

Aisles streaked out from the bank of cashier computers in the central court like massive wheel spokes. Spotlights tangoed back and forth, shouting sale prices. Above each aisle LED boards flashed row numbers. B-5. F-92. V-1.

Where to go first? Always the most enjoyable decision. Sandra took a deep breath and plunged in. The air cooled dramatically the further in she went. The roots of her hair unclenched and she sighed with happiness. The glacial air-conditioning licked her bare arms and she shivered. The coolness and peace soothed her jangled brain. Such an awful morning. She frowned. What was it that had disturbed her so much? It couldn't have been that bad if only ten minutes at Grafton's had made her forget.

What did she need for Doc Hurt's office? Tea? Coffee filters?

She snorted. Perhaps he could wear coffee filters over his face to meet patients for the next few weeks. Those cuts all over his face he'd come in with a couple of days ago were off-putting for the patients. He insisted he'd cut himself shaving – but she'd never seen shaving cuts like that. Perpendicular? She decided that it was none of her business.

What should she get for dinner tonight? She wasn't that interested in food. She hated the feeling of turgid fullness after you ate. Like a stuffed salmon.

But *shopping* for food, that was another thing.

What were the contents of her refrigerator at the moment? Sandra closed her eyes and tried to visualize the small humming white box in her kitchen. Her imaginary pale hand went to open it and brushed past all the polished heart-shaped rocks stuck magnetically to the front. She opened the door and stared inside. One plastic lemon with a trickle of juice inside it sat in the side drawer, two waxed containers of strawberry yoghurt resided on the top shelf, and a bottle of mint vinaigrette dressing lay on its side on the bottom shelf. She started to close the door and spotted the two cubes of ancient Gro-Meat lurking in the back.

She felt disgusted with herself. She couldn't remember the sell-by dates for any of it. She should keep fresh food. She should throw out the vinaigrette too, as it was cohabiting with something furred and furious.

What a muck-up. Doc Hurt was right.

She rarely had milk to offer with coffee when people dropped in. If she had any, it was usually off. Whenever she thought to check a carton by wafting it in front of her nose, something always smelt as though it had died inside. *Eeeuuuuch.*

Powdered milk was the answer. She'd get some today. She hoped it wasn't made of plastic. It tasted like it. She was afraid to think of how much plastic went into making food these days. Your system would eventually fill up with plastic and push all the real stuff out. Plastic veins. Plastic heart . . .

Doc Hurt always told her she had far too much imagination for such a young girl. She wished he would stop telling her she was a mess-up, though. It destroyed her confidence. 'You could never get a job anywhere else,' he always said, after she made a little mistake or two. 'Agree with me, Sandra. You know I'm right.'

She always agreed with him as, after all, he was her boss. It wasn't like there were hundreds of jobs out there for someone with her limited experience. And she did do a good job sometimes. 'Patients like me,' she reassured herself.

How long had she worked for him? She couldn't even remember. She must have started right after school, or something like that. She was much too busy to worry about such silly things. It was okay working there, except for his nasty comments. You had to feel sorry for him.

After all, they had the same background. He reminded her when he thought she was getting too full of herself.

'We were both foster children, weren't we, Sandra? Our parents didn't want us. Threw us out with the garbage. That's why we work so well together. We have each other.' Dr Hurtigger had smiled at her kindly.

She gave him a tremulous smile. Surely her parents hadn't thrown her out with the garbage.

'And our little experiments, of course,' he continued.

Your experiments. Not mine. Sandra couldn't remember her real parents. She became aware recently of how many large gaps her memory actually held. She had read a quiz last week in a women's magazine in Doc Hurt's waiting room: 'Evaluate Your Life and Career.' She'd tried to do just that, but was unable to come up with many pertinent details. What life? What career?

Doc Hurt told her she forgot more than she remembered. She was lucky to be employed by him, he said.

She had asked him once if he knew who her original parents had been. He was busy preparing a donor for a multiple implant, and she hoped he'd answer without thinking.

'Who were your parents? I have no idea.' He looked unconcerned 'Drug addicts, I think.'

Yeah, right. It would have been nice if her parents had been

213

royalty or something. Just too busy to bring her up. Too many difficult affairs of state. Multitudes of brothers and sisters fighting over the crown. *Typical. Everyone always wants to be a princess.* Maybe she'd been one in another life. One could always dream. She wondered what the doctor's parents were like. She decided it was safe to ask him as he was busy situating one of the implant buds.

'Who were your parents? Do you know, Dr Hurtigger?'

His hands tucked a bud on the donor's shoulder. Sandra moved some of the woman's tangled blonde hair out of his way. He nodded his thanks.

'French-speaking . . . Turn over, Marina, there's a good girl . . . Good people . . . they're why I went into medicine . . . Sandra, can you swab out the incision here? Yes, that's right. Just there. Spray it with that stuff in the blue bottle. Antiseptic. Not the flea spray. That's the green bottle. You're such a . . .'

I know I know. Sandra got tired of hearing him tell her what a waste of space she was. Sometimes she substituted the term in her ead with little mental asterisks. ****-up. It made her feel less like grinding her teeth or smacking him. She should feel grateful to him. He'd given her a job and he let her get involved with all his important operations. All kinds of medical things that she hadn't expected him to let her do. She was allowed to give injections and make incisions. She had even been allowed to implant a wriggling hand bud into the latest donor's other shoulder. She'd love to be a doctor.

It wasn't worth taking his constant belittling. She should look for another job. There had to be somewhere else she could work. It was time for a change.

Enough lallygagging around! Get shopping, girl. What was first? She didn't like to make lists. Trying to improve her memory was much more productive. She set off towards one of the aisles on the north side. Her shoes squeaked on the polished floor. The cart swerved. *Clackety-clackety-clackety.*

Vinaigrette was first. With herbs. Which aisle? Aisle B-5. That was no test. Too easy.

Squeaking and clacking down the cereal-filled A aisles, she turned right to get to the Bs. B-1. B-2. B-3. There was no hurry. She knew exactly where everything was. It was boring just going up and down all the aisles one by one, chucking things in her trolley. That was for simps, as the Doc said. Simpletons. Make it entertainment. Besides, remembering where each product resided was a good mental exercise. She didn't know why her memory was so good here at the shop when it seemed to lie down in the dust and die in front of Doc Hurt.

Test yourself. Herb vinaigrette. Aisle B-5. Left-hand side. Third row up. There it was. Next to the mayonnaise. She sighed happily. No contest at all. She wished everything at work was in such perfect order.

What a mess Doc's office was. You could never find anything. His filing system was a travesty. Whenever she tried to convince him that, with computers, they didn't need paper back-ups of everything, he became irritatingly obstinate. And he wouldn't even keep them in any discernible order. Whenever she tried to get them sorted, he came in like an unalphabetized whirlwind and changed everything round. She got steamed up just thinking about it. Especially his bills. He had an entire cabinet filled with boxes and boxes of gas and electricity bills stuffed randomly in bunches. Whenever she tried to sort them by date, he came in and whiffled them all up.

The only files he kept in good order were his red files. The current ones he kept locked in his desk. Despite her hatred of filing, she'd offered to sort them for him, sure that they would be in as bad a state as his other files.

'Don't worry about them, Sandra, I know exactly where everything is. I don't want you messing with my own system. Keep your hands off my private files.'

No need to get snarky. The disorganization in the office drove her mad. Whenever Doc needed anything in a hurry he'd yell, which made her nervous. If only his files were in order, then she could find something for him quicker and he wouldn't yell, breathing down her neck, warm spittle spraying the back of her head.

'Now!' he'd shriek. 'I want that Zimmerman file N-O-W. Now!'
She must remember to buy some Stress-Vite.

Here at Grafton's everything was in its place. Orderly. Items neatly stacked into inviting symmetrical displays. Pyramids of cans. Columns of jars. She never missed an aisle, despite her haphazard way of shopping. She never missed anything, not even KittyPrint cat food. She knew exactly where everything was. *What a life. When tins of cat food were your best friends.*

The vinaigrette was right where she expected it to be. One item down. Next. *Rice.*

That would be Aisle D-2. First row down. Right side. Sandra rounded the corner with ease, making a slightly self-conscious 'vroom-vroom' noise under her breath. Besides a princess, she'd always fancied being a glamorous female racing-car driver in another life. Either that or Ginger Rogers. Bending down, trying hard to be as elegant as Ginger, she scooped up Fred Astaire in her arms. She adored old movies. She deposited Fred in her cart, gazing fondly at him despite his uncanny resemblance to a bag of rice.

That was odd. Fred Astaire wasn't a bag of rice at all. He was a sad-looking sack of dried chick peas, seemingly just as surprised to be in her trolley as she was to see them there.

The chick peas were where the rice should be. Wasn't she in aisle D-2? Confused, she looked up at the identifying markers. Aisle D-2. She hadn't become lost. What was going on? They *never* moved anything in this store. That's why she kept coming back. A tiny razor-edged shard of panic sliced into her. A trickle of sweat crept down the back of her neck and steamed in the cool air. She wanted to sit down. Leaning against the trolley, she rubbed her eyes hard and waited till the panic passed.

Daydreaming idly, Sandra watched fragments of a familiar woman's body float by. The curve of her breast, the dip of her waist . . . The fragments were hazy. If she reached out, she could touch her.

Opening her eyes, Sandra felt uncomfortable. *Why am I day-dreaming about women? How embarrassing.*

Pushing the trolley, she felt tainted. She hoped nobody could tell by the look on her face what she'd been thinking about. *I should be thinking about men.*

Fighting the recalcitrant trolley with new vigour, Sandra forced herself to be calm. She had to find out what had happened to the rice. Clacking through the aisles, she searched for a shelf-stacker. Thankfully, there was one in Aisle D-3, arranging boxes of crackers. 'Where have you taken them?' she demanded.

The man turned round and raised his fists in mock challenge. 'Pardon?'

'Did you know the rice is in the wrong place?'

'We've reshuffled a few things to see if sales improve.' He lowered his fists and grinned. 'It was my idea. I'm the new assistant manager.' Exceedingly pleased with himself, he turned back to his stacking. Belatedly, he remembered that perhaps he should be helping her, and he turned back. 'Can I help you find something?'

'You haven't moved anything else, have you?' she choked out.

'Go and have a look at Aisle G-14.' He waved with a box of crackers. 'We've stopped that silly garden effect. It's much better now.'

Sandra felt punched in the stomach. She had loved the way the vegetables had always been arranged. Just like a real garden right in the middle of all the canned goods, with hand-written markers stuck into each vegetable section. 'Corn-on-the-Cob – 4 CCs, Real Lettuce – 3 CCs.'

She'd always wanted to be a gardener. She had suggested to Doc Hurt that they make a garden in the patch behind the office, but he always refused. 'We have more important things to grow there.'

Sandra was sick of all the weird implant people who came into the office to grow new body parts. That Luca gave her the shivers whenever she saw her being dug up. The other one, Marina, wasn't yet an in-patient. Dr Hurtigger was excited about her, though. She must be having another multiple implant. He acted funny around her. Excited, yet calm, as if he'd been expecting her.

'Right on schedule.' He'd marked something on a red file. The personal red file in his desk that he wouldn't let her see. She'd tried sneaking up behind him once to see what the files said. All she could see was, 'In Progress'. *Boring*.

How could that woman have ten hands put on herself? What could possibly make these people sign up for something like that? The money? They must just not care about themselves. Otherwise, how could they? It must be the money. That's why Sandra had tucked the envelope of City Credits back into Marina's pocket when she'd tried to return them. She was sure the woman needed them. She didn't even have a shirt on when she came in, for heaven's sake.

The other one. Luca. Shivers ran up and down Sandra's spine. Why would she volunteer to have parts of herself cut off? Did she have no feelings?

Sandra knew Luca had volunteered for the experiment, as Dr Hurtigger told her. He insisted that Luca felt not one iota of pain. Still, being kept in a box? Sandra couldn't do it. Just being in a small room gave her the heebie-jeebies.

She wished she could read Marina's file. Doc Hurt was so excited about her. What was next? Something creative, she bet. He was nothing if not creative. He loved working with people.

Sandra wished he'd left the mouse alone. Thinking about it depressed her.

Rolling the trolley along, she arrived at Aisle G-14 and felt almost unbearable pain. Instead of the beautifully organized vegetable plots, there were now large bins filled with heaps of different vegetables all mixed together. Green peppers sat jammed unsociably close to flaccid, unhappy-looking carrots. Depressed-looking onions leaned against aubergines dull with despair. The broccoli was the worst: a few sorry-looking specimens slumped in dejected heaps. Before, the broccoli had been carefully massed together in a vast undulating sweep of verdancy. Sandra would brush her fingertips lightly over its rough flowering ends, close her eyes and breathe in the fresh scent that wafted to her nostrils. She could imagine the sun on her shoulders and the dusky smell of upturned earth.

They'd also put mixed jars of fruit and vegetables on a shelf above the fresh ones, in a pathetic effort at decoration. Sandra looked up in despair. White asparagus tips floating in brine. They looked like the fingers Dr Hurtigger had thrown out last week.

Rat-brain lychees.

Jars of mushy peas. Mashed green, slimy . . . *Get a grip, Sandra*.

She tightened her fingers around the trolley handle. She had to get out of this aisle. She was losing all sense of proportion. Dr Hurtigger's body bits were invading her refuge and even creeping into the jars of vegetables. Acrid sweat trickled freely under her thin shirt.

She changed her mind. The asparagus didn't look like fingers at all. They looked like Dr Hurtigger's lips. In some misguided idea of making him be nicer to her, she'd tried to kiss him once when they locked up for the evening. After all, he wasn't unattractive. Rather nice-looking when he made an effort. He patted her shoulder, telling her to get some sleep. She hadn't felt rejected, but had hurried back to her flat, wiping her mouth with the back of her hand. His lips had been so . . . wet. Like tinned asparagus.

Sandra felt her hands trembling. She had better get the shopping done and go home. She wasn't feeling well. Grafton's wasn't calming her down today. The disorder was ripping the scabs off her peace, and she had to get out of there.

The only item left to get was Gro-Meat from the anti-vegetarian section. Aisle S-14. Shouldn't be a problem. Gro-Meat should be on the fourth shelf up on the left on S-14. It was in green boxes the shape of the animal it was to represent. Cow-shaped. Pig-shaped. Goat-shaped. Cellophane windows let you look inside at the little stamped cubes. It looked a lot like tofu and was comfortingly easy to cook. You dropped a cube into some water and watched it swell up to its intended shape. Very nutritious. And fun for kids. Sandra usually loved it, feeling no more than a kid herself sometimes.

It was like seeding and growing your own meat. Your own animals.

Sandra entered the mouth of Aisle S-14 and walked towards the Gro-Meat.

Thinking of animals reminded her of the mouse she'd helped to escape that morning.

Watching Doc Hurt grow the ear on the mouse had made Sandra feel uncomfortable. For some reason, it bothered her more when experiments were done on animals than on people. Maybe because people asked for their implants, and animals didn't. And at least people got paid.

She watched the doctor prod the sweating mouse with the electric shock inducer. He switched it on and a blue flame shot from the metal tip to the tightly curled thing that looked like a dried apricot on the mouse's back. The mouse screamed. Sandra winced. She watched with sick fascination as with every prod and accompanying electric shock the human ear unfurled and puffed up. It became more full and pink as the mouse became more limp and grey. She watched the tiny star-shaped paws clench and unclench. Within about ten minutes, the ear attained adult growth, although damp and unsure of itself. The mouse lay still, panting heavily.

Dr Hurtigger told her to clean up and get the mouse back in its cage. He had to write up his reports.

Go on. Get up, mouse.

The mouse had certainly paid heavily for letting Doc catch it. He hadn't finished paying either. Now that Doc Hurt had Luca to play with and Marina to plan for, he didn't need the mouse any more.

'Kill it,' he told her. 'Or I will.'

Sandra reached into the mouse's cage, towards the shivering grey bundle in the corner. He was trying to chew some of the wires that ran just outside. Delicately, she tried to pull the wire bits out of his mouth, but he kept his mouth clamped shut on them. His eyes whirled in fright. She let go and touched the tip of his earlobe with her little finger. The mouse trembled.

Go on, mouse. Go. Sandra left the cage door open and deliberately turned away and walked towards the door. *Go.*

She didn't know if he could survive in the wild, but he deserved a chance. Far more of a chance than that woman buried underneath her feet. She could hear Luca tapping. She hoped the noise wasn't upsetting the mouse. How could that woman have signed up for this treatment?

'When I come back, mouse, you be gone. Okay?'

She shut the door.

Sandra's unease increased as she continued up Aisle S-14. Things were looking better. Everything was the same so far. The slabs of meat and offal were in their usual places. Chunks of stewing beef. Greyish purple liver. Finger-sized tubes of smokable dried cow's brains. They were like magic mushrooms that gave you crazy hallucinations. Her friend, Juliana, had made her try them once.

Juliana was great fun. It was a shame she'd moved away, although probably better for her health, Sandra thought. Before she'd gone, they'd been out every Tuesday, Thursday and Saturday night. Juliana cheered her up. They used to try on each other's clothes all the time.

'What are those *awesome* scars all over you, Sandra?' Juliana was fascinated. Sandra knew she would be. Whenever they went out dancing, Juliana was always pointing out the men with scars. 'Look at that one,' she'd say, nudging Sandra painfully in the ribs. 'Awesome-looking knife scar on his face! Wonder what he's been doing.' They'd both shiver.

Juliana had convinced Sandra to let the scars all hang out. 'Be brave! Wear them like you love them. Don't hide them. Be proud.' She said. 'Make the best of your assets.'

Sandra took her advice once and wore a dress with cut-outs. Usually she wore things that hid the scars around her neck. The ones down her back. Around her arms. Around the tops of her legs. *I'm like a huge cut-price rag doll.*

There must have been some horrendous accident. It must have happened when she was really young. Dr Hurtigger didn't know anything about it.

'Bring a man home from the club,' Juliana urged. 'You'll see, men love scars. Oddities.'

'You're sick, Juliana.'

'They'll go mad, I tell you.'

They did. Or, actually, one did when she'd brought him home. When she'd undressed, he came over and kissed each and every one of the scars. He traced them with fascinated fingers. 'Keerist,' he breathed, 'what have you done to yourself?'

She couldn't tell Juliana that she had chickened out of the next part and asked him to leave. It was embarrassing being a virgin at her age. Juliana would laugh.

She had pretended to Juliana that the man had stayed. 'Wow,' she told her. 'Fantastic.'

At least the man didn't have wet lips like Dr Hurtigger.

Juliana used to read their tarot cards. Some woman down the street had given her a pack. It was fun. Sandra hooted with laughter at the garbage Juliana made up.

'You will be reborn among flames. You are two people in one. You will be a saviour.'

Like she said. Garbage. But fun. Too bad Juliana wasn't here to read the cards for her now. She wished she could read her own. Maybe she could find someone to do it for her. Find out if she'd get a better job. Have a better life. Tell her why she always dreamed about women. One woman in particular.

Sandra went as far as looking up 'Palmists' in the phone book once. She'd stopped by the time she reached the Bs. The first name on that page was an improbable 'Madame Berengaria'.

What a silly name. It put Sandra right off. With a name like that, the woman had to be a fake. Sandra gave up on that idea. She couldn't go and have her cards read by someone with a stupid name.

Sandra reached the Gro-Meat. What used to be the Gro-Meat section.

It had all changed. Everything was in the wrong place. Chaos. Disorder. Bits everywhere. The Gro-Meat animals were all mixed. Cows with pigs. Horses cantering next to goats. Oh, God. A tiny

Gro-Meat cow's head lay on its own, disconnected from its body. Raw and unexpanded. Fragments of horse tails. A head. All messed up.

As she stared around her in horror, she remembered suddenly why the morning had gone so badly. Dr Hurtigger had asked her to come with him to Camden Town Transport station. To collect some donations, he had said.

'Hurry up, Sandra. Stop lallygagging around. I have to get back before my next appointment. You'll have to help me carry some stuff back to the office before you take off for the afternoon. C'mon. Strike a trot.'

Following him down the platform, she cast a quick look over the edge on to the tracks and felt faint. She never took the Transport if she could avoid it. The smells down here bothered her. Urine. Decaying food. Damp. They leeched on to her skin with fusty fingers. It was dark so she couldn't see details, but the tracks gleamed at her. They looked oddly familiar and menacing at the same time. Tiny shapes skittered between the rails. It brought the woman back into her head.

The woman. And other shadows that had been pressing more fervently to be heard lately. Shadows of a person raising a hand holding some kind of horrifying weapon with predatory claws at one end. Bashing it down on someone . . . something . . .

'Sandra!'

She'd walked on the back of Dr Hurtigger's shoes. She put her hand on his back to steady herself and quickly removed it when she felt the sweaty dampness of his shirt. *Why was he sweating? It was so cool down here.*

'Please, Dr Hurtigger, can I go back to the office? I'm feeling ill all of a sudden.' She looked up at him.

'You do look pale. All right. Go back to the office and wait for me. I'll do all the work as usual. Just leave.'

Sandra hurried out of the Transport station accompanied by huge waves of relief. All the way back to the office she considered her options. The shadows wouldn't leave her alone. She decided she'd give Dr Hurtigger her notice when he got back. She wanted to leave even if she didn't have another job to go to.

Sandra sat at her desk, rubbing silver whorls in the top while she waited for him. Her hands wouldn't keep still. When he came in she'd –

There he was. She stopped moving her hands. 'Dr Hurtigger! Can I have a minute?'

He carried on walking past her desk. He was balancing several bulky parcels in his arms.

'Dr Hurtigger?'

'Can't you see I'm busy?'

'Can I have a minute?'

'Certainly you *can*, Sandra.' He kept walking.

'I meant *may* I have a minute?'

'That's better.' He stopped and turned, looking at her with unreadable eyes. 'I have something important to ask you . . . to tell you . . .'

'Hurry up. I have to dissect that mouse you killed earlier. Is it ready?'

At Sandra's hesitant nod, he smiled. 'It's culling day today and I have to get back to Luca. She's ready to burst. I think we'll be able to cut off her head soon and use the rest of her as a nutrient host.'

Sandra felt sick. Why had she ever agreed to work for this . . . she forgot the words she was looking for. Oh, yes. Sick bastard.

'Well?'

'I'd like to give my notice. Two weeks. That should give you plenty of time to find someone else.'

'Impossible, I'm afraid.'

'Why?'

'Sorry, dear, I don't have enough time to train another receptionist. Besides, you'll be pleased I didn't let you leave when you see what's coming up. We'll be famous! In all the papers. You'd like that, wouldn't you? Your real parents might see and will be sorry they didn't want you.'

Sandra felt cold rage taking over her apologetic whimpering. 'But –'

'No. I don't want to hear another word about it.'

'You can't prevent me from leaving!' Sandra stood up, tall and proud. She pushed one of the files off her desk, and it landed in a flutter of papers on the floor by his feet.

'I can.' He gave a heavy sigh at the interruption to his schedule and went into his office. Sandra heard him unlock his desk drawer and pull out a file. It must be from 'Ongoing'.

He came back out and slapped a dusty red file on her desk. She didn't move.

'Open it.'

She couldn't.

'I didn't want to have to show you this. But you know the old movie phrase, "I made you, dear, I can unmake you"? It's a stupid hackneyed phrase, but one I find extremely apt in the circumstances. I grew you, Sandra, and I can certainly ungrow you.'

What?

He smiled at her and went out of the door.

Sandra looked down at the file. She was afraid to open it. *Don't be stupid.* She picked up the file and ran her thumbnail over the embossed cover. Very fancy, she thought.

'Project A9XXB,' a tinny voice croaked.

She had forgotten about the old speaking files. In her surprise at hearing the voice, she tilted the file and a photograph slipped out, landing on the floor at her feet. She bent down and picked it up by the edges. It was a picture taken of an 'incident' on the Transport line. After a suicide. The carnage on the photograph made her feel sick. She moved her fingers so that they wouldn't touch any of the 3-D colour. Bits lay on the tracks that looked like . . . There was a head lying there. With her own face. No, it wasn't hers. It was a man's face. Herbert's face.

She wasn't Hurtigger's mess-up. She was Hurtigger's scrape-up.

Sandra remembered who she was.

Who he was. *I'm him.*

Jump jump jump. The woman standing next to Herbert that day on the Transport platform had said that inside his head. You have no hope, no joy. Was she talking to him or herself? Didn't matter. His wife was leaving him . . . his daughters . . . jump step off ease the pain. One foot edged closer.

No i can't do it.

The muscles in his buttocks clenched. One more step. Jump man go. Soaring. *Upwards i flap my arms i fly.*

The swirling of the train's air rushing past him carrying hair and tiny flecks of skin stung his face like boiling raindrops. The flash of white-hot impact . . . the train driver's frightened face. Hitting the glass window. Impact. Nothing. Dark. Cool. Cold. Peace. Flicker of heat. Sizzling no go away stop i'm tired a bolt of heat the size and shape of an arm.

It tastes of silver. Electric prickling. Laser beams sewing him back together. A face. Hurtigger's face. Not Hurtigger's face . . . her face . . . his wife's face . . .

Why did you have to leave me?

Robby and his mother entered S-14. Sandra heard them whispering, through the grey haze of fright which was banging inside her head. The boy came over and tapped her shoulder. He asked her a stupid question and she got rid of him. She heard him running back to his mother.

'Mummy,' the boy said in a loud whisper, 'look at that woman. I think she's crying about the razzwherries. I asked her why she was so sad, and she tolme, Mum, she tolme she's loss her berry.'

Sunstroke

LUCA

A man with wings large enough and duly attached might learn to overcome the resistance of the air, and conquering it succeed in subjugating it and raise himself upon it.

LEONARDO DA VINCI

Something huge and dark passed across the surface of the sun, a ponderous invasion. The thing shifted. Retreated. Advanced.

Luca blinked several times, hoping it was just an irregular shadow floating past the round opening above her. She knew that air hole like it was her own mother. How could she not, when she spent all her waking hours fixating on it? Praying that the man wouldn't shut it off in some arbitrary display of playfulness or power. The opening was round and the size of a baby's fist. Glittery dust motes trickled past the corrugated edges into Luca's box during the day. Sun was hope, rounded and solidified. So was the air hole.

Parting her lips slightly, Luca wished she could suck the sun down into her mouth and tuck it into her cheek. It would taste of buttery caramel and burnt sugar. She'd keep it safe. Tickle the surface of it with her tongue and bite it gently, feeling its chewy golden resistance.

She was afraid most when the light faded from view every night. The minuscule drops of gold darkened and became just dim promise somewhere above. Luca spent the hours of darkness training her eyes on the spot where she thought it had been and beseeching it to come back. Praying that when day arrived the glowing sun wouldn't have gone away.

In the morning the golden roundel would appear, at first faint . . . then brighter . . . relief and warmth ebbing down, bathing Luca in its radiance. It was still there. The air hole hadn't been blocked off.

The dark thing moved again and sliced the orb of sun in half.

An eclipse, that's what it was. Something was blocking the sun. Her one link to the outside world. Her lifeline. Her air hole.

'Move!' Luca yelled.

The eclipse shifted. Fluttered. Breathed. It solidified into a shape. An object. An eye . . . an ear . . . an eye again . . . No, it's a mouse. An eclipse in the shape of a mouse with a human ear on its back. *I'll start thinking I'm Napoleon next.*

The mouse was looking at her through the air hole.

Luca opened her mouth and screamed as loud as she could. The mouse was going to block her air hole. She squeezed her eyes shut, feeling tiny crumbs of grit and dried tears that she couldn't wipe. When she ran out of screaming breath, she stopped. And heard something. The mouse? A high keening sound. Luca cracked open one eye. The mouse's mouth was open too, and it was screaming.

It. Was. Afraid. Of. Her.

Things must be bad.

'I'm sorry, mouse,' Luca attempted. She felt apologetic that she'd scared it so badly. It had closed its tiny rose-tinted mouth, but was still shaking. Luca cleared her throat. Her voice felt alarmingly unstable. Screaming for such extended periods of time didn't facilitate dulcet tones. She tried again.

'Help me?' she murmured. 'Please, mouse? I don't like it here.' *Go bite that sonofabitch with poisoned teeth and make sure he dies in agony. But get me out first.*

Luca managed her first laugh in ages. As she chuckled, her ribcage pressed against the top of her container, reminding her that she had to laugh small. *See? Bonkers. Here I am begging a mouse to get me out of here.* These were childhood nightmares gone all surrealistic and drug-induced, that was for sure. Abruptly Luca stopped chuckling. *Don't laugh.* Excessive emotion could kick off regeneration. *Houston, we have lift-off.*

She'd wait out the mouse. It would go soon, she hoped.

An hour passed. The mouse didn't go. On the other hand, it didn't seem that interested in blocking off her air hole either. Luca started hoping, in between the times that she hoped it would move its little mouse bottom as far away as possible, that it *would* block the air hole. Get it over with. *Kill me*.

Suffocate her. *Go on. Make my day*.

Eclipse the sun. *Move, mouse*!

The mouse remained unmoved.

She wouldn't be able to stand things as they were much longer. *Maybe if I hold my breath until I die*.

Just as she'd tried to punish her mother when she was small, Luca tried holding her breath as long as possible, but sneaky shreds of air leaked out. She gave up and gazed at the mouse again. It looked startled. As startled as a mouse could look with an ear like a waving hand wafting above it. No wonder it didn't move away from the air hole. Whenever it moved, the ear leaned tortuously. Luca felt a sharp pang of sympathy. It must feel awful, as if your guts were being pulled out from within you with a crochet hook.

Do you want to join me for a spot of suicide pact, mouse?

She got the funny impression, from a dark shadow crossing the mouse's face, that the idea wouldn't go amiss. That was, of *course*, if the mouse could understand English. And was into thought transference. Luca chortled. Could mice have Talk-Lang chips embedded in them, too? She'd worked as a temp for two weeks for Talk-Lang. Bunch of crooks. They upgraded their dodgy chips every two weeks to make people buy the new and improved version. They all talked about what crap the chips really were. They tested them on people in the hospital no-hoper wards.

She hoped nobody was taken in by the chip advertisements in the Transport stations. Utter crap. She should know. She'd designed the ads. Working as a computer-design temp brought you into contact with all kinds of iffy products. Once Luca had worked for a rice manufacturer and was astonished to find out what actually went into rice. She hadn't thought plastic would be one of the ingredients.

The products and companies all blended in after a while. The bicycle inner-tube packing company. Myriad failing banks. The bakery advertising campaign. It was all rather depressing, but enjoyable in a macabre way. It was fun being a temp. You never had to talk to people if you didn't feel like it. If you hated the job, you could just up and leave. If someone came up and was snippy to you, a little half-smile from you was all that was necessary. You could leave. *I'm off. Watch my dust.*

Continuity was a problem. Working for so many places you lost the capacity or the will to look for a permanent job. Luca had stopped looking. Your CV began to look quite fractured and frenetic, too. Personnel people always gave her condescending looks over the tops of their glasses while they read it. They told her with a contemptuous sneer how 'American' her CV was. Americans changed jobs a lot. Not like Brits, who worked their whole sorry lives in the same job. If they could *get* a job, that is. Personnel people always acted as if she was a bad smell wafting through their offices, but Luca wasn't bothered. If Americans took less guff from obnoxious companies, she was all for them.

Temping at the flotation tank place hadn't worked at all. They had wanted her to try out the different services before she designed the ads so that she could tell the clients exactly how the tanks felt. The flotation tanks. The Fear tanks.

Oh, Jesus. Get into a tiny enclosed place, filled with primeval slime or whatever it was . . . saline solution? Think about what you were frightened of, and then be surrounded by the damn things? Immersion therapy. Kill or cure. No, thanks.

Luca thought the idea had merit, but there was no way she'd ever try it. Being afraid of small enclosed spaces, she couldn't force herself into the tiny tank. The flotation tank boss, Rita, told her they couldn't employ her if she couldn't try them. You had to know the product before you could advertise it.

'Plenty more where you came from who'd be willing.'

'I'm off,' Luca had responded with relief. 'Watch my dust.'

Perhaps Dr Hurtigger visited the Fear tanks and got his best ideas there.

Dr Hurtigger. He had sucked her into this. He and the diet clinic temp job.

Thinking about him made Luca's panic return. Her breathing rate increased and the surrounding box walls shrank, pressing with clammy chumminess against her. Nervous sweat sprang in droplets from her, and the walls pressed closer with obsequious ardour. They became a friendly pooch, lolloping up to her, panting with doggy breath, butting her leg with his head . . . suddenly becoming a slavering beast, shagging her leg with that look of apologetic desperation.

The mouse looked at her. Black serene eyes.

Calm yourself. Breathe deeeeeply. Luca attempted the relaxation techniques she'd learned during her two-week stint at the hypnosis-tape place. They specialized in positive-thinking capsules you inserted in your ear to relax you. A voice would intone, as she did now, *You're lying on a sunny beach with loads of space around you. The air is warm and brushes your skin gently. Ocean waves crash upon the sandy shore.*

It was hard to visualize something she'd never seen. She breathed deeply, trying to capture the marine smell. The salty tang.

She smelt mouse instead. Damp earth. And her own unpleasantly rancid sweat.

Hypnosis and positive thinking couldn't work if you had distractions. Perhaps distraction was a good thing in these circumstances. If she couldn't distract herself, she'd think about where she was. How many tons of earth surrounded her? Think of the rinky-dink, small, tiny, minuscule, cramped, undersized, diminutive, miniature, little, puny box that she was locked into.

NO! The capsules said to shout no whenever you had bad thoughts. They never said anything about what to tell yourself should you wake up one morning buried alive. With only an air hole and an eerie mouse for company. Seriously remiss, she thought. You could develop a whole new marketing strategy. Hypnosis for the tortured? Positive thinking for captured victims? Creative visualization for rodents?

Luca found herself warming to both the mouse and its companion ear. It was only one ear, after all. It wasn't as if there was a whole crop of them. She wondered if the ear had been implanted, or whether it had been thought-generated. He was obviously the mad doctor's handiwork.

'You're a he-mouse, aren't you?' Luca addressed the bits of him that she could see through the hole.

The mouse's front paw tips were slung over the edge of the hole's rim. The paws looked manly.

Luca squinted up at him. He was wrinkly around the extremities, as if he'd lost weight recently. It gave him a vulnerable appearance, like a woman whose tights sagged at the ankles.

'I can tell you're a man-mouse. Your whiskers look macho. Besides, he wouldn't have implanted an ear that big and butch on a she-mouse.'

A pleasant, accommodating look settled on the mouse's features.

Luca found herself wanting to know who he was. 'What's your name?' *It could be anything.*

He wiggled his whiskers at her. Luca smiled. It was almost as if he could understand her. That would be a pleasant fiction. She would die buried in some bizarre version of a Sunday gardening experiment, chatting with a rodent.

Not a normal rodent. No, indeed. A rodent with an ear on its back.

Luca laughed until she was breathless.

At least she could see what kind of body part was on *him*. She couldn't look down to see what *she* had on *her*. She could feel them. What was it this time? A testicle between the toes, tickling her with springy pubic hair? A nice little nose in her armpit? A pervasive elbow in the groin?

Just thinking about them made her itch.

Itching was how each began.

After your thought processes betrayed you by being just that bit too detailed and creative, the regeneration process started. Cells gathered around a chosen spot and communed. Had a little soirée in your system. Consulted with each other. Decided on the best result.

It would start as a tiny itching. The feel of an incipient cold sore. A tingle. A tiny golden bell of warning. *Ding-a-ling.*

Luca winked at the mouse. 'Sing along with Luca's bells.' *Ding ding ding-a-ling.*

The mouse blinked, uncomprehending.

She had wondered when he was finally going to blink. He hadn't blinked or moved in ages. Just sat there, gazing at her like a meditative sphinx.

I'm not a freak show. 'Stop staring.'

She could never scratch the itch when it started. That was the problem about being in such a small box. Her arms and legs were pinned in position and she could only move her head left and right. Luca couldn't understand how the Japanese could sleep in those businessmen's hotels in Tokyo. She'd read about them. It sounded as if they were buried alive for one night in boxes just like her own. You couldn't move and the terror pressed down upon you until you felt as if everything in the world was above you and your body was light as air underneath. Falling. Plummeting deeper. Plunging into an abyss of terror where there was no sun and no escape.

Stop! She must remember not to dwell too long on one subject. If she did, the tingles became painful chancres. Then small lumps. Burning pieces of coal under her skin. The lumps erupted and became . . .

The mouse opened his mouth and clattered his teeth loudly.

As if to distract her.

'Thanks, mouse. You're a pal.' It was so hard trying to keep your thoughts from settling in one place too long. Almost as hard as keeping your mind totally blank. The more you pushed thoughts from your mind, the more forcefully they insisted on being heard. And if thoughts crept in, chancres crept out.

Dr Hurtigger was so excited when he lifted her lid and she'd grown a new crop of whatevers. At her first crop removal, he hopped from side to side on both feet, as thrilled as a small boy carrying his plastic farming bucket and scything knife.

'These are the results of intelligence. You're a bright woman, Luca,' he said. 'I like that in a person. A thinker.'

The harvesting felt no worse than the growing, even though Dr Hurtigger told her with regret that he couldn't use the normal anaesthetic on her.

'It would dull the synapses,' he said. 'Sorry, old girl. We want you to keep springing forth with these little beauties.'

He sprayed some stuff down the air hole fifteen minutes before he opened her box to paralyse all her muscles.

'Can't have you leaping for freedom now, can we?' He laughed, soft affection wrapping her like a cloak of slime. 'You're my masterpiece, so far. You'll be having some companions soon. We'll think about what's to be done with you after my other work in progress is ready.'

Luca burned with sympathy for the new work in progress.

At least the burning of the blade reminded Luca she was still alive and not in some horrible nightmare. After he finished with the scythe, Dr Hurtigger smoothed Heal Cream on to the wounds on her flaccid body. His hand was surprisingly gentle. It was so pale. Almost anaemic-looking. Did he stay in the dark all the time, too? Was he an albino? He said darkness was more productive.

'Do you know how people used to grow oyster mushrooms?' he chatted as he smoothed the cream.

Luca didn't reply. Her jaws were paralysed, too. She didn't think he needed an answer. He seemed perfectly happy with his one-sided conversations.

'You ordered special seeds from a catalogue. Black specks that looked like ants when you poured them into your palm. Oh, sorry. I guess that spot is tender still.'

Luca wished she could open her mouth and scream. His fingers continued to massage the cream on additional sore spots.

'You dipped a roll of toilet paper into a sink filled with water,' Dr Hurtigger continued. 'Not a used one, a new one. Until it was sopping wet. Then you lifted it out, pried apart a couple of layers without ripping them and sprinkled seeds randomly inside. Next you placed the whole contraption into a box, sealed it and put it as far back into a dark closet as possible. You couldn't risk air or light getting to the seeds.'

Or?

'Otherwise the spores would escape, wouldn't they?' he said, as if in answer to her silent question. Luca winced as the doctor's hand hit a sensitive spot.

Dr Hurtigger grinned at her, gums gleaming. 'You waited, and every few days you'd slice off a new crop of delicious mushrooms! How do you like that? Such prolific donors, those rolls of toilet paper.' He beamed as he put the cap back on the tube of cream.

She could see him still smiling as he closed her lid. Dr Hurtigger set the locking-pad device by pressing his hand on it. It beeped to register that the process was complete. She could hear him scatter earth over the top of the box, keeping the air hole free with a piece of paper rolled up into a tube.

'Bye-bye, Luca. Keep your chin up.'

Luca had heard him laughing enormously at his own joke as he walked away, his steps fading.

Luca wondered if she had the capacity to kill. She supposed that if you were locked up in enough small places and enough people did bad things to you it was possible. Only *you* were allowed to do bad things to yourself. Others joining in wasn't fair.

The mouse looked nervous.

'I was wondering if I had the capacity to kill Dr Hurtigger, not you.'

She imagined that the mouse looked relieved.

He did, surprisingly enough.

'What are you afraid of, mouse?' *I used to be afraid of so much.*

Being incarcerated seemed to have overridden most of her previous fears. Or at least coalesced them all into one quivering lump.

'What are you afraid of, Luca?' Dr Hurtigger had asked her at the diet-clinic interview. He seemed more interested in her thought processes than the other places at which she'd worked. She put that down to his medical background. He was a doctor. Of course he had a fascination with people's minds.

'Lots of things,' Luca said. She bet she'd be out on her ear after that admission, just like at the flotation tank place. She was a bad liar.

The doctor looked thrilled. 'Will you tell me about some of

them? Most of our clients are afraid of many things. Living. Dying. Gaining weight. Now that being larger is more fashionable, lots of people have let themselves go. Not like you.' He looked pointedly at her slight build and continued, 'But it becomes hard to keep control. Only a certain amount of fat is acceptable in today's society. Beyond a certain point, it's too much.' Dr Hurtigger paused briefly and then said, as if struck, 'Wouldn't it be helpful if you went through some of the diet treatments while you're here, so that you can better understand what we do?'

Luca preferred just doing the work and getting paid. 'Yes, please. It would be so exciting to experience your methods.' Smiling brightly, Luca wanted to stick her fingers down her throat and gag. 'I'd love to.' *To get this job, of course.*

Turning down that job at the flotation tanks had been a luxury she couldn't afford too often. Her C C account was strapped this week. Luca hoped the treatments wouldn't take long. She was happy with her eating disorders, thank you very much. She just needed a job.

'First, tell me more about those fears you mentioned.' Dr Hurtigger's mouth smiled. Luca figured his eyes would catch up eventually. He looked harmless enough, in a fish-like way.

'I can empathize with your patients and their fears. I'm obsessive about my weight sometimes.' Luca looked to see if she was giving him what he wanted.

Nodding with concerned sympathy, he motioned for her to continue. 'Go on. That's just like the other patients here. The Hurtigger Clinic is specifically for people who are obsessive about their weight. We deal with various other medical areas, but I won't bother you with that now.'

Luca had always been terrified of gaining weight and had done some stupid things in the past to avoid it. Flirting with bulimia had taken up a large part of her life for a few years. She had even become a vegetarian for two weeks, thinking that meat was making her bloat.

'Never eat anything which, if thrown on the floor, excites a dog,' Luca had once proclaimed to her ex-boyfriend. She had read that in the *Evening Standard*. The saying had impressed her.

He hadn't been impressed. But that was towards the end of their relationship. He told her she was too cold. Although it broke her heart into pieces at the time, now that she had a lot of time to think, she was glad it had ended. When she thought about it now, the tone of his voice had sounded awfully practised. As though he'd said the same thing many times before. Almost as if it was his way of exiting every relationship. His signature kiss-off.

The kiss-off was done in a restaurant, where he held her hand and sipped a glass of Sancerre *Blanc et Noir*.

'You can't mean it.' Luca felt as if he had punched her in the stomach.

'Sorry, Luca.' He took another sip, rolling the wine around in his mouth with a pleased expression on his face.

'Sorry for what? Sorry that you've brought me to a restaurant that has rubbery tiramisu or that you're leaving me?'

'We could have gone somewhere else.' He sounded aggrieved.

'Would it have made you feel better to break the news to me over a superior wine list?'

'Stop it. Can't you react like a normal woman? Cry? Beg me to stay? Instead you whinge about the tiramisu. Haven't you heard me?'

Luca recited, in a sulky monotone, 'I have no warmth. You feel frozen by my lack of response.'

'That's it. Do you understand what I'm saying?'

'If you want to leave, then do. It's my flat. Give me back my keys.'

He looked uncomfortable. 'I've got more stuff than you. I thought you —'

'It's my flat. If you don't want to be with me, then leave. I won't try to change your mind. If it's fate that you're to be with me, you will be. If it's not, you won't.'

'Yes. Yes. You can't change fate. I know. You tell me that all the time. Well, I'm fated to get up and leave this table. You're fated to watch me leave. I want to warm myself by going outside.'

'It's snowing.'

'Like I said, I want to warm myself.' He finished the Sancerre in one gulp and stood up.

Everybody thinks they're a comedian. 'Go then.' *Don't leave me.*

She had taken all the breadsticks at the table and broken them into tiny pieces. She was afraid to be alone.

'What else are you afraid of?' Dr Hurtigger appeared so pleased with her.

Luca racked her brain for more resident terrors. Death scared her. Ever since she'd seen that man jump in front of the train. He had been right next to her, standing beside a woman on his other side. The two of them looked as if they were in some silent form of communication, which had culminated in the man's jump. Luca had smelt his fear. It smelt like hot tar. The woman disappeared in the furore that erupted when the thump of the body hitting the train window was heard. Was that other woman afraid of death now, too? Luca couldn't help wondering.

Death was such an arbitrary hair's breadth away. One inch closer to or further from a train platform. One box buried underground here or there. One Transport strike more or less. The man had jumped on a strike day.

'And?' Dr Hurtigger prompted.

She'd always been afraid of mice, too. Ever since that horrid boy next door had found a dead mouse and brought it home. He had arranged it into a running position and frozen it in a plastic bag.

Because she ran over his invisible fort with her bicycle one day, he galloped up behind her and popped the frozen mouse down the neck of her new red LycraSyl blouse. The heat from her body began to defrost it. As she ran around in a frenzy trying to get it out of her blouse, the mouse's legs had scrabbled, the melting ice trickling down her spine.

Finally Luca managed to get her shirt off. She threw it at the little pig-face, who was laughing himself sick safely behind the neighbour's Rottweiler. She swore she'd get that boy some day. Addison was his name. Addy.

Dr Hurtigger's interest was seductive. Luca sat back and thought further about what he was asking. He was right. Fear crippled you.

Fear of food made you do such stupid things. Once she'd bought one of the diet tapeworms advertised in the back of a women's magazine. The ad promised that the worm could grow up to thirty feet long inside your intestines. Every bit of food you cared to throw at it would be snapped up in its maw, leaving you to remain thin, pale and interesting.

When it arrived in its sterile packaging, it was only two centimetres long. She cut it out of the plastic and dropped it into saline solution to reactivate it. Seeing it wiggle cheered her. It looked no more threatening than a worm at the bottom of a bottle of tequila. Before she could chicken out, she popped the reactivated worm into her Diet Sainsbury's Hot Chocolate, and drank the whole thing down.

She had to get the tapeworm removed long before it reached its full growth. The sensation was too unpleasant and her work suffered. The worm grew with phenomenal speed. After only two weeks, it was an unpleasantly full feeling in her guts. When she brushed her teeth at night, she opened her mouth wide and peered in the mirror. Could you see it? Would there be little glowing eyes down there? Yuck. Even losing ten pounds wasn't worth keeping it.

The removal wasn't much fun. She refused the poisoning option as she didn't want to risk it dying while it was inside her. If that happened, you had to wait while the thing was excreted, section by section. She decided on the easier option, but getting the tapeworm to exit the business end of her body rather than her mouth, which would have choked her, took ages. It had to be tempted out with a bit of cheese.

Dr Hurtigger was so sympathetic. He assured her that their diet methods were different from the norm, but amazingly effective. 'Don't be concerned if we act harsh with you during the treatment. It will all be a pretence just to show you.' At Luca's inquiring look, he continued, 'We've found that clients need to be locked up and pushed around. If you give them too much choice, they fail with their diets.'

Luca wondered if that grey-haired woman she'd seen charging around the halls on her way into the interview was one of the patients. She was probably doing her daily jog, or something. She had long flowing silver hair. Luca ran her hands through her own short spiky red hair and sighed. She liked long hair.

'Shall we get started?' Dr Hurtigger waved to the door. 'Sandra will take you away and fit you out with the prison garb.' He winked. 'Act the part! You'll be a sullen patient, truculently refusing all efforts to help you. Have fun.'

After Luca had been outfitted and manacled by the doctor's assistant, Sandra led her to another office. Without a word, she indicated that Luca should sit in the blue-velvet wing chair facing an imposing steel desk with matching chair. Luca relaxed into the chair and watched Sandra walk to the door. She had an odd, almost mannish walk, which contradicted her slight feminine build and frosty-tipped fingernails.

Dr Hurtigger came in, passing Sandra, clearing his throat and pushing up his sleeves. He went and sat down behind the steel desk. 'Come here,' he ordered.

Luca uncoiled herself obediently from the recesses of the chair. 'If I must,' she spat, as she sauntered towards him. Playing the resistant patient was fun. She hadn't acted since she was a kid. As Luca walked towards him, she pretended she was as tall and pale as a strand of fettucini. She screamed disdain for the man at the desk with every slow and considered step.

Luca noticed that a pearl of sweat was trickling down Dr Hurtigger's neck. It disappeared into the folds of his white coat. Why did he look so nervous? The tinkling sounds of her restraint chains amused her.

'Hurry up,' Dr Hurtigger snapped. 'Don't take all day about it.'

Luca snorted. 'How fast would you walk with manacles clamped around your ankles?' She tried to sound exactly as a peeved overweight patient would – the same buttery, even tones, the same faint stench of insubordination ebbing towards him.

'This is for your own good.'

'Of course.' Her face was calm as milk.

He took a deep breath and picked up a glass ampoule that had been lying on his desk. Leaning forward, he showed it to Luca. 'Haägen Dazs – *circa* 1996,' the curled label read. He smoothed it with one pale finger. 'Triple Chocolate Brownie Peanut Butter Overload.'

'This will hurt me a lot more than it'll hurt you.' His voice stretched uncomfortably around the words. 'That's what we do to bulimics. You shouldn't have tried the tapeworm trick.' His eyes glittered with what looked like venom. 'Stand up straight,' he ordered.

The doctor certainly was getting into his part.

Setting down the ampoule, Dr Hurtigger wiped one sweaty hand on the back of his trousers. 'We know.' He picked up the ampoule and flicked off the silver cap. 'When you stop gaining weight, it's the first thing we suspect.'

Luca laughed. 'I lost ten pounds at least.'

'You have to stop fighting us.' He held up the ampoule to the light and admired the tiny milky drop that clung to the inside of the glass. 'You will lose weight our way or not at all.'

Luca watched Dr Hurtigger with curiosity. Despite the nervousness, he was playing the game well. Authoritative dictator diet-clinic doctor.

'I'm getting tired,' she said. 'Can we stop now?'

She felt a hand come up from behind her and stuff a rag in her mouth. Sandra's hand. Stopping must not be an option.

Dr Hurtigger talked about different options as he shut her into the box. Luca tried to think that it was a sick joke or over-enthusiastic diet methods. She gave up those ideas when he shut the lid of the box and started to trickle earth on top.

'I'm not burying you alive,' he said soothingly. 'I have to make sure you're in the dark, can't escape, and nobody can find you. The police, were they actually to find this room, would think it a fine example of a medieval wine cellar.'

Luca heard bottles clinking. Dr Hurtigger's eye wove into view above her. 'I won't let you suffocate,' he added comfortably. 'I've left you a nice air hole to breathe through. Right under the window so you can catch some sun.'

It took Luca months to give up hope that he would let her go. He brought her out of the box periodically, but not with any silly ideas of freeing her. She was brought out for experiments.

'Perfect. You're nice and white and squidgy now. The nutrients I've been spraying down the hole have really plumped you up. Time for the mushrooms!'

At her look of horror, he laughed. 'Just kidding. Can't you take a joke? I wouldn't implant mushrooms on you. Give me *some* credit.'

During the escalation of the experiments, he fiddled with this and changed that. She was kept blindfolded and gagged when her box was uncovered and she was lifted out. He continued to use the paralysing spray. But sometimes he'd leave the dosage low so that she could still speak.

He took off her gag when he started culling her body of the growths. He talked to her as he worked.

'You're an equal partner, Luca,' he told her earnestly. 'Talk to me. Tell me what you're feeling.'

'I feel like bashing your face in.'

'That's not very sociable.' Tutting, he rolled her over to reach a growth on her side. Although she didn't know what was erupting from her, she felt dull pain that flared into a burning orange radiance when the knife was used to slice off whatever it was.

'Damn,' he muttered. 'I couldn't get the root of this one. I'll have to dig around with the knife tip. Sorry.'

The point of the knife bit into her flaccid body like shark's teeth. She wanted to twist away from the burning poison of the knife, but could only scream. The rest of her body remained paralysed.

He muttered to himself. Luca wasn't sure if he was talking about past experiments or planning new ones. He rambled on about different people. He seemed angry with people from his past.

'They'll see,' he said with smug satisfaction. 'The project I started when you were just a little girl is about to come to fruition.' Waving the scythe, he flicked a few drops of Luca's blood on to her face.

Dr Hurtigger noticed her blinking, and he gave her a top-up spray of the paralysing juice. 'Can't have you popping out for a jog, now can we?' he asked her cheerfully.

Luca wished she could see what he'd grown on her. He was careful to keep her blindfolded until just before he shut her box lid.

'If you see what they are, you might start fixating on them when you're in your box. Thoughts are catalysts and I don't want them popping out willy-nilly. Controlled growth, that's what I want.'

No comment.

'I'm like God, aren't I, Luca? I have power over so much. The electrical current of life itself.'

Luca felt sick at the mention of the current.

He mumbled about his parents. They must annoy him because he chopped more aggressively when speaking about them.

'I told them I'd be a success,' she caught once. 'My experiments are better than theirs.'

Oh, Jesus. Were his parents fruitcake body-part farmers? Did it run in the family?

Three other names made up the bulk of his muttering.

A name, something like 'Merino', came up the most. She figured highly in his future plans. A jewel on the crown of abominations.

Slice. Slice. 'Electricity is the catalyst for the two of them,' Dr Hurtigger confided to Luca. He dropped another whatever in a nutrient bath. Plop plop fizz fizz.

Luca yearned to see what it was he had just taken off her. *Two of who?*

Merino apparently had a sister. Win or some-such. She had apparently been overexposed. Too much electricity.

'Thank goodness I still had Merino.' He giggled. 'Poor Win. She'll have trouble if she ever gets angry.'

Luca thought about the two names. Win and Merino. They

twisted throughout his conversation on and on and on. Luca grew sick of them. There was a third name that she couldn't catch.

'Merino's the one to place me in the history books, Luca. She was totally successful with the second stage of the experiment except for a hitch near the end. She's ready for the third and final stage shortly. I'm ready to call her back in.' He looked down at her. 'Are you wondering why such a delightful young woman would keep coming back to me? Easy . . .'

Making a last cut with a flourish, he put down the scythe.

'During the first stage I implanted her with a call-back feature. She comes back whenever I'm ready. I couldn't keep her until she matured. The Board wouldn't agree to the residency expense.'

Dr Hurtigger wiped his hands. He began to put away his equipment, rinsing his dishes and scythe. Luca heard him running water. He continued talking as he clattered metal pans. When he tucked Luca's box back into the ground and took off the blindfold, she shut her eyes. She couldn't bear to look at him. He chuckled as he closed the lid. 'She'll make up for everything soon. She and . . .'

Luca lost the last name again as he sprayed her with time-release nutrient spray and slapped the locking pad with his palm.

Luca had listened to his footsteps recede. He'd return. He was as regular as a metronome.

Hurtigger's footsteps approached. Luca saw the mouse's head jerk sharply towards the door. The doctor was back for the next culling.

'Get lost, mouse! He's coming!' Luca hissed.

The eclipse went suddenly and Luca's sun was once more whole. She felt a strange sense of loss.

She heard Dr Hurtigger rattling around the room.

'Where is that damned mouse? I don't have time for this . . .' mumble mumble ' . . . can't keep Luca waiting.' The box lid creaked open and Hurtigger's pallid face peered in at her. 'Oooh, we have a lovely bunch today! More than ever.' He rubbed his hands together and set to work. 'I'll have to mouse hunt after I finish here. Even though you've replaced him in my affections and experimental regard lately, I can't let him wander about. He might scare the cleaning woman.'

Dr Hurtigger's hands approached her face with the blindfold. 'I'll have to catch the little bugger and put him to sleep. I've no more use for him.'

When Dr Hurtigger had finished the culling session and gone mouse hunting, Luca lay in the dark feeling helpless. Her air hole remained round and empty. She felt bereft. Positive thinking didn't get you anywhere. She balled her hands into fists and pounded against the lid until she could feel blood leaking down between her fingers. She longed to put her fingers in her mouth for comfort.

She used to believe she could fly while she walked to school. If you strained really hard, you could fly above the crowd. That was positive thinking. See where it had got her then and see where it was getting her now.

Nowhere. Not a sausage. Living with hope is killing me. *I want to die*. Luca closed her eyes wearily.

Frantic chittering roused her. The mouse was looking down at her. He had wire stuck in one of his teeth. She wished she could help him get it off.

Had the mouse been watching somewhere while Hurtigger did his business? Did he watch Hurtigger close the lid, lock it and go off hunting for his escaped experiment?

'Get lost, mouse! He'll be back to look for you.'

The mouse left. Luca felt better. At least one of them could escape.

She heard scraping above her. Tiny fistfuls of dirt were scratched off the lid and pushed to the side. Mouse? He was near the edge by the locking pad. Luca listened without comprehension, and suddenly it clicked. He was scrabbling over the locking pad. It wasn't random meandering. He was clearing dirt off the pad.

He walked round and round on it, obviously trying to set off the unlocking mechanism. Luca heard the frustrated tick-tack sound of his claws. After several minutes her exhilaration died.

The pad must need a human's touch to set it off. The mouse's weight was too insubstantial even with the human ear.

The mouse must have come to exactly that conclusion at the same instant as Luca. She heard him retreat to the far end of the lid and take a running approach to the locking pad. His claws galloped above her, running the entire length of the box. Then silence, when he must be soaring in the air . . . twisting . . . falling . . . landing ear-first right smack on the locking pad.

The lock unclicked. *Houston, we again have lift-off!*

Luca lay back. It was no use. She didn't have the strength to push open the lid. The sun darkened. The mouse looked anxiously down the hole at her. Luca looked up at him. He had strained to fly above the crowd. For her. He'd succeeded.

She had to try.

If he can live with that ear, I can live with whatever.

That doesn't mean Hurtigger has to live.

'Okay, mouse, shift yourself. I don't want you falling over yourself when I spring like a phoenix out of here.' The sun became round.

Afraid to try, in case it was a cruel fantasy, Luca hesitated before she pressed her palms against the inside of the lid. She didn't have much room to manoeuvre as she couldn't bring her arms towards her chest to use the power of her elbows. Could it be done? She drew her knees up to use them for extra leverage.

Luca sensed the mouse's tension outside her box. His ear must be fluttering with tension. 'Hurry,' she sensed him urging her. 'We don't have much time.'

Luca pushed, her body shuddering with effort. Lying in a box for ages hadn't done her muscles much good. Hearing footsteps in the hall, she decided her muscles worked after all. Adrenaline was a powerful motivator. She pushed the lid upwards and a shower of dirt slid off. She sat up and found herself eye to eye with the mouse. His eyes gleamed and dirt encrusted his ear.

A tiny smut rested on his nose.

She reached over. He didn't flinch. She bet he was the only one who wouldn't flinch. Everyone else would when they saw her. She brushed the smut off his nose. 'They can watch our dust, mouse.'

Luca picked him up and placed him next to her neck, tucking him behind her hair. She'd been in the box so long that her spiky hair had become longish lank hair. She hoped it wasn't unpleasant for him. 'Sorry, mouse, I haven't had a chance to wash.'

Luca brushed her hair over him to create a curtain. It was difficult to cover the ear too. She didn't have the thickness of hair to deal with that. She hoped nobody noticed that she had three ears.

Climbing out of the box, she rested several times. Her muscles took an awful lot of convincing to work. They hadn't totally atrophied but they were terribly weak. Swinging her legs over the edge of the box, she rested again.

An amused woman's voice erupted from the other side of the room.

'Just look at that! I've got to shake your hand. You're the best one I've seen.'

Sandra was standing at the door, her tea-coloured hair swept up in a loose ponytail. She held a broom, as if she'd been sent to sweep the laboratory. Her other hand was outstretched towards Luca.

The mouse chittered by her neck.

You're right. I'm not really in a position to annoy her, am I? Luca stuck out her hand. 'Nice to meet you.'

The woman smiled. 'Likewise.' She shook Luca's outstretched hand. 'Nice to meet *all* of you. I think you're going to need some of my cling-film to flatten some of them if you're leaving.'

Luca looked down. In the adrenaline of escaping, she'd forgotten that she now could.

Looking down was a mistake.

Tabling the Motion

DYSIS

'All right,' she said calmly, 'I'll thcream
then. I'll thcream, an' thcream, an' thcream
till I'm thick.

RICHMAL CROMPTON

'Just Wynne,' she said, her voice halting the squabbling in the meeting room as effectively as if she'd shot a pistol into the air. 'I'm here to apply for a job as an electrician.'

Dysis stood well back in the hallway, chuckling. That girl possessed a superb sense of drama. *What an entrance!* Admiringly, Dysis shook her grey curls and looked at the young woman she and Ricker had followed all day. The strike mess earlier had created the ideal opportunity to go up and talk to her. There she was, bellowing in the middle of the crowd with her dress and stomach billowing around her. Flames and sparkles shot from her head giving the impression of a fiery Medusa. Dysis still hadn't a clue how she did it. It couldn't just be special effects. A child born of this woman would be a smashing one, she was sure.

It had been a long time coming. When Ricker had asked her to work part-time in the gene clinic, at first she'd been reluctant. She already had so much to do. But Ricker convinced her that it would be the chance to utilize resources more effectively. If they received a gene request for a child from either Estra, Wynne or Marina, she'd be in the perfect place to alter the chromosomes. Besides, they just weren't getting enough donors from any of their existing sources. People weren't going to diet clinics any more.

'A chance to begin the abnormality at source,' he had crowed. 'Think of the possibilities if we can tamper with a child from the beginning. And one that comes from an already enhanced parent!'

Dysis was so proud of Ricker. He worked so hard. The Board should treat him better. She had been worried about him lately. His hands had a tremor that hadn't been there before. His eyes were manic. As for their own relationship, they weren't spending as much time together, which saddened her. Perhaps if she could get this baby for him successfully, things would improve.

To pretend that Ricker was a tourist in order to approach Wynne this afternoon had been inspired. He was so full of ideas, that man. Dysis beamed with admiration. A tourist! When you were Canadian, even if you had lived in London for donkey's years, people still assumed you had just blown in on the last boat.

'How long are you visiting?' they burbled, willing to overlook your temerity in being one-of-those people who came in to suck up the welfare system. Use up the taxes. Move into bed-and-breakfasts with all your myriad family and distant cousins.

Forty-seven years, you donkey brains. I pay my taxes. Not that she was bitter or anything, mind you.

Watching Wynne was fascinating. She was poised like a charred ballerina about to fly on stage. She stood at the entrance to the Arbitration Meeting room, her muscles corded with tension. Her soot-smeared hand clutched the side of the doorway, as if to brace herself, and the other hand curved round to cradle her child.

Wynne's dress was a mass of scorched flowers and shreds of material. The blue faded to black in sections, and the flower petals were an angry burnt scarlet. One shoe was missing, and her hair looked as if it had been through a high wind sideways. An unidentified odour crept apologetically from her, which made Dysis feel queasy. *What is that?* A smell of burning and dampness like wet leaves . . .

Wynne suddenly cried out in dismay, clutching her stomach with both arms and looking down in horror. Dysis saw what she was looking at. The damp peaty smell had been Wynne's waters breaking. She was about to have her baby.

Not in front of all these people! Dysis panicked. What if they all ran out into the hall? They'd go and find a doctor, wouldn't they? She pressed her substantial figure into the wall as far as possible and held her breath. There wasn't time to run. The noise level increased in the room but nobody ran out. They seemed shocked immobile. The fuss they started making then was comical. Hadn't they ever seen a baby being born?

Probably not, she reflected. Babies weren't born in the normal way any more. They had to be requested well in advance. What balderdash was invented in the name of futuristic medical advances.

Would they know what to do? Curious, Dysis leaned forward and peered inside the room. Wynne didn't notice her – she was trying to wipe up the puddle underneath her with part of her burned skirt. She kept overbalancing with the swaying of her huge stomach and had to put out a hand to brace herself.

Dysis squinted. Her eyes weren't as sharp as they used to be. Ricker's eyesight was going too. Whenever they went to bed, they had to make sure they placed both pairs of spectacles within easy reach on the bedside table. It never failed, though: one pair of glasses always wandered off. You patted around blindly in the morning but the darned things must get up in the middle of the night and fling themselves on to the floor. You swung one foot out from under the covers, stepped carefully and *smaaaaassssh!* that's where they were. It was best to have several pairs of glasses.

Ricker got so annoyed when she stepped on his glasses that she tried to put off his finding out for as long as possible. Surreptitiously she'd shove the mangled bits of metal and smashed lenses underneath the bed. Snicking her foot back under the covers, she would reach over to distract him from getting up. There were lots of nice ways to distract a man in the morning. He flushed such a pretty pink colour when she rubbed his tooty-frooties. His arms crept around her and he forgot all about finding his glasses.

They had never used those ridiculous gene-request places to have a child. There were much better ways of getting one. How did you expect to rear a healthy well-rounded child when you submitted a cold and calculated request for it?

'Quick, get her on the table!' she heard an enterprising young woman shout. Wynne was pulled into the room by several pairs of arms and hustled up on to the shiny mahogany table. Cups of water, pocket computers, thought recorders and the ubiquitous symbolic pads of paper and fake yellow pencils were swept aside.

'What do we do next?' a man cried, panic making his voice high and young-sounding.

'Should we fetch hot water?' someone asked. 'Blankets?'

'Don't be stupid,' someone else replied. 'That was only in old movies. We need dry ice.'

Dysis chuckled with ill-humoured glee. This ought to be entertaining.

'I can't be having this baby,' Wynne's thin voice cried, above the noise of the crowd. 'My delivery appointment at the gene clinic isn't until Sunday! I'm not supposed to be having it yet . . . Ooooooooow!'

Time and tide wait for no man, Dysis thought. *Or electricity and childbirth.*

Thank the Good Lord and his spotty dog she'd found Wynne again.

Dysis had been frantic when she had lost her in the Transport tunnels an hour before. She walked back and forth in front of the LOT building next to the tunnel entrance, scanning all the people hurrying past. She clutched her handbag close to her body and made sure the top button of her dress was closed, in case of roaming pickpockets and sex maniacs. She peered into the foyers of the nearest buildings. One led to a hospital, and she hurriedly backed out. Despite the very real necessity for continued association with hospitals, the odours in them repelled her. Nurse Johnson always carried that medicinal smell with her when she brought them bodies.

In her effort to find Wynne, Dysis accidentally stepped on the back of several people's shoes. One woman swung her head round when Dysis trod on her. Her eyes looked manic and Dysis could have sworn upon her mother's grave that when the sheet of lank hair swung, it revealed that the woman had three ears. Dysis had no time to waste and pushed past, muttering an apology.

She was overwhelmed with relief when Wynne reappeared at the mouth of the tunnel access door, but stunned by her appearance. Something had happened to her down there. Dysis cooed in proprietary alarm. She hoped whatever it was hadn't harmed the baby.

She waved frantically for Ricker to get the car, and followed

Wynne up the stairs into the LOT building, staying well back in the hallway when she burst open the door to the Arbitration Meeting room.

Dysis watched as Wynne was arranged on the table.

Not very private, is it, honeybun? Lying there with your skirt up to high noon, your frooty-tooties hanging out for all the world to see. I bet you wished you'd never burst in there, huh?

People bustled around the supine woman, for all the world like the cast of a TV medical drama.

Some hospital delivery this was going to be. The thought of the last hospital she'd been in almost plunged her spirits down to her sensible grey lace-ups. She hadn't been in a hospital for ages. Twenty-five years or thereabouts. Since she'd brought little Timmy home. Just stepping into the hospital foyer before had brought it all back. The same multitudinous slapping of rubber-soled shoes. The same acrid medicinal smells.

The sharp scent of disinfectant had drifted past her during that last visit to the hospital. Dysis had waited for ages in the waiting room. She wrinkled her nose in distaste and settled back into the hard plastic seat. The friction created an embarrassing 'blu-uuuurrrrrrp' sound as she shifted. Scanning the chair-filled room to see if anyone thought it was *her* making a rude noise, she prepared to volunteer the information that it had been an aeroplane overhead, but the other people looked as if they hadn't noticed.

There weren't many people. Just one tired-looking young girl of seventeen or eighteen, wearing tight purple jeans and a gauzy shirt far too revealing to be worn out in public. Why, she could see her breasts through the fabric! Dysis tsked in disapproval. *Slut.*

Next to the hussy was a little boy with a runny nose and a line of grizzle that wouldn't quit. Dysis couldn't figure out how old he was. Two? Three? Why was he still wearing a diaper then? He should be out of them by now, surely. How old were children when they started talking?

'Mummy,' he whined, 'wanna go home!'

Dysis was surprised. The woman looked far too young and irresponsible to be anyone's mother. She did have pretty blue hair, the colour of the frosted plums that used to grow in Papa's garden. *I bet it's not her real colour.*

Dysis patted her own short greying curls absentmindedly, thinking to herself that her new wig was really quite fetching. It had cost the earth. But what was life for if you couldn't give yourself occasional treats? She'd passed the maternity ward on the way here. Catching a glimpse of herself in the glass, she'd been pleasantly surprised. 'Hello, you old thing.' She smiled to herself, baring her new platinum dentures. They were somewhat glary and flamboyant for a forty-year-old, but she could chomp apples and corn-on-the-cob now like nobody's business. It was a shame all her teeth had fallen out so early – a nasty side effect from all the chemical substances she and Ricker used. That and the passive electricity she absorbed when administering shocks. Those jolts made your teeth quake in their sockets. Apparently.

She was surprised at how much like her mother she looked. Broad, shelf-like bosom upholstered in a loud floral print, closed modestly at the neck with three delicately pretty pearl buttons in the shape of love knots. Small pale eyes and a sweet shy smile. She turned sideways and focused her attention on her stomach. She smoothed one hand, and then the next, with viciously chewed fingernails, over her stomach. She wished she weren't so blobby. It looked as if she were pregnant. And she never had been. Not once! She'd been careful. Most women of her age had several children by now. Sudden fierce anger curdled her satisfaction.

Dysis twisted the pearl buttons as she sat and shifted uncomfortably in the plastic seat. A sudden sharp itch craved attention from somewhere down the middle of her back. She moved repeatedly back and forth against her chair to try to scratch at the bra strap digging into her without the young mother noticing. Her bra didn't fit. She'd grown out of it. Fat just seemed to pile right on. She was always growing out of her clothes.

Good thing Ricker liked his woman with lots of handles to

grab. She should lose a few pounds. More than a few. The doctors had told her she had to lose weight or else.

Or else. Such silly useless little words. Such empty threats. If people threatened, they should have something to threaten with. Something significant. Not empty threats.

Coming today had taken a lot of effort and willpower. She had spent enough time in hospitals as a child.

A huge wave of exhaustion hit her and she yawned, her jaw cracking loudly in the room's silence. Hospital waiting rooms always had that indefinable air of tedium. Random piles of musty out-of-date magazines with gleaming smiles and missing pages. Querulous children carping at their mothers. Like that one sniffling and snorting next to her now. The boy left his inattentive mother and shuffled up to Dysis, staring at her rudely. 'You're fat,' he said. *He must be older than three.*

'Why hello there to you, too, cute little man,' she said, bouncing him a huge rubbery smile. He looked up at her with sulky eyes. Drool criss-crossed his face like silvery snail tracks and gave his face the surprising impression of a road map.

'Would you like a piece of chocolate, sweetness? I think I've got some somewhere.'

Dysis rustled in her large leather handbag and, at the same time, gave the child's mother a conspiratorial wink. She always had problems with winking, so her face contorted awkwardly and both eyes squeezed shut. Not the most effective wink. She hoped the girl was reassured. 'We've got to keep the wee kiddies happy. These long waits are always so distressing for them, don't you think?' The girl, who had first looked tense and suspicious, relaxed. Her shoulders slumped and she brushed a lank strand of hair back behind one ear.

'Timmy's not had his lunch yet, and we've been here for absolutely . . . *absolutely* hours. They told us we had to come in for that new multi-jab. The one that covers all childhood diseases. Supposed to prevent just about everything a child could pick up. Chicken-pox, measles . . . Thank the nice lady.'

Timmy had grabbed the piece of dusty chocolate Dysis had

found, unwrapped and was holding out to him. He stuffed it in his wet, pink-rimmed mouth and ignored them both as he masticated.

'Timmy!' his mother snapped. She threw an apologetic glance at Dysis. 'It's so difficult to teach them manners these days. I get so awfully, *awfully* tired. I'm a student, you know.'

A student of something worthless, Dysis was sure. She hated people who repeated themselves. *Repeated themselves*. 'I'm sure it won't be long now,' Dysis said, as she patted Timmy's head gingerly.

'You're a fine-looking young man, aren't you?' Surreptitiously she wiped her hand on her slightly too tight skirt in case he had head lice, as so many children had these days. Or 'cooties', as they had called them in her day.

'Dysis has cooties! Dysis has cooties!' the nasty little brats had cried in the school yard and had danced around her fat pink ten-year-old self. Dysis remembered it as plain as day. Cringing in the middle of the circle of jeering children, their eyes and mouths cruelly flashing at her, fingers pointing without letting up. At her. All the time at her.

She had a good memory. She remembered everything.

Timmy gaped and stuck his finger up his nose with baleful disinterest.

Nasty little toad, Dysis thought. *I bet you've got cooties. You should be smacked*. A good hiding never hurt anyone. Look how well *she*'d turned out, after all. Sure, you could go overboard. Hadn't her foster father whispered to her before he died that he'd perhaps disciplined his children 32 per cent too much? 32 per cent too much! How had Fospop arrived at that figure? Had he counted? Multiplied? Did he mark each episode in a little black book?

> *Dysis—*
> *Tuesday / one punishment.*
> *Thursday (big day) / five punishments.*

It was more like 98 per cent too much.

Fosmom hadn't helped.

'Wait till your father gets home and has his dinner,' Fosmom had shrieked at Dysis, waving her wooden spoon. Spaghetti sauce spattered the cheerful daisy-patterned wallpaper.

'You're in big and I mean B-I-G trouble now!'

Fosmom clonked her on the top of her head for emphasis, the spoon tangling in her hair. Tomato sauce dribbled down the side of Dysis' face, mingling with hot tears that refused to stop.

Dinner was poisoned for her from that point on, even if it was her favourite lentil soup with ham hocks and carrots.

'Pass the salt, please,' Fospop addressed the table. Dysis' hand shook as she passed it to him. She couldn't swallow past the corrosive lump of fear lying fallow in her throat, much less eat the food in front of her, knowing what was to come later. It always did.

Fospop shook his head with distress as he took off his worn black belt and coiled it around his fist. 'You talked back to your mother, Dysis.' Rueful sadness further thinned his already slender lips, and he ran his free hand through his sparse hair, making it stick straight up like ruffled swamp grass. 'You were bad. That's not allowed. I'll have to teach you a lesson.'

Dysis wanted to pee. So badly, she thought she'd wet her pants if she didn't go. 'I'm sorry, Fospop. I won't do it again, I promise.' At the shuttered look on his face, she trailed off and pressed both her legs together.

'Tell me what you need.' His voice was cold and distant.

'No, please . . .' she begged faintly.

'*Tell me what you need.*'

Dysis whispered, 'I need to be whipped.'

'Louder. I can't *hear* you!'

'I NEED TO BE WHIPPED.'

He whipped her then and didn't stop until she screamed. Dysis knew, from previous experience, that if she held on and refused to give him the satisfaction of screaming, he'd keep on, his face growing more and more furious. She didn't recognize him when he got that angry. His face became as puffed and purple as a blowfish. When she finally couldn't bear it any more and screamed, his anger escaped as if chased out by demons. The livid purple colour ebbed away from his face.

'Well?' he asked.

'Yessir?'

'What do you say?'

'Thankyousir.'

'You're welcome, sweetheart. Any time.' He smiled at her, his eyes softening. He patted her on the head and went off to read the paper. The spot on her head where he had patted her burned for hours afterwards. As strong a burn as the welts on her back from the metal belt buckle.

Dysis shifted uncomfortably in her plastic seat. The waiting was doing her head in and her bra strap still itched. Why had Fosmom let him whip them so often? Was she afraid his anger would turn on her if she intervened? Would his belt buckle wrap around her? Surely Fosmom could have done something when Fospop had broken Dysis' arm. She and her brother had been playing with the cat.

Dysis loved playing with cats. Fluffy was great fun to experiment with.

'Look, Ricker,' she said. 'I'll show you something.'

'I'm playing with her,' he whined. 'You can have her after.'

Dysis grabbed Fluffy and pulled. Her larger mass meant that Ricker lost the other end of the cat quickly.

'Watch,' she said, over his wailing. Trapping Fluffy between her knees, she tore a strip of newspaper and put it around the cat's stomach like a paper belt. Taping the ends closed, she put the cat down on the floor. Fluffy, in paroxysms of relief, leaped to her feet and raced for escape. At least the front part of her did.

'Jeez,' Ricker said, awed. 'What have you done?'

Proudly, Dysis told him how you could interrupt a cat's nerve transmission from its head to its back legs. 'Easy-peasy,' she said. 'See? The paper's not even tight. Teddy down the street showed me how.'

They watched Fluffy desperately attempting to get up and walk, but the hind end of her body just lay behind her with slug-like torpor. She made a low growling moan and tried to drag her body across the floor. Being paralysed from the waist down made it difficult.

Dysis shrieked with laughter while Ricker looked on in horrified fear. She reached down and whipped off the piece of paper and Fluffy streaked away, all four legs scrabbling.

'See?' she said. 'Fluffy's fine.'

'Now she's gone and I was playing with her,' Ricker snarled. Dysis had to smack him to shut him up. His crying would attract undue attention. Their squabbling got out of hand and Ricker saw Fospop looming up behind Dysis before she sensed his presence.

'I was sleeping,' Fospop said, his voice a deep icy lake. You could drown in just those three words. Drown with no hope of being saved. 'You woke me up.'

'Sorrysirwediddenmeanit,' both she and Ricker muttered.

Fospop was not appeased. 'You deserve to be punished. Tell me what you need.'

'We need to be whipped,' they chorused with resignation.

Dysis thought Timmy would profit from a whipping. One of Fospop's silver belt buckle specials. The boy had stopped putting his fingers up his nose, but his whining was becoming louder and more annoying. He wanted to sit on his mother's lap. He wanted to get down. Changed his mind. Got back up and kicked his mother's purple-clad legs with angry feet.

'Timmmmeeeeeeee!' she cajoled.

Timmy whined right back in the exact same tone. 'Mummmmmmeeee!'

The escalating pitch of a child's crying was enough to drive someone to murder, Dysis thought.

Finally Timmy's mother had had enough, and shoved the squirming noisy bundle off her lap. Picking up a magazine, she waved it in the direction of some toys on the floor across the room.

'Go on, Timmy darling, leave Mummy in peace for five minutes.' Rolling her eyes and smiling at Dysis in friendly collaboration, she sighed. 'We mothers have so much to put up with,' the smile seemed to say.

Timmy's diaper made him walk slightly bow-legged, a mewling John Wayne. He trundled past Dysis, on his way to the distant panoply of toys. Dysis cast a quick sideways glance at his mother and saw that she was deep into '40 Ways to Enchant A Man'. Sneakily, she moved one of her feet, clad in their sensible grey lace-ups and tan lisle stockinettes, out in front of the boy. In his fascination with the promise of new toys to break, he didn't see the carefully situated obstruction. When one pudgy foot butted into Dysis' ankle, over he crashed, smacking his head against one of the plastic chairs. Dysis snatched her leg back and sprang up.

'The poor wee mite!' Over his mounting screams and accusing looks, she gazed worriedly at Timmy's mother, who had dropped her magazine as she was about to discover the thirty-eighth way to enchant a man. Frantic, the girl squatted down next to Timmy and threw her arms around him. 'Timmy. Sweetie. Darling! Let me kiss the boo-boo better. Here's Mummy's little snookums.' She looked up at Dysis with dejected panic when his screams continued and his face went an angry shade of fuchsia.

Dysis sat down again, making that horrible plastic squeaking noise. At least she didn't have to worry if people thought she had made a rude noise. Nobody could hear anything above the siren-like shrieking.

'Quick. Go and get him some water,' she urged. 'That'll make him feel better. I'll watch the poor darling for you.'

'Oh, but I can't leave my baby.' Timmy's mother looked flustered and very young. 'It's far, far too much bother for you.'

'Don't be silly. I've got nothing else to do except wait, have I? I won't let anyone else walk off with him. I promise. Go along now and fetch him a nice refreshing glass of water.' Dysis stretched her smile across her face in what she hoped was a reassuring manner.

Timmy's mother looked apologetically at Dysis, her thoughts flitting transparently across her face. '*Such a nice older woman who smiles so sweetly at Timmy,*' Dysis imagined she was thinking. She bet her face reminded the girl of her own mother. She knew she had a comforting aura.

The girl's smile was tremulous. 'I'm dying for a cigarette, and we've been waiting so long. I'm afraid Timmy's not good at waiting. Maybe some water *would* help. Would help.'

'No problem whatsoever,' Dysis assured her. 'Timmy and I will be best buddies by the time you come back, won't we, honeybear?' Timmy's wailing escalated to an even higher pitch and his mother looked embarrassed.

'Get along with you.' Dysis flapped her plump pink hands in the direction of the hallway. 'We'll be just fine.'

With a grateful look, Timmy's mother got up and hurried out of the room. As she disappeared from sight, Dysis compressed her lips together. 'What kind of a mother would leave her child with a stranger?' She gathered up her things with controlled speed and grabbed Timmy's sticky hand, jerking him roughly to distract him. 'Come on, sweetie-pie. High time we left this nasty old smelly hospital, isn't it? Time to go for a visit to Auntie Dysis' house.' Timmy looked disenchanted at the idea, but became co-operative when Dysis let him peep inside her handbag at the big bag of chocolates wrapped in crinkly blue paper. His sobs quietened and a smile appeared on his tear-streaked, snail-tracked face as he reached greedily for the chocolates.

Dysis snapped her handbag shut. 'Not yet, hon. Wait till we get in the car.'

Squaring her shoulders, she marched down the hall with Timmy a foot soldier holding reluctantly to her hand. She turned down the deserted hallway she'd investigated earlier. People passed. Nurses. Doctors. Visitors. Mothers. When they arrived at the side door, she pushed it open. Ricker was waiting in their antique Ford Yazaboo. She hustled Timmy into the car, started it up and introduced him to Ricker.

'This is our new little son, honeybee. Ricker Hurtigger, this is Timothy Hurtigger. Timothy Hurtigger, this is your new daddy, Dr Ricker Hurtigger, Ph.D. Now, let's drive like the wind!' She locked the doors carefully with the automatic control next to her seat and wrapped a paisley scarf around her head. Tying the ends into a neat bow, she turned to look into the back seat.

'Another chocolate, Timmy sweetness?' she asked sweetly. 'Or a toffee? Tell me what you need.'

The woman giving birth on the meeting-room table needed something, that was for sure. Dysis dragged her attention back to the present. The people milling around Wynne were useless. She uttered small mewling cries of pain as she thrashed from side to side. Her face and hair dripped with sweat. The skirt of her dress was rucked up to her waist and her pink bikini underwear lay discarded on the floor.

Dysis crept closer and peered through the doorway at Wynne. Gaping journalists and LOT employees and management staff were ranged around her. Dysis noticed that the view of Wynne's business end was scrupulously avoided by the men. The only person brave enough to man the search for the baby's head was a short stocky woman with a Press badge pinned to her T-shirt. She was gingerly patting Wynne's knee. 'Don't worry,' she quavered. 'I'm sure things will be fine.'

Things were *not* going to be fine if everyone milled around like flies around a fresh cowpat. It was time to make her move. Dysis held her head high, pushed her handbag straps further up her plump arm and marched in. 'You called for a doctor?' she boomed.

Surprised faces turned towards her. 'Noooooo,' someone said in a faint voice. 'I don't think anybody called for one. Did they?' Everyone looked at each other, doubt and embarrassment flooding their panicked faces.

Dysis busily pushed past everyone. 'Never you mind who did and who didn't.' Just bombast over them, that was the ticket. Now was her last chance to secure this damn baby. It would make a fine replacement for Timmy, who'd been ungrateful enough to take off after only ten years. This one wouldn't escape.

Circumstances were working out far better than she could have hoped.

Pushing up her sleeves, Dysis went to where Wynne's head

was cradled in someone's greasy cast-off LOT jacket.

'Hello, honeychild,' she cooed. 'Time for you to use your own pressure tactics now. Bear down, dear. Bear down.'

Wynne's stomach rippled and she gasped. The small journalist standing at the table end between Wynne's legs cried out with excitement.

'Something's coming! An ear . . . no, an eye . . . a head . . . No, no, it's a . . .'

The sound of the journalist fainting didn't deter Dysis at all. Shoving the unconscious woman aside with her foot, she whipped Wynne's charred flower-bedecked skirt up over her head and bent down to peer short-sightedly at what was arriving.

'Oh, my,' she said, shocked exhilaration turning her even pinker than usual. 'Ricker will be *so* pleased.'

Paperwork

RICKER

He spoke with a certain what-is-it
in his voice, and I could see that,
if not actually disgruntled, he was
far from being gruntled.

P. G. WODEHOUSE

'Hints for Successful Grafting and Budding,' he said, into the mobile recorder's metallic mouth. 'By Dr Rickman Hurtigger, Ph.D.' About to continue, Ricker changed his mind and rewound the tape. Nodding for it to commence voice activation, he tried again.

'Topical Tips for . . .' His voice trailed off. *Boring*.

Ricker's distorted reflection gazed at him mockingly from the depths of his metal desk. He could smell disdain wavering from it. It had the stench of milk that had gone off. Yet another odour of failure joining the others in his stuffy office. He knew he should fling open the windows. Spring clean. 'Budding and Grafting'. The words had the sound of spring. But no. That title wouldn't work either.

Medical reports were the worst thing about being a doctor. He would survive very happily if he never had to do another in his entire life. They were the bane of his existence. People just didn't realize how much doctors had to put up with. The ubiquitous red tape. He knew he had a responsibility to record everything, but he resented the time it took him away from his real love, research and development. The Board drove him mad with their grasping fingers. They scrabbled around anything he did, wanting more and more and . . .

Well, what then? You had to begin a report with an appropriately impressive title. If it wasn't a grabber, the Board members would do as they constantly threatened. His report would go in the trash, as would his chances of promotion. Heck. There would go his job.

Think of a title, you old fool. If you didn't get the head right, you may as well throw the rest of the body on to the scrap heap. *Besides, when one is a perfectionist, only the perfect title is acceptable.*

Ricker felt tidal waves of acid slap against the walls of his stomach. He had to strike a trot and finish this up. Shaking his head to rid it of the tendrils of self-pity wafting through it, he rewound his tape again.

There wasn't time to get into yet another black mood. Besides, it didn't make for sparkling reports if he felt put upon while he wrote them. Depression muffled the clarity of one's words like a wet towel. There wasn't time to do the thing twice. Lots to do. Dysis would be bringing Wynne's baby back. Marina would be recalled in three days. The hanging hook room needed to be swept. Luca's excess extremities needed to be eliminated.

No. He'd forgotten. Not Luca. She'd gone. The rejection pained him. *No time for self-pity. Dysis will be back soon.* First things first. He had to finish this report or he'd never get the funding from the Board for the next stage.

'Electrically Stimulated Enhanced Scion Propagation By Emotion Regeneration?' he tried. His reflection shook its greyish head with regretful doubt. That title wasn't specific enough. Too wordy. Board members were accountants, not scientists. They'd glaze over if they heard that. He couldn't risk annoying them. Sweat collected under his armpits and the faintly rank smell disgusted him. It reminded him that he'd been remiss in the bathing department lately. Too busy. Too many things to do. Flapping his arms up and down to try to dry the wet patches, he spoke firmly into the recorder. 'Emotionally Linked Scion Propagation Generated By Electric Stimulation.'

He wiped his forehead with a damp wrist and noticed he had crescent moons of dried blood under his fingernails. He picked up a pen cap and tried to get some of it out with the sharp tip. The fragments refused to budge. Luca was hanging on and she wasn't even here.

No. That title wouldn't work either. The Board had specifically requested a report that could be adapted for public release. They were ready to commence leaking selected items of information to the general public, who were far too idealistic and naïve to be let into the whole picture in one go. Little things to get them used to growing new body parts. When the public got used to the smaller experiments, the Board could make them aware of the massive problem of lack of donors. Then its real agenda could be leaked. Developing a constant regenerating donor source.

If they leaked the news items too quickly or in the wrong order, there would be a typical hue and cry about human and animal rights. Cruelty. Didn't people realize that a few always had to suffer for the good of the many? Did they think medical advances were obtained without sacrifice? Did they think he enjoyed cruelty?

The public would eventually become used to the idea of budding and grafting on animals and then . . . *pam ʒow whap* . . . they'd hit them with a gradually increasing plethora of altered humans. The mouse had been good PR. He'd been on TV shows. Cereal packets. There had even been a toy mouse manufactured with a removable foam-rubber ear.

The sour feeling in Ricker's stomach increased. Bloody mouse. How had it escaped? Had he forgotten to close the cage? He couldn't remember. Ricker hadn't needed the mouse any longer, but it wouldn't be good for publicity if his experiment was found wandering down a road, starving or limping or anything. Hopefully it wouldn't get far. It couldn't. Not with that ear.

It was the work of ten to do the experiments, keep the subjects from wandering away, try to keep socially acceptable experiments within the public eye yet push the boundaries outside that eye. After all, if you didn't push boundaries, how did the public expect you to stay ahead? To respond to more advanced need. Accidents. Deformities. Illness. And that wasn't even taking into account all the paperwork.

Ricker had been disappointed when the Board told him they didn't think Mr John Q. Public was ready to hear about incident scrape-ups. He'd had to put off the release of the experiment findings until the public was more accepting. Collecting random suicide-victim extremities from the Transport tracks, combining them with live donors and generating fusion with electricity. What was frightening about that? Sandra wasn't frightening. Luca is. *Was.*

He couldn't tell the Board she'd escaped as well. How had she broken out? How *had* Luca and the mouse both escaped? It niggled him. Had he forgotten to bolt their cages? So much admin made him absent-minded. He hoped it wouldn't come down to him. Be found at fault. There would be an inquiry, he was sure. He sighed with gusto. He was an artist. Not a paper pusher, hospital attendant, cook and bottle washer, report writer, cage cleaner, jail attendant and everything on God's green earth.

He twisted his hands together and noticed that they were shaking. The Board would kill him if they found out. Fire him for sure. If the public caught wind of Luca before they were ready, he was done for. The Big Boss wouldn't take any excuses about forgetfulness.

'There's no such thing as *forget*,' they'd bellow. 'You did it deliberately!'

They'd make him the subject of yet another experiment. He wouldn't be able to take another.

Hopefully Luca wouldn't go to the media. She had to know he was only doing it for science. She couldn't be selfish enough to think she was above sacrificing herself to the common good. He *was* doing it for science anyway. Science and Dysis. *I'm getting too old for this stress.*

What about Dysis? She was already doing so much for him. Even filling in all the computerized time sheets the Board had requested. He'd been so furious, when they'd sent their memo requesting them that Dysis had to physically restrain him from throwing his paper copies out of the window. She was already doing enough. Keeping him from total disintegration. Not a small contribution.

Paperwork doesn't write itself. Get on with it. This report was a two-parter. Besides wanting a generalized description of the different implantation methods, the Board wanted a complete accounting on his research and experiments to date. Before they'd give him any more funding, they wanted to make sure he was going in the right direction. They were checking up on him. The imposition angered him.

Can't have that. Anger is so destructive. He snickered. It wasn't as if he'd start creating flower hybrids or something. He was a professional. He knew the importance of the project. *Stop procrastinating.*

'Emotional Scion Regeneration,' he said finally, and nodded at the recorder to indicate acceptance. Not an exciting title, but one that should be acceptable to Big Boss man. BB was just the kind of idiot who'd thrive on bland titles. But, then, if it made him loosen his grip on the City Credits, Ricker would make the titles as bland as Gro-Goat if he had to.

He hated it when the Big Boss man phoned. Ricker knew when it was him on the line. The beep of the telephone sounded different. He always debated whether to answer and get it over with or let his answering machine do the talking. Wasn't that what they were for? To screen calls?

One word from BB was enough to curdle any lurking good mood.

'Hellooooo, Dr Hurtigger,' he always sighed, every syllable as damp and slithery as warm spit. His sighs would waft through the phone wire and plop wetly near Ricker's feet.

Ricker shuffled his feet and sat up straighter in his chair. He'd better get going or BB would call him. Stretching both arms up in the air, he rotated them in several huge circles to get his blood circulating. Dropping his arms down, he began to speak. 'These are the highlights of an article I will be submitting for the January issue of *Creative Implants* magazine. I will also be sending it to two other publications, *Donor – Donee* and *Language Chip Implantation Monthly.*'

Ricker rubbed his forehead. That should convince them he meant business. Seed the knowledge. Disseminate. Decimate. Words words words. What came next? The intro stuff was covered now. Putting the recorder down, he rubbed his tired eyes and ran one hand over his left cheek, where the worst cuts were. Although they were healing, the itching drove him crazy. Is this what some of his experimentees felt? Idly, he traced one of the perpendicular cuts Estra had inflicted.

Maybe I should try using a razor instead of a culling scythe. You could get some interesting effects, he reflected. Besides, he didn't want to get stuck in a rut. An opportunity for creativity within his work excited him.

Ricker hadn't expected Estra to come back and attack him last week the way she had. She hadn't been scheduled for recall and he thought he'd sorted her out years ago. He was just too soft-hearted to deal with her in the way he should have. His foster parents would have told him that.

When the doorbell had rung, he hadn't even bothered to check the front-door security screen. He was expecting a pizza delivery. Meat-free vitamin-enriched medium with peppers and extra cheese. He felt proud that he and Dysis had managed to become vegetarians. They did their part against cruelty to animals.

He hadn't recognized her at first. The woman facing him when he answered the door looked like an apparition. A wild, blood-drenched hand-waving one. He couldn't understand what she was saying. Something about how he wouldn't get away with destroying her family. Which family? How was he supposed to keep all their names in his head? He wasn't a telephone book.

'Do you want some City Credits?' he asked. 'Although I don't give to beggars at my door.' He spoke loudly for the benefit of any listening neighbours. The woman muttered more names. Merino and Win. He recognized her then. Estra had come to rescue her nieces years ago with that boy – what was his name? Timmy? No, that had been his name before Dysis renamed him. Colwyn? Colton?

Estra was doing something to her hand and mumbling again.

Oh, do speak up, woman! Ricker squinted down to see what she was doing. He felt something liquid splash on to his shoes. Moving his feet back in disgust, he wondered if she was incontinent. He looked down.

The splashing liquid was blood. A lot of it.

He looked back at her hands. She was slashing at the left hand with one of two silvery razors she held between the clenched fingers of the right. The skin of the palm under attack undulated. Whenever she'd slice down one side, ripples would shiver up the other. There was a round dark area in the middle. Ricker couldn't see any details, but he thought something moved inside it. He blinked to clear his vision.

One of Estra's razors appeared to slip and she grunted in pain. With a small silver flash, the blade disappeared.

Ricker took the opportunity to slam the door shut. She was trying to kill herself on his doorstep and get him implicated. That must be it.

Estra pounded at the door. 'I need to talk to you,' she yelled.

He leaned against the door. She couldn't hurt him. She was too small and inconsequential.

'Throw down the razors. If you do, I'll help you. Bandage your hand up. Talk to you about your self-destructive problem. You need psychological –'

'I only have one left.'

'What?'

'Here.' She threw down the razor against the door frame. He could see the tip of it protruding underneath. It was slimed with her blood, a slick candy-red colour.

'The other one too.'

'It's gone. He has it.'

There are so many sickos in this city. Unable to resist, he opened the door. 'You need help.'

Estra leaped at him, almost cracking her head against his chin. She thrust her hand up in front of his face. He gazed in fascination. A raging seething eye, striated with bloody cuts, blinked at him from around the edges of a blade that appeared to be erupting from her palm. It looked oddly familiar. The edges of torn skin around the eye fluttered and breathed like flower petals.

As he stared, the razor flicked towards him. Fingers held the other end of it. Not Estra's fingers. A man's fingers leaped from the centre of her palm.

Ricker was impressed. 'How —'

He hadn't realized he was cut until seconds later when his face started to burn. The razor had been so sharp, it had snicked through his cheek like a hot culling scythe through butter. Good thing he'd ducked. His face would have been filleted by now. Leaning forward, he reached for Estra.

Expecting him to back away, she pushed forward trying to keep her hand in front of his face. He took hold of her arm and pulled, hoping to unbalance her. It worked. She fell forward with the extra weight of the hand erupting from her palm, the razor still clutched in its bloody fingers.

Ricker looked around for a weapon. A pair of scissors? He didn't want to do battle with a pair of scissors against a razor. A gun? Only children had them. He spotted something. The scraper tool he'd liberated from Estra and Colton when they'd come to get Marina and Wynne. He'd insisted on the tool as part of the trade. It was heavy and metallic, with steel claws on one end. He had it resting on one of his bookshelves for decoration. A souvenir of sorts.

Ricker ran to the shelf and hefted the scraper claw in both arms. Turning back, he saw that she was scrambling to her feet. Swinging the claw in an arc above his head in an Olympian manner, he advanced towards her. *How can they use these things all night? It weighs more than a small child!*

His aim was off and he was out of shape. He couldn't keep the heavy claw in a true arc. It fell, hitting Estra a glancing blow on the side of her head. She sagged to the floor and lay still. The only movement came from the third hand, which retreated, drawing itself inwards, covering itself with bloody petals of skin.

Ricker had noticed that, as it withdrew, it still clutched the razor.

The hand had reminded him of someone. Who was it? He knew those fingers. The nails were chewed down almost obscenely short. The skin bulged over the shreds of remaining nail.

Daniel?

Ricker reached into his desk drawer and got out his Ongoing

files. Reaching inside one, he pulled out a photograph. Yes, that was him. Looking at it depressed him. Daniel had been one of his disappointments.

He'd gone a bit funny after a hand implant grew inwardly and almost killed him. Ricker had to get him out of London so that nobody would hear about it. Paris seemed a good idea as he couldn't speak French. They hadn't had Talk-Lang chips back then, so he had thought he couldn't get into trouble.

Unfortunately, Daniel had had some problems in France. 'Domestic violence and public fracas,' the police had said. Very unsettling. The Board hustled Daniel out of Paris and demanded that Ricker place him somewhere else.

Ricker thought Scraper detail would be perfect. It solved the immediate problem of watching over Wynne and Estra and making sure that Marina was sent away. Daniel started out in great form, ingratiating himself into the family and marrying Estra. But somehow he'd managed to activate strong emotion in Estra and her implanted emotion generator had misfired. Hers had been an earlier version, done through the diet clinic. It wasn't as finely tuned as the later upgraded versions.

Estra had somehow managed to trap Daniel inside her. Ricker was fascinated by what she'd done. Should he recall her? No time, no time. He didn't want to be in her shoes when Daniel got out, though. Not with his vicious temper.

Luckily, although Estra and Wynne were misfired experiments, Marina was still intact. An egg waiting to hatch. Calling her back for the second stage – the hand implantation trial – had worked. The third stage would be in three days.

Whenever he had foster children, or anyone in for eating disorders, he'd give them vitamin shots. Inside the fluid was a dissolved microscopic call-back chip, which travelled through the victim's bloodstream. It solidified and activated when Ricker was ready for them. As so many experiments were long-term ones, you had to be sure you could get people to return without excessive force. No dragging them kicking and screaming through the streets, attracting unwelcome attention. All you had to do was dial their telephone number and hang up. They'd think it was their own idea, but somehow they'd find you and come back.

Call-back had been one of his finest inventions and the Board had been impressed, despite themselves. He'd received a 1000 City Credit bonus for its development. He would have more time for things like that if they'd only take away this onerous paperwork.

Ricker sat back in his chair, filled with a pleasurable sense of power. Being able to call people back was like being God, or a director working on some huge elemental play. One character went off-stage, but he could make them return. At his own whim. The Board's whim, he amended.

He'd activated Luca's recall already, but she hadn't made her way back to him yet. It could take time.

He wasn't infallible, after all. He felt tired. So many projects. So little time. Projects were stacking up in his in-tray. He straightened up. Dysis would be back soon. She wouldn't be happy if he hadn't finished the report. Her fury was not something to mess around with.

'Grafting Basic,' Ricker said into the recorder. Restless, he looked over at the TV. Some background noise would help. An approximation of an admiring crowd. Turning on the TV with a nod, he continued. 'The first problem is how to successfully graft body parts from one person, the donee, on to another person, the donor. The bigger problem is the shortage of available donors, which explains the urgency of developing our own source. My initial project using Transport incidents addressed this problem, but it wasn't a permanent solution. We can't expect people to jump in front of trains often enough to suit our purposes.'

Ricker stopped speaking and the recorder clicked off. He rewound the tape. It was too soon for that aspect to be brought out and it sounded a touch unsympathetic. He sat back in his chair and mused. His reflection in the desk looked tired. He didn't recognize himself any more.

Sandra had been his second attempt at melding scraped-up bits to live donors using electrical current. The first trial had misfired.

The woman had wandered off when Ricker wasn't looking. Dysis had been upset at the loss of resources, but Ricker wasn't that bothered. He wished the poor thing well, but he didn't have time to look after every single experiment. He had buried Luca to keep her from wandering off, though. She was too valuable a short-term prize.

Yet she'd still managed to get out. He felt like a man trying to keep the ocean in his arms. His family were all spilling away from him in great gushes. *Too old. Too tired.*

A sombre TV voice broke into his concentration. 'Reports of the day,' the newscaster said with sly importance. 'Flotation tank accident last week – inquiry to be launched.' The voice paused. 'Woman steals baby. News at eleven.'

Ricker was pleased. Dysis must be hard at work, securing Wynne's baby for him. He hadn't wanted to count only on Colton sending it to him when he found out it was severely deformed. No sense restricting one's options. Besides, if you want something done right, you have to do it yourself. Or send your sister, he amended. *To work, man.*

He tried to loosen his collar with one finger. Was he puffing up with stress or were his clothes shrinking?

'The most common errors committed by beginning grafters are easily avoided.'

More waffle to comfort the public.

'Grafts are most successful between members of the same species, such as human on human. Some body parts can be grafted on to a similar species, such as chimpanzee on human, or less commonly, to different species altogether. I have an experiment in process at the moment which combines different species. I am hoping for modestly positive results.'

Don't give too much away.

'In the past, grafts between different species didn't form a union and never survived long enough to make a desirable result. I'm hoping to change that.'

The next part of the report should be easy. Ricker could recite these in his sleep.

'Tips for successful grafting. A grafting knife needs to be razor-sharp. I test my knife by shaving hair from my arm. If it won't shave, the knife isn't sharp enough. Don't test a sharpened grafting knife with your thumb, or you may need sutures! Our knives are sharpened professionally, and I touch up the edge with a leather razor strop. A dull cutting implement will guarantee grafting failure. I recommend a knife designed specifically for grafting. These are honed on one side, leaving the other side flat. With such a blade, it is easier to make a smooth cut.'

I would have needed a special knife for Luca's head. Arms and legs were one thing, but you can't be sloppy when cutting off heads. Maybe if I don't tell the Board she's gone, I can convince them to spring for a specialized knife? Marina's worth the expense.

Sourly, Ricker bet that they'd tell him to stick with the tools at hand. Tight-fisted old gremlins. It would serve them right if he hacked away with antique butter knives.

'Implants should be removed as soon as they're matured. Place them in a plastic bag with a damp paper towel, and seal the bag. If left in artificial light, the implants die within minutes, but in a shady, cool spot, they should last several days. Implants can survive for several months in the refrigerator if kept moist.'

The glory closet was like a refrigerator. It was always cold in there.

'Rootstock should be kept in the dark for several weeks before and after grafting.'

Keep them in the dark like mushrooms.

'Go on, little Ricky, into the glory closet!' He could still hear his foster mother. Fosmom had put him and Dysis in the closet a lot when they were bad. Never at the same time so that they could comfort each other.

She sharpened her knife on a huge sharpening strop. *Skreeeek skreeeek.*

The sound made Ricker feel sick. He was never sure if she'd do it or not. He peered through the glory hole in the door. It was small and round and made him feel like screaming to be let out. What if he ran out of air? Fosmom stomped over to the closet, the floor trembling underneath her substantial weight. He backed away as far as possible from the opening. The hole now seemed yawningly massive and accessible.

'Out with it,' she cooed. 'Stick out whichever body part you don't mind losing.'

Ricker kept quiet. He smelt the sickly sweetness of her honeysuckle perfume. It made him want to retch.

'Can't decide?' she continued. 'You have ten minutes to pick one then.' *Skreeeek skreeeek*.

He went over all the body parts and extremities he possessed. Everything. In the end, he stuck out one finger. Anything else was insupportable.

Fosmom laughed and clattered her knives before putting them away. He crouched in a pool of urine and cried, snot and tears collecting on his upper lip until she let him out of the closet.

Dysis prevented him from killing himself after one of the glory closet episodes. He had dressed up in Dysis' ruffled ballerina tutu and stretched her pink ballet slippers over his feet. Pressing blue thumb tacks into his ear lobes for adornment and clutching a silvery starred wand for good luck, he opened the window and stood teetering on the ledge.

I can fly, he thought. I will fly away from here.

Dysis had convinced him not to jump.

When they were old enough, they left together and stayed that way. Who else could understand their mutual nightmares? At first they had slept together for comfort. In time it had turned to something else.

Thinking about Dysis was not getting this report finished.

'When cutting, use the knife tip to make a single sweeping cut. This results in a smoother cut than whittling, sawing or pulling the blade. Cut imperfections will prevent a good match of scion to stock, and will reduce success rate.

'Unprotected cut surfaces will dry out in seconds, preventing a good graft union from forming, so it is important to make your cuts, match them together, and wrap the graft as soon as possible.

I like to wrap a graft within ten seconds of the time I start to cut.

'Practice is necessary to make perfect grafts. For practice, I cut scions and reattach them elsewhere on the same person. I can make up to twenty practice grafts on one person, if they have enough body mass. I try to practise on the species I intend to graft. If I'm budding people, I don't practise on animals, which have an entirely different feel under the knife.'

That was certainly true. Luca felt far different from the mouse.

'I wrap grafts with cling-film, which has the advantage of being readily available and not having to be unwrapped later, since the scion will eventually grow and split the cling-film. It also sticks to itself, making it unnecessary to tie off the end.

'If callus tissue develops on all the cut surfaces, the graft is ready to be unwrapped. Callus is the wound-healing tissue, and looks like a small blob of white or pale tan spongy material.'

'Marina Callus.' I could call her that in the report we eventually release to the public.

Ricker placed the recorder on his desk with a sigh. The first part of the report was done. He let thoughts of Marina suffuse him.

When Marina was back here where she belonged, he could begin with the third stage. Activation. Fifteen years of delving into the lower reaches of the emotional scale would have prepared her well.

When she was reactivated, emotions would generate a constant supply of fresh body parts. When she experienced sadness, she'd have growth. Despair. Another growth. The endless possibilities thrilled him. Body parts would battle for space on her body like drowning people in a lifeboat.

He hadn't been able to resist the additional twist of genetic contact regeneration. Besides emotions generating just part-growths, he thought he'd found a way to grow entire people. It wasn't perfected yet, but it was getting there. A few tests were necessary.

For instance, if some man experiencing a rush of negative emotion brushed up against Marina in the Transport, she would absorb his genetic information and grow another version of him inside herself.

Or that's what Ricker hoped.

At present, it was only genetically linked family members that would set off the internal growth. He paused. There were problems with that scenario. It would be difficult to keep several members of a family together.

It was much easier splitting them apart. Look how easy it had been to separate Marina's family. Just feed Estra and Colton one or two white lies fifteen years ago and *splam* . . . they'd all splattered apart like water dropped into boiling oil.

He'd find out in a few days whether he'd done it correctly. When he activated Marina and drew her family together. Seeing each other for the first time in fifteen years would certainly be an event. *What a family reunion* . . .

There were so many different experiments he could carry out with her. Which to do first? The partials? The internals? Ricker would have to work closely with the timings. He was fine with the body-part removal as he'd had enough practice, but he still had to work out the timing for the internals. When did he liberate the internal person before it destroyed the external person? He had to find a way of harvesting without killing the donor. Cruelty-free culling.

Although the Board hadn't thought he was ready to try this stage of the experiment, he'd show them. Growing just partials was inefficient. Melding scrape-ups with donors was inefficient. Marina would be the way to super-efficiency. And job security. All she needed to commence the next stage was a jolt of heavy enough electricity. He could get that from LOT's track system.

Ricker heard a light tapping at the door. *I have no time. Go away!*

Marina's emotional state should be perfect now. She'd lived alone and away from her family for enough years. Her emotions were raw and intact. She'd be like a fine wine. Matured. Woody. If she'd been able to stay with her family, she would have had pallid emotions. Happiness. Contentment. Security. What a waste those would have been. Ricker wanted her to have the whole range of negative emotions. Guilt. Depression. Hate. She'd grow hordes of creative implants with those. And once she started she wouldn't be able to stop. Eventually she could subsist just as a torso. Then she'd have the room to grow new heads, arms and legs. Whole people. Something for everyone just from one donor!

He couldn't wait to stop with the scrape-ups. They were so messy. Dysis always clucked when he came home with gunk under his nails.

Marina, my little seedling. He hoped he hadn't waited too long or not long enough. It was so hard to be sure. Experimentation was a difficult business.

Whoever was knocking at the door wouldn't go away. Ricker banged his arms down on his desk. He clenched his hands into fists, digging the nails into his palms. You just couldn't get any work done with these constant interruptions.

As suddenly as his rage started, it ebbed away. It might be Dysis, back with Wynne's baby. Perhaps her hands were full. He didn't want to risk her anger.

She was too important to lose. He had nobody else. She was family. The others were his family but they kept leaving. Luca and the mouse had been family. Sandra was trying to go. Children always rejected their parents. It seemed to happen to him more than most.

Only Marina was left. *I'm losing control. It's all getting away from me . . .*

Ricker swung open the door, ready to give Dysis a hand. Only it wasn't Dysis and the baby at the door. To Ricker's surprise, it was a woman who looked familiar. Blonde. Dancer's legs.

'Dr Hurtigger?' she asked. 'I'm Terza. Don't you remember me? You reattached my hand a few weeks ago. I brought you something to thank –'

He went through the file cabinets in his mind. *Click. Clang.* Open and shut those empty drawers. *Now I'm getting short-term memory loss.*

'Yes, yes, of course I remember you,' he said, stretching out his hand. *Whoever you are.*

She put hers in his hand and shook it. He saw the faint pink scar like a bracelet around her wrist. *They're like homing pigeons. Coming back to Papa.*

'Dr Hurtigger,' she asked. 'Why are you wearing a dress?' Her face was slightly pink, as if she was embarrassed to be bringing up such a minor issue.

Oh, Jeez. Ricker's hand flew up to his hair. He was still wearing his wig. The Dysis clothes. In all the confusion over finishing the report he'd forgotten to change himself back with the CompuLook machine.

Part Three

Life can only be understood backwards,
but it must be lived forwards.

SØREN KIERKEGAARD

Team Spirit

TERZA
ESTRA
LUCA
ZEBEDIAH
CECILIO
WYNNE

*She wrenched from her brow a diamond
and eyed it with contempt, took from
her pocket a sausage and contemplated
it with respect and affection.*

CHARLES READE

'Not that there's anything wrong,' Terza said, 'with a man wearing a dress.' She felt a hysterical giggle pushing its way up and out that she didn't think she'd be able to stop. She wished now she'd never come. Dr Hurtigger was just standing there at the door in his grey wig and flower-strewn dress. How embarrassing. She'd obviously caught him in at a very private moment.

'I –' Dr Hurtigger stopped. 'Dysis . . .' The colour drained out of his face leaving two rosy dollops on his wrinkled cheeks. The wig, with which he was fiddling, was askew. Terza felt terrible. She wanted to reach over and straighten it for him. Give him some dignity.

She gazed down at his feet, unable to look at the thickly made-up face. The hair on his legs was visible through the tan-coloured tights he was wearing. She felt sick and opened her mouth to say goodbye. She saw that he seemed more miserable than she felt. His mouth quivered.

'Don't cry,' she said. 'Your mascara will smear.'

He seemed surprised at how matter-of-fact she sounded.

'I . . . Dysis – '

Terza threw back her shoulders. She owed this man, and she was damned if she'd let a little cross-dressing come between friends.

'Yes,' she said to him, with a careful smile, 'I'd like to come in. Like I said, I have something for you.'

When Dr Hurtigger didn't move from the doorway, she politely but firmly pushed past him, pulling Addy after her. 'C'mon, Addy. Follow Mummy.'

Dr Hurtigger looked shell-shocked, but recovered enough to

clear papers off some chairs scattered in forlorn disarray around the office. Terza sat Addy down in one of them. When his head lolled to the side, she bolstered it up with a small foam cushion that she took out of her handbag. She also took out a Kleenex and dabbed at the drool oozing from the corner of his mouth. Carefully, she put one hand on his lap. The other handless arm she let hang at his side.

Straightening the immaculate black LycraSyl suit she was wearing, Terza sat down in the other chair across from the doctor. 'I'm sorry, Dr Hurtigger,' she said. 'My husband is not the man he was.'

'I can see that.' He paused and brushed a hand across his face, smearing his lipstick. 'What happened?'

'The flotation tanks –' she began.

The telephone rang. The beep sounded high-pitched and demanding. She watched Dr Hurtigger flinch and saw that his hands were trembling. *What's he so scared of?*

The phone beeped again, imperious in the stuffy calm of the office.

'Aren't you going to answer it?' she asked.

He started. 'Of course.'

He waved past Addy at the telephone screen on the wall. She noticed with amusement that he flicked off the visuals. He must not want the other person to see that he was dressed like an old lady.

Was he actually cross-dressing, or had one of those CompuLook machines gone wrong? It had been known to happen before. Just like making faces at your little brother. If the wind blew in the wrong direction while you had your face all screwed up like a pig, you'd stay like that for ever. That's what mothers said. Terza would probably say it to her children, if she ever had any. Looking over at Addy, she shivered. Not with him! What a mistake that marriage had been.

She glanced over at Dr Hurtigger, who was sitting forward in his chair as if he was about to take off. He'd switched on the personal speaker. Damn. She would have loved to hear what was making him break out into such a sweat. His too-tight dress had expanding rings of sweat under each armpit. He didn't make a very attractive woman, she thought. His eyes were slightly too close together and the wig was unflattering. Why had he chosen such a large doughy body? Such a shelf-like bosom? Such unfashionable clothes? She peeked under the desk. Clunky shoes. She made a tiny *moue* of distaste. You couldn't dance in those.

The doctor nodded. 'Yes, BB. Luca's almost ready. I can't send pictures yet . . .' Dr Hurtigger's sweat stains become sweat moons. ' . . . because the camera flash would halt the growths. As soon as . . . Yes, sir. Of course. No, the time sheets aren't ready either . . .' Sweat constellations. 'Soon.'

When Dr Hurtigger waved to hang up and turned back to Terza she saw, to her extreme consternation, that he was crying. Muddy drips of mascara crawled down his face, giving him the look of some nightmarish ghoul from an old film.

'I can't –' he began.

'What's wrong?'

Dr Hurtigger's face collapsed. 'That's it. They want Luca and she's gone. The mouse . . . My time sheets.' He started to gulp in distress. Terza jumped to her feet and came round the desk. She patted his shoulder in as comforting a manner as she could manage.

'They want the pictures of Luca to be released. They want the public prepared for my biggest project. She's gone. What am I going to do?' He cried like a child and put his bewigged head down on his desk. His flower-printed shoulders heaved.

Terza put both arms around him. 'Who?' she asked. 'Tell me.'

Dr Hurtigger had lost every shred of the authority and confidence she had been so impressed by a few weeks before. When she had looked up at him from the stretcher before her operation, she had known she was in safe hands. But now? He was a mess. How could she help? He'd done so much for her, fixing her hand like that after Addy had almost decimated her career. Dr Hurtigger hadn't even charged her. He'd waved his hand at her and told her to get going before he changed his mind. She was so grateful.

How could she ever have continued her dancing school with only one hand? She had a scar around her wrist, which some of her male dance students seemed fascinated by.

'Tell me,' she said, drawing Dr Hurtigger's head to her bosom. He sniffled against her as she rubbed his back comfortingly. Eventually he told her. The slip-ups. The problems. The admin gone into over-drive. He was all ready to do the big experiment that would impress the Board, but they'd fire him when he told them he'd lost Luca. They were very strict in their requirements for public knowledge. Information about her had to be released prior to the final experiment. If he couldn't give them Luca, he might as well quit. She'd disappeared into thin air. Someone had helped her out of that box. It couldn't have been Sandra. She didn't know how the box release worked.

None of it made much impression on Terza. It sounded distasteful, but she was certain that he knew what he was doing. He was a doctor, after all.

'And Dysis?'

He even told her about being Dysis. She was the mother he never had. The lover. The sister.

'I change myself into her with the help of the CompuLook machine.'

'I bet tons of people have whole families inside them,' she comforted.

'What am I going to do?'

Terza sighed. All men became children in the end. Here Addy was wearing nappies, and now Dr Hurtigger was asking her to tell him what to do. She'd spent so many years of her life thinking that you depended on men. They were there to lean on because they knew all the answers. But if she leaned on either of these men, they'd keel over in a flailing heap of drool, tears and foundation garments.

All right. It was up to her. Perhaps her thank-you gift to him would be more welcome than she'd anticipated.

'Wait.'

She sat and thought for a minute. The only sounds in the room were Dr Hurtigger's occasional sniffles and Addy humming to himself.

'Wouldn't the Board forget about Luca if you did something spectacular and released your big project early?'

'But the public . . . the Board doesn't want me to work on it yet.'

'Take a risk! Who says you have to follow rules? I never have.'

She looked at Addy as she said that. He had been her one attempt at following rules. Her parents had wanted her to marry him. 'Nice boy,' they'd said. 'Think of your biological clock.' Bugger her biological clock. Addy was a bully. At first, she only expressed her unhappiness with a little mild flirtation with his friends. Colleagues. Then some strategic dancing with certain selected salsa students convinced them that she might welcome a little dalliance.

'Oh, sorry,' she'd say, twinkling up at them when they broke apart from her all flushed and embarrassed. 'Did I make you uncomfortable?' Speechless, they'd look as startled as rabbits when she brushed a hand delicately against the hardness developed during the dance. 'Mmm. How nice . . .' she'd murmur.

She'd had plenty of offers.

Terza knew Addy thought she was cheating on him. It was fun teasing him. Leaving shreds of evidence around to drive him mad. It was exciting. She had presumed it would drive him to violence, but she hadn't expected the episode at the flotation tanks. She hadn't known he'd try to maim or kill her. Good thing he'd been distracted by those floating things she'd seen with him in the tank.

When he'd phoned her suggesting a tandem soak, she sensed something would happen. She hoped it would turn out to be a session of sexual tank antics. She didn't expect his fury, the fight to the death and thrashing around they'd ended up doing. She'd lost a hand in the fracas when he'd slammed the tank lid. But so had he.

She managed to get out of the tank. He didn't and swallowed a lot of water. She waited until he was sure to have drowned before calling the hospital. Unfortunately, the ambulance service showed up in record time and they'd managed to revive him.

He was in a vegetative state for weeks. Eventually the doctors told her Addy had suffered brain damage from lack of oxygen while in the water. Nurse Johnson informed her of the options. As his wife, Terza had the choice of letting him die, taking him home to live with her or . . .

Nurse Johnson whispered the last choice, 'Donate him to science as a live donor.'

Terza thought of Dr Hurtigger and how difficult it must be to find willing donors. She thought of the note she had received from Marina – the woman who'd grown her hand for her – telling her to be careful. Terza looked at Addy and remembered the incessant pressure on the back of her head. Whenever she was dressed up and ready to go to dance class, her make-up carefully applied, Addy would grab her.

'You have to,' he would say, as he pushed her to her knees in front of him. The fingers of his other hand bit painfully into her shoulders. 'You're my wife and you have no choice.'

She had a choice now. Going over to Addy, she took his good hand and hauled him up. Leading him around the desk, she placed his hand in Dr Hurtigger's. 'Merry Christmas.'

'I couldn't possibly . . .' he began.

'Of course you can. You can give him to the Board in place of Luca.'

'He'd have to sign a living will. A donor card.'

'No problem.' She smiled and ran her fingers through her hair. Noticing her wedding ring, she twisted it off her finger and dropped it into an ashtray on Dr Hurtigger's desk.

'He can write,' she said. 'I'll help him.' Taking out a pen from her purse, she closed Addy's flaccid fingers around it.

'Well?' she asked. 'Do you have anything for him to sign?'

Dr Hurtigger scrabbled around in a desk drawer and pulled out a form. Pushing it over the top of the desk for them to sign, he began to look much more cheerful.

Terza brought Addy's hand up to the form and moved it to produce an approximation of his signature. 'Messy,' she said, cocking her head slightly to the side, 'but it's close enough to his signature.' She winked at Dr Hurtigger. 'He'd be so pleased to know he's contributed to medical advancement.'

'Thank you,' he said. 'It's so kind of you. And of Addy, of course.'

'It was odd,' she said. 'In the water, as he was trying to drown me, he told me I'd killed him in a previous life and would do it again. He said you can't change fate. But by choosing Nurse Johnson's third scenario, I'm showing him that you can. I'm not vindictive. I'm not allowing him to die. Although he's brain dead, his body will live for science.' She paused to take a breath.

'Admirable sentiments,' he said.

'He'll die in order to help someone else live.' She paused and then gave Dr Hurtigger a warm look. 'Thank you for reattaching my hand.' She flexed her hand and wiggled the fingers. 'I couldn't have continued my dance classes without you. It would have been impossible to get another job. I can't do anything else.'

Dr Hurtigger smiled vaguely. 'I'm sure you have plenty . . . I have to figure out what goes next. So much to do.'

'One thing at a time,' she said, with firmness. 'Too many things at once. No wonder you're dithering all over the place.'

He brushed back a grey curl. 'I wish Sandra was like you. Everything is so unorganized here.'

'It helps to be organized.' Terza watched Addy drool. 'You have more time to yourself when you are. Now that I . . . I might take some night classes.'

Dr Hurtigger stood up, obviously anxious to get to work.

'Do you have any idea when you'll work on Addy?' She felt a flicker of emotion. She wanted to make sure she'd never have to see him again. This certainly beat divorce. You had to face both families then. Be branded a failure at marriage.

'Accident,' she'd tell them sadly. 'Addy has left us for a better place.' She'd cry. She looked good when she cried. Dewy and fresh. Her nose didn't turn red and tomato-like as some women's did. She prided herself on her nice little nose.

'Perhaps I can use him,' Dr Hurtigger mused, 'to see if I can kick off my girl's automatic regeneration. If I implanted something from every one of her family members on to him, then I wouldn't need her whole family to be around. Similar genetic contact from her family could be accomplished in one person.'

Terza was confused. 'I don't understand.'

'I'd like to eventually have it be anyone's genetic contact, but the Board hasn't given me enough funds to go down that avenue. But Addy might be my catalyst. Much more cost effective!'

'You'd have Addy touch her over and over again?'

The doctor frowned. 'Yes. I think the best thing would be to cage him in with her. That might work. After all, I wouldn't want to run the risk of losing him.'

'Addy can't escape without a brain, at least.' She twinkled up at him. 'That should make you feel better.'

Dr Hurtigger looked at her. 'You're so understanding. I've never been able to talk to anyone else about my experiments like this before.'

She hoped he wasn't flirting with her. She flexed her hand in front of her again and glanced at Addy. 'I admit, I would have felt funny about some of these experiments before. I used to be a real campaigner against animal testing when I was a teenager, but now I can see the benefits.'

'You've made my day, Terza.'

'It's nothing.' She stood up, buttoning her jacket and making sure the brief skirt was smooth over her hips and covering everything important. 'I'd better go. Class in an hour.'

'Wait a sec.' He stood up, too. 'I'll walk you out. I just have to make one phone call.'

She watched as he went over to the telephone screen, switched on the Manual button and punched in some numbers. The phone rang at the other person's house and a woman's answering machine picked up. 'Hello,' it said. 'Marina here. I'm not in at the moment but . . .'

Marina? That couldn't possibly be the same woman who had grown her hand and written her that friendly warning note?

Dr Hurtigger hung up the phone. 'Recall commenced. I'd better head over to the Emergency Department. I don't know when she'll come in. Could be anywhere from twenty minutes to twelve hours.'

'Was that the same Marina who grew my hand for me?' Terza asked. Concern bubbled up inside her.

He cast her a quick look. 'It is, but don't worry. She volunteered for this. She can't wait.' He paused. 'I get the impression she's one of those kinky women who fantasize about being touched by hordes of people . . . made love to by several men at the same time. You know . . .'

Terza relaxed. 'I certainly wouldn't know! I'm not one of those women.'

'Of course not, Terza.' The corners of his mouth turned up and his confidence looked restored. 'Shall we go?' At her nod of assent, he walked over to Addy. 'There's a shortcut through to the hospital from my waiting room.' Taking hold of Addy's arm, he made a clucking noise, as if summoning a horse. 'Gee up now, Addy. Let's go.'

Addy dribbled in response as he obediently stood up.

'Dr Hurtigger?' Terza felt uncomfortable.

He stopped in the doorway. 'Yes?'

'Don't you think you should change out of that dress or,' she wanted to be kind, 'put some new mascara on?'

He looked down at himself.

'Silly me.' He laughed. 'I'd forget my head if it wasn't already attached. Good thing you're here. Wait just a sec. I've got to cover the cuts Estra gave me with some more foundation. Damn woman could have really done me some damage. I've also got to get out of this girdle. It feels like a prison sentence.'

'Such a silly thing to do.' Giuseppe coughed and Estra felt reluctant sympathy. The damp in these cells must be making his lungs worse.

'Are you all right over there, Kingpin?'

He coughed again, obviously an attempt for additional sympathy.

'I'm fine,' he said, in a wretched voice.

'Have you finished being pathetic?' Estra asked.

He answered meekly, 'Yes.'

She continued, as if he hadn't interrupted, 'What else *could* I do? I had to try to kill that man. He's responsible for decimating my family in the past and I had to get to him before he destroyed the rest. Having Daniel inside me has to be useful for something.' She gave a small bitter laugh. 'Fifteen years of having a man hacking his way out of you to kill you.' She paused. 'Can you imagine what that's like? I haven't had a good night's sleep since it happened. It must be like having a child kick inside you. I'm afraid if I fall asleep too deeply that he'll pick faster and somehow get past the cling-film I've wrapped around my hand to cover him up.' She leaned her head against the bars, which were cold against her forehead.

'I still can't understand how cling-film could slow him down,' Giuseppe said, 'or even how it could happen in the first place.'

'Nor me,' she said. 'All I know is that I was terribly angry when I wished him away from me. Things happen when I'm angry. It sets something off. It has since I was young.' She paused. 'Ever since my stay in the clinic.'

'What clinic?'

'I was anorexic when I was a girl. I thought I was fat. Kept looking in the mirror and seeing flesh flowing out of me in torrential floods. I felt out of control.' As she told him that, she looked down at her arm, and pinched a fold of skin with her fingers. *Still too flaming fat. But not as bad as before.*

'What did that have to do with anger?'

She stayed silent for an instant. 'The woman in charge at the diet clinic talked to me a lot about anger and why I was trying to starve myself. You can do a lot of damage with rage. Against yourself as well as other people.'

'Yes . . .'

She waited for him to continue, the bars warming under her hands. She rubbed a bar with one fingertip, watching the flakes of rust fall.

' . . . Cecilio's still angry with me. I don't know if he'll come to help us get out. I tried calling and his answering machine was full. As if he hasn't been home in a while. Or he's just not answering me.'

'Don't worry, Kingpin,' she said. 'I didn't expect your son to ride up on a white horse and rescue us.'

'It would have been nice.'

'But unrealistic.'

'Probably.'

A large rust flake flicked off and settled on her lip. She brushed it away and watched it float down to the ground. 'I've thought of a way to get out.'

'How?'

'If you'll help me. I can't do it myself.'

'Anything, Estra.'

'Help me slash my wrist with a sharpened piece of urine bucket.' *It's the only way.*

'WHAT?'

Estra heard a thud, as if something was hit against the bars.

'Not to kill myself. I don't have that luxury. If I'm hurt, they'll take me to the hospital, which is next door to Dr Hurtigger's clinic. I want to set Daniel on him again. He's my only weapon. I have to pay him back for destroying my family.'

'Oh, Estra. How can you expect me to do what you ask?'

'Are you refusing?'

Silence.

'Kingpin?'

'Are you sure it won't hurt?'

'Course not. Don't forget, I can do things when I'm angry. At the very least, I can make it stop hurting.' *Hopefully. I haven't tried that yet.*

'I'll make sure not to annoy you in future. Don't want to make you mad.'

Estra giggled.

Giuseppe sounded glad he'd made her laugh. 'How —?'

'If I pass over the piece of bucket, can you try to saw through my wrist?' *I can't do it myself. I'll faint.*

Giuseppe swore at great length and volume in Italian. 'You're not doing it now, are you?'

'I will if you don't help, and I'll do a worse job with only one hand to do it. I'll die horribly, raggedy bits of wrist everywhere, screaming and leaking blood all over the place. Some puddles of it could leak into your cell.'

'Give it here.'

'Kingpin?'

She heard him kick the bars sullenly. 'Ouch.' He must have hurt his toe. 'What?'

'You won't take my piece of metal away?'

Giuseppe hesitated. 'No.'

'You'll do it? Please? I don't have anyone else.'

'How can slashing your wrists help, Estra?'

'I didn't say cut my wrist completely. Just nick it enough to get it bleeding. They'll take me to the hospital for stitches. I'm used to pain. Come on, Kingpin, you've seen the cuts in my hand! I won't bleed to death. I told you. I can do things when I'm angry.'

'Okay.'

'Okay you've seen them or okay you'll help me?'

'*Porca miseria,*' he mumbled.

'Kingpin?'

'Okay.'

'*Grazie.*' She paused. 'Thank you.'

'Estra?'

'What?'

'You have to promise me something.'

'Anything, Giuseppe.'

'When they slam you back in jail for life for murder or assault or whatever, promise you'll marry me.'

'In prison?'

'In prison.'

'If you insist.'

'I do.'

'Italians are so pushy,' she said.

'I'd kiss you if you were here.' He made a smoochy kissing sound.

Estra laughed. 'Yeah, I know. Ravish me against the urine bucket.'

'Not yet. First I'd —'

'I'd kiss you back.' Her voice was quiet. 'Hold my hand.'

'Give it here, then.'

She reached out and felt her hand enclosed in his warmer one. 'Will you do it? I can't do it myself.'

'Yes. But if you let yourself die, I'll kill you.'

She held a piece of her skirt up against her mouth to smother her laughter.

When the prison doctor carried Estra away on the stretcher, she tried to turn her head to see Giuseppe in his cell. She wanted to smile and thank him, but she felt alarmingly weak. It had taken longer than they had expected for the guards to come. Giuseppe had to scream very loudly before they came. Because he'd been yelling about Cecilio so much, they thought he was going on about his son again.

They were past his cell before she could catch a glimpse of him. All she caught before her eyes closed was a grey moustache like a dove flickering between the bars.

She wanted to sleep. She hoped Giuseppe had noticed that she'd tucked the toilet paper rose behind her ear.

'I detest moustaches, Kingpin,' she whispered.

Luca tickled the mouse with the ends of a lock of hair and then brought it over her top lip like a moustache. She pushed the hair behind her ear and looked around the police-station waiting room with apprehension. She always fiddled with her hair when she was nervous. Would they believe her?

She felt the mouse's nose push into her grimy fingers for comfort.

Trying to keep her mind blank while she was in public did her head in. She wanted to control the growths until she saw the police. She had to show them.

It took all the energy she had, but at least the growths were at bay temporarily. She didn't think the clamouring flood of things would allow themselves to be held back for much longer, though. The chancres made their presence known under her skin with burning impatience. The itching sense of internal poison made her flesh creep. She wanted to scratch but was afraid it would dislodge the thin skin of control.

The policeman at the front desk had laughed when she told him why she was here. 'You're here to report what?' He looked down his red nose at her. 'Is this a prank?' He held himself back from her as if she smelt.

I probably do smell. Wouldn't you stink after a few months in a box? 'No.' She wavered and cleared her throat. It was hard to talk. 'It's no joke.'

'You're telling me that every time you get angry or think, or whatever, little animals pop up all over you?' The man scratched his crotch with lazy insolence. 'Show me.'

Luca pulled up her shirt to leave her midriff bare. 'Look. I'll let one of them come out now.' She waited. The man waited. She felt the mouse hold his breath, waiting.

Nothing happened. The growths, so anxious to erupt when she didn't want them, refused to fire. Luca wanted to scream.

'Sure,' the policeman said, with a smirk. 'Of course. Uh-huh. Well, you just wait here until my colleague comes off break. I'm sure he'd love to fill out a report about you, your little animals and this Dr Harbinger person.'

'Hurtigger,' she said.

'Whatever.'

She sat down again and waited. The clock ticked by. She felt dirty. Months of grime coated her skin. No wonder the policeman didn't believe her. She looked like a vagrant.

The mouse ruffled her hair. She reached up and scritched under his chin. She was a vagrant with three ears. Would he want to stay with her? She'd thought of releasing him into the wild, but didn't think that was such a hot idea. He'd make too big a target for hunters. She and the mouse could live together. It wasn't like she was going to have much of a social life after this. *Maybe I can grow you some little brothers and sisters.*

After five minutes the policeman, still staring at her contemptuously, waved at the phone to make a call.

'Chief . . .' he said.

She stood up. She'd waited long enough. She walked out of the room and down the hall. Bursting from the front door of the police station, she hurried down the street. As she walked she could feel the chancres sprouting. They were angry at being held back. Something was growing on the left side of her ribcage. She reached in to scratch, and something gave her a sharp nip. *Whatever it is, it has teeth.*

She'd have to forget about reporting Dr Hurtigger for now. She had to get to the hospital. Would they be more likely to help or would a veterinary surgeon? She needed them to help her mouse, too. She reached up to brush hair out of her eyes and felt something on her forehead.

Something was growing on her face.

Hospital, now.

Zebediah almost fell off his woman's shoulder when she started to run, despite his relatively stable perch next to her neck.

He tried to grip on to fronds of her hair but swung alarmingly. His ear became tangled in her hair and he started to slide. His woman's hand came up to brace him.

What consideration. Zeb felt proud. She knew what was due to someone in his exalted position.

No. Zeb smacked his forehead with a paw. No no no. He'd forgotten. She was the emperor, not him. Or maybe she was a god. Goddess. Who else could create a whole Noah's Ark full of animals on her own body? He hadn't liked that whiff of snake emanating from somewhere around her waist. He hoped it couldn't get loose. If he could smell the snake, the snake could probably smell him. He wondered if it could smell his fear. Probably. Zeb could smell it, and the odour wasn't pleasant. Like decayed insects.

He hoped she was taking him somewhere safe. He didn't feel

safe, what with the precarious nature of his position, and the snake lurking somewhere below. Maybe she could grow him a new wife to thank him for getting her out of the big coffin thing. A new wife couldn't complain about Zeb's human ear, as she herself would have a great whopping human embedded on her. He closed his eyes and swayed with the movement of the woman's body.

I want Zimne back.

At least they were out of that police place with the bad smells. He wondered why the woman had taken him there. Police couldn't help. They smelt obstinate. The man at the desk had exuded scorn. Zeb sneezed. He hadn't liked that man. He had heard part of the phone conversation as Luca ran from the room. His hearing was so much better than normal now.

'Chief,' the man said on the telephone, 'Mr B B, there's someone you'll have to pick up. One of Hurtigger's . . .'

Zeb couldn't pick up any more as they were out of hearing range.

He hoped she was going somewhere near the Man's laboratory. His hospital. Whatever it was. Zeb had decided on a plan. He wasn't important any more. His family was gone. Zimne didn't need him for the kids. He'd go on a suicide mission. Chew the wires in the place where the Man was and cause an electrical fire. Burn him and the hospital right up.

He knew the goddess would agree.

Despite being in a hospital, and the pain of having Marina lie on top of his various wires and tubes, Cecilio didn't remember when he'd ever felt so happy.

Being a hand implanted on to someone had been horrifying at first. When he pushed from the sticky warmth inside her body up through her skin, he'd felt sure that it must hurt her. How could it not? He tried not to burst through impatiently, although he craved the light. Just a finger at a time. Softly. Slowly.

The sense of dislocation of being in two places had been exhausting. The effort to keep both body and hand together sapped his strength. He started wishing his body would die so that he could stay on Marina. He'd never been this close to a woman before. Inside her. On her. Around her. He had once thought sex must be like that, but now he didn't even care. What he felt was something he never wanted to be without again.

He couldn't make Marina understand at the end, but he'd decided to let his body die. Unfortunately, withdrawing all the strength from his body, causing it to die, also affected him. He had hoped that wouldn't happen, but he no longer had the strength to try to keep both alive.

Dying in two places was weird.

He blinked his eyes now with contented happiness. He'd never been good at science or biology. He didn't know what was happening to him. All he knew was that the woman in his arms at this moment was in the right place. Her hair smelt of woodsmoke. He parted his lips to try to taste the smell. To savour it and roll it around in his mouth.

He couldn't believe his luck when he'd woken up and found he'd been implanted on the woman from the Transport station. The one he'd tried to talk to but couldn't speak to from panic and lack of English. He'd almost passed out right on her shoulder from shyness and nerves when he'd become aware of who she was. She was Marina.

He had to thank her now. To tell her how he felt. To thank her for being her. He couldn't just lie here holding her like some pathetic lump. He had to say something. He needed words. The words bubbled up inside him to the tune of his ventilator.

In. *You*. Out. *Are*. In. *My*. Out. *Life*.

'You caused my life to begin,' he started to say. 'Don't ever leave me.'

He'd forgotten about the Talk-Lang chip. It whirred into operation and spat out the words around his throat tubes.

'You caused my death,' he said. 'Leave me.'

He saw the shock in her face just before the electricity went out. The beeping of his breathing machine slowed. Faltered.

Oh, no . . .

He saw her turn towards the opening in the curtains. It was

becoming difficult to breath. He saw her turn away from him. *No. Come back.*

'Mother,' he heard her say, through a haze of whiteness, 'is that you?'

She turned back to him, pain flooding her pale face. 'I know I shouldn't have tried to keep you,' she said. 'It's my fault. Everything is.'

Don't go, Marina! I didn't mean that! His Talk-Lang chip didn't work at all now. His words spilled out in a torrent of Italian. Apparently she knew Italian less than sign language. Or was he talking at all? He couldn't tell. The air was becoming thicker. Glutinous. He couldn't breathe.

The beeping in the room stopped. Silence.

Marina?

Watching the woman take her child to safety as she lay on the meeting-room table, Wynne felt the same sense of loss that had crushed her when Marina was sent away so long ago. She didn't know what Marina had done to be sent away, but it must have been bad. Mama refused to speak of it and Wynne eventually gave up trying.

Her loss now felt far more elemental, though. Her child. Wynne felt the warm electric thing pull from deep inside her. It crept around the empty spaces her newly vacated baby had left and ebbed slowly upward. She looked down and noticed her grounding wires splayed out along the floor. Picking them up and hanging them over her arms, she tried to get off the table.

Having given birth ten minutes before, she hadn't the strength and fell back.

'Please,' she said. 'Someone help me get up.'

The people in the room continued to stare. At both her and at the door where, minutes before, two women had been struggling. A small woman with tea-coloured hair and turquoise fingernails and a large, matronly woman with grey hair. Wynne had thought she was a doctor or midwife when she'd first appeared between her legs. Her face had looked familiar. But the eyes had been rolling and mad. She'd tried to snatch her child even when half of it was still within her.

Wynne closed her eyes as waves of cramp crashed inside the beach of her body. The placenta must not have come out. Isn't that what happened next? She tried to sit up and look, but fell back again. What did a placenta look like? She'd never seen one. A water balloon? Jellyfish? If she could hurry up and eject the thing, she could go to find her child in the hospital.

She felt woozy. Lightly pressing her fingertips on the table next to her, she felt dampness. Lifting her hand in front of her face, she realized that the dampness was blood. It felt as if the pool she lay in was spreading. Becoming deeper. Waves of blood were crashing over her head.

'Please, somebody . . .'

A woman placed a cool hand on her damp forehead. Wynne opened her eyes and looked up at her. She couldn't see her face. All she could see was a Power to the People T-shirt.

'Your father went next door,' the woman said. 'To get an ambulance for you.'

'Don't be stupid. He's dead,' Wynne whispered. 'The woman who took my child to the hospital . . .'

'. . . says she's your father.' The woman took her hand off Wynne's forehead. 'Don't look at me. I'm just relaying the message she said to give you.'

Soft red waves of lethargy crept over Wynne and she wanted to sleep. 'Papa's dead.'

Family Reunion

COLTON
SANDRA
BERRI
RICKER
GIUSEPPE
MARINA

*The world breaks everyone and afterward
many are strong at the broken places.*

ERNEST HEMINGWAY

'You can't miss her,' Herbert said, after he'd reached the hospital and found a nurse. 'My daughter is the one bleeding in the middle of the table. Hurry!'

The nurse looked at him with amused scepticism. He could tell she thought he was nuts. She didn't realize he was a man inside a woman's body. How could she? He couldn't just announce to everyone, 'I'm Herbert. Not Sandra.' The nurse probably wondered how a girl in her late teens could have a daughter old enough to give birth. It didn't matter. She didn't matter. His daughter mattered. He drew himself up. 'I'm older than I look. Appearances can be deceiving.' He peered at the small badge on the pocket of her uniform. 'Please, Nurse Johnson? Send an ambulance.'

She nodded finally and he felt himself sag with relief. 'Give me the child. I'll transfer it to the new-borns' wing.' She held out her arms into which Herbert placed his squirming bundle.

'I'm a grandfather.' He couldn't help giving the nurse a huge smile. After all, as a teenage girl how often did you get to be a grandfather?

That done, he set off to locate his son-in-law. Flagging down a taxi-moto, he jumped in and gave the domed driver the address he'd found for Colton in Doc Hurt's files. The silver dome swivelled round and whistled at Herbert's legs in automatic flattery. Herbert dragged his skirt hem down as far as it would go and clamped his knees together. Glaring at the dome until it turned away, he knew it would take some time to get used to being a man when he was actually a woman. Or a woman, when he was actually a man. The whole thing gave him a pounding headache. *I may be a Herbert but my body is a Sandra.*

Women's clothes were so hard to organize. All he'd ever worn as Herbert had been Scraper overalls. Not much difficulty there. All this wind rustling up your private parts. No wonder women wore that tinge of surprise on their faces so often. It wasn't because they had wind. It was wind itself rustling up, brushing aside scraps of lacy underwear with rough impatience and thrusting inside with casual probing fingers. He'd wear boxer shorts under skirts. That would foil the wind.

The sensation of losing and gaining a life and a family in one day was an unsettling one. His brain felt crowded and uncertain. As Sandra, here he had been wishing to be a princess and have real parents, and now he had two daughters, grandchildren . . . a wife. A wife living with an Italian named Imolo. The name roiled around in his guts as if he'd heard it yesterday. To him, it *was* yesterday. Berri's betrayal felt fresh and unsliced.

Don't cry, you wassock. You'll ruin your makeup. 'Are we almost there?' he asked, knocking on the back of the dome's head.

The dome swivelled towards Herbert and attempted an approximation of an insouciant grin. 'Yup,' it said, with chummy familiarity.

Herbert rolled his eyes in amusement. An American taxi-moto. A British one would have been furious at anyone having the temerity to tap the back of its dome.

Losing Berri had crushed him, but he hadn't intended to jump in front of the train. After he had overheard her telling Marina she was leaving with Imolo, he went for a walk. A sad and lonely walk, but not with the intention of any flamboyant final leap. He had walked along the platform at Archway Transport station, kicking candy wrappers somersaulting past. He paused to unstick a piece of paper clinging to his shoe, straightened up and looked right into Estra's face. Berri's sister was looking right through him at something black and frightening. He fell into the misery in her eyes and couldn't find his way out. He knew he must jump. When the rumbling train approached, he stepped off into it.

Had Doc Hurt given her the ability to make men fly with one look, or had she had it all along? The doctor's results were inconsistent. His disorganization meant results were wildly divergent and his reports were scrappy. The only mark of consistency running throughout Dr Hurtigger's work was his Sword of Damocles burning a swathe through Herbert's family.

Watching buildings flash past his window, Herbert couldn't decide whether or not he'd been done a favour by being brought back to life. Being scraped up off the tracks, combined with a dead teenage girl and zapped to life with electricity in some macabre approximation of Frankenstein was not something you were prepared for. *I'm Frankensandra. Bloody hell.*

That in itself could convince one to jump. But then again, Herbert reflected with glum certainty, killing himself hadn't worked the first time. The gruesome nature of his creation and the futility of trying to fix things swept over him like a cold wind.

When Doc Hurt had dropped his bombshell and stomped out, Herbert had been floored. He sat in the office, his family battling for room inside his head. The red file with his and Sandra's names on it lay cradled in his lap. Getting up, he stumbled over to Doc Hurt's desk. Even if your existence had just been flushed down the toilet, you couldn't let your standards slip. As he'd thought, the doctor had been in such a hurry to leave, he had forgotten to lock his desk drawers. The Ongoing drawer wasn't shut completely.

Opening it and riffling through the files, he noticed that, in Doc Hurt's typical manner, they were in unalphabetized chaos. Sorting them, he recognized several names.

Timmy Kaneen a.k.a. Colton Massey
Dario Insenga a.k.a. Cecilio Insenga
Luca Timmerman

Herbert was glad he'd helped Luca and the mouse escape. It had been a tiny fragment of rebellion at the time, but now he felt a blaze of satisfaction at having saved two subjects from final cut.

Estra Considine
Wynne Considine
Beryl Considine
Herbert Considine a.k.a. Sandra Johannis
Marina Considine

Fate was cruel. Herbert hadn't just assisted with Marina's implant operations, he'd even helped to insert her self-destruct chip. Sandra had been jealous of her. The thought of it sickened him. When Marina returned sporting the dying hand frilling from her shoulder, Sandra had been awed by the fervour with which she and the hand had fought separation. It had moved her so much, she had slipped the envelope of City Credits back in Marina's pocket.

Shaking her head with sorrow, he continued straightening the files.

Ricker Hurtigger a.k.a. XXXXX a.k.a. XXXXX.

Doc Hurt had his own ongoing file? What were all these crossed-out aliases for? Herbert pulled out the file and opened it. What he read in the first few paragraphs stunned him. So that was it. That explained a lot. Bemused, he shut the drawer and left the office. There must be some way to help his newly remembered family. But how? Pushing through the glass door, he crashed into someone running past.

'Sorry,' they both said.

'Can you help me?' the woman begged. 'A woman's giving birth in the LOT building. It's by natural means and none of us knows how to help.' She wiped her forehead with the bottom of her T-shirt. Herbert noticed it was stained with something suspiciously like blood.

'I'm a doctor,' Herbert told her. *Sort of.*

The best thing to do was to see the woman and then go next door to the hospital to get an ambulance. Following her into the building and into the room, his breath caught in his throat with the amazingly incredibly wonderful coincidence. It was Wynne lying on the table. His Wynne. Although he hadn't seen her since she was a child, he'd recognize that peppermint-tinted face anywhere. Not that he could see much of it. She was surrounded by milling people and a large grey-haired woman was kneeling between her legs like a huge preying mantis. *Dysis.*

She must be about to snatch the child for one of Doc Hurt's experiments.

318

No! There was no way he'd let the mad doctor tamper with yet another generation of his family.

'Get away from my grandchild!' he forced from between clenched teeth. Dysis ignored him. She was singing to herself.

'Oh, what a lovely bunch of coconuts . . .' She giggled in a manic, high-pitched tone.

'Dysis!' Herbert said.

She turned to look at him. 'Sandra. Glad you could make it. I need a hand here.' She beckoned him closer and pointed. Herbert looked. A tiny leg protruded from Wynne. *Two. Three?*

'The gene splicing worked,' Dysis said. 'Ricker will be so pleased. But the birth will be more difficult. You'll help me . . .'

Herbert squared his shoulders and gave her a ferocious look. 'You will not lay a hand on either my daughter or my grandchild.'

She chortled. 'You helped work on your other daughter.'

Herbert felt sick. He hadn't just laid a hand on Marina, he'd helped implant one on to her.

'Things are different now,' he said. 'Get away from her.' He tried to push Dysis off the table. She swung a meaty fist and thumped him in the midriff, driving all the air from his lungs in a painful burst.

'I'm bigger than you, dear,' she said.

He bent over and tried to gulp back elusive scraps of air. He noticed the T-shirted woman looking down at him, concerned.

'Stop her,' Herbert begged, between gulps. 'She's going to steal the baby!' The woman looked from him to Dysis, confusion warring with scepticism. Dysis rolled her eyes and smiled at the woman in complicity.

'The poor girl is obviously a nutter,' she said.

'I'm Wynne's father.' Herbert clenched his fists in frustration, noticing that one of his sparkle-tipped fingernails had broken off. It grinned up at him from the floor by his feet, a tiny razor-blue smile. Wynne moaned, distracting Dysis. Scooping up the fingernail fragment, Herbert jabbed the fingernail into Dysis's plump neck.

She swore and slapped a hand on her neck. The T-shirted

woman looked from her to Herbert. She must have seen something in his eyes that satisfied her. She pursed her lips and whistled, a piercing screech that snatched the attention of everyone in the room.

'The old woman's trying to steal the baby,' she said.

'Noooo,' Wynne moaned.

Herbert forgot about Dysis. He went over and touched Wynne's cheek. 'Bear down, darling. It'll be over soon.' He hoped. *Those three legs didn't look good*.

She looked up at him with surprise. Another contraction rippled through her body. Gritting her teeth, she pushed. Herbert noticed Dysis gripping one of the baby's legs.

'Push!' she ordered.

As the baby erupted in a slither of fluids, Wynne screamed. At the sudden lack of resistance and slipperiness of what she clutched, Dysis fell backwards off the table. The T-shirted woman immediately sat on her and a crowd of people with press badges grabbed her arms and legs. She thrashed like a beached porpoise in outraged fury.

'I've pulled her genes off. The child is mine!'

Herbert quickly cut the umbilical cord with a penknife somebody passed him.

Noticing the growing puddle of blood seeping from Wynne, Herbert wrapped the wailing bundle he held in someone's discarded LOT jacket. He turned to the T-shirted woman. 'I'm going to get an ambulance for Wynne.'

At that moment, Dysis managed to heave everyone off. 'I'm afraid I have no more time to assist the birth,' she said huffily. 'Things to do. Phone calls to make.' She grabbed her handbag and limped out.

'She doesn't matter,' Herbert told the woman. 'It's Dr Hurtigger we've got to worry about. Tell Wynne . . .' Her eyes were shut and her breathing was faint. ' . . . that her father will sort everything out. I'll get Colton. I know where he lives.'

At the knock on the door, Colton let his breath out with relief.

Wynne was back. He hurried to the door. Why was she knocking? Maybe she wanted to surprise him. Opening the door, he looked with surprise at the young woman with tea-coloured hair standing there.

'Hello, Timmy Kaneen a.k.a. Colton Massey,' she said. 'Come with me,' she continued. 'It's about Wynne. I'll explain on the way.'

On the way to the hospital, Colton saw the woman looking askance at his chaos box. He supposed not everyone wore a cardboard box with the word CAULIFLOWER emblazoned on the sides. He didn't bother explaining he needed it to go outside.

'I know where your mother is,' the woman said to him. 'I saw her address in Dr Hurtigger's files. I work for him. I'm Sandra . . . Herbert.'

Colton felt faint. 'My mother?'

'Yes.' She paused. 'And another thing. I'm your father-in-law, believe it or not.'

Colton didn't, but she refused to answer any further questions. She told him in a tired voice that she wanted to help them all before she left.

'Thank you for coming to get me,' Colton said. 'My wife means everything to me.'

The girl patted his shoulder. 'I know. You're a good boy, Timmy . . . Colton. You've taken good care of my daughter.'

Despite his worry for Wynne and unease with this odd girl, Colton felt warmed by her approval.

When they arrived at the hospital, they passed the children's ward. Looking through the glass window, Colton squinted his eyes. Little fists and legs flailed.

'We have to find Wynne.'

They found her in an emergency-room cubicle. When they pushed back the curtains, Wynne was being fed blood pellets by a nurse. Her face brightened when she saw him. 'Colton!' she cried. 'And . . .' She looked at the woman following him. 'You're the person who got rid of that awful grey-haired woman.' She shivered. 'Thank you.'

'No need to thank me. I'm your father,' Herbert said.

Wynne's mouth dropped.

The nurse popped another blood pellet into it. 'Just a few more,' he coaxed. 'You lost a lot of blood.'

Wynne swatted her hand away with impatience. 'I thought someone said something like that when I was drifting in and out. Colton, do you know what she's talking about?'

Colton looked blank.

Wynne narrowed her eyes. 'My father's dead. And besides,' she pointed out, 'fathers don't have breasts.'

'That woman trying to get your kid was Dr Hurtigger's sister. Don't you remember her from when he kidnapped you?'

Her face blanched. 'He always did the experiments. I never saw anyone else.'

Herbert continued, 'After we got you both back, and I heard your mother was going away, I . . .' He looked as if he found it hard to continue under her clear gaze. ' . . . I felt there was nothing more for me. I jumped in front of a train. Doc Hurt got me after that. I was a scrape-up experiment. He regenerated me. Scraped the bits off the track, stuck me on to another person, prodded me with electricity and here I am.'

Wynne looked sceptical. 'If it *is* you, why didn't you come back before?'

'I just found out.' He shot her an agonized look. 'Is your mother with Imolo?'

'No.'

'No?'

'Mother lives alone. She always has.'

Colton saw Herbert looked sick. 'But she said . . .'

Wynne was impatient. 'Mama never went away with anyone. She lives by herself not far from here and reads palms.'

'Reads what?'

'Palms. Go and see her. She'll know if you're you. She never stopped missing Papa and I hardly see her. She says she's always busy watching over things. I don't know what.'

'I will.' Herbert smiled grimly. 'I'll freshen my make-up first. I'll come back and check on you before I go.'

When her so-called father stepped out of the cubicle, Wynne looked up at Colton with tired eyes. 'Mama will know.' She paused. 'Have you seen . . . ?'

Colton knew exactly what she was asking. 'They're beautiful,' he said. 'Absolutely perfect. A boy and a girl. When I first saw them their legs were all tangled. I thought they were Siamese twins or something. Scared me to death.'

Wynne reached her arms up towards him. 'Kiss me.' When he didn't move towards her, she cast him a quizzical look. 'I'm grounded, don't worry,' she said. Her eyes clouded. 'What's wrong?'

Colton had to tell her. He couldn't live with the secret of his involvement with her kidnapping lying fallow between them any more. Besides, with the doctor and Dysis roaming around like mad bookends, she might find out.

'I have to tell you something,' he said. *She'll hate me.*

She shot him an unreadable look. 'I know already,' she said. 'You were scraping in the tunnel one night and I saw you pick up one of the tunnel mice. You held it out to me and I remembered you in the other tunnel. Smiling. Holding out another mouse.'

He covered his face with his hands. 'I'll go.'

'You can't leave,' she said. 'You have responsibilities. A family.'

He dropped his hands. 'But . . .'

She coughed. 'Colton, we're each other's family. Are you trying to tell me you don't love me?'

He was stung. 'Of course not!'

'Well, then.' She gave him a fond look. 'That's sorted. Besides, who will watch the children while I go to work at LOT?' She laughed.

'I didn't think –'

'Oh, ye of little faith. They told me in the meeting that I could enter the training programme.'

'Congratulations.' He hugged her.

'So now I've got something on you, I can bribe you into baby-sitting when I'm working.'

'Bribe away. When they're older, I'll take them to visit Mummy at work.'

'All three with your own boxes?' she asked, her eyes twinkling.

'No. It's cosier to share. Like sardines.'

'What shall we call them, Colton?'

'How about Bonnie and Clyde?'

'Who are they?'

'Old friends.'

Suddenly the lights went out and they heard a woman's voice from the next cubicle. 'Cecilio? You can't die twice.' A moment of silence within the blackness. 'Mother? Mother, is that you?'

Wynne felt for Colton's hand. 'That's Marina's voice.' Colton could feel her hands trembling with shock.

Footsteps ran past the cubicle, making the curtains flutter. They both turned and saw a woman with long silver hair run past them in a flash of blue-green skirts.

'And Mama,' Wynne said, with incredulity. 'What's going on?'

A voice quavered from the next-door cubicle. 'Please get someone,' it begged. 'Cecilio's dying.' The curtain parted and Marina's face peered at them. All the colour drained from her already pale, tear-stained face. 'Wynne? It can't be.'

At that moment, Herbert flipped the curtain and came back in. 'Some woman just ran past me and almost knocked me down.'

'Sandra, what are *you* doing here?' Marina asked.

'I'm not Sandra. I'm Herbert,' he replied. 'Papa for short.'

'That's Marina's voice,' Ricker said to himself as he walked through the corridors. He had to pull Addy along as he kept lagging behind to look at all the bright colours. At hearing Marina's voice, Ricker's heart jumped. He hadn't even needed to activate her recall chip. She was right here in the hospital. He pushed past the curtains into the cubicle containing her voice. Impatiently, he pulled Addy after him. 'C'mon, you big lump.'

What a pain it was having to drag along one experiment while you retrieved the other. They were just queuing up. He giggled. *Can't keep track, can't keep track.*

At least Terza had reminded him to get changed. How could he exert authority in a dress? Besides, his grey wig rode up at the back and made his head itch. He always had to wash his hair with dandruff shampoo after he'd worn it. He hated seeing white specks settling on his shoulders like snow. No authority when you had dandruff. That's probably why he couldn't get Wynne's baby from LOT's meeting room. He hadn't been exerting enough authority.

'Sit, Addy.' Ricker shoved him into a plastic chair. 'Heel.' He walked towards Marina, who was peering into the cubicle next door. 'Come with me.' He grabbed her arm. 'You have no choice.'

'She has,' someone cried. People erupted from all sides. Sandra and Colton from the right. Wynne tottering behind them. Estra burst in from the left. Her hands were manacled, but from between them the razor blade flashed again, as did the man's fingers, working frantically. Daniel glared at Ricker from between them.

Now that Ricker knew who it was inside Estra, he wasn't surprised. He had known Daniel would show up some day and try to pay him back. Hadn't Daniel warned him years ago? 'I'll get you – I'll get you no matter what I have to do,' he'd said. And here he was erupting from his wife's hands. It wasn't Estra trying to pay him back for her family, it was Daniel trying to get him back for his own mistreatment. Ricker sighed. Nobody appreciated him or his work. He tried to edge backwards, but people blocked his exit. Noise erupted from the corridor.

He swung his elbows in fury and pushed through the people blocking him. He stopped, stunned, when he saw who stood outside the cubicle. It was Luca. The mouse was perched on her, for all the world like a child riding on its father's shoulders. When she saw him, her face blanched and she took off. At that instant, he felt a razor slice across his cheek, neatly crossing the cut he'd received from Estra before. He screamed and put his hands to his face.

'Don't kill him, Aunt Estra!' Marina cried. 'He has to save Cecilio.'

Ricker's cheek burned. The razor must be duller than last time. He hadn't remembered it hurting this much before. Everyone was trying to hurt him when all he ever tried to do was help them. Didn't they understand? It was nothing personal. An acrid cloud of injustice and indignation swirled around him. After all, that's why he was here today. His mother had told him over and over when she'd signed him over to BB and the medical service. He had to continue her work and help others. *Mother!*

He started to cry in big gulping sobs.

Marina came up to him and slapped him across the face.

Shocked, Ricker stared at her. His lower lip wobbling. 'Why did you do that?' Fat tears mixed with the blood trickling down his face.

'Cecilio needs your help.'

'I can't do anything,' he said. 'I'm bleeding to death.'

'You can do that later. You have something else to do first.'

Ricker was so surprised at her new-found authority that he obediently followed her over to the man's bed and felt his pulse.

'He's dead.'

Marina let out a howl. Ricker put both hands over his ears. *What a hellish racket!*

Footsteps come running down the hall. A woman with long silver hair burst into the cubicle.

'Mama?' Wynne and Marina said in unison.

Sandra looked sick. 'I was just coming to look for you.'

Ricker's head hurt. Was every single member of this family roaming around the hospital? The call-back to Marina must have gone into universal mode and recalled the entire Considine family.

'I had to come back,' the woman said. 'To see if he was really dead. To see if I'd pulled the right – '

Marina looked stunned. 'You pulled his plug?'

Berri bowed her head. 'I did it to protect you. Ask Estra.'

Marina looked at Estra, who nodded, and then back at her mother. 'Protect me from what?'

Ricker interrupted, smiling with genial kindness at Estra and Berri, 'Automatic regeneration. That's right. If we prod Marina with electricity, it'll start working.' He laughed so hard that he started to hiccup.

Everybody seemed lost for words until Addy burped. Everyone stared at him. He stuck out his tongue.

'Nyaah nyaah,' he said clearly.

Marina stared intently into Ricker's eyes. 'You owe me,' she said. 'If it's true and I'm going to start sprouting things, why can't you do me one favour?'

Sandra walked up next to her and put her arm around her for support. She looked pointedly at Addy. 'You could fuse Cecilio to Addy. He doesn't look as if he'd notice.'

'Impossible.' Ricker tried to giggle, but it came out as a cough. 'A hand couldn't force his personality on to an entire body.'

Sandra walked up and shook him by the shoulders. 'You know it's possible,' she said calmly.

He looked into her eyes. She knew what was written in his files. She must have seen it. 'You don't have to be so pushy,' he said, flustered.

At that point, Nurse Johnson came into the cubicle. 'What's going on?' she asked. 'Who are all these people?' Spotting Ricker, she nodded to him with complicity. 'Oh, it's you.' She winked. 'I'll keep the rest of the doctors away from this cubicle.'

When she left, the weight of everyone's regard fell upon him again. It was always like this. Everyone wanted so much from him. Expected so much. The need to fill other people's needs was such a crushing burden.

'My hand's trembling,' he said. 'I might make a mistake.' He held it up. 'See?' They began to surround him, walking slowly. Glaring. Obligating him. Expecting. *Don't hurt me*.

He started to hyperventilate. He crouched on the floor and covered his head with both arms. The cut on his cheek felt like a chasm. Wind whistled through it in and out in-and-outinandout. The buzzards in his mind began to circle and he opened his mouth to shriek. *Make them go away, Mummy!*

Up from behind him he felt a shadow. A box came over his head and settled down over his shoulders. 'Here,' Colton said. 'This should help.'

The box walls were warm from Colton's skin. It smelt brown and safe. The cardboard was soft from wear, the edges dulled into soft chamois. Ricker felt his rapid heartbeat calm. The buzzards circling him flew away. He stood up, adjusting the box on his shoulders.

'If I'm to operate on Cecilio. 'I'll need Sandra's assistance.'

He nodded.

Taking what he needed from the shelves lining the one non-curtained wall, he brought up his arms like a conductor. 'Addy, pop yourself up here next to Cecilio. Breathe into this mask. We'll help you count to three.'

He looked over his shoulder at Marina. 'You have to understand, I don't know who will be the dominant victor of the body. Cecilio or Addy.'

'One, two, three,' they all counted aloud.

Throughout the whole operation, Berri's eyes roamed over everyone in the cubicle. She marvelled to see her two daughters and her son-in-law in one room again.

Berri had given up trying to keep the red-handed man from her daughter. Marina seemed to want him, and everyone else supported her. She was outnumbered, she decided. The Cecilio hand had been removed and was now attached to Addy. The dead Cecilio body lay on the side table. He looked exactly like his father. Berri felt a pang. He had been her flesh and blood, after all. What remained of him was now attached to that drooling blob.

Berri felt a touch on her arm. It was the girl who had helped Dr Hurtigger operate. The one he called Sandra.

'Berri, I have to tell you something.'

'What?'

'I'm Herbert.'

Berri became furiously angry. 'What kind of sick joke are you playing?'

'It's no joke.' The girl paused. 'Believe me, Berengaria.'

Berri sat down on the floor and bruised her tailbone. Only Herbert knew that name.

She looked up into the girl's eyes, which were looking calmly back at her. There was something . . . She blanched and felt faint. It was the look Herbert had given her the time she'd agreed to marry him. 'Herbert?' she whispered.

The girl reached down and traced Berri's face with one sparkly fingernail. 'You didn't go to Imolo, after all.' His smile split her face in half.

Berri forgot to breathe. 'No.'

Imolo. Giuseppe. Whatever his name was. He had been Estra's dalliance, not hers. Berri had promised not to tell anyone, even Herbert.

Right before Berri's wedding, she'd convinced Estra to take a holiday with her. Estra, normally so shy in England, somehow let loose in Italy. She went around with a waiter named Patrizio for a few days. Then she'd fallen madly in love with a pastry chef.

'He has great hands,' she giggled to Berri, when she dropped into the hotel after three days' absence to get some clothes. 'Fantastic technical expertise. He must have had a lot of practice.'

Practice makes pregnant. As her sister became.

'What will I do?' Estra begged her.

Berri helped her, in her role as responsible older sister. Besides, it was her fault. She was the catalyst. If she hadn't taken her to Italy, it never would have happened.

Estra didn't co-operate much. She refused the abortion pills Berri bought for her. She wanted to keep the child. Berri convinced her it was impossible. Children that weren't requested from the Gene Board were far too imperfect and unpredictable.

'Give it up for adoption.'

'But . . .'

'You'll have more children. You're only nineteen. There's plenty of time.'

Berri took Estra to an extractor clinic. Estra made her promise not to tell anyone. Even Herbert. 'I won't tell,' Berri said. 'Don't worry.'

The baby was extracted and put into the baby hatcher. Berri and Estra came every other day to watch the baby in its glass container.

'See, Estra,' Berri said. 'It's happy.' The baby floated in lazy circles and gurgled inside the tank, bubbles rising to the surface of the liquid. They waved and watched it smile in gummy delight.

When the baby hatched, Berri made the arrangements to give the child to social services. Estra put her foot down. 'I want it to go to its father.'

Berri was so relieved that Estra had stopped saying she wanted to keep it that she agreed. 'What's his name?'

'Imolo Giuseppe Insenga. I'll write his name down for you.'

'How do you know he's the father?'

'The other man and I used spray-on birth control. Imolo and I forgot.'

Estra let her disgusted silence speak for her.

'We didn't think about birth control. Besides . . .'

'What possible reason could you have for being so stupid?'

'We were married.'

'*What?*'

With hesitant guilt, Estra told her. 'He asked me to marry him after only three days. I was having so much fun I said yes. We went to one of those all-night register offices. You could choose three different services. We chose the most expensive one. It turned out it was the same service as the other two, just delivered at a slower pace. It lasted twelve minutes.'

'You married him in between going to the museums and restaurants with me?'

'Don't worry. We came to our senses. Imolo seemed relieved when I told him I'd made a mistake.'

Imolo had been perfectly willing to take the baby when Berri brought him. 'My wife will take care of him,' he said. 'She won't mind.'

His wife? She looked at his hand and saw the wedding ring. No wonder he'd been relieved when Estra wanted out. He was already married.

His wife had been good about Cecilio, Giuseppe reflected. Although she never forgave him.

It's a shame Cecilio wasn't biologically his son, although he felt like the son of his heart. Amalea didn't know that he was sterile due to a childhood bout of mumps. He hadn't had the multi-jab kids received these days. He didn't want to upset her. He knew she wanted children. She'd feel better if he brought Cecilio home.

He smiled fondly. Cecilio's mother's name was Hester. He got the feeling it wasn't her real name, but it didn't matter. He'd really fallen for her in a big way. She must have been with someone else around the same time as him, though, if she'd become pregnant. He was surprised to feel slightly hurt. That's why he didn't follow her to England and try to convince her to stay married. He might even have left his other wives for her. She was different from the others. He'd looked up the name 'Hester Williams' in the information *YP* for England, but there were none listed so he gave up and directed his attention towards bringing up his new son.

Giuseppe tried to push away the thought of Hester. That was all in the past. At long last he had finally found a woman who cared for him, despite knowing how imperfect he was. How odd. Falling in love with a woman he'd never met.

Would the prison allow him to leave the cell long enough to bake the wedding cake? He ran through all his mental recipes. What ingredients could he cadge from the kitchen? Would Estra like Kahlua walnut carrot cake with cream-cheese frosting?

He hoped she was safely in the hospital and away from that man she thought had set out to destroy her family. Surely the man wasn't as bad as she thought? Flexing his fingers to loosen their arthritic stiffness, he noticed his wedding ring.

Start as you mean to go on. Twisting the heavy gold ring off his finger, he reached into his pocket and drew out the other seven he carried around for luck. *Don't lie to yourself. Spares.*

331

Going over to his bucket, he dropped the rings with a ceremonial flourish into it. They made tiny plinking sounds and stared up at him owlishly. That wouldn't do. He fished them out, with a large wad of toilet paper. Going over to the refuse slot in the wall, he rolled them through one by one. No more spares.

He paced back and forth in his cell, practising the marriage vows. It made him worry less about Estra.

'Will you take this man?'

He hoped Estra would still want to when she came back. She'd be his last wife. The best one to be.

'Will you take this man over by the electric socket?' Dr Hurtigger asked Marina. 'We've got to give him a jolt to get him started.'

She rolled Cecilio's stretcher to the side. 'Here?'

'Marina, you have to leave immediately,' Berri cried. 'If you absorb any passive electricity, you'll start growing things.'

'I'll risk it,' Marina threw out. 'Besides, you can't tell me what to do. You haven't been around in years.'

'She did it for you,' Estra said in a low voice.

Marina didn't have time to deal with her complicated feelings towards her mother. She looked over at Dr Hurtigger. He was rubbing a tiny crescent-shaped red mark on the back of his neck. She wondered what it was. 'Is that true?'

'Well, yes,' he said. 'You have a few . . . modifications which might mean you'll sprout . . . things if you encounter any random electrical current. I don't know if it'll work or not.' He sighed and spoke with resigned bitterness. 'After all, I screwed up with Wynne. That's why she keeps shooting off sparks. An overabundance of current.'

Berri interrupted, 'Won't you go, Marina, just in case? We'll watch over your friend.'

'No.'

'Well, if you have things sprouting all over you, don't say I never warned you.'

'You can gloat later.'

'I wouldn't gloat!'

Marina giggled under her breath. *Families. Who'd have 'em?*

'Haven't you all forgotten the electricity is off, and they haven't managed to get the emergency generators going yet?' Colton said. 'We have nothing to give Cecilio a jolt with.'

'Except me,' Wynne said from her bed.

They all turned to look at her.

Ricker looked at Wynne, the one he'd messed up so badly years before. A reminder of failure. BB had really screamed about that one.

The painful unceasing clamour in his head had faded for the first time in ages. How could just wearing a box do this? He'd probably be wearing it in jail, if these people had anything to do about it. He looked forward to it in a mild sort of way. It might be okay there. Dysis couldn't follow him. He was tired of her. She made him do such awful things. He couldn't totally absolve himself from responsibility – but she made everything worse. Increased the intensity. Whispered in his ear. 'C'mon, honeybun. *Tell me what you need!*'

Wynne looked at Marina. 'I can do it,' she said. 'If I get angry enough or . . .'

' . . . feel other strong emotion,' Estra continued for her.

'Would it help if I told you I hated you, Wynne?' Marina asked.

Wynne gave her a slight smile. 'No, sorry.' She laughed. 'We should be able to generate some strong emotion. There's enough in this cubicle to set off an H-bomb. I've just had twins, my sister's in love with a hand, my mother and my aunt are attempted murderers, my father's dressed as a woman, and a mad doctor in a box ends up attaching the dead hand to some drooling man. Isn't that enough?'

Colton sniffed. 'What about me? Don't I rate?'

She squeezed his hand. 'I was just getting to you. Help me up, Colton,' she said. 'I need to start my electrical career.'

After being helped over to the stretcher holding the new Addy–Cecilio combination, she took hold of both its hands. She squeezed her eyes shut and concentrated, cajoling the thing within her to come. Slowly, ever so slowly, it crept upwards. Ten minutes went by. Fifteen. The thing was stalled somewhere around her solar plexus. She felt bleary with fatigue.

'Anything?' she asked.

'His eyelids fluttered once,' Estra said helpfully.

She sagged. 'It's not working, Marina. I'm sorry. It's not coming.' She felt terrible for not being able to help.

Marina twisted her hands together. 'It probably wouldn't have worked. A hand couldn't take over an entire body.'

'I'm not sure,' Dr Hurtigger said, rocking on his heels, his box swaying with the rhythm. 'It's never worked before.'

Sandra walked over and punched him in the box. 'Yes, it has,' she said.

Dr Hurtigger looked nervously down at her. He seemed about to speak when Marina threw down the plastic ether bottle she was clutching. 'It's probably best it didn't work. I couldn't have stood it if the man turned out to be Addy. There I'll be with things growing all over me. After risking absorbing all the electricity, it won't even be worth it, because it won't have been for Cecilio. I'll end up with nothing as usual,' she said bitterly. 'Just like when I was a child. You all left me, and now Cecilio's gone and left me as well!' Her voice wobbled and she turned and ran.

'Wait,' Sandra called. 'Dr Hurtigger has something to tell you –'

Marina ran down the corridor, and only stopped when she developed a pain in her side. *I could jump in front of a train like my father did.* Her sense of the ridiculous tried to kid her back to good humour. 'I'll hold my breath until I die,' her psyche taunted. Pausing to catch her breath, she sat down on a bench just outside the hospital exit. A woman with a small dog by her side sat at the other end with a stony expression on her face. Marina tried to calm down. As soon as she caught her breath, she'd leave. Go back to her old life. She'd been stupid and unrealistic to think anything else was possible.

'Waaaaaaah,' her psyche teased her. 'You're a pathetic mewling baby. You don't deserve to have a family to love you. A man.'

Cecilio loved me.

Something cold and wet shoved into her hand. Opening her eyes, she looked down at the tiny lap-sized dog sitting between her and the other woman. It was licking her hand with a raspberry tongue and gazing up at her with adoration. A lock of its hair was tied up loosely in a bedraggled pink bow. A green collar with yellow diamond shapes encircled its neck.

Marina patted it. 'Nice doggie,' she said. It exuded friendliness. And hair, she thought, when she saw it on her jeans.

'Is your dog ill?' she asked the woman. 'It seems to be losing an awful lot of hair.'

The woman stood up. 'Do you want to see what's wrong with my dog?' she snapped, spreading her arms wide. 'Look, no hands.'

The dog had risen with her. It wriggled from side to side, and nipped the woman's elbows playfully. Its green collar was a glossy diamond-back snake, which twisted out from somewhere under the woman's shirt. The dog only had front paws to brace himself on the woman's hip as the rest of him was embedded in her side.

'I'm sorry,' Marina said. 'I didn't understand.'

'How could you?' the woman said. 'Nobody does.' Brushing hair out of her eyes, she amended bitterly, 'Except for Mouse here. Everybody else – those doctors – Well, don't call me Luca. Call me Multi-pet. They don't want to remove them, they're too fascinating apparently.'

Marina stared at the mouse Luca had pointed to under her hair. It was *him*.

He chittered down at her like a king demanding obeisance. She could swear he smiled at her. *You're that mouse on TV.*

'Sorry. Must go,' Luca said. 'Have to see a man about a dog.'

She turned and marched away, canine companion bobbing happily by her side. Someone with a guide dog passed them and Luca's barked wildly down into the big dog's bemused face. Luca ignored them both.

Marina stared after her.

Could she live with things like that growing out of her? If that woman could, so could she. It's not that the woman looked thrilled with them. In fact, she obviously hated them. But the mouse hadn't cared.

Cecilio wouldn't care, would he? If it was him. She sighed and stood up. She had to give him the chance, even if she risked the electricity and Addy came back. If it was Addy, she'd help him anyway. She still felt slightly guilty at having kicked him out of her flat that night. He *had* held her all night, as she'd asked. He hadn't made fun of her when she'd cried.

Marina went back inside the hospital and walked with slow, steady deliberation down the corridors towards the Emergency Department. Just before she entered the cubicle, she gave her palm a quick once-over. She must have made the right decision. Long straight love line crossing the fate line. So okay. Whatever happened, it didn't mean she was trapped. She had choices.

I can't just leave Addy and Cecilio half alive. Neither of them deserves it. Steeling herself, she walked in and brushed past the others. Stopping at Addy and Cecilio's stretcher, she stood looking at the man's hand and then his face. It was a handsome face, she supposed. Long straight nose with flaring nostrils. Not too many errant hairs escaping from the nostrils. Full, petulant lips. Dark hair. Darker stubble. Could she love the Addy body with the Cecilio hand?

'You can't be him,' Marina whispered. The man's eyes were closed, and he was as pale as the sheets he lay upon. He was a whole collection of men. Like her. Made up of disparate parts. Was his situation any worse than hers? Although genetically contaminated, she was alive, he wasn't. She was the catalyst for this man dying. A catalyst responsible for so much. For the splitting apart of her entire family. Her father's death. Her mother's loneliness.

Don't catalysts deserve to be happy, too?

Marina turned round and smiled at the people ranged around her, all wearing anxious expressions. Except for Dr Hurtigger, who looked beatific inside his box. Colton was hugging his arms to himself as if he missed his box and perhaps wished he hadn't given it away.

She looked at her palm again. If the line was so insistently straight, then didn't it mean it all turned out right in the end? Picking up Cecilio's hand, she noticed his life line was still long. Was palmistry all a con? Here he was dead and his life line stretched like a motorway across his palm. The hand was cold. Not cold cold. But cold. Lukewarm.

'What are we waiting for?' she asked in a loud voice. 'It doesn't matter whether it's Addy or not. We have to try again. Wynne?'

Her sister looked miserable. 'But it didn't work before. I wasn't strong enough.'

Marina waved her hand as if to show how insignificant that fact was. 'What are Estra and I? Dog liver? We've been mucked around with too. Perhaps we might not have the electrical abilities you have, but just consider us like catalystic converters.'

Estra jumped off the bed. 'Have we decided whether it's anger or the other –?'

'Dunno,' Wynne answered. 'I seem to get a little with normal emotions, but rage really kicked it off last time.' She shot Colton a look as he tapped her arm inquiringly. 'I'll tell you about what happened in LOT later.'

'Are you angry now, Wynne?' Marina asked.

'No. More disappointed that I failed before.'

'Can you get angry?'

'I don't know.' Wynne looked doubtful.

Marina grinned. 'I hate your guts. You were a terrible sister.'

'Not working.'

'Aunt Estra?' Marina started to look despairing.

'I'm not angry enough either.'

'Look at Dr Hurtigger,' Marina suggested.

'He's just pathetic.'

'But think of what our family could have been without him.'

'We could have destroyed it ourselves,' Berri said from the back.

Marina glared at the doctor. 'He helped.'

'Split up our entire family,' Wynne added. 'Almost destroyed Colton, kidnapped you and me, not to mention all the other people we don't even know about.' *And the mouse.*

Wynne's eyes were becoming dangerously green.

Berri spoke up again from the back. 'Estra, I told Herbert about Imolo.'

Aunt Estra's eyes went ballistic.

Dr Hurtigger stood up. 'It probably wouldn't work. In the end it would probably be Addy anyway, and you remember the state he was in.' He started edging towards the curtain. 'While you're discussing it, if you'll excuse me, I have an office to close down and a wig to burn. Thanks for the loan of your box, Colton. I'm borrowing it and shall return it to you when I'm safely back –'

'You're not going anywhere,' Herbert said. He turned to face everyone. 'I hoped Doc Hurt would help without me having to tell you about it, but he knows all about melding a hand to a person, don't you?' He glared at Dr Hurtigger, who raised his eyebrows.

'I don't know what you mean.'

'You've been dead a long time, haven't you?' Herbert raised his delicate chin and flicked back a sheaf of his tea-coloured hair. The others in the cubicle were stunned into silence.

'That's being rather personal, Sandra dear. Just because the job hasn't worked out.'

'It wasn't you who figured out how to combine people and generate live growths, it was your foster mother, wasn't it? When you had that taxi-moto accident back when you were a boy. Your foster mother cut your hand off as it was the one piece of you still relatively unscathed, and she implanted it on to a woman's body.'

'I don't know what you're talking –' Dr Hurtigger looked faint. He reached up and tugged an earlobe thoughtfully. 'I remember nothing about that.'

'You do. Your mother made you touch a live Transport rail with a fingertip one morning. The massive burst of electricity combined the two of you. You lived. The woman died. Dysis Jenkins, her name was.'

Dr Hurtigger made a choking sound. Herbert ignored him. 'I suggest you, your sister and your aunt get a move on. Cecilio has a damned good chance of surviving. Doc Hurt is proof of that. But, Marina, you still run the risk . . .

'I told you so,' Berri muttered.

'I heard that,' Marina said. 'You promised you wouldn't gloat.'

Colton snickered.

Marina beckoned Estra and Wynne to come and stand next to her. 'I'll take the risk. Wynne? Are you ready?'

'I think so.'

They moved the man's stretcher nearer to Estra's bed. Wynne took hold of her sister's cool hand, and her aunt's warmer one. Estra and Marina both picked up one of the man's hands. 'Wait a second,' Wynne said. 'Colton, could you . . .?' Colton came over and lifted Wynne's grounding wires. He wound them around her neck like a Christmas wreath, kissed her quickly and stepped back as sparks started to crackle from her.

Wynne closed her eyes and relaxed. She didn't have to worry about failing, it would work this time with their help. As she relaxed, warmth burgeoned up inside her, splitting into shards of white-hot brilliance. For the first time she didn't resist and the thing crawled up her spine, at first reluctant and wary, then gaining in confidence. Looking around the faces of her family, Wynne felt exasperated contentment. It would work. Everything would work.

She tried to shake off Marina's hand. She couldn't risk . . . But Marina wouldn't let go. Wynne gave up and let the thing rip. Torrents of flame shot through her body, raced down her arms, and burned through the circle of hands into the man.

Marina watched the electricity enter the man's body. The union at his wrist turned a furious red and smoke curled from it. Both of his hands twitched and he opened his eyes.

She could barely breathe. 'Cecilio?'

He looked up at them with blank and uncomprehending eyes.

Marina let go of the others' hands and leaned over the stretcher. Nobody breathed.

'Addy?' Marina tried again.

The man's eyelids flickered.

'*Cecilio*? Is that you in there? Addy?'

She dropped to her knees and leaned her head against the stretcher by the man's side and moaned. She felt something. A hand twining itself gently into her hair and tugging. A familiar touch. Or was it? She was so afraid to look up. The disappointment was too great.

She drew a ragged breath.

The hand moved. She felt a weak tapping on her cheek and then a hand cupped her shoulder. As Cecilio had.

She sat up abruptly. The man's eyes blazed at her. He made a garbled sound. She leaned closer. He made the same sound. A tiny bead of moisture glistened at the corner of his mouth. She couldn't understand what he was saying. It was still garbled. Addy. *It isn't Cecilio.*

Marina felt an itch burn on her leg. Reaching down to scratch, she wondered if it was a stress rash or if it was something starting to hatch. A hand? A foot? A horse's hoof?

Herbert came up behind her and put a blue sparkle-tipped hand on Marina's shoulder. 'I forgot to tell you – I made Dr Hurtigger take out Cecilio's Talk-Lang chip while you were outside. They always cause problems. I should know, Luca used to work for the company that made them.' She paused. 'I'm sorry, Marina, but if it's Cecilio he won't speak English.'

Marina looked up at Herbert and back down at the man's face. He made another unintelligible sound. She leaned closer. He lifted his hand and made those funny hand movements. Sign language.

Ti amo, Marina.

The End

For now . . .

*A person may be indebted for a nose
or an eye, for a graceful carriage or a
voluble discourse, to a great-aunt
or uncle, whose existence he has
scarcely heard of.*

WILLIAM HAZLITT